FLOODGATE

'Schiphol airport had just disappeared, its place taken by a wave-rippling lake that stretched almost as far as the eyes could see.'

Amsterdam Schiphol airport is under floodwater. Aircraft are trapped and silent. This is the opening scene in FLOODGATE, Alistair MacLean's gripping new adventure story of bombing and blackmail set in Holland, a country vulnerable to flooding.

A sinister terrorist group, the FFF, has caused the chaos. The aim of the organization is not to murder. It is to demonstrate the destruction it can cause by blowing up strategically placed dykes and so reduce the Netherlands to a state of fear and helplessness. And ripe for blackmail.

It is Lieutenant Peter van Effen's mission to sabotage their plans. Van Effen is a detective working undercover amongst the notorious Krakers – criminal gangs who specialize in drugs, in prostitution, in arms deals. He also heads the Amsterdam bomb disposal squad.

Using his specialist knowledge in explosives and with the help of two friends, flamboyant George and young Vasco from Utrecht, van Effen attempts to infiltrate the FFF. The price for failure – the flooding and annihilation of Holland.

In FLOODGATE, master storyteller Alistair MacLean draws the reader through a labyrinth of truths and false trails in a tense compelling novel, a masterpiece of contemporary suspense.

Alistair MacLean

FLOODGATE

COLLINS
8 Grafton Street, W1
1983

William Collins Sons & Co. Ltd
London · Glasgow · Sydney · Auckland
Toronto · Johannesburg

BRITISH LIBRARY CATALOGUING IN PUBLICATION DATA
MacLean, Alistair
Floodgate.
1. Title
823'.914[F]   PR6063.A248
ISBN   0 00 222754 1

First published 1983
© Alistair MacLean 1983

Photoset in Linotron Plantin by
Rowland Phototypesetting Ltd
Bury St Edmunds, Suffolk

Made and printed in Great Britain by
William Collins Sons & Co. Ltd, Glasgow

TO
DAVID & JUDY

Prologue

The two oddly similar incidents, although both happening on the night of February 3rd, and both involving army ammunition storage installations, had no discernible connection.

The occurrence at De Doorns in Holland was mysterious, spectacular and tragic: the one at Metnitz in Germany was a good deal less mysterious, unspectacular and faintly comic.

Three soldiers were on guard at the Dutch ammunition dump, set in a concrete bunker one and a half kilometres north of the village of De Doorns, when, about one-thirty in the morning, the only two citizens who were awake in the village reported a staccato burst of machine-pistol fire – it was later established that the guards were carrying machine-pistols – followed immediately by the sound of a gigantic explosion, which was later found to have blasted in the earth a crater sixty metres wide by twelve deep.

Houses in the village suffered moderately severe damage but there was no loss of life.

It was presumed that the guards had fired at intruders and that a stray bullet had triggered the detonation. No traces of the guards or supposed intruders were found afterwards.

In Germany, a group calling themselves the Red Army Faction, a well-known and well organized band of terrorists, claimed that they had easily overcome the two-man guard at the US Nato arms dump near Metnitz. Both men, it had been claimed, had been drinking and when the intruders had left both were covered with blankets – it had been a bitterly cold night. The US Army denied the drinking allegation but made no mention of the blankets. The intruders claimed that they had acquired a quantity of offensive weapons, some so advanced that they were still on the secret list. The US Army denied this.

The West German press heavily favoured the intruders'

account. When it came to penetrating army bases, the Red Army Faction had an impressive record: when it came to protecting them, the US Army had an unimpressive one.

The Red Army Faction customarily list the nature of their thefts in meticulous detail. No such details of the alleged secret weapons were published. It has been assumed that, if the Faction's account was true, the US Army or the US Army through the German government, had issued a stop order to the press.

One

'It is clear that it is the work of a madman.' Jon de Jong, tall, lean, grey, ascetic and the general manager of Schiphol airport, looked and sounded very gloomy indeed and, in the circumstances, he had every justification in looking and sounding that way.

'Insanity. A man has to be deranged, unhinged, to perform a wanton, mindless, pointless and purposeless task like this.' Like the monkish professor he so closely resembled, de Jong tended to be precise to the point of pedantry and, as now, had a weakness for pompous tautology.

'A lunatic.'

'One sees your point of view,' de Graaf said. Colonel van de Graaf, a remarkably broad man of medium height with a deeply trenched, tanned face, had about him an unperturbability and an unmistakable cast of authority that accorded well with the Chief of Police of a nation's capital city. 'I can understand and agree with it but only to a certain extent. I appreciate how you feel, my friend. Your beloved airport, one of the best in Europe –'

'Amsterdam airport *is* the best in Europe.' De Jong spoke as if by rote, his thoughts elsewhere. 'Was.'

'And will be again. The criminal responsible for this is, it is certain, not a man of a normal cast of mind. But that does not mean that he is instantly certifiable. Maybe he doesn't like you, has a grudge against you. Maybe he's an ex-employee fired by one of your departmental managers for what the manager regarded as a perfectly valid reason but a reason with which the disgruntled employee didn't agree. Maybe he's a citizen living close by, on the outskirts of Amsterdam, say, or between here and Aalsmeer, who finds the decibel level from the aircraft intolerably high. Maybe he's a dedicated environmentalist who

9

objects, in what must be a very violent fashion, to jet engines polluting the atmosphere, which they undoubtedly do. Our country, as you are well aware, has more than its fair share of dedicated environmentalists. Maybe he doesn't like our Government's policies.' De Graaf ran a hand through his thick, iron-grey hair. 'Maybe anything. But he could be as sane as either of us.'

'Maybe you'd better have another look, Colonel,' de Jong said. His hands were clenching and unclenching and he was shivering violently. Both of those were involuntary but for different reasons. The former accurately reflected an intense frustration and anger; the latter was due to the fact that, when an ice-cold wind blows east-north-east off the Ijsselmeer, and before that from Siberia, the roof of the main concourse of Schiphol airport was no place to be. 'As sane as you or I? Would you or I have been responsible for this – this atrocity? Look, Colonel, just look.'

De Graaf looked. Had he been the airport manager, he reflected, it would hardly have been a sight to gladden his heart. Schiphol airport had just disappeared, its place taken by a wave-rippled lake that stretched almost as far as the eyes could see. The source of the flooding was all too easy to locate: close to the big fuel storage tanks just outwith the perimeter of the airport itself, a wide breach had appeared in the dyke of the canal to the south: the debris, stones and mud that were scattered along the top of the dyke on either side of the breach left no doubt that the rupture of the containing dyke had not been of a natural or spontaneous origin.

The effect of the onrush of waters had been devastating. The airport buildings themselves, though flooded in the ground floors and basements, remained intact. The damage done to the sensitive electric and electronic machinery was very considerable and would almost certainly cost millions of guilders to replace but the structural integrity of the buildings was unaffected: Schiphol airport is very solidly built and securely anchored to its foundations.

Aircraft, unfortunately, when not operating in their natural element, are very delicate artifacts and, of course, have no means at all of anchoring themselves. A momentary screwing of de Graaf's eyes showed that this was all too painfully evident. Small planes had drifted away to the north. Some were still floating aimlessly around. Some were known to be sunk and out of sight, and two had their tail-planes sticking up above the water – those would have been single-engined planes, carried down head-first by the weight of the engines in their noses. Some two-engined passenger jets, 737's and DC9's, and three-engined planes, Trident 3's and 727's had also moved and were scattered randomly over a large area of the airfield, their noses pointing in every which direction. Two were tipped on their sides and two others were partially submerged, with only parts of their upper bodies showing: their undercarriages had collapsed. The big planes, the 747's, the Tri-Stars, the DC10's, were still in situ, held in position by their sheer massive weight – these planes, fuelled, can weigh between three and four hundred tons. Two, however, had fallen over to one side, presumably because the undercarriages distant from the onrush of water had collapsed. One did not have to be an aeronautical engineer to realize that both planes were write-offs. Both port wings were angled upwards at an angle of about twenty degrees and only the roots of the starboard wings were visible, a position that could only have been accounted for by the fact that both wings must have broken upwards somewhere along their lengths.

Several hundred yards along a main runway an undercarriage projecting above the water showed where a Fokker Friendship, accelerating for take-off, had tried to escape the floodwaters and failed. It was possible that the pilot had not seen the approach of the flood waters, possible but unlikely: it was more likely that he had seen them, reckoned that he had nothing to lose either way, continued accelerating but failed to gain lift-off speed before being caught. There was no question of his plane having been engulfed: in those initial stages, according to observers, there had been only an inch or two of water fanning out over the airfield but that had been enough to make the Fokker aquaplane with disastrous results.

Airport cars and trucks had simply drowned under the water.

The only remaining signs of any wheeled vehicles were the projecting three or four steps of aircraft boarding ramps and the top of a tanker: even the ends of two crocodile disembarkation tubes were dipped forlornly into the murky waters.

De Graaf sighed, shook his head and turned to de Jong who was gazing almost sightlessly over his devastated airfield as if still quite unable to comprehend the enormity of what had happened.

'You have a point, Jon. You and I are sane, or at least I think the world at large would think so, and it is not possible that we could have been responsible for such appalling destruction. But that doesn't mean that the criminal responsible for this wanton destruction is insane: we will doubtless find, either through our own efforts or because he chooses to inform us, that there was a very compelling reason for what he did. I shouldn't have used the word "wanton" there, you shouldn't have used words like "mindless" and "pointless". This is no random, arbitrary, spur-of-the-moment act of an escaped mental patient: this is a deliberately calculated act designed to produce a deliberately calculated effect.'

Reluctantly, as if by a giant effort of will, de Jong looked away from the flooded airfield. 'Effect? The only effect it has on me is one of sheer outrage. What other effects could there be? Do you have any suggestions?'

'None. I've had no time to think about it. Don't forget I've only just come to this. Sure, sure, we knew yesterday that this was promised, but like everyone else, I thought the idea was so preposterous as to be not worth considering. But I have two other suggestions. I suggest that we'll achieve nothing by staring out over Lake Schiphol: and I suggest we're not going to help anyone or anything by hanging around here and getting pneumonia.' De Jong's briefly pained expression showed what he thought of the term 'Lake Schiphol' but he made no comment.

The staff canteen was an improvement on the roof-top inasmuch as there was no wind but it wasn't all that much warmer. All electric heating had inevitably been short-circuited

12

and the butane heaters that had been brought in had as yet had a minimal effect on the chilled atmosphere. An abundance of hot coffee helped: something rather more sustaining, de Graaf reflected, would have been in order, but for those with a taste for schnapps or jonge jenever the presence of the airport manager had a markedly inhibiting effect. As became his ascetic appearance, de Jong was a lifelong teetotaller, a difficult thing to be in Holland. He never made a point of this, he had never even been heard to mention this, but, somehow, people just didn't drink anything stronger than tea or coffee when de Jong was around.

De Graaf said: 'Let's summarize briefly what we know. It has to be brief because we know virtually damn all. Three identical messages were received yesterday afternoon, one to a newspaper, one to the airport authorities – in effect, Mr de Jong – and one to the Rijkswaterstaat of the Ministry of Transport and Public Works.' He paused briefly and looked across at a burly, dark-bearded man who was placidly polluting the atmosphere with the smoke from what appeared to be a very ancient pipe. 'Ah! Of course. Mr van der Kuur. The Rijkswaterstaat Deputy Projects Engineer. How long to clear up this mess?'

Van der Kuur removed his pipe. 'We have already started. We seal off the breach in the canal with metal sheeting – a temporary measure only, of course, but sufficient. After that – well, we do have the best and biggest pumps in the world. A routine job.'

'How long?'

'Thirty-six hours. At the outside.' There was something very reassuring about der Kuur's calm and matter-of-fact approach. 'Provided of course that we get a degree of cooperation from the tugboat men, barge men and private owners whose boats are at the moment resting on the mud at the bottom of the canal. The boats that settled on an even keel are no problem: those which have fallen over on their sides could well fill up. I suppose self-interest will ensure cooperation.'

De Graaf said: 'Any loss of life in the canal? Or anybody hurt?'

'One of my inspectors reports a considerable degree of high

13

blood pressure among the skippers and crews of the stranded craft. That apart, no one was harmed.'

'Thank you. The messages came from a man or a group signing themselves FFF – it was not explained what those initials were meant to stand for. The intention, it was said, was to demonstrate that they could flood any part of our country whenever and wherever they wished by blowing up a strategically placed dyke and that accordingly they intended to give a small scale demonstration that would endanger no one and cause as little inconvenience as possible.'

'As little inconvenience! Small scale.' De Jong was back at his fist clenching. 'I wonder what the devil they would regard as a large scale demonstration?'

De Graaf nodded. 'Quite. They said the target was Schiphol and that the flooding would come at 11 a.m. Not one minute before eleven, not one minute after. As we know, the breach was blown at precisely 11 a.m. At police headquarters, quite frankly, this was regarded as a hoax – after all, who in his right mind would want to turn Schiphol airport into an inland sea? Perhaps they saw some symbolic significance in their choice – after all, the Dutch navy defeated the Spanish navy at this very spot when the present Schiphol really was a sea. Hoax or not, we took no chances. The canal was the obvious choice for any saboteur so we had both sides of the north bank of the canal closely examined. There were no signs of any kind of disturbance that could have indicated a preparation for the blowing of the dyke. So we assumed it was some kind of practical joke.' De Graaf shrugged, palms uplifted. 'As we know too late nothing was further from the mind or minds of the FFF than fun and games.'

He turned to the man seated on his left side. 'Peter, you've had time to think. Have you any idea – sorry, gentlemen, sorry. Some of you may not know my colleague here. Lieutenant Peter van Effen. Lieutenant van Effen is my senior detective lieutenant. He is also an explosives expert and, for his sins, the head of the city's bomb disposal squad. Have you figured out yet how it was done?'

Peter van Effen was an unremarkable figure. Like his boss,

he was just over medium height, uncommonly broad and looked suspiciously as if he were running to fat. He was in his mid or late thirties, had thick dark hair, a dark moustache and an almost permanent expression of amiability. He didn't look like a senior detective lieutenant, in fact he didn't even look like a policeman. Many people, including quite a number of people in Dutch prisons, tended to take van Effen's easy-going affability at its face value.

'It didn't take much figuring, sir. Anything's easy with hindsight. But even had we had foresight there was nothing we could have done about it anyway. We'll almost certainly find that two boats were tied up bow to stern alongside the north bank. Unusual, but there's no law, say, against an engine breakdown and a sympathetic owner of a passing vessel stopping to lend a hand. I should imagine that we'll find that those boats were almost certainly stolen because there is traffic on the canal and any habitual waterway user would have been able to identify them.

'The two boats would have been very close or even overlapping, leaving a clear, hidden area where scuba divers could work. If this took place during dusk or night-time, as I'm sure it did, they would have bright lights on deck and when you have those on, anything below gunwale level is in deep shadow. They would have had a drilling machine, something like the ones you use on oil-rigs only, of course, this one would have been on a very small scale and operated horizontally not vertically. It would have been electrically powered, either by batteries or a generator, because the exhausts of a petrol or diesel plant make a great deal of noise. For an expert, and there are literally hundreds of experts operating on or around the North Sea, this would have been a childishly simple operation. They would drill through to, say, a foot of the other side of the dyke – we may be sure they would have taken very careful measurements beforehand – withdraw the bit and insert a waterproof canvas tube packed with explosives, maybe just plain old-fashioned dynamite or TNT, although a real expert would have gone for amatol beehives. They would then attach an electrical timing device, nothing elaborate, an old-fashioned kitchen alarm clock will do very well, plug the hole with mud and gravel – not that there would be a chance in a million of anyone ever looking there – and sail away.'

'I could almost believe, Mr van Effen, that you master-minded this operation yourself,' van der Kuur said. 'So that's how it was done.'

'It's how I would have done it and within the limits of a slight variation that's how they did it. There is no other way.' Van Effen looked at de Graaf. 'We're up against a team of experts and the person directing them is no clown. They know how to steal boats, they know how to handle them, they know where to steal drilling equipment, they know how to use that equipment and they're obviously at home with explosives. No wild-eyed, slogan-chanting cranks among this lot: they're professionals. I've asked head office to notify us immediately if they receive any complaints from factories, wholesalers or retailers of the theft of any equipment from the manufacturers or distributors of drilling equipment. Also to notify us of the theft of any vessels from that area.'

'And beyond that?' de Graaf said.

'Nothing. We have no leads.'

De Graaf nodded and looked down at the paper he held in his hands. 'That message from the mysterious FFF. No indication whatsoever as to the reason behind this threatened – now actual – sabotage. Just a warning that nobody should be at ground level at 11 a.m. this morning and that all planes should be flown out yesterday afternoon or evening to adjacent airfields as the needless destruction of property formed no part of their plans. Very considerate of them, I must say. And even more consider-ate, Jon, was the phone call you got at nine o'clock this morning urging you to evacuate all those planes immediately. But, of course, we all knew it was a hoax, so we paid no attention. Would you recognize that voice again, Jon?'

'Not a chance. It was a woman's voice, a young woman and speaking in English. All young women speaking English sound the same to me.' Fist clenched, de Jong gently thumped the table before him. 'They don't even hint at the reason for carrying out this – this monstrous action. What have they achieved by this action? Nothing. Absolutely nothing. I repeat that any person or persons who behave in this fashion have to be mentally unbalanced.'

Van Effen said: 'I'm sorry, sir, I disagree. I do agree with what the Colonel said on the roof – they're almost certainly as sane as any one. No one who is mentally unbalanced could have carried out this operation. And they're not, as I said, wild-eyed terrorists throwing bombs in crowded market-places. In two separate warnings they did their best to ensure that neither human lives nor property would be put at risk. That was not the behaviour of irresponsible people.'

'And who, then, was responsible for the deaths of the three people who lost their lives when that Fokker Friendship cart-wheeled and crashed on take-off?'

'The saboteurs, indirectly. One could equally well say that you were, also indirectly. It might be argued you might at least have considered the possibility that the threat was not a hoax, taken even the most remote possibility into account and refused permission for the Fokker to take off at exactly 11 a.m. But that permission was given, personally I understand, by you. It is as certain as certain can be that the saboteurs had carefully checked landing and take-off schedules and made sure that there were no planes either taking off or landing at or near that time. That Fokker was the private plane of a German industrial-ist and was therefore not listed on the scheduled departures. I suggest, Mr de Jong, that it's futile to ascribe the blame for those three deaths to anyone. Sheer bad luck, an unfortunate coincidence in timing, an act of God, call it what you like. There was nothing planned, nothing calculated, no motive behind those deaths. It was nobody's fault.'

De Jong had substituted finger-drumming for table thump-ing. 'If those evil men were as considerate as you say, why didn't they postpone the explosion when they saw people boarding the plane?'

'Because we don't know that they were in a position to see anything and, even if they were, they were almost certainly unable to do anything about it. Had the explosives been activated by a radio-controlled device, sure, they could have

17

stopped it. But, as I told you, I'm pretty certain it was an electrical timer and to de-activate that they would have had to assemble a boat, scuba gear and diver – and all in broad daylight – in a matter of minutes. In the time available, that would have been impossible.'

There was a faint but unmistakable sheen of sweat on de Jong's forehead. 'They could have phoned a warning.'

Van Effen looked at de Jong for a long moment, then said: 'How much attention did you pay to the previous warning this morning?'

De Jong made no reply.

'And you've just said that the saboteurs have achieved nothing, absolutely nothing, by their action. I know you're upset, sir, and it seems unfair to press the point, but can you really be so naive as to believe that? They've already made a considerable achievement. They have achieved the beginnings of a climate of fear and uncertainty, a climate that can only worsen with the passing of the hours. If they've struck once, apparently without a blind bit of motivation, are the chances not high that they will strike again? If they do, when? If they do, where? And, above all, there's the why. What overpowering reason do they have to behave as they do?' He looked at de Graaf. 'Soften up the victim but keep him in suspense as to your purpose in behaving in this fashion. It's a novel form of blackmail and I see no reason why it shouldn't work. I have the strong feeling that we are going to hear from the FFF in the very near future. Not to state the reasons for acting as they do, certainly not to make any specific demands. Dear me, no. Not that. That's not the way you conduct psychological warfare. One turns the wheel that stretches the rack very, very slowly over a calculated period of time. Gives the victim time to ponder more deeply about the hopelessness of his situation while his morale sinks lower and lower. At least that's how I believe they operated in the Middle Ages – when using the actual instrument, of course.'

De Jong said sourly: 'You seem to know a lot about the workings of the criminal mind.'

'A little.' Van Effen smiled agreeably. 'I wouldn't presume to tell you how to run an airport.'

18

'And what am I to understand from that?'

'Mr van Effen just means that a cobbler should stick to his last.' De Graaf made a placatory gesture with his hand. 'He's the author of the now established text-book on the psychology of the criminal mind. Never read it myself. So, Peter. You seem sure the FFF will contact us very soon, but not to tell us about themselves or their objectives. Tell us what? The where and the when? Their next – ah – demonstration?'

'What else?'

A profound and rather gloomy silence was ended by the entrance of a waiter who approached de Jong. 'Telephone, sir. Is there a Lieutenant van Effen here?'

'Me.' Van Effen followed the waiter from the canteen and returned within a minute and addressed himself to de Graaf.

'Duty sergeant. Apparently two men reported their boats missing some hours ago. Pleasure boat owners. The sergeant who took their complaint didn't think it necessary to notify our department. Quite right, of course. The boats have now been recovered. One, it would seem, was taken by force. The boats are in our hands. I told them to take a couple of finger-print men aboard, return the boats to the owners but not to allow the owners aboard. If you can spare the time, sir, we can interview the two owners after we leave here: they live less than a kilometre from here.'

'A promising lead, yes?'

'No.'

'I don't think so either. However, no stone unturned. We may as well go now and –'

He broke off as the same waiter reappeared and approached him. 'Phone again. For you this time, Colonel.'

De Graaf returned in a matter of seconds. 'Jon, have you such a thing as a shorthand typist?'

'Of course. Jan?'

'Sir?' A blond youngster was on his feet.

'You heard the Colonel?'

'Yes, sir.' He looked at de Graaf. 'What shall I say?'

'Ask her to take that phone call and type it out for me. Peter, you have clairvoyance, the second sight.'

'The FFF?'

'Indeed. The press, I need hardly say. The FFF have their publicity priorities right. Usual anonymous phone call. The sub-editor who took the call was smart enough to tape-record it but I'd be surprised if that is of the slightest help. A fairly lengthy statement, I understand. Shorthand is not my forte. Let us possess our souls in patience.'

They had possessed their souls for not more than four minutes when a girl entered and handed a type-written sheet to de Graaf. He thanked her, looked briefly at the sheet and said: 'Action this day would appear to be their motto. This, I understand, is their statement in full and a fairly arrogant example of its kind it is, too. This is what the FFF says:

'"Next time, perhaps, the responsible citizens in Amsterdam will listen to what we say, believe what we say and act accordingly. It is because you did not believe what we said that a misadventure occurred today. For this misadventure we hold Mr de Jong entirely responsible. He was given due warning and chose to ignore that warning. We deplore the unnecessary deaths of the three passengers aboard the Fokker Friendship but disclaim all responsibility. It was not possible for us to arrest the explosion."' De Graaf paused and looked at van Effen. 'Interesting?'

'Very. So they had an observer. We'll never find him. He could have been in the airport but hundreds of people who don't work here visit here every day. For all we know, there could have been someone outside the airport with a pair of binoculars. But that's not what is interesting. The four first-aid men who brought in the most seriously injured passengers did not know at the time whether the three men who were later pronounced dead were, in fact, dead or alive. Two of them, I understand, died after admission, but none was officially pronounced dead until the doctor certified them as such. How did the FFF know? Neither the doctor nor the first-aid men could have been responsible for leaking the news for they would be the obvious suspects and all too easily checked on. Apart from them, the only people who knew of those deaths are in this room.' Van

Effen looked leisurely around the sixteen men and three women seated at the canteen tables then turned to de Jong.

'It hardly needs spelling out, does it, sir? We have an infiltrator here, an informant. The enemy has a spy in our camp.' Again he carried out the same slow survey of the room. 'I do wonder who it can be.'

'In this room?' De Jong looked both disbelieving and unhappy at the same time.

'I don't have to repeat the obvious, do I?'

De Jong looked down at his hands which were now tightly clasped on the table. 'No. No. Of course not. But, surely, well, we can find out. *You* can find out.'

'The usual rigorous enquiries, is that it? Trace the movements of every person in this room after the Fokker crashed? Find out if anyone had access to the phone or, indeed, used a phone? Sure, we can do that, pursue the rigorous enquiries. We'll find nothing.'

'You'll find nothing?' De Jong looked his perplexity. 'How can you be so sure, so sure in advance?'

'Because,' de Graaf said, 'the Lieutenant has a policeman's mind. Not a bunch to be under-estimated, are they, Peter?'

'They're clever.'

De Jong looked from de Graaf to van Effen then back to de Graaf. 'If someone would kindly explain . . .'

'Simple, really,' de Graaf said. 'It hasn't occurred to you that the FFF didn't have to let us know that they knew of the deaths. Gratuitous information, if you like. They would know that we would know this. They would know, as the Lieutenant has just pointed out, that we would know that someone had informed them and that someone would have to be one of us. They would be certain that we would check on the possibility of someone here having made a phone call, so they made certain that no one here made a phone call. He passed the word on to an accomplice who is not in this room: the accomplice made the call. I'm afraid, Jon, that you have another mole burrowing away inside here. Maybe even more. You are aware, of course, that every word of our conversation will be reported back to the FFF, whoever they may be. We will, naturally, go through the

21

motions and make the necessary routine enquiries. As van Effen says, we will, of course, draw a blank.'

'But – but it all seems so pointless,' de Jong said. 'Why should they be so devious so as to achieve nothing?'

'They're not really devious and they do achieve something. A degree of demoralization, for one thing. More important, they are saying that they are a force to be reckoned with, that they can infiltrate and penetrate security when they so choose. They are giving the message that they are a highly organized group, one that is capable of carrying out any threats that it chooses to make and one that is to be ignored at our peril.

'Speaking of threats and perils, let's return to the FFF's latest phone call. They go on to say: "We are sure that the Dutch people are well aware that, in the face of an attacker determined to bring it to its knees, it is the most defenceless nation in the world. The sea is not your enemy. We are, and the sea is our ally.

'"You will not need reminding that the Netherlands has about 1300 kilometres of sea dykes. A certain Cornelius Rijpma, president of the Sea Polder board in Leeuwarden, in Friesland, is on record as saying some months ago that the dykes in his area consist of nothing more than layers of sand and that if a big storm comes they are certain to break. By a 'big storm', one would assume that it would have to be a storm of the order of the one that breached the delta defences in 1953 and took 1,850 lives. Our information, supplied to us by the Rijkswaterstaat, is that –'

'What! What!' Van der Kuur, red-faced and almost incoherent with anger, was on his feet. 'Are those devils daring to suggest that they got information from us? Dastardly! Impossible!'

'Let me finish, Mr van der Kuur. Can't you see that they're using the same technique again, trying to undermine confidence and demoralize? Just because we know that they have contacts with one or more of Mr de Jong's staff is no proof that they have any with your people. Anyway, there's worse to come. They go on: "Our information is that a storm of not more than 70% of the power of the 1953 one would be sufficient to breach the dykes. Mr Rijpma was talking about vulnerable dykes. Of the Netherlands' 1300 kilometres of dykes, almost exactly three hundred have deteriorated to a critical condition. By the best estimates, no repairs will be carried out to the threatened dykes for another twelve years, that is to say, 1995. All we propose to do is to accelerate the advent of the inevitable."'

De Graaf paused and looked around. A chilled hush seemed to have fallen over the canteen. Only two people were looking at him: the others were either gazing at the floor or into the far distance; in both cases it was not difficult to guess that they didn't like what they saw.

'"The dykes cannot be repaired because there is no money to repair them. All the money available, or likely to be available in the future, is being sunk or will be sunk into the construction of the East Scheldt storm-surge barrier, the last link in the so-called Delta plan designed to keep the North Sea at bay. The costs are staggering. Due to gross original underestimates, cost over-runs and inflation, the likely bill will probably be in excess of nine billion guilders – and this massive sum for a project that some engineering experts say will not work anyway. The project consists of 63 lock-gates fitted between enormous, 18,000 tonne, free-standing concrete pillars. The dissident experts fear that heavy seas could shift the pillars, jam the locks and render the barrier inoperable. A shift of two centimetres would be enough. Ask Mr van der Kuur of the Rijkswaterstaat."'

De Graaf paused and looked up. Van der Kuur was on his feet again, every bit as apoplectic as on the previous occasion: the thought was inevitable that van der Kuur's normal air of pipe-puffing imperturbability was a very thin veneer indeed.

'Lies!' he shouted. 'Rubbish! Balderdash! Defamation! Calumny! Lies, I tell you, lies!'

'You're the engineer in charge. You should know. So, really, there's no need to get so worked up about it.' De Graaf's tone was mild, conciliatory. 'The dissidents the FFF speak about – they have no hydraulic engineering qualifications?'

'The dissidents! A handful. Qualifications? Of course. Paper qualifications! Not one of them has any practical experience as far as this matter is concerned.'

Van Effen said: 'Does anybody have on this project? Practical experience, I mean. I understood that the East Scheldt involved completely untested engineering techniques and that you are, in effect, moving into the realms of the unknown.' He raised a hand as van der Kuur was about to rise again. 'Sorry. This is all really irrelevant. What is relevant is that there is a mind or minds among the FFF that is not only highly intelligent but has a clear understanding about the application of practical psychology. First, they introduce the elements of doubt, dismay, dissension and the erosion of confidence into Schiphol. Then they apply the same techniques to the Rijkswaterstaat. And now, through the medium of every paper in the land, this evening or tomorrow morning, and doubtless, through television and radio, they will introduce those same elements into the nation at large. If you ask me, they have – or will have – achieved a very great deal in a very short space of time. A remarkable feat. They are to be respected as strategists if not as human beings. I trust that the traitor in our midst will report that back to them.'

'Indeed,' de Graaf said. 'And I trust the same traitor will understand if we don't discuss the steps we plan to undertake to combat this menace. Well, ladies and gentlemen, to the final paragraph of their message and incidentally, no doubt, to introduce some more of what the Lieutenant referred to as doubt, dismay, dissension, erosion of confidence or whatever. They go on to say: "In order to demonstrate your helplessness and our ability to strike at will wherever and whenever we choose, we would advise you that a breach will be made in the Texel sea dyke at 4.30 p.m. this afternoon."'

'What!' The word came simultaneously from at least half a dozen people.

'Shook me a bit, too,' de Graaf said. 'That's what they say. I don't for a moment doubt them. Brinkman' – this to a uniformed young police officer – 'contact the office. No urgency, probably, but check that people on the island know what's coming to them. Mr van der Kuur, I'm sure I can leave it to you to have the necessary men and equipment to stand by.' He consulted the sheet again. 'Not a big operation, they say. "We are sure that damage will be minimal but it might behove the citizens of Oosterend and De Waal to stand by their boats or take to their attics shortly after 4.30. Very shortly." Damned arrogance. They end up by saying: "We know that those names will give you a fairly accurate idea as to where the charges have been placed. We defy you to find them."'

'And that's all?' van der Kuur said.

'That's all.'

'No reasons, no explanations for those damned outrages? No demands? Nothing?'

'Nothing.'

'I still say we're up against a bunch of raving maniacs.'

'And I say that we're up against clever and very calculating criminals who are more than content to let us stew in our own juice for the time being. I wouldn't worry about the demands, if I were you. These will come in due time – their time. Well, nothing more we can achieve here – not, on reflection, that we have achieved anything. I bid you good day, Mr de Jong, and hope that you'll be back in operational services some time tomorrow. It'll take days, I suppose, to replace the machinery ruined in your basements.'

On their way out, van Effen made a gesture to de Graaf to hold back. He looked casually around to make sure that no one was within earshot and said: 'I'd like to put tails on a couple of gentlemen who were in that room.'

'Well, you don't waste time, I will say. You have, of course, your reasons.'

'I was watching them when you broke the news of the proposed Texel breach. It hit them. Most of them just stared away into space and those who didn't were studying the floor. All of them, I assume, were considering the awful implications. Two did neither. They just kept on looking at you. Maybe they didn't react because it didn't come as any news to them.'

'Straws. You're just clutching at straws.'

'Isn't that what a drowning man is supposed to do?'

'With all the water that's around, present and promised, you might have picked a less painful metaphor. Who?'

'Alfred van Rees.'

'Ah. The Rijkswaterstaat's Locks, Weirs and Sluices man. Preposterous. Friend of mine. Honest as the day's long.'

'Maybe the Mr Hyde in him doesn't come out until after sunset. And Fred Klassen.'

'Klassen! Schiphol's security chief. Preposterous.'

'That's twice. Or is he a friend of yours, too?'

'Impossible. Twenty years' unblemished service. The *security* chief?'

'If you were a criminal and were given the choice of subverting any one man in a big organization, who would you go for?'

De Graaf looked at him for a long moment, then walked on in silence.

Two

Bakkeren and Dekker were the names of the two boat-owners who had been involuntarily deprived of their vessels during the previous night. As it turned out, they were brothers-in-law. Bakkeren was phlegmatic about the borrowing of his boat and not particularly concerned by the fact that he had not yet been allowed to examine his boat to see what damage, if any, had been done to it. Dekker, by contrast and understandably, was seething with rage: he had, as he had informed de Graaf and van Effen within twenty seconds of their arrival at his suburban home, been rather roughly handled during the previous evening.

'Is no man safe in this godforsaken city?' He didn't speak the words, he shouted them, but it was reasonable to assume that this was not his normal conversational custom. 'Police, you say you are, police! Ha! Police! A fine job you do of guarding the honest citizens of Amsterdam. There I was, sitting in my own boat and minding my own business when those four gangsters –'

'Moment,' van Effen said. 'Were they wearing gloves?'

'Gloves!' Dekker, a small dark, intense man, stared at him in outraged disbelief. 'Gloves! Here am I, the victim of a savage assault, and all you can think of –'

'Gloves.'

Something in van Effen's tone had reached through the man's anger, one could almost see his blood pressure easing a few points. 'Gloves, eh? Funny, that. Yes, they were. All of them.'

Van Effen turned to a uniformed sergeant. 'Bernhard.'

'Yes, sir. I'll tell the finger-print men to go home.'

'Sorry, Mr Dekker. Tell it your way. If there was anything that struck you as unusual or odd, let us know.'

'It was all bloody odd,' Dekker said morosely. He had been, as he had said, minding his own business in his little cabin, when he had been hailed from the bank. He'd gone on deck and a tall man – it was almost dark and his features had been indistinguishable – had asked him if he could hire the boat for the night. He said he was from a film company and wanted to shoot some night scenes and offered a thousand guilders. Dekker had thought it extremely odd that an offer of that nature should have been made at such short notice and with night falling: he had refused. Next thing he knew, three other men had appeared on the scene, he'd been dragged from the boat, bundled into a car and driven to his home.

Van Effen said: 'Did you direct them?'

'Are you mad?' Looking at the fiery little man it was impossible to believe that he would volunteer information to anyone.

'So they've been watching your movements for some time. You weren't aware that you were under surveillance at any time?'

'Under what?'

'Being watched, followed, seeing the same stranger an unusual number of times?'

'Who'd watch and follow a fishmonger? Well, who would think they would? So they hauled me into the house –'

'Didn't you try to escape at any time?'

'Would you listen to the man?' Dekker was justifiably bitter. 'How far would you get with your wrists handcuffed behind your back?'

'Handcuffs?'

'I suppose you thought that only police used those things. So they dragged me into the bathroom, tied my feet with a clothes line and taped my mouth with Elastoplast. Then they locked the door from the outside.'

'You were completely helpless?'

'Completely.' The little man's face darkened at the recollection. 'I managed to get to my feet and a hell of a lot of good that did me. There's no window in the bathroom. If there had been I don't know of any way I could have broken it and even if I had there was no way I could shout for help, was there? Not with

God knows how many strips of plaster over my mouth.

'Three or four hours later – I'm not sure how long it was – they came back and freed me. The tall man told me they'd left fifteen hundred guilders on the kitchen table – a thousand for the hire of the boat and five hundred for incidental expenses.'

'What expenses?'

'How should I know?' Dekker sounded weary. 'They didn't explain. They just left.'

'Did you see them go? Type of car, number, anything like that?'

'I did not see them go. I did not see their car, far less its number.' Dekker spoke with the air of a man who is exercising massive restraint. 'When I say they freed me, I meant that they had unlocked and removed the handcuffs. Took me a couple of minutes to remove the strips of Elastoplast and damnably painful it was, too. Took quite a bit of skin amd my moustache with it too. Then I hopped through to the kitchen and got the bread knife to the ropes round my ankles. The money was there, all right and I'd be glad if you'd put it in your police fund because I won't touch their filthy money. Almost certainly stolen anyway. They and their car, of course, were to hell and gone by that time.'

Van Effen was diplomatically sympathetic. 'Considering what you've been through, Mr Dekker, I think you're being very calm and restrained. Could you describe them?'

'Ordinary clothes. Rain-coats. That's all.'

'Their faces?'

'It was dark on the canal bank, dark in the car and by the time we reached here they were all wearing hoods. Well, three of them. One stayed on the boat.'

'Slits in the hoods, of course.' Van Effen wasn't disappointed, he'd expected nothing else.

'Round holes, more like.'

'Did they talk among themselves?'

'Not a word. Only the leader spoke.'

'How do you know he was the leader?'

'Leaders give orders, don't they?'

'I suppose. Would you recognize the voice again?'

Dekker hesitated. 'I don't know. Well, yes, I think I would.'

'Ah. Something unusual about his voice?'

'Yes. Well. He talked funny Dutch.'

'Funny?'

'It wasn't – what shall I say – Dutch Dutch.'

'Poor Dutch, is that it?'

'No. The other way around. It was very good. Too good. Like the news-readers on TV and radio.'

'Too precise, yes? Book Dutch. A foreigner, perhaps?'

'That's what I would guess.'

'Would you have any idea where he might have come from?'

'There you have me, Lieutenant. I've never been out of the country. I hear often enough that many people in the city speak English or German or both. Not me. I speak neither. Foreign tourists don't come to a fishmonger's shop. I sell my fish in Dutch.'

'Thanks, anyway. Could be a help. Anything else about this leader – if that's what he was?'

'He was tall, very tall.' He tried his first half-smile of the afternoon. 'You don't have to be tall to be taller than I am but I didn't even reach up to his shoulders. Ten, maybe twelve centimetres taller than you are. And thin, very very thin: he was wearing a long rain-coat, blue it was, that came way below his knees and it fell from his shoulders like a coat hanging from a coat-hanger.'

'The hoods had holes, you say, not slits. You could see this tall man's eyes?'

'Not even that. This fellow was wearing dark eye-glasses.'

'Sun-glasses? I did ask you to tell me if there was anything odd about those people. Didn't you think it odd that a person should be wearing a pair of sun-glasses at night?'

'Odd? Why should it be odd? Look, Lieutenant, a bachelor like me spends a lot of time watching movies and TV. The villains always wear dark glasses. That's how you can tell they're villains.'

'True, true.' Van Effen turned to Dekker's brother-in-law. 'I understand, Mr Bakkeren, that you were lucky enough to escape the attentions of those gentlemen.'

'Wife's birthday. In town for a dinner and show. Anyway, they could have stolen my boat any time and I would have known nothing about it. If they were watching Maks here, they would have been watching me and they'd know that I only go near my boat on weekends.'

Van Effen turned to de Graaf. 'Would you like to see the boats, sir?'

'Do you think we'll find anything?'

'No. Well, might find out what they've been doing. I'll bet they haven't left one clue for hard-working policemen to find.'

'Might as well waste some more time.'

The brothers-in-law went in their own car, the two policemen in van Effen's, an ancient and battered Peugeot with a far from ancient engine. It bore no police distinguishing marks whatsoever and even the radio telephone was concealed. De Graaf lowered himself gingerly into the creaking and virtually springless seat.

'I refrain from groaning and complaining, Peter. I know there must be a couple of hundred similar wrecks rattling about the streets of Amsterdam and I appreciate your passion for anonymity, but would it kill you to replace or re-upholster the passenger seat?'

'I thought it lent a nice touch of authenticity. But it shall be done. Pick up anything back in the house there?'

'Nothing that you didn't. Interesting that the tall thin man should be accompanied by a couple of mutes. It has occurred to you that if the leader, as Dekker calls him, is a foreigner then his henchmen are also probably foreigners and may very well be unable to speak a word of Dutch?'

'It had occurred and it is possible. Dekker said that the leader gave orders which would give one to understand that they spoke, or at least understood, Dutch. Doesn't necessarily follow, of course. The orders may have been meaningless and given only to convince the listener that the others were Dutch. Pity that Dekker has never ventured beyond the frontiers of his own homeland. He might – I say just might – have been able to identify the country of origin of the owner of that voice. I speak two or three languages, Peter, you even more. Do you think, if

31

we'd heard this person speaking, we'd have been able to tell his country?'

'There's a chance. I wouldn't put it higher than that. I know what you're thinking, sir. The tape-recording that this newspaper sub-editor made of the phone call they received. Chances there would be much poorer – you know how a phone call can distort a voice. And they don't strike me as people who would make such a fairly obvious mistake. Besides, even if we did succeed in guessing at the country of origin, how the hell would that help us in tracking them down?'

De Graaf lit up a very black cheroot. Van Effen wound down his window. De Graaf paid no attention. He said: 'You're a great comforter. Give us a few more facts – or let's dig up a few more – and it might be of great help to us. Apart from the fact, not yet established, that he may be a foreigner, all we know about this lad is that he's very tall, built along the lines of an emaciated garden rake and has something wrong with his eyes.'

'Wrong? The eyes, I mean, sir? All we know for certain is that he wears sun-glasses at night-time. Could mean anything or nothing. Could be a fad. Maybe he fancies himself in them. Maybe, as Dekker suggested, he thinks sun-glasses are *de rigueur* for the better class villain. Maybe, like the American President's Secret Service body-guards, he wears them because any potential malefactor in a crowd can never know whether the agent's eyes are fixed on him or not, thereby inhibiting him from action. Or he might be just suffering from nyctalopia.'

'I see. Nyctalopia. Every schoolboy knows, of course. I am sure, Peter, that you will enlighten me at your leisure.'

'Funny old word to describe a funny old condition. I am told it's the only English language word with two precisely opposite meanings. On the one hand, it means night-blindness, the recurrent loss of vision after sunset, the causes of which are only vaguely understood. On the other hand, it can be taken to mean day-blindness, the inability to see clearly except by night, and here the causes are equally obscure. A rare disease, whatever meaning you take, but its existence has been well attested to.

32

The sun-glasses, as we think of them, may well be fitted with special correctional lenses.'

'It would appear to me that a criminal suffering from either manifestation of this disease would be labouring under a severe occupational handicap. Both a house-breaker, who operates by daylight, and a burglar, who operates by night, would be a bit restricted in their movements if they were afflicted, respectively, by day or night blindness. Just a little bit too far-fetched for me, Peter. I prefer the old-fashioned reasons. Badly scarred about the eyes. Cross-eyed. Maybe he's got a squint. Maybe an eye whose iris is streaked or parti-coloured. Maybe wall-eyed, where the iris is so light that you can hardly distinguish it from the white or where the pupils are of two different colours. Maybe a sufferer from exophthalmic goitre, which results in very protuberant eyes. Maybe he's only *got* one eye. In any event, I'd guess he's suffering from some physical abnormality by which he would be immediately identifiable without the help of those dark glasses.'

'So now all we've got to do is to ask Interpol for a list, world-wide, of all known criminals with eye defects. There must be tens of thousands of them. Even if there were only ten on the list, it still wouldn't help us worth a damn. Chances are good, of course, that he hasn't even got a criminal record.' Van Effen pondered briefly. 'Or maybe they could give us a list of all albino criminals on their books. They need glasses to hide their eyes.'

'The Lieutenant is pleased to be facetious,' de Graaf said morosely. He puffed on his cheroot, then said, almost wonderingly: 'By Jove, Peter. You could be right.'

Ahead, Dekker had slowed to a stop and now van Effen did also. Two boats were moored alongside a canal bank, both about eleven or twelve metres in length, with two cabins and an open poop deck. The two policemen joined Dekker aboard his boat: Bakkeren boarded his own which lay immediately ahead. Dekker said: 'Well, gentlemen, what do you want to check first?'

De Graaf said: 'How long have you had this boat?'

'Six years.'

33

'In that case, I don't think Lieutenant van Effen or I will bother to check anything. After six years, you must know every corner, every nook and cranny on this boat. So we'd be grateful if you'd do the checking. Just tell us if there is anything here, even the tiniest thing, that shouldn't be here: or anything that's missing that should be here. You might, first, be so good as to ask your brother-in-law to do the same aboard his boat.'

Some twenty minutes later the brothers-in-law were able to state definitely that nothing had been left behind and that, in both cases, only two things had been taken: beer from the fridges and diesel from the tanks. Neither Dekker nor Bakkeren could say definitely how many cans of beer had been taken, they didn't count such things: but both were adamant that each fuel tank was down by at least twenty litres.

'Twenty litres each?' van Effen said. 'Well, they wouldn't have used two litres to get from here to the airport canal bank and back. So they used the engine for some other purpose. Can you open the engine hatch and let me have a torch?'

Van Effen's check of the engine-room battery was cursory, seconds only, but sufficient. He said: 'Do either of you two gentlemen ever use crocodile clips when using or charging your batteries – you know, those spring-loaded grips with the serrated teeth? No? Well, someone was using them last night. You can see the indentations on the terminals. They had the batteries in your two boats connected up, in parallel or series, it wouldn't have mattered, they'd have been using a transformer, and ran your engines to keep the batteries charged. Hence the missing forty litres.'

'I suppose,' Dekker said, 'that was what that gangster meant by incidental costs.'

'I suppose it was.'

De Graaf lowered himself, not protesting too much, into the springless, creaking passenger seat of the ancient Peugeot just as the radio telephone rang. Van Effen answered then passed the phone across to de Graaf who spoke briefly then returned the phone to its concealed position.

'I feared this,' de Graaf said. He sounded weary. 'My minister wants me to fly up with him to Texel. Taking half the cabinet with him, I understand.'

'Good God! Those rubber-necking clowns. What on earth do they hope to achieve by being up there? They'll only get in everyone's way, gum up the works and achieve nothing: but, then, they're very practised in that sort of thing.'

'I would remind you, Lieutenant van Effen, that you are talking about elected Ministers of the Crown.' If the words were intended as a reprimand, de Graaf's heart wasn't in it.

'A useless and incompetent bunch. Make them look important, perhaps get their name in the papers, might even be worth a vote or two among the more backward of the electorate. Still, I'm sure you'll enjoy it, sir.'

De Graaf glowered at him then said hopefully: 'I don't suppose you'd like to come, Peter?'

'You don't suppose quite correctly, sir. Besides, I have things to do.'

'Do you think I don't?' De Graaf looked and sounded very gloomy.

'Ah! But I'm only a cop. You have to be a cop and a diplomat. I'll drop you off at the office.'

'Join me for lunch?'

'Like to, sir, but I'm having lunch at an establishment, shall we say, where Amsterdam's Chief of Police wouldn't be seen dead. La Caracha it's called. Your wife and daughters wouldn't approve, sir.'

'Business, of course?'

'Of course. A little talk with a couple of our friends in the Krakers. You asked me a couple of months ago to keep a discreet, apart from an official, eye on them. They report occasionally, usually at La Caracha.'

'Ah! The Krakers. Haven't had much time to think of them in the past two months. And how are our disenchanted youth, the anti-everything students, the flower men, the hippies, the squatters?'

'And the drug-pushers and gun-runners? Keeping a suspiciously low profile, these days. I must say I feel happier, no that's not the word, less worried when they're heaving iron bars and bricks at our uniformed police and overturning and burning the odd car, because then we know where we are: with this unusual peace and quiet and uncharacteristic inactivity, I feel there's trouble brewing somewhere.'

'You're not actually looking for trouble, Peter?'

'I've got the nasty feeling I'm going to find it anyway. Looking will be quite unnecessary. Yesterday afternoon, when that call came from the FFF, I sent two of our best people into the area. They might come across something. An off-chance. But the crime in Amsterdam is becoming more and more centralized in the Kraker area. The FFF would you say qualify as criminals?'

'Birds of a feather? Well, maybe. But the FFF seem like pretty smart boys, maybe too smart to associate with the Krakers, who could hardly be called the intellectual Titans of crime.'

'The FFF. So far we've got a pretty tall fellow, with maybe something wrong with his eyes and maybe of foreign extraction. We've practically got it all wrapped up.'

'Sarcasm ill becomes you. All right, all right, no stone unturned, any action is better than nothing. What's the food like at La Caracha?'

'For that area, surprisingly good. I've had a few meals –' He broke off and looked at de Graaf. 'You are going to honour us at the table, sir?'

'Well, I thought, I mean, as Chief of Police –'

'Of course, of course. Delighted.'

'And no one will know where I am.' De Graaf seemed cheered at the prospect. 'That damned radio phone can ring its head off for all I care. I won't be able to hear it.'

'Nobody else will be able to hear it either. That damned phone, as you call it, will be switched off the moment we park. How do you think the dockland citizens are going to react when they hear a phone go off in this relic?'

They drove off. By and by de Graaf lit another cheroot, van Effen lowered his window and de Graaf said: 'You have, of course, checked up on the proprietor of La Caracha. What's he called?'

'He prefers to be known just as George. I know him moderately well. He's held in high regard among the local people.'

'A kindly man? A do-gooder? Charitable? An upstanding citizen, you would say?'

'He's reputed to be a ranking member of three, perhaps four, successful criminal organizations. Not drugs, not prostitution, he despises those and won't touch them: robbery, it is said, is his forte, usually armed, with or without violence according to the amount of resistance offered. He, himself, can be extremely violent. I can testify to that personally. The violence, of course, was not directed at me: you have to be out of your mind to attack a police lieutenant and George is very far from being out of his mind.'

'You do have a genius for picking your friends, associates, or whatever you call them, Peter.' De Graaf puffed at his cheroot and if he was ruffled in any way he didn't show it. 'Why isn't this menace to society behind bars?'

'You can't arrest, charge, try and convict a man on hearsay. I can't very well go up to George with a pair of handcuffs and say: "People have been telling me stories and I have to take you in." Besides, we're friends.'

'You've said yourself that he can be excessively violent. You can pull him in on that.'

'No. He's entitled to eject any person who is drunk, abusive, uses foul language or is guilty of causing an affray. That's the limit of George's violence. Ejection. Usually two at a time. The law says he can. We are the law.'

'Sounds an interesting character. Unusual, one might say. Two at a time, eh?'

'Wait till you see George.'

'And how do you propose to introduce me?'

'No need to emphasize the police connections. Just Colonel de Graaf. This is, shall we say, a semi-official visit.'

'I may be recognized.'

'Colonel, there isn't a self-respecting criminal in this city who wouldn't recognize you at a distance of half a kilometre. When their kids are misbehaving they probably whip out your picture, show it to their offspring and tell them if they don't mend their ways – the bogieman will come and get them.'

'Extremely witty. You're not exactly unknown yourself, Peter. I'd be curious to know what the – ah – criminal element hereabouts think about you.'

'You don't have to be curious. They think I'm bent.'

The unprepossessing entrance to La Caracha was located halfway down a lane so narrow that not even a car could enter it. The cracker plaster of the tiny entrance porch, the fading and peeling paint belied the bar room that lay beyond. This was well lit and clean, with gleaming knotted-pine walls, half-a-dozen tables, each with four small armchairs instead of the usual metal or plastic seats, a semi-circular bar flanked by fixed stools and, beyond the bar, the barman. When one looked at him one forgot about the rest of the room.

He was huge. Very tall and very broad he probably weighed in about a hundred and thirty kilos. He wore a rather splendid Mexican sombrero – one assumed there was some connection between the barman's headgear and the vaguely Latin American name of the restaurant – a white shirt, a black string tie, an open black waistcoat and black leather trousers. The absence of a gun-belt and a holstered Peacemaker Colt struck a discordant note. The eyes were dark, the bushy eyebrows black and the equally black moustache, equally bushy, luxuriant and dropping down past the corners of his mouth, perfectly complemented the spectacular sombrero. The craggy face appeared to have been hacked from granite by an enthusiastic but ungifted stone-mason. He was the epitome of all those 'wanted' portraits that used to adorn the walls of nineteenth century western American saloons.

'That's George?' Van Effen didn't bother to answer the superfluous question. 'When he ejects them two at a time I assume he uses only one hand.'

George caught sight of them and hurried round the corner of the bar, a wide, welcoming smile revealing startlingly white teeth. The nearer he approached, the bigger he seemed to become. His hand was out-stretched while he was still quite some distance away.

38

'Welcome, Peter, my friend, welcome. *And* Colonel van de Graaf. My word, this is indeed an honour.' He pumped the Colonel's hand as if he were a twin brother he hadn't seen for twenty years.

De Graaf smiled. 'You know me then?'

'If there is anyone in the city who doesn't recognize our Commissioner of Police he must either be blind or never read newspapers or magazines. Peter, as of this moment, my reputation is made.' He looked at de Graaf and dropped his voice. 'Provided, of course that this is not an official visit.'

'Purely unofficial,' de Graaf said. 'Regard me as the Lieutenant's guest.'

'It is my pleasure to celebrate this auspicious occasion,' George said. 'Borreltje, jonge jenever, whisky, beer, wine – La Caracha has an excellent wine cellar. No better in Amsterdam. But I recommend my bessenjenever, gentlemen. Ice just beginning to form on the top.' He touched his lips. 'Incomparable.'

So it proved, and in the quantities that George supplied it the bessenjenever – red-currant gin – was as formidable as it was incomparable. George remained with them for a few minutes, discoursing freely on a variety of subjects but mainly and inevitably about the dyke breach that had brought back into existence the long-vanished Haarlem lake.

'No need to look for the perpetrators of this crime among the professional criminals of the Netherlands.' George sounded very positive. 'I use the word "professional" because one would have to exclude the pitifully amateurish criminals among the Krakers, hot-headed madmen capable of any atrocity, no matter how many innocents suffer, in the name of their crazy and woolly ideals, totally amoral lunatics, mindless idiots who love destruction for destruction's sake. But they are not Dutchmen, though they may have been born in this country: they're just members of a terminally sick sub-culture that you'll find in many other countries.

'But I don't think they're responsible for the Schiphol flooding. However much one may deplore the action of the saboteurs one has to admire the clear-headed intelligence that lies behind it. Nobody with a clear-headed intelligence would ever dream of associating with the retarded morons who make up the Krakers, though that's not to say the Krakers couldn't be employed in some subordinate capacity where they wouldn't be allowed to know enough to do any damage. But no Dutchman, however criminally minded, would or could have been responsible. Every Dutchman is born with the belief, the certain knowledge, that our dykes are inviolable: it is an act of faith. I am not – what is the word, gentlemen? – I am not xenophobic, but this is a foreign-inspired idea being carried out by foreigners. And it's only the beginning. There will be further atrocities. Wait and see.'

'We won't have to wait long,' de Graaf said. 'They're going to breach the Texel sea dyke at four-thirty this afternoon.'

George nodded, as if the news had come as no surprise to him.

'So soon, so soon. And then the next dyke, and then the next, and the next. When the blackmail demands come, as come they must, for nothing other than blackmail can lie behind this, they will be horrendous.' He glanced towards his bar where a group of men were making urgent signals that they were dying of thirst. 'You will excuse me, gentlemen.'

'An extraordinary fellow,' de Graaf said. 'He would have made a splendid politician – he could hardly be accused of being at a loss for words. Strange type to be a criminal alleged to be associated with violence – he's an intelligent and clearly well-educated man. So, on the other hand, were a number of famous – notorious, rather – and highly successful criminals in the past. But I find him especially intriguing. He seems well into the criminal mind but at the same time he thinks and speaks like a cop. And he got on to the possibility that those criminals might come from another country in a fraction of the time that it took us to arrive at the possibility – and, unlike us, he had nothing to help or guide him towards that conclusion. Maybe you and I are fractionally less clever than we like to think we are.'

'Maybe you should hire George, on an ad hoc basis, substantive rank of sergeant, as a dyke-breach investigator. Rather a fine title, don't you think?'

'The title is fine, the idea is not. Set a thief to catch a thief –

the idea never did work. Do not jest with your superior in his hour of need. Speaking of need, when do we eat?'

'Let's ask.' George had returned with fresh supplies of bessenjenever. 'We'd like lunch, George.'

'The Colonel will eat here? La Caracha is doubly honoured. This table will do?'

'I'm expecting Vasco and Annemarie.'

'Of course.' George picked up the drinks tray and led the way up four steps into a dining room, bright, cheerful and so small that it held only two tables. George produced a menu. 'Everything is excellent. The Rodekool met Rolpens is superb.'

'Shall we have the superb, Peter?' de Graaf said.

'Fine. And, George, as our chief of police is with us, I think the expense account could stand a bottle of reasonable wine.'

'Reasonable? Do I believe my ears? A superb wine to go with a superb dish and strictly on La Caracha. A Château Latour, perhaps? I have said that there is no better cellar than mine in the city. Equally beyond dispute is the fact that I have far the best Bordeaux cellar.' George handed them their aperitifs. 'Sharpen your appetites, gentlemen. Annelise, I promise, will excel herself.'

When George left de Graaf said: 'Who's Annelise?'

'His wife. Less than half his size. He's terrified of her. A wonderful cook.'

'She is aware of his, what shall we say, extracurricular activities?'

'She knows nothing.'

'You mentioned a Vasco and an Annemarie. Those, I assume, are your informants. George seems to know about them.'

'He knows them pretty well. They're friends.'

'Does he also know that they're working under-cover for you?' Van Effen nodded and de Graaf frowned. 'Is this wise? Is it politic? Is it, dammit, even professional?'

'I trust George.'

'Maybe you do. I don't have to. To say you have the best Bordeaux cellar in Amsterdam is to make a pretty large claim. That would cost money, a great deal of money. Is he into the highjacking and smuggling rackets too or does he earn enough from his extra-curricular activities to buy honestly on the open market?'

'Look, sir, I never said George was a rogue, thief, crook, gangster or whatever. I was only quoting the neighbourhood opinion of him. I wanted you to make up your own mind about him. I do think you already have, only you still have reservations owing to the fact that you have a nasty, devious, suspicious mind which is why, I suppose, you're the city's Chief of Police. Annelise knows nothing about George's extra-curricular activities, as you call them, because there are none. George has never earned an illegal guilder in his life. He's totally straight and if every man in Amsterdam were as honest as he is you'd join the unemployed by nightfall. I was certain you'd caught on to this when you said he thought and spoke like a cop. He is – or was – a cop, and a damned good one, a sergeant in line for his inspectorate when he decided to retire last year. Phone the Chief of Police in Groningen and find out who he'd give a bag of gold for to have back on his staff.'

'I am staggered,' de Graaf said. He didn't look staggered, he just sat placidly puffing his cheroot and sipping his bessenjenever as if van Effen had been discussing the weather or crops. 'Different. Yes, different.' He didn't say what was different. 'Might have given me some kind of warning, though.'

'Thought you'd guess, sir. He's got cop written all over him. At least he had until he grew his moustache after retirement.'

'Any specialities?'

'Drugs and counter-terrorism. I should have said drugs then counter-terrorism.'

'Drugs? The only drug in the province of Groningen comes out of a gin bottle. Here's the place for him. Or, if I take you rightly, was. Why was he taken off. Who took him off?'

'Nobody. Nature took him off. To be a successful drugs cop you have to be able to merge unobtrusively into your background. You've seen him. He wasn't built to merge into anything.'

'What's more, they've never even *seen* a terrorist up north.'

'They're not all that thick on the ground down here either,

sir. Maybe that's why George resigned – no challenge, nothing left for him to do.'

'A waste. An intelligence like that devoting its life to serving up superfluous calories to already overweight Amsterdamers. Could be useful. Maybe there's something to your idea of ad hoc recruitment. In an emergency, could always have him co-opted.'

'Yes, sir. I thought that to co-opt anyone you required a committee, a quorum.'

'There's only one committee and quorum in the Amsterdam police force and I'm it. If you think he could be of help, just ask me. In fact, don't bother to ask me. I'm hungry.'

'Ah, yes. George normally serves up hors d'oeuvre. Maybe he thought there was no urgency.' He surveyed de Graaf's ample frame. 'Superfluous calories. However . . .' He rose, opened a wooden cupboard door to reveal a refrigerator, opened this and said: 'Half a smoked salmon. Smoked trout. Mountain Ham. Gouda, Edam, and a few other odds and ends.'

'There are no limits to the heights you might reach, my boy.' Some time later, the first sharp edge of his appetite temporarily blunted, he said: 'If you're too busy or too cowardly to accompany me to Texel, may one ask what you intend to do.'

'Depends on what I learn from Annemarie and Vasco. If, of course, anything. On balance, however, I think I'll go and do what poor George couldn't, merge unobtrusively among the Krakers in their garden suburb.'

'You! You're mad. The unchallenged *bête noire* of Krakerdom. Two minutes after your arrival all activity and conversation will wither on the vine.'

'I've been there more than once in the past and the vine has remained unaffected. I don't wear this rather nice pin-stripe you see before you or my official uniform. I wear another uniform. My Kraker uniform. I don't think I've ever discussed my wardrobe with you before.' Van Effen sipped some more bessenjenever. 'I've a sealskin jacket with lots and lots of tassels and a coonskin hat with a wolverine's tail attached to the back. Rather dashing, really.' De Graaf closed his eyes, screwed them tightly shut and then opened them again. 'The trousers are made of some other kind of skin, I don't know what it is, with lots of little leather strips down the sides. Moccasins, of course. Those were a mistake. The moccasins, I mean. They leak. Then my hair and my moustache are blond, not platinum, you understand, that would attract too much attention.'

'The rest of your outfit doesn't?'

'The dye is impervious to any rain-storm. Have to use a special detergent to get it off. A painful process. Then I wear half a dozen rings, solid brass, on my right hand.'

'That the hand you hit people with?'

'Among other things I'm a Green Peace, anti-nuclear, environmental pacifist. I also have a multicoloured bead necklace, double chain, and an earring. Only one earring. Two are passé.'

'This, some day, I must see.'

'I can get you one like it, if you like.' De Graaf closed his eyes again and was saved further comment by the arrival of George with lunch. George served the Rodekool met Rolpens, opened the Château Latour with a suitably reverential air and departed. The meal was a simple one, red cabbage, rolled spiced meat and sliced apple, but, as George had promised, splendidly cooked: as was customary in Amsterdam there was enough food for four. The wine, also as George had promised, was superb.

They had just finished when George brought in coffee. 'Annemarie is outside.'

'Bring her in, please.'

Annemarie was a young lady of undeniably striking appearance. She wore a roll-necked pullover of indeterminate colour which had once, perhaps, been white. It was about four sizes too large for her, a defect she had tried to remedy by hauling a three-inch studded belt tightly about her midriff. As she had a rather slender waist, the effect was incongruous in the extreme: she resembled nothing so much as a potato bag that had been tied around the middle. The faded and patched blue jeans were fashionably frayed at the cuffs and she teetered, rather than walked, into the room on a pair of stained short leather boots with ludicrously pointed high heels. The condition of her streaky blonde hair showed that she regarded combs as an unnecessary luxury. The jet-black mascara had been applied

44

with a heavy hand, as had the turquoise eye-shadow. The ghastly pallor of her face, which could only have been caused by an over-enthusiastic application of some cheap powder, was in stunning contrast to the two circular red patches on her cheeks, which equally owed nothing to nature. The lipstick was purple and the blood-red nail varnish, which showed to advantage when she removed the cigarette holder from between her stained teeth, was chipped and flaking. The nose-wrinkling smell of her cheap perfume suggested that she had been bathing in it, although the impression was overwhelming that she hadn't bathed in anything for a very long time. Her brass earrings tinkled as she teetered.

Van Effen looked at de Graaf, but de Graaf didn't look at him: he was either mesmerized or petrified by the apparition before him. Van Effen cleared his throat, loudly.

'This is Annemarie, sir.'

'Yes, yes, Annemarie.' De Graaf was still staring at her, and it was by a visibly conscious effort of will-power that he turned his head to look at van Effen. 'Of course, of course. Annemarie. But there are one or two things I haven't had the opportunity yet to discuss with you and –'

'I understand, sir. Annemarie, my dear, would you mind for a few minutes – I'm sure George will give you something.' She blew a long puff of smoke, smiled and tottered from the room.

'Annemarie, my dear.' De Graaf sounded and looked appalled. 'Annemarie, my dear. You in your Kraker uniform and that – that creature, what a couple you would make. Level headed, I'd always thought you, eminently sensible – this must be some kind of joke. Where on earth did you pick up that hussy, that harlot, that harridan, that ghastly spectacle? God, that make-up, that bordello perfume!'

'It's not like you, sir, to go by appearances. Snap judgments –'

'Snap judgments! Those preposterous shoes. That filthy jersey that was built for – for a gorilla –'

'A very practical jersey, sir. That way no one would suspect the existence of the Biretta automatic she carries strapped beneath her waist.'

45

'A Biretta! That creature, that spectacle – she carries an automatic? That – that caricature of a human being carries a gun? You must be mad.' He drew deeply on his cheroot. 'No, you're not mad. I'm not complaining, Peter, but it's been a shock to my system.'

'I can see that, sir. Should have warned you, I suppose. She does have rather an effect on people who make her acquaintance for the first time. That awful harridan is in fact a rather lovely young lady, or would be if she soaked in a bath for about an hour. She's very nice, charming really, intelligent, speaks four languages, is a university graduate and is also a lady police-woman from Rotterdam. Don't you see, sir, I'm making a point. If she can fool the Chief of Police, who has become Chief of Police by, among other things, being fooled by fewer people than anyone else around, she can fool anyone.'

'How did you come by this paragon?'

'Exchange basis. Not a very fair exchange, really. I knew she'd spent six months underground in Rotterdam, and we had no one comparable up here. It wasn't easy but my opposite number down there is a friend of mine.'

'Why wasn't I informed of this?'

'Because you gave me a free hand, remember. I would have informed you if there had been anything to report. So far there has been nothing. Didn't want to bother you with trifles.'

De Graaf smiled. 'I doubt whether the young lady would care to be called a trifle. Have her in, would you?'

Van Effen did so and de Graaf waved her courteously to a seat. 'Sorry you were kept waiting. You know who I am?'

'Of course. Colonel van de Graaf. My boss.' The slightly husky voice was low and pleasant, at complete variation with her appearance.

'Lieutenant van Effen told you?'

'He didn't have to, sir. I work for him and I know he works for you. And I've seen your picture dozens of times.'

'That outfit you're wearing, Annemarie. Don't you feel it makes you look rather conspicuous?'

'Among the people I'm supposed to be investigating? I can assure you, sir, that compared to some of the clothes worn

46

there, mine are low key, positively understated. Isn't that so, Peter?'

'Ah! Peter, is it? A lowly ranker addresses my senior Lieutenant by his given name?'

'On orders, sir. We've been out a couple of times together –'

'Among your – ah – friends?'

'Yes, sir.'

'I wish I had seen that.'

'We do form rather a striking couple. I told Annemarie that it would be unwise to call me Lieutenant in such company but to call me Peter and always think of me as Peter. That way you don't make mistakes. Someone drummed this into me years ago.'

'I was the drummer. I understand that you carry a gun, young lady. You can use it?'

'I was trained at the police range.'

'Ever used it?'

'No. And I must admit I hope I never have to.'

'Would you use it?'

'I don't know. If it was to stop someone from killing a person, well, perhaps, yes. But I couldn't kill a person. I don't like guns. I'm afraid I'm not very brave, sir.'

'Nonsense. Your sentiments do you credit. Feel exactly the same way myself. And it takes a brave girl to venture into Krakerland.'

She half-smiled. 'That's where the roll-neck comes in so useful. They can't see the pulse in my neck.'

'Rubbish. How are things among your friends? Anything untoward or exciting afoot.'

'They're not a very exciting lot, sir. Rather dull, really. Most of them are not the social rebels and anti-authority storm-troopers they would like to be thought to be. Of course, there are the drug-pushers and drug-users, and there is a hard core that trade in armaments, selling Russian small-arms to the Irish Republican Army and other disaffected elements. But Peter has told me not to bother about the arms-running side.'

'Disaffected elements? I rather like that. So, Peter, the young lady does not concern herself with gun-running. Why?'

47

'*You* ask *me*, sir? America, Russia, Britain, France trade in arms – legally – to the tune of billions of dollars yearly. The Israelis do it, as do the Iranians, Libyans and God knows how many other countries. All with their government's blessings. Who are we to become all God-fearing, moralistic and holier-than-thou when private enterprise move in on a tiny scale? Anyway, I know you're not really interested in that side, and that the only things you really are interested in are drugs and those mysterious and increasing threats to the Royal family and members of the Government.'

'Yes, yes, of course. Anything interesting to report on any of these fronts?'

Annemarie shook her head. 'Vasco – you've heard of Vasco?'

'Yes. Never met him, though. Supposed to meet him today. In fact I thought I was meeting him with you.'

'I thought so, too. We'd arranged to meet in a café close by here almost an hour ago. No signs, which is most unlike Vasco.'

'This friend of yours – he's a dyed-in-the-wool true-blue Kraker?'

'Well, he seems to be but he can't be, can he? They have some kind of leaders, nobody with any personality or charisma, a kind of loose council, and Vasco appears to be a member or close to it. But he says he's basically against them and I believe him. After all, he works for you. Sort of.'

'But you're in two minds about him?'

'My intelligence, if I have any, says that – well, I'm ambivalent about him. My instincts trust him.'

'Peter?'

'Her instincts are right. He's a cop. Detective sergeant.'

'A policeman.' Annemarie's lips were compressed, her eyes angry. 'Thank you. Thank you very much.'

'Don't be childish,' van Effen said. 'You told him you were a policewoman?'

She didn't answer and de Graaf said hastily: 'It's the need-to-know principle, my dear. He didn't even tell me. I take it he thinks I didn't need to know. You were about to say something about Vasco?'

'Yes. Could be important. I don't know. He told me late last night that he thought he had a lead. He said he had been approached by one of the council, a person who knew that he, Vasco, moved quite often about the outside world – to them, everything beyond their suburban boundaries is the outside world. He said he was being taken to a meeting about midnight to meet someone important. I don't know who the person was.'

Van Effen said: 'Who was the person who approached him? Can you describe him?'

'I can describe him, all right. Short, balding, pepper-and-salt beard and a bad squint in his right eye.'

De Graaf looked at van Effen. 'Another eye disorder, but this one for real. This person have a name?'

'Julius.'

'Julius what?'

'Just –' She hesitated. 'Julius Caesar. I know it's crazy, but then they're crazy. Nobody out there ever uses his real name. Right now, as far as names are concerned, they're going through an historical phase. That's the kind of follow-my-leader sheep they are. We've got Alexander the Great, Genghis Khan, Charlemagne, Lord Nelson, Helen of Troy, Cleopatra – I could go on. They go for macho men or beautiful women, everything that they're not. Anyway, Julius Caesar.'

Van Effen said: 'And that's all you know? No indications as to what kind of lead it was?'

'No.' She pursed her lips. 'That's not to say that he didn't know.'

'An odd comment to make,' de Graaf said. 'What do you mean?'

'Nothing. I just don't know whether he knows or not.'

'Dear me.' De Graaf studied her quizzically. 'You don't trust your fellow officer?'

'He doesn't trust me.'

'Well, once again, dear me. This does make for a happy relationship in the field.'

Van Effen said: 'Sergeant Westenbrink doesn't distrust her. It's just that three years working under-cover tends to make you secretive, a loner.'

'Westenbrink, is it. I thought I knew all my sergeants.'

49

'He's from Utrecht, sir.'

'You cast a wide net. Lieutenant van Effen, Annemarie, works on the same principle as Vasco, whose name, I feel quite certain, is not Vasco. The need to know. How can you be hurt when you see me being treated in this cavalier fashion?'

George entered, apologised, picked up a phone set from a side table and placed it in front of Annemarie. She lifted the receiver, listened to the crackling voice for all of two minutes, said: 'Thank you. Five minutes,' and hung up.

Van Effen said: 'The Hunter's Horn, I presume. What's the message from Vasco?'

'The Hunter's Horn.' De Graaf frowned. 'I trust that's not the Hunter's Horn that –'

'There's only one – ah – establishment of that name in Amsterdam. Beggars can't be choosers. Apart from La Caracha it's our only safe house in Amsterdam. A private connection, Colonel. The fair name of the Amsterdam police department remains unbesmirched.'

'Not to know,' de Graaf muttered. 'Not to know.'

'You're half right,' Annemarie said, almost reluctantly. 'It was the Hunter's Horn. But it wasn't Vasco.'

'Never said it was. I said "What's the message from Vasco?" It was Henri. Henri, sir, is the owner. Vasco is under observation but whoever is tailing him didn't know, wasn't to know, that it's virtually impossible to follow Vasco without Vasco being aware of it. So he couldn't come here. The person or persons following him would have raised their eyebrows if they saw you here: they'd have gone into shock if they'd found me, which would have been a small disaster for us and the end of the usefulness of both Vasco and yourself. So the only place left for Vasco was the Hunter's Horn. Even there he couldn't use the telephone for he would still be being watched. So he wrote a small note for Henri who did the telephoning. You're to ask me a question and you're to give Henri my answer inside five minutes.'

Annemarie sighed. 'Did you have to spoil it for me?' Then she brightened. 'But you didn't get it all, did you?'

'I'm brilliant at deducing the obvious. I'm not clairvoyant.

50

The rest, what I didn't get, can wait, including the reasons why Vasco is going to call me back.'

'I didn't say that?'

'Henri did. The message.'

She made a *moue*. 'It went like this. Two tails. Understand can't ditch. Meet two –'

De Graaf interrupted. 'What was that meant to mean?'

'Westenbrink's shorthand, I imagine,' van Effen said. 'Only two ways of getting rid of his tails. He could throw them into the nearest canal, which he's perfectly capable of doing or he could easily have lost them which he is again perfectly capable of doing. Either course of action would have ended any connection he's succeeded in making.'

Annemarie went on: 'Meet two, three men four-thirty Hunter's Horn.' She pushed across a piece of paper.

'*Stephan Danilov*,' van Effen read. '*Pole. Radom. Explosives expert. Oil well fires. Texas.* Clear enough. Interesting, sir?'

'It is indeed. How do you feel about blowing up banks?'

'Should be interesting to see the law from the other side. They'll bring along a Polish speaker, of course.'

Annemarie said: 'You think this is a Polish criminal group.'

'No. Just to check on me.'

'But if they speak to you in –'

'If they speak to him in Polish, my dear,' de Graaf said, 'He'll answer in Polish, in which language he's very fluent. Your friend from Utrecht, Peter, of course knew this.'

Annemarie said: 'But – but you'll be recognised. Everybody in that – that ghetto knows you, I mean, knows who you are.'

'Ninny. Sorry, but, please. If you think I'm going to present myself as Lieutenant van Effen you can't be feeling too well. I shall, in the best traditions as befits the circumstances, be heavily disguised. I shall put on about twenty kilos – I have a suit and shirt designed to cope with the excess avoirdupois – fatten my cheeks, tint hair and moustache, wear a sinister scar and a black leather glove. That's to disguise the fearful scars and burns I sustained when – let me see, yes, of course – when I was putting out this oil fire in Saudi Arabia or wherever. It's remarkable what a single black glove does. It becomes the focal point for identification in nearly everyone's mind and if you're not wearing it, you're not you, if you follow me. And don't call Krakerdom a ghetto – it's an insult to decent Jews.'

'I didn't mean to –'

'I know. I'm sorry. Call Henri, tell him it's OK and to let a few minutes pass before giving Vasco the nod.'

She made the call and hung up. 'Everything seems all right. A few minutes.' She looked at van Effen. 'You already have all the details you want. Why have Vasco make the call?'

'Why have Vasco make the call?' Van Effen tried to look patient. 'Vasco goes back every afternoon to this empty block of flats that they've taken over under so-called squatters' rights. He's been under surveillance since his meeting with the council or whatever they call themselves since last night and it's a safe assumption that he'll remain under surveillance until the time of the meeting in the Hunter's Horn. How's he supposed to have communicated with me to arrange this meeting? Telepathy?'

De Graaf cleared his throat and looked at Annemarie. 'You must forgive our Lieutenant his old-world gallantry. Do you go back to the dreadful place now?'

'Very soon.'

'And you stay there overnight?'

She gave a mock shudder. 'There are limits, sir, to my loyalty to the police force. No, I don't sleep there at nights.'

'No raised eyebrows among the fraternity?'

'Not at all, sir. I have a gentleman friend who comes calling for me every evening. The Krakers understand this sort of thing.'

'And you go back in the morning?'

'Yes, sir.' She put her hand to her mouth to cover a smile but de Graaf had seen it.

'You are amused, young lady.' His tone had lost some warmth.

'Well, yes, I am a little, sir. Your voice and expression of disapproval and disappointment. This friend is really a very gallant gentleman. Especially as he's married.'

'Inevitably.' De Graaf was not amused.

'He takes me to his cousin's house, leaves me there and comes for me in the morning. That's why he's gallant, because he's very much in love with his own wife. His cousin, Colonel de Graaf, is a lady.'

De Graaf said: 'The Chief of Police is in his usual condition, namely, out of his depth.' He was noticeably relieved. 'You will, of course, Peter, have carried out a check on this cousin, this lady?'

'No I have not.' Van Effen spoke with some feeling. 'I wouldn't dare.'

De Graaf frowned briefly then leaned back and laughed. 'Behold our intrepid Lieutenant, Annemarie. He's terrified of his young sister. So you're staying with Julie?'

'You know her then, sir?'

'My favourite lady in all Amsterdam. Except, of course, for my wife and two daughters. I'm her godfather. Well, well.'

The phone rang. Van Effen picked it up and listened for perhaps half a minute then said: 'Can anyone overhear my voice if I speak?' Apparently nobody could for van Effen said: 'Say that you'll give me half a minute to think it over.' At the end of that period van Effen spoke again: 'Say to me: "Stephan, I swear to you it's no police trap. My life on it. And if it were a police trap what would my life be worth then? Don't be silly."'

A few moments later van Effen said: 'That was fine. Will you be coming with them? Fine? Be sure to tell whoever comes with you – I'm sure it won't be the gentlemen who have you under surveillance at the moment – that I have a police record in Poland and have a United States extradition warrant out against me. I shall be wearing a black leather glove.' He hung up.

'Nice touch about the police record and extradition warrant,' de Graaf said. 'Nice criminal touch and two statements they have no way of checking on. You will be carrying a gun, I assume?'

'Certainly. It would be expected of me and I'll have it in a shoulder holster that should make it obvious to even the most myopic that I am armed.'

Annemarie said doubtfully: 'Perhaps they will take it off you before discussions start. Just as a precaution, I mean.'

'One must take a chance about those things. I shall be brave.'

'What Peter means,' de Graaf said drily, 'is that he always carries a second gun. It's like his single glove theory, that people only concentrate on one thing at a time. It's in that book of his, I'm sure. If a person finds a gun on you he's got to be almost pathologically suspicious to start looking for another.'

'It's not in the book. I don't put thoughts like those in criminal minds. Curious, sir, that we'll both be engaged in something interesting at exactly four-thirty – you and the Minister, schnapps in hand, peering down at the Texel sea-dyke from the safety of your helicopter seats while I am entering the lion's den.'

'I'd switch with you any time,' de Graaf said morosely. 'I should be back from Texel by six – damn all I can do up there anyway. Let's meet at seven.'

'Provided we both survive – you the schnapps, me the lions. The 444 would be in order, sir?'

De Graaf didn't say that the 444 would be in order: on the other hand he didn't say it wouldn't.

Three

The Chinook helicopter, a big, fast experimental model on demonstration loan from the US Army of the Rhine, suffered from the same defect as other, smaller and less advanced models in that it was extremely noisy, the rackety clamour of the engines making conversation difficult and at times impossible. This wasn't helped by the fact that it had two rotors instead of the customary one.

The passengers were a very mixed bag indeed. Apart from de Graaf and his Justice Minister, Robert Kondstall, there were four cabinet ministers, of whom only the Minister of Defence could claim any right to be aboard. The other three, including, incredibly, the Minister of Education, were aboard only because of the influence they wielded and their curiosity about things that in no way concerned them. Much the same could have been said about the senior air force officer, the brigadier and rear-admiral who sat together behind de Graaf. Flight evaluation purposes had been their claim. The evaluation tests had been completed a week ago: they were along purely as rubber-neckers. The same could be said of the two experts from the Rijkswaterstaat and the two from the Delft Hydraulics laboratory. Superficially, it would have seemed, their presence could be more than justified, but as the pilot had firmly stated that he had no intention of setting his Chinook down in floodwaters and the experts, portly gentlemen all, had indicated that they had no intention of descending by winch or rope ladder only to be swept away, it was difficult to see how their presence could be justified. The handful of journalists and cameramen aboard could have claimed a right to be there: but even they were to admit later that their trip had hardly been worthwhile.

The Chinook, flying at no more than two hundred metres and

55

about half a kilometre out to sea, was directly opposite Oosterend when the sea dyke broke. It was a singularly unspectacular explosion – a little sound, a little smoke, a little rubble, a little spray – but effective enough for all that: the Waddenzee was already rushing through the narrow gap and into the polder beyond. Less than half a kilometre from the entrance to the gap an ocean-going tug was already headed towards the breach. As the pilot turned his Chinook westwards, presumably to see what the conditions were like in the polder, de Graaf leaned over to one of the Rijkswaterstaat experts. He had to shout to make himself heard.

'How bad is it, Mr Okkerse? How long do you think it will take to seal off the break?'

'Well, damn their souls, damn their souls! Villains, devils, monsters!' Okkerse clenched and unclenched his hands. 'Monsters, I tell you, sir, monsters!' Okkerse was understandably upset. Dykes, the construction, care and maintenance of, were his *raison d'être*.

'Yes, yes, monsters,' de Graaf shouted. 'How long to fix that?'

'Moment.' Okkerse rose, lurched forwards, spoke briefly to the pilot and lurched his way back to his seat. 'Got to see it first. Pilot's taking us down.'

The Chinook curved round, passing over the waters flooding across the first reaches of the polder and came to hover some fifteen metres above the ground and some twenty metres distant. Okkerse pressed his nose against a window. After only a few seconds he turned away and gave the wave off signal to the pilot. The Chinook curved away inland.

'Clever fiends,' Okkerse shouted. 'Very clever fiends. It's only a small breach and they chose the perfect moment for it.'

'What does the time of day matter?'

'It matters very much. Rather, the state of the tide matters. They didn't pick high tide, because that would have caused heavy flooding and great destruction.'

'So they can't be all that villainous?'

Okkerse didn't seem to hear him. 'And they didn't pick low tide because they knew – how, I can't even guess – that we would do what we are just about to do and that is to block the gap with the bows of a vessel. Which is what we are about to do with the bows of that ocean-going tug down there. At low water the tug probably wouldn't have found enough water to get close to the dyke.' He shook his head. 'I don't like any of this.'

'You think our friends have inside information?'

'I didn't say that.'

'I suggested that to your friend Jon de Jong. That those people have either an informant in or somebody employed in the Rijkswaterstaat.'

'Ridiculous! Impossible! In *our* organization? Preposterous!'

'That's more or less what Jon said. Nothing's impossible. What makes you think your people are immune to penetration? Look at the British Secret Service where security is supposed to be a religion. They're penetrated at regular intervals and with painful frequency. If it can happen to them with all their resources, it's ten times more likely to happen to you. That's beside the point. How long to seal the breach?'

'The tug should block off about eighty per cent of the flow. The tide's going out. We've got everything ready to hand – concrete blocks, matting, divers, steel plates, quick-setting concrete. A few hours. Technically, a minor job. That's not what worries me.'

De Graaf nodded, thanked him and resumed his seat beside Kondstaal. 'Okkerse says it's no problem, sir. Straightforward repair job.'

'Didn't think it would be a problem. The villains said there would be minimal damage and they seem to mean what they say. That's not what worries me.'

'That's what Okkerse has just said. The worry is, of course, that they can carry out their threats with impunity. We're in an impossible situation. What would you wager, sir, that we don't receive another threat this evening?'

'Nothing. There's no point in wondering what those people are up to. They'll doubtless let us know in their own good time. And there's no point, I suppose, in asking you what progress you've made so far.'

De Graaf concentrated on lighting his cheroot and said nothing.

Sergeant Westenbrink wore an off-white boiler suit, unbuttoned from throat to waist to show off a garishly patterned and coloured Hawaiian shirt, a Dutch bargee's cap and a circular brass earring. Compared to those among whom he lived and had his being, Vasco, van Effen thought, looked positively underdressed but was still outlandish enough to make himself and the two men sitting opposite him across the table in the booth in the Hunter's Horn look the pillars of a respectable society. One of them, clad in an immaculately cut dark grey suit, was about van Effen's age, darkly handsome, slightly swarthy, with tightly-curled black hair, black eyes and, when he smiled – which was often – what appeared to be perfect teeth. Any Mediterranean country, van Effen thought, or, at the outside, not more than two generations removed. His companion, a short, slightly balding man of perhaps ten or fifteen years older than the other, wore a conservative dark suit and a hairline moustache, the only really and slightly unusual feature in an otherwise unremarkable face. Neither of them looked the slightest bit like a bona fide member of the criminal classes but, then, few successful criminals ever did.

The younger man – he went, it seemed, by the name of Romero Agnelli, which might even have been his own – produced an ebony cigarette-holder, a Turkish cigarette and a gold inlaid onyx lighter; any of which might have appeared affected or even effeminate on almost any man: with Agnelli, all three seemed inevitable. He lit the cigarette and smiled at van Effen.

'You will not take it amiss if I ask one or two questions.' He had a pleasant baritone voice and spoke in English. 'One cannot be too careful these days.'

'I cannot be too careful any day. If your question is pertinent, of course I'll answer it. If not, I won't. Am I – ah – accorded the same privilege?'

'Certainly.'

58

'Except you can ask more what you consider pertinent questions than I can.'

'I don't quite understand.'

'Just that I take it that we're talking on a potential employer employee relationship. The employer is usually entitled to ask more questions.'

'Now I understand. I won't take advantage of that. I must say, Mr Danilov, that you look more like the employer class yourself.' And indeed, van Effen's over-stuffed suit and padded cheeks did lend a certain air of prosperity. It also made him look almost permanently genial. 'Am I mistaken in thinking that you carry a gun?'

'Unlike you, Mr Agnelli, I'm afraid I'm not in the habit of patronizing expensive tailors.'

'Guns make me nervous.' The disarming smile didn't show a trace of nervousness.

'Guns make me nervous, too. That's why I carry one in case I meet a man who is carrying one. That makes me very nervous.' Van Effen smiled, removed his Biretta from its shoulder holster, clicked out the magazine, handed it to Agnelli and replaced his pistol. 'That do anything for your nerves?'

Agnelli smiled. 'All gone.'

'Then they shouldn't be.' Van Effen reached below the table and came up with a tiny automatic. 'A Lilliput, a toy in many ways, but lethal up to twenty feet in the hands of a man who can fire accurately.' He tapped out the magazine, handed this in turn to Agnelli and replaced the Lilliput in its ankle holster. 'That's all. Three guns would be just too much to carry about.'

'So I should imagine.' Agnelli's smile, which had momentarily vanished, was back in place. He pushed the two magazines across the table. 'I don't think we'll be requiring guns this afternoon.'

'Indeed. But something *would* be useful.' Van Effen dropped the magazines into a side pocket. 'I always find that talking –'

'Beer for me,' Agnelli said. 'And for Helmut, too, I know.'

'Four beers,' van Effen said. 'Vasco, if you would be so kind –' Vasco rose and left the booth.

Agnelli said: 'Known Vasco long?'

59

Van Effen considered. 'A proper question. Two months. Why?' Had they, van Effen wondered, been asking the same question of Vasco.

'Idle curiosity.' Agnelli, van Effen thought, was not a man to indulge in idle curiosity. 'Your name really is Stephan Danilov?'

'Certainly not. But it's the name I go by in Amsterdam.'

'But you really are a Pole?' The elder man's voice, dry and precise, befitted his cast of countenance which could have been that of a moderately successful lawyer or accountant. He also spoke in Polish.

'For my sins.' Van Effen raised an eyebrow. 'Vasco, of course.'

'Yes. Where were you born?'

'Radom.'

'I know it. Not well. A rather provincial town, I thought.'

'So I've heard.'

'You've heard? But you lived there.'

'Four years. When you're four years old a provincial town is the centre of the world. My father – a printer – moved to a better job.'

'Where?'

'Warsaw.'

'Aha!'

'Aha yourself.' Van Effen spoke in some irritation. 'You sound as if you know Warsaw and are now going to find out if I know it. Why, I can't imagine. You're not by any chance a lawyer, Mr – I'm afraid I don't know your name?'

'Paderiwski. I am a lawyer.'

'Paderiwski. Given time, I would have thought you could have come up with a better one than that. And I was right, eh? A lawyer. I wouldn't care to have you acting for my defence. You make a poor interrogator.'

Agnelli was smiling but Paderiwski was not. His lips were pursed. He said brusquely: 'You know the Tin-Roofed Palace, of course.'

'Of course.'

'Where is it?'

60

'Dear me. What have we here. The Inquisition? Ah. Thank you.' He took a glass from a tray that a waiter, following Vasco, had just brought into the curtained booth and lifted it. 'Your health, gentlemen. The place you're so curious about, Mr – ah – Paderiwski, is close by the Wista, on the corner of the Wybrzeze Gdanskie and the Slasko-Dabrowski bridge.' He sipped some more beer. 'Unless they've moved it, of course. Some years since I've been there.'

Paderiwski was not amused. 'The Palace of Culture and Science.'

'Parade Square. It's too big.'

'What do you mean?'

'Too big to have been moved, I mean. Two thousand, three hundred rooms are a lot of rooms. A monstrosity. The wedding-cake, they call it. But, then, Stalin never did have any taste in architecture.'

'Stalin?' Agnelli said.

'His personal gift to my already long-suffering countrymen.' So Agnelli spoke Polish, too.

'Where's the Ethnographic Museum in Warsaw?'

'It's not in Warsaw. Mlociny, ten kilometres to the north.' Van Effen's voice was now as brusque as Paderiwski's had been. 'Where's the *Nike*? You don't know? What's the *Nike*? You don't know? Any citizen of Warsaw knows it's the name given to the "Heroes of Warsaw" monument. What's Zamenhofa Street famous for?' An increasingly uncomfortable Paderiwski made no reply. 'The Ghetto monument. I told you you'd make a lousy lawyer, Paderiwski. Any competent lawyer, for the defence or the prosecution, always prepares his brief. You didn't. You're a fraud. It's my belief that you've never even been in Warsaw and that you just spent an hour or so studying a gazetteer or guide-book.' Van Effen placed his hands on the table as if preparatory to rising. 'I don't think, gentleman, that we need detain each other any longer. Discreet enquiries are one thing, offensive interrogation by an incompetent, another. I see no basis here for mutual trust and, quite honestly, I need neither a job nor money.' He rose. 'Good day, gentlemen.'

Agnelli reached out a hand. He didn't touch van Effen, it was just a restraining gesture. 'Please sit down, Mr Danilov. Perhaps Helmut *has* rather overstepped the mark but have you ever met a lawyer who wasn't burdened with a suspicious, mistrustful mind? Helmut – or we – just happened to choose the wrong suspect. Helmut, in fact, has been in Warsaw but only, as you almost guessed, briefly and as a tourist. I, personally, don't doubt you could find your way about Warsaw blind-folded.' Paderiwski had the look of a man who wished he were in some other place, any place. 'A blunder. We apologize.'

'That's kind.' Van Effen sat down and quaffed some more beer. 'Fair enough.'

Agnelli smiled. Almost certainly a double-dyed villain, van Effen thought, but a charming and persuasive one. 'Now that you've established a degree of moral ascendancy over us I'll reinforce that by admitting that we almost certainly need you more than you need us.'

Not to be outdone, van Effen smiled in turn. 'You must be in a desperate way.' He lifted and examined his empty glass. 'If you'd just poke your head round the corner, Vasco, and make the usual SOS.'

'Of course, Stephan.' There was an unmistakable expression of relief in his face. He did as asked then settled back in his seat.

'No more interrogation,' Agnelli said. 'I'll come straight to the point. Your friend Vasco tells me that you know a little about explosives.'

'Vasco does me less than justice. I know a great deal about explosives.' He looked at Vasco in reproof. 'I wouldn't have thought you would discuss a friend – that's me, Vasco, in case you've forgotten – with strangers.'

'I didn't. Well, I did, but I just said it was someone I knew.'

'No harm. Explosives, as I say, I know. Defusing bombs I know. I'm also fairly proficient in capping well-head oil fires but you wouldn't be approaching me in this fashion if that was your problem. You'd be on the phone to Texas, where I learnt my trade.'

'No oil fires.' Agnelli smiled again. 'But defusing bombs – well that's something else. Where did you learn a dangerous trade like that?'

'Army,' van Effen said briefly. He didn't specify which army.

'You've actually defused bombs?' Agnelli's respect was genuine.

'Quite a number.'

'You must be good.'

'Why?'

'You're here.'

'I am good. I'm also lucky, because no matter how good you are the bomb you're trying to defuse may be your last one. Peaceful retirement is not the lot of a bomb disposal expert. But as I assume you have no more unexploded bombs than you have oil wells, then it must be explosives. Explosives experts in Holland are not in short supply. You have only to advertise. That I should be approached in a clandestine fashion can only mean that you are engaged in activities that are illegal.'

'We are. Have you never been? Engaged, I mean?'

'All depends upon who defines what is illegal and what is not and how they define it. Some people hold definitions which are different from mine and wish to discuss the matter with me. Very tiresome they can be, those alleged upholders of justice. You know what the British say – the law is an ass.' Van Effen considered. 'I think I put that rather well.'

'You've hardly committed yourself. May one ask – delicately, of course – whether this discussion you are avoiding has anything to do with your vacationing in Amsterdam?'

'You may. It has. What do you want me to blow up?'

Agnelli raised his eyebrows. 'Well, well, you can be blunt. Almost as blunt as you can be, shall we say, diplomatic.'

'That's an answer? An explosives expert is good for only one thing – exploding things. You wish me to explode something? Yes or no?'

'Yes.'

'Two things. Banks, boats, bridges, anything of that kind I'll blow up and guarantee a satisfactory job. Anything that involves injury, far less death, to any person I won't have any part of.'

'You won't ever be called upon to do any such thing. That's also a guarantee. The second thing?'

'I don't seek to flatter you when I say that you're an intelligent man, Mr Agnelli. Highly intelligent, I should think. Such people are usually first-class organizers. To seek the help of a last minute unknown to help you execute some project that may have been in the planning stage for quite some time doesn't smack to me of preparation, organization or professionalism. If I may say so.'

'You may. A very valid point. In your position I would adopt the same disbelieving or questioning attitude. You have to take my word for it that I am a member of a highly organized team. But, as you must well know, the best-laid plans etc. An unfortunate accident. I can explain to your satisfaction. But not just at this moment. Will you accept our offer?'

'You haven't made one yet.'

'Will you accept an offer of a job in our organization, on, if you wish, a permanent basis, on what I think you'll find a very satisfactory salary plus commission basis, your special responsibility being the demolition of certain structures, those structures to be specified at a later date.'

'Sounds *very* businesslike. And I like the idea of commissions, whatever they may be. I agree. When do I start and what do I start on?'

'You'll have to bear with me a little, Mr Danilov. My brief for this afternoon is only of a limited nature – to find out, if, in principle, you are prepared to work with us, which I'm glad to say you seem to be. I have to report back. You will be contacted very shortly, sometime tomorrow, I'm sure.'

'You are not the leader of this organization?'

'No.'

'You surprise me. A man like you acting as a lieutenant – well, this leader I must meet.'

'You shall, I promise.'

'How will you contact me? No phones, please.'

'Certainly not. You will be our courier, Vasco?'

'My pleasure, Mr Agnelli. You know where to reach me any time.'

'Thank you.' Agnelli stood up and gave his hand to van Effen. 'A pleasure, Mr Danilov. I look forward to meeting you tomorrow.' Helmut Paderiwski didn't offer to shake hands.

As the door closed behind them, Sergeant Westenbrink said: 'I need another beer, Lieutenant.'

'Peter. Always Peter.'

'Sorry. That was pretty close. The ice was very thin at times.'

'Not for a practised liar. I rather gather that you've given them the impression that I'm a desperate and wanted criminal?'

'I did mention that there was the odd extradition warrant out for you. But I didn't forget to emphasize your generally upright and honest nature. When dealing with your fellow criminals, of course.'

'Of course. Before you get the beer, I have a phone call to make. Well, get it anyway.'

Van Effen went to the bar and said to the man behind it, 'Henri, a private call, if I may.'

Henri, the proprietor, was a tall, gaunt man, sallow of countenance and lugubrious of expression. 'You in trouble again, Peter?'

'No. I hope someone else will be, soon.'

Van Effen went into the office and dialled a number. 'Trianon? The manager, please. I don't care if he is in conference, call him. It's Lieutenant van Effen.' He hung on for a few moments. 'Charles? Do me a favour. Book me in as from a fortnight ago. Enter it in the book, will you, in the name of Stephan Danilov. And would you notify the receptionist and doorman. Yes, I expect people to be enquiring. Just tell them. Many thanks. I'll explain when I see you.'

He returned to the booth. 'Just booked myself – Stephan Danilov, that is – into an hotel. Agnelli pointedly did not mention anything about where I might be staying but you can be sure that he'll have one of his men on the phone for the next couple of hours if need be, trying to locate me in every hotel or pension in the city.'

'So he'll know where you are – or where you're supposed to be.' Vasco sighed. 'It would help if we knew where *they* were.'

'Should know soon enough. There's been two separate tails on them ever since they left the Hunter's Horn.'

Van Effen, appearance returned to normal, asked the girl at the *Telegraph*'s reception desk for the sub-editor who had taken the FFF's first telephone message. This turned out to be a fresh-faced and very eager young man.

'Mr Morelis?' van Effen said. 'Police.'

'Yes, sir. Lieutenant van Effen, isn't it? I've been expecting you. You'll be wanting to hear the tapes? Maybe I should tell you first that we've just had another message from the FFF, as they call themselves.'

'Have you now? I suppose I should say "The devil you have" but I'm not surprised. It was inevitable. Happy tidings, of course.'

'Hardly. The first half of the message was given over to congratulating themselves on the Texel job, how it had happened precisely as they had predicted and with no loss of life: the second half said there would be scenes of considerable activity on the North Holland canal, two kilometres north of Alkmaar at nine o'clock tomorrow morning.'

'That, too, was inevitable. Not the location, of course. Just the threat. You've taped that, too?'

'Yes.'

'That was well done. May I hear them?'

Van Effen heard them, twice over. When they were finished he said to Morelis: 'You've listened to those, of course?'

'Too often.' Morelis smiled. 'Fancied myself as a detective, thought maybe you would give me a job but I've come to the conclusion that there's more to this detecting business than meets the eye.'

'Nothing struck you as odd about any of the tapes?'

'They were all made by the same woman. But that's no help.'

'Nothing odd about accents, tones? No nuances that struck you as unusual?'

'No, sir. But I'm no judge. I'm slightly hard of hearing, nothing serious, but enough to blunt my judgment, assuming I had any. Mean anything to you, Lieutenant?'

'The lady is a foreigner. What country I've no idea. Don't mention that around.'

'No, sir. I rather like being a sub-editor.'

'We are not in Moscow, young man. Put those tapes in a bag for me. I'll let you have them back in a day or two.'

Back in his office, van Effen asked to see the duty sergeant. When he arrived van Effen said: 'A few hours ago I asked for a couple of men to be put on a Fred Klassen and Alfred van Rees. Did you know about this, and if you did, do you know who the two men were?'

'I knew, sir. Detective Voight and Detective Tindeman.'

'Good. Either of them called in?'

'Both. Less than twenty minutes ago. Tindeman says van Rees is at home and seems to have settled in for the evening. Klassen is still on duty at the airport or, at least, he's still at the airport. So, nothing yet, sir.'

Van Effen looked at his watch. 'I'm leaving now. If you get any word from either, a positive not negative report, call me at the Dikker en Thijs. After nine, call me at home.'

Colonel van de Graaf came from a very old, very aristocratic and very wealthy family and was a great stickler for tradition, so it came as no surprise to van Effen when he approached their table wearing dinner jacket, black tie and red carnation. His approach bore all the elements of a royal progress: he seemed to greet everyone, stopped to speak occasionally and waved graciously at those tables not directly in his path. It was said of de Graaf that he knew everybody who was anybody in the city of Amsterdam: he certainly seemed to know everybody in the Dikker en Thijs. Four paces away from van Effen's table he stopped abruptly as if he had been transfixed: but, in fact, it was his eyes that were doing the transfixing.

That the girl who had risen from the table with van Effen to greet de Graaf had this momentarily paralysing effect not only on de Graaf but on a wide cross-section of the males of Amsterdam and beyond was understandable. She was of medium height, wore a rather more than well-filled ankle-length grey silk gown and no jewellery whatsoever. Jewellery would have been superfluous and no one would have paid any attention to it anyway: what caught and held the attention, as it

67

had caught the riveted attention of the momentarily benumbed Colonel, was the flawless classical perfection of the features, a perfection only enhanced, if this were possible, by a slightly crooked eye-tooth which was visible when she smiled, which seemed to be most of the time. This was no simpering and empty-headed would-be Miss Universe contender, churned out with repetitive monotony by a Californian-style production line. The finely chiselled features and delicately formed bone structure served only to emphasize the character and intelligence they served only to highlight. She had gleaming auburn hair, great hazel eyes and a bewitching smile. It had, at any rate, bewitched the Colonel. Van Effen cleared his throat.

'Colonel van de Graaf. May I introduce Miss Meijer. Miss Anne Meijer.'

'My pleasure, my pleasure.' De Graaf grabbed her outstretched hand in both of his and shook it vigorously. 'My word, my boy, you are to be congratulated: where *did* you find this entrancing creature?'

'There's nothing to it really, sir. You just go out into the darkened streets of Amsterdam, stretch out your hands and – well, there you are.'

'Yes, yes, of course. Naturally.' He had no idea what he was saying. He seemed to become aware that he had been holding and shaking her hand for an unconscionably long time for he eventually and reluctantly released it. 'Remarkable. Quite remarkable.' He didn't say what he found remarkable and didn't have to. 'You cannot possibly live in this city. Little, my dear, escapes the notice of a Chief of Police and I think it would be impossible for you to be overlooked even in a city of this size.'

'Rotterdam.'

'Well, that's not your fault. Peter, I have no hesitation in saying that there can be no more stunningly beautiful lady in the city of Amsterdam.' He lowered his voice a few decibels. 'In fact I would come right out and say that she is the most stunningly beautiful in the city, but I have a wife and two daughters and these restaurants have ears. You must be about the same age as my daughters? May I ask how old you are?'

'You must excuse the Colonel,' van Effen said. 'Policemen are much given to asking questions: some Chiefs of Police never stop.'

The girl was smiling at de Graaf while van Effen was speaking and, once again, van Effen could have been addressing a brick wall. 'Twenty-seven,' she said.

'Twenty-seven. Exactly the age of my elder daughter. And *Miss* Anne Meijer. Bears out my contention – the younger generation of Dutchmen are a poor, backward and unenterprising lot.' He looked at van Effen, as if he symbolized all that was wrong with the current generation, then looked again at the girl. 'Odd. I know I've never seen you but your voice is vaguely familiar.' He looked at van Effen again and frowned slightly. 'I look forward immensely to having dinner with you, but I thought – well, Peter, there were one or two confidential business matters that we had to discuss.'

'Indeed, sir. But when you suggested we meet at seven o'clock you made no exclusions.'

'I don't understand.'

The girl said: 'Colonel.'

'Yes, my dear?'

'Am I really such a hussy, a harlot, harridan and ghastly spectacle? Or is it because you don't trust me that you want to speak privately with Peter?'

De Graaf took a pace forward, caught the girl by the shoulders, removed one hand to stop a passing waiter and said: 'A jonge jenever. Large.'

'Immediately, Colonel.'

De Graaf held her shoulders again, stared intently into her face – he was probably trying to equate or associate the vision before him with the creature he had met in La Caracha – shook his head, muttered something to or about the same nameless deity and sank into the nearest chair.

Van Effen was sympathetic. 'It comes as a shock, I know, sir. Happened to me the first time. A brilliant make-up artist, don't you think? If it's any consolation, sir, she also fooled me once. But no disguise this time – just a wash and brush-up.' He looked at her consideringly. 'But, well, yes, rather good-looking.'

69

'Good-looking. Hah!' De Graaf took the jonge jenever from the waiter's tray and quaffed half the contents at a gulp. 'Ravishing. At my age, systems shouldn't be subjected to such shocks. Anne? Annemarie? What do I call you?'

'Whichever.'

'Anne. My dear. I said such dreadful things about you. It is not possible.'

'Of course it's not. I couldn't believe Peter when he said you had.'

Van Effen waved a hand. 'A loose translation, shall we say?'

'Very loose.' Wisely, de Graaf did not pursue the subject. 'And what in heaven's name, is a girl like you doing in a job like this.'

'I thought it was an honourable profession?'

'Yes, yes, of course. But what I meant was – well –'

'What the Colonel means,' van Effen said, 'is that you should be an international stage or screen star, presiding over a Parisian salon, or married to an American oil millionaire – billionaire, if you like – or a belted English earl. Too beautiful, that's your trouble. Isn't that it, Colonel?'

'Couldn't have put it better myself.'

'Dear me.' Anne smiled. 'Doesn't say much for your Amsterdam girls. You mean you only employ ugly girls?'

De Graaf smiled for the first time that evening. 'I am not to be drawn. The Chief of Police is famed for his powers of recovery. But you – you – among those dreadful Krakers and dressed like a – like –'

'Harlot? Hussy?'

'If you like, yes.' He put his hand on hers. 'This is no place for a girl like you. Must get you out of it. Police is no place for you.'

'One has to earn a living, sir.'

'You? You need never earn a living. That, Anne, is a compliment.'

'I like what I'm doing.'

De Graaf didn't seem to have heard her. He was gazing at some distant object out in space. Van Effen said to the girl:

'Watch him. He's at his most cunning when he goes into a trance.'

'I am not in a trance,' de Graaf said coldly. 'What did you say your surname was?'

'Meijer.'

'You have a family?'

'Oh, yes. The usual. Parents, sisters, two brothers.'

'Brothers and sisters share your interest in law and order?'

'Police, you mean. No.'

'Your father?'

'Again police?' She smiled as a person smiles when recalling someone of whom they are very fond. 'I couldn't imagine it. He's in the building business.'

'Does he know what kind of business you are in?'

She hesitated. 'Well, no.'

'What do you mean, well, no? He doesn't, does he? Why?'

'Why?' She seemed to be on the defensive. 'He likes us to be independent.'

'Would he approve of what you are doing? And that was no answer you gave me. Would he approve of his darling daughter mingling with the Krakers?'

'Is this what it's like to be a suspect, sir, and to be grilled? Am I supposed to have done something wrong?'

'Of course not. Would he approve?' The entranced Colonel of a few minutes previously could have belonged to another world.

'No.'

'You put me in a quandary. I don't like you being in this. You, apparently, do. Your father wouldn't. To whom should I listen – you or your father?'

'The question hardly arises, sir. You don't know my father.'

'Child!'

'What does that mean. I don't understand.'

'I know your father. Very well. We've been friends for over thirty years.'

'Impossible! You can't know him. You've only just met me and you didn't even know me.' She was no actress and was visibly upset. 'This is – this is a trick of some kind.'

71

'Annemarie.' Van Effen touched her arm. 'If the Colonel says he's a friend of your father, then he is. Come on, sir.'

'I know. When next you write or phone, Anne – if you ever do – give my warmest regards to David Joseph Karlmann Meijer.'

Her eyes widened. She opened her mouth as if to speak, closed it again and turned to van Effen. 'I think it's my turn for a jonge jenever.'

De Graaf looked at van Effen. 'My old friend David – we've gone sailing, fishing, skiing, hunting over the years – we were even up exploring the Amazon before this young lady here was born – owns a huge construction company. He also owns one of the biggest cement factories in the Netherlands, oil refineries, tankers, an electronics firm and God knows what else. "One has to earn a living, sir,"' he mimicked. 'Earn a living! Cruel, cruel landlord throwing the poor orphan out into the snow. Ah!' He turned to look at the maître d' at his elbow. 'Good evening. The young people will choose for me. But, first, another jonge jenever.' He looked at Annemarie. 'Must have something to cry into. They say gin is best.'

After the orders had been taken and the maître d' and his minions departed, van Effen said: 'You have a scenario, sir, and you don't like what you see.'

'I don't like it at all. Two things. If anything happens to this young lady – well, David Meijer's wrath is fearful to behold – and it's considerably worse to be the object of it. Secondly, disguise or no disguise, Anne's identity may be discovered. It can happen, as you know all too well, Peter: a slip of the tongue, an unguarded reference, some careless action, there are too many possibilities. What a windfall for a penniless Kraker or even worse, a professional kidnapper. Her father would pay five, ten million guilders to get her back. Do you like it, Peter?'

Van Effen made to speak, then glanced at the waiter who stood by his side.

'Lieutenant van Effen. Phone.'

Van Effen excused himself. De Graaf said: 'Well, do *you* like it?'

'Not the way you put it but – I don't want to seem impertinent, sir, to disagree with my boss, but I think you put it too strongly. I've been doing this kind of work for some months in Rotterdam and nothing has ever happened to me there. And while there may be no Krakers down there, the criminal element are a great deal tougher than they are here. I'm sorry, Colonel, but I think you exaggerate the dangers. I'm rather good at disguises – you as much as said so yourself. I have a gun. Best, of course, is that no one in Amsterdam knows me.'

'I know you.'

'That's different. Peter says that you know everyone – and you must admit that it was a very remote chance that you knew my father.'

'I could have found out easily enough. Peter knows?'

'Only my name. Not who I am, not until you spoke about it just now. I must say he didn't seem particularly surprised.' She smiled. 'He could, of course, have been unconcerned or uninterested.'

'You're fishing for compliments, my dear.' She made to protest but he held up his hand. 'In your case, indifference is impossible. The Lieutenant cares very much for people. That doesn't mean he goes around showing it all the time. It's a learned habit. I know he didn't know. I'm equally sure Julie does.'

'Ah. Julie. Your favourite lady in all Amsterdam?'

'I now have two favourite ladies in all Amsterdam. With the usual provisos, of course.'

'Your wife and daughters, of course.'

'Of course. Don't stall. You're very good at stalling, you know, Anne, at diverting me from the topic at hand, which is you, and don't give me those big innocent eyes.'

'Julie knows,' she said. 'How did you know that, sir?'

'Because I know Julie. Because she's clever. Because she's a woman. Living so close to you she's bound to notice things that others wouldn't. Clothes, jewellery, personal possessions – things the average working girl wouldn't have. Even the way you speak. Fine by me if Julie knows, she'd never tell anyone, I'll bet she's never even told her brother. You like living there?'

'Very much. And Julie, also very much. I think she likes me, too. I have the honour to sleep in the bedroom that used to be

73

Peter's. I believe he left about six years ago.' She frowned. 'I asked her why he'd left, it couldn't have been an argument, they're obviously terribly fond of each other, but she wouldn't tell me, just said I'd have to ask Peter.'

'Did you ask him?'

'No.' She shook her head very firmly. 'One doesn't ask the Lieutenant personal questions.'

'I agree that he does rather give that impression. He's quite approachable really. No secret about his departure – he left to get married. Marianne. Loveliest girl in Amsterdam, even although I do say it about my own niece.'

'She's your niece?'

'Was.' De Graaf's voice was sombre. 'Even in those days Peter was the best, most able cop in the city; far better than I am but for God's sake don't tell him so. He broke up a particularly vicious gang of people who specialized in a nice mixture of blackmail and torture. Four brothers, they were, the Annecys. God knows where they got their name from. Peter put two of them away for fifteen years. The other two just vanished. Shortly after the conviction of the two brothers, someone, almost certainly one or both of the two brothers that had not been brought to justice, placed in Peter's weekend canal boat a huge bomb wired up to the ignition switch – same technique as was used by the murderers who assassinated Lord Mountbatten. As it happened, Peter wasn't aboard his boat that weekend. But Marianne and their two children were.'

'Dear God!' The girl's hands were clenched. 'How awful. How – how dreadful!'

'And every three months or so since that time he receives a postcard from one of the two surviving Annecy brothers. Never any message. Just a drawing of a noose and a coffin, a reminder that he's living on borrowed time. Charming, isn't it?'

'Horrible! Just horrible! He must be worried to death. I know I would. Wondering every night when I go to sleep – if I could sleep – whether I would wake up in the morning.'

'I don't think he worries much – if he did he'd never show it – and I know he sleeps very well. But that's the reason – although he never mentions it – why he doesn't return to live with Julie.

74

He doesn't want her to be around when the bomb comes through his window.'

'What a way to live! Why doesn't he emigrate somewhere, live under an assumed name?'

'If you ever get to know Peter van Effen – really know him, I mean – you'll wonder why you ever asked that question. Anne, you have an enchanting smile. Let me see it again.'

She gave a puzzled half-smile. 'I don't understand.'

'He's coming back. Let me see how good an actress you are.'

And, indeed, when van Effen returned to the table she was smiling, a person at ease with the world. When she looked up and saw the expression – more accurately, the total lack of expression – on his face she stopped smiling.

'About to ruin our dinner, are you, Peter?' de Graaf shook his head. 'And such a splendid meal we've ordered.'

'Not quite.' Van Effen smiled faintly. 'Might put us off our third bottle of Bordeaux or Burgundy or whatever. Perhaps even the second bottle? First, let me put you briefly in the picture as to what happened earlier today. Yes, sir, I'll have some wine, I feel I could do with a mild restorative. I've been offered a job – at, I'm sure, a far higher salary plus than I'm ever likely to get in this police force – to blow something up. What, I don't know. Could be the Amsterdam–Rotterdam bank for all I know. Maybe a boat, bridge, barge, barracks, maybe anything. Haven't been told yet.

'As you know, Vasco had brought those two characters to the Hunter's Horn this afternoon. Prosperous and respectable citizens, but, then, no successful criminal ever looks like one. We were all very cagey and crafty, toing-and-froing, sparring and giving nothing away for most of the time. Then they made me this definite offer of a job and I accepted. They said they would have to report back to their superiors but would definitely contact me tomorrow and give me details of the job to be done and what my rewards would be for this. Vasco was to be the courier. So we shook hands like gentlemen and parted with expressions of goodwill and mutual trust.

'I had two sets of tails waiting at a discreet distance from the Hunter's Horn. I've had a report –'

'Goodwill and mutual trust?' Annemarie said.

De Graaf waved a hand. 'We tend to use figurative terms in our profession. Proceed, Peter.'

'I've had news of both sets of tails. The first say that they lost Agnelli and Paderiwski – that's what they called themselves –'

'Good God!' de Graaf said. 'Agnelli and Paderiwski. A famous industrialist and a famous pianist. Aren't they original?'

'That's what I thought. Lost them in a traffic jam, they say. Claimed that they hadn't been spotted. Pure accident. The report about the other two makes me wonder, to say the least.'

' "About" the other two?' de Graaf said. 'Not "from"?'

'About. They were found in a darkened alley. Barely able to call for help, barely conscious. Unable to move and both in agony. Both men had had both kneecaps smashed. A sign used in Sicily and certain American cities that some people don't like being followed and that those who were doing the following won't be doing it again for some time to come. They weren't knee-capped – no guns. Iron bars. They're under surgery. Neither man will be able to walk for months, neither will ever be able to walk properly again. Nice, isn't it, sir. And a new development in our fair city. Another instance, one supposes, of the steady advance of American culture.'

'Crippled?' Annemarie's voice was low, barely above a whisper. 'Crippled for life. How can you – how can you joke about such things.'

'I'm sorry.' Van Effen looked at her, saw that some colour had gone from her face, and pushed her glass closer to her. 'Take some. I'll join you. Joking? I can assure you I never felt less funny in my life. And it's not just an American practice, sir: it's become a very popular pastime in Northern Ireland in the past two or three years.'

'So your other tails were almost certainly given the slip and nothing accidental about it.' De Graaf sampled his Bordeaux and the distressing news didn't appear to have upset him unduly for he smacked his lips appreciatively. 'Excellent. Our friends seem to have a considerable expertise in both evasive and direct action. Professionals. And gone to ground. Ah. All is not lost. The Chateaubriand. You said you would share this with me, my dear.'

She appeared to give a tiny shudder. 'I know it's trite, silly, but I don't think I could eat a thing.'

'Maybe the moles will come out of their burrows tomorrow,' van Effen said. 'I'm still hoping that they will keep their promise and make contact with me.'

Annemarie stared at him, almost blankly. 'You must be mad,' she said in a low voice. She seemed genuinely puzzled. 'Either they'll come and give you the same treatment, perhaps worse, perhaps dispose of you permanently, or they won't come at all. After they carried out that savage attack on those poor men they could have examined them and found out that they *were* policemen. They must have been carrying something that would identify them as policemen, even guns. Were they carrying guns?' Van Effen nodded. 'Then they'll know you are a policeman because they'll know you must have had them followed since they left the Hunter's Horn. You like the idea of suicide?' She reached out and touched de Graaf's wrist. 'You mustn't let him do it, sir. He'll be killed.'

'Your concern does you credit.' It was van Effen who answered and he seemed quite unmoved by her plea. 'But quite uncalled for. The villains don't necessarily know that I set the tails on their tracks. They might not even have noticed them until long after they'd left the Hunter's Horn and would have no reason to connect me with them. That's one thing. The other thing is the fact that though the Colonel is your father's friend that doesn't give the father's daughter the right to advise the Colonel. A fledgling policewoman. A Chief of Police. It would be laughable if it weren't so presumptuous.'

She looked at him, her eyes hurt as if she had been struck, then lowered her gaze to the tablecloth. De Graaf looked at van Effen, shook his head slightly, then took the girl's hand.

'Your concern *does* do you credit. It does. But it doesn't give me much credit in your eyes. None. Look at me.' She looked at him, the hazel eyes at once solemn and apprehensive. 'Van Effen is absolutely correct. The foxes have to be flushed from their covers and this, at the moment, seems the only way to do it. So Peter will go – I would never order him to go – and with my consent. Good heavens, girl, do you think I would use him as live bait, a lamb to the slaughter, a Daniel in the lion's den, a tethered goat for the tiger? My word, I do have a way with metaphors. I guarantee, my girl, that, when and if the meeting does take place, both the Hunter's Horn and the surrounding area will be alive with invisible armed men. Invisible to the ungodly. Peter will be as safe as a man in a church.'

'I know. I'm silly. I'm sorry.'

'Pay no attention to the Colonel's comforting words,' van Effen said. 'I shall probably be riddled with bullets. Police bullets. Unless it's pointed out to them that I'm in disguise. Ironic if they shot the wrong man. Same outfit as before. Just let them concentrate on the black glove. That's me.'

A waiter approached their table. 'Sorry, Lieutenant. There's another call for you.'

Van Effen was back inside two minutes. 'Well, no surprise, surprise. The FFF, again, mysterious message, no doubt stepping up their demoralizing campaign. They say there *could* be some havoc wreaked along the North Holland Canal tomorrow at Alkmaar at 9 a.m., but they have made no guarantee that there will be. All they have promised is that there will be some quite considerable activity.'

De Graaf said: 'That was all?'

'All. I see. Seems utterly pointless and meaningless. What the devil do you think they're up to now?'

'It's not pointless. That's just the point – to make us wonder and worry about just what the devil they *are* up to now. They want to create uncertainty, confusion and demoralization and it would seem to me that they're going the right way about it. Speaking of the FFF, sir, how was your pleasure trip to Texel this afternoon?'

'Complete waste of time. I was accompanied, as you more or less predicted, by a bunch of old women.'

'You don't intend to be at Alkmaar at 9 a.m. tomorrow?'

'I intend to be in Amsterdam at 9 a.m. tomorrow. What am I supposed to do? Lurk around and nab anyone who looks as if he

78

is acting suspiciously, such as gloating over the scene of the crime?'

'An unpromising course of action. You've got friends in the University, sir. Specifically, in the linguistics department?'

De Graaf said to Annemarie: 'I'm supposed to look startled at this sudden switch and ask "why on earth do you ask that?" ' He looked at van Effen. 'Well, why on earth *do* you ask that?'

'I listened to the FFF's tapes in the *Telegraph*'s office earlier on this evening. A woman's voice. A young woman, I would say. And not Dutch, I'm sure.'

'Interesting. Very. Back to our mysterious foreigners again. Any educated guesses as to the country of origin of the caller?'

'That's the trouble, sir. I speak the odd language, sure, but I'm not what you might call an educated linguist. Regional accents, nuances, pronunciation – that is quite definitely not my field.'

'And you think the university could help?'

'It's a chance, sir. As you say, no stone unturned. The tapes are in my office.'

'I'll do what I can. You may as well get to your feet, Peter. A purposeful waiter comes your way.'

Van Effen rose, met the waiter, spoke briefly and moved on. When he took his seat again, he said: 'The opposition is stirring. Whatever opposition that might be. That was my hotel, the Trianon. Message relayed through the office of course.'

De Graaf said patiently: 'And how long have you been staying in the Trianon, Lieutenant? You have been evicted from your own apartment?'

'The register book says that I have been there for two weeks. I arranged that about five o'clock this afternoon.'

'Dear, dear. Falsifying register books is a civil offence.'

'I've no time to be arrested at the moment. Romero Agnelli or one of his men must have been very busy phoning around and have at last located me as staying at the Trianon. They have posted a watcher in the shadows – in a little old Fiat, actually. I have arranged for another watcher to watch the original. Well, I can't disappoint them. I shall turn up there later on tonight.'

'You lead an active life,' de Graaf said. 'I assume that you do not intend to spend the night there?'

'You assume correctly, sir. I shall park my car at the back of the hotel, where I shall be picked up by a police taxi and deposited at the front door. Then I pass through the hotel, exit by the rear entrance and drive home. It's a nuisance, no more.'

'And here, again,' de Graaf said, 'comes your own private and personal nuisance. My word, you *are* popular tonight.'

Van Effen looked, sighed, rose, spoke briefly to the waiter again and disappeared towards the telephone booths.

'The same opposition stirs yet again,' he said on his return. 'Ah, a brandy. Thank you, sir. That was Sergeant Westenbrink – Vasco. Message again via the office, of course. Agnelli has been in touch with him. They would, they say, very much like to meet me at 11 a.m., tomorrow morning. Same place. This can mean one of two things.'

'I know what it means,' de Graaf said. 'Either they're on to us or they're not on to us. It is quite possible that they had no idea that they were being shadowed ever since leaving the Hunter's Horn this afternoon. On the other hand it's perfectly possible that they did know. If they did, they can have only one purpose in wanting to meet you, to see how much you know, what danger your knowledge offers and how best they can eliminate this danger. It should, I imagine, be all very discreet. And, if they suspect you and suspect that you in turn suspect them, they're being clever, for in that case one would have expected them to opt for a neutral rendezvous, for if they suspect you're an undercover policeman or working as an agent for the police then they must automatically suspect that the Hunter's Horn is a police hang-out. But, of course, to go elsewhere would be to tip their hand that they know.' De Graaf sighed. 'All very devious and complicated. Designed to spread confusion and doubt on all hands. Maybe they've been taking lessons from the FFF. Or vice versa. Another brandy, Peter? No? In that case I suggest we be on our way. I expect we shall be having a rather long day tomorrow. Do you have any particular plan for this young lady tomorrow?'

'I shall think up some onerous task by and by. As yet, no.'

'Um.' De Graaf pondered. 'You, Anne, are, of course, seen quite often in the company of Sergeant Westenbrink.'

She smiled. 'I find it difficult to think of him other than as Vasco. Yes, of course. We have to talk and it seems the best – and also the easiest – thing to do it openly.'

'Quite. Do you come and go as you like there?'

'Of course. That's the whole point of being us. No hours, no rules, no regulations. You do as you like, you're as free as the air.'

'It would cause no undue comment if you were not to turn up for a day, even two days?'

'No.' She hesitated. 'Am I supposed to be intelligent and guess what you're getting at, sir?'

'You're intelligent enough. It's just that you lack the training and experience to have a nasty, devious, suspicious mind, such as is possessed by Lieutenant van Effen, and I hope you always will.'

Annemarie shook her head, almost imperceptibly, then looked questioningly at van Effen who said: 'The Colonel is right, you know.'

'I don't know. That is, I'm sure he's right, but I don't know what he's right about. If you're having fun with me, I don't think it's very fair.'

'We aren't having fun with you, Annemarie. Teasing or diminishing people is not our idea of having a good time. Look. All this is a matter of connections. It's at least possible – I'd say a fifty-fifty chance – that Agnelli and company are on to us. In that case, Vasco is also under suspicion because he introduced them to me. And because you are known to associate with Vasco you, in turn, come under suspicion.

'What the Colonel's suggesting is that you lie low for a day, maybe even two. Depends how things develop. I have the feeling, irrational, perhaps, that the development is going to be very rapid indeed. It's not a pleasant thought for the Colonel or myself that you should fall into those people's hands. Think of those two detectives, the tails who ran out of luck. We already know that those people are ruthless, that the inflicting of pain is a matter of indifference to them. It may even be a downright pleasure. How would you care to be taken by them and tortured? I am not trying to scare you, Annemarie. I'm talking about something that's halfway between a possibility and a probability.'

'I think I've already told you.' Her voice was very quiet. 'I'm not particularly brave.'

'And then they'd know who it was they had on their hands. They'd be over the moon. Another lovely blackmailing trump in their hands in addition to their still undisclosed trumps. Apart from your own health, you'd be putting us in an impossibly difficult situation.'

'Couldn't have put it better myself,' de Graaf said.

She smiled faintly. 'I'm a coward. I'll do what I'm told.'

'Not told, my dear, not told,' de Graaf said. 'Just a suggestion.'

Again the faint smile. 'It sounds like a very good suggestion to me. Where shall I stay?'

'With Julie, of course,' van Effen said. 'An unobtrusive armed guard will be lurking in the vicinity. But before you go into purdah, as it were, there's one thing I want you to do for me.'

'Of course.'

'I want you to go to Vasco in the morning. Tell him what we've told you and tell him to disappear. I know where he'll disappear to and I'll contact him there when it's safe to.'

'I'll do that.' She was silent for a moment. 'When you asked me to do something for you and I said "of course" – well, I wish now I hadn't. You see what you've done to me, Peter. I'm a quivering wreck.'

'You're not quivering and for a wreck you look in pretty good shape to me. You may be jumped on there and then your gallant fellow Krakers would look the other way?'

'Yes.'

'We are accustomed to those injustices, are we not, Colonel? Nothing will happen to you. You'll be under constant surveillance, and by constant I mean sixty seconds every minute. The trusty Lieutenant van Effen, suitably disguised – not the Hunter's Horn disguise, of course – and lumbered with his usual arsenal – there's a thought for you, Colonel. I think I'll carry a third gun tomorrow when I meet Agnelli and his friend or friends. They already know that –'

'That you carry two guns,' de Graaf said, 'and so their minds will, of course, be pre-conditioned against the idea of you carrying a third. It'll be in your book, of course.'

'Of course, it's not. One mustn't put such thoughts in the minds of the criminal element. But, yes, that's the idea. So, no problem, Annemarie. I won't be further away than five metres at any time.'

'That's nice. But you've put all sorts of unpleasant thoughts in my head. I could be jumped on, in your words, anywhere and any time between here and Julie's house.'

'More injustice. No worry. I will transport you there in the safety and comfort of my own limousine.'

'Limousine!' de Graaf said. 'Comfort! My God!' He bent a solicitous eye on the girl. 'You have, I trust, not forgotten your air cushion?'

'I don't understand, sir.'

'You will.'

They left the restaurant and walked along the street until they came to the Colonel's car, parked, as usual, in a no parking area. De Graaf kissed the girl in what he probably regarded as an avuncular fashion, said goodnight and climbed into his gleaming Mercedes. The back seat of his Mercedes. Colonel de Graaf, inevitably, had a chauffeur.

Annemarie said: 'I understand now what the Colonel meant about an air cushion.'

'A trifling inconvenience,' van Effen said. 'I'm having it fixed. Orders. The Colonel complains.'

'The Colonel does like his comforts, doesn't he?'

'It may not have escaped your attention that he was built for comfort.'

'He's very kind, isn't he? Kind and courteous and considerate.'

'It's no hardship to be all those things when the object of them is as beautiful as you.'

'You do have a nice turn of speech, Lieutenant.'

'Yes, I do, rather.'

She was quiet for a moment, then said: 'But he is rather a snob, isn't he? A fearful snob.'

'In the interests of discipline, I must speak severely. You can't expect me to condone, far less agree with, denigrating remarks about our Chief of Police.'

'That wasn't meant to be denigrating. It was just an observation. I refuse to get to the stage where I must watch every word I say. This is still an open society. Or is it?'

'Well, well.'

'Go on. Say it. "Spoken with spirit" or something like that.'

'I don't think I will. But you're about as wrong with your snobbism as you were about your warm-hearted Arthur bit.'

'Arthur?'

'Our chief's first name. Never uses it. I've never figured out why. Regal connotations. Sure he's kind and thoughtful. He's also tough, shrewd and ruthless, which is why he is what he is. And he's no snob. Snobs pretend to be what they are not. His is a very ancient, very aristocratic and very wealthy lineage which is why you'll never find me contesting a restaurant bill with him. He was *born* with the knowledge that he was different, the one per cent of the one per cent. Never occurs to him to question it. He's convinced that he radiates the spirit of democracy.'

'Tough or not, snob or not, I like him.' She spoke as if that settled the matter, without specifying what the matter was.

'Arthur, as you may have observed, has a way with the ladies. Especially when he's off-duty, which is what he considered himself to be tonight.'

'Are you never off-duty? Am I always a policewoman?'

'Never thought about it that way. But I will. Think about it, I mean.'

'You're too kind.' She lapsed into silence and remained that way for the rest of the drive. Only van Effen spoke. He called up his office and requested an armed guard for his sister's house.

It was not difficult to understand why de Graaf had said that Julie van Effen was his favourite lady in all Amsterdam. With hair dark and shining as a raven's wing, a delicately moulded face and high, rather Slavonic cheek-bones, she was far more than just merely good-looking but her attraction for de Graaf, as for a great many others, almost certainly lay in her laughing dark eyes and laughing mouth. She was almost permanently good-humoured – except when she encountered injustice, cruelty, meanness, selfishness and quite a few other things of which she disapproved, when she could become very stormy indeed – and seemed to love the whole world with the exception of those who encountered her formidable disapproval. She was one of those rare people who radiated happiness, a quality that more than tended to conceal the fact that below it all lay a fine intelligence. Cabinet Ministers do not habitually employ dim-witted secretaries and Julie was a Cabinet Minister's secretary, private, personal, confidential and discreet.

She was also very hospitable and wanted to cook them a meal as soon as they had entered. It was easy to believe that this multi-talented young lady was also a cordon bleu chef, which, in fact, she was. She then offered sandwiches and desisted only when she learned that they had already eaten.

'The Dikker en Thijs, was it? Well, the police always did know how to look after themselves. For a working girl, it's new herring, red cabbage and sausage.'

'For this particular working girl,' van Effen said, 'it's the ministerial canteen. A gourmet's paradise, so I'm told – we cops aren't allowed near the place, of course. Julie, alas, has no will-power – well, you've only to look.' Julie, had in fact, as nearly perfect a figure as it was possible to imagine. She treated this badinage with a lofty contempt, ruffled his hair in the passing and went to the kitchen to prepare some coffee and a café schnapps.

Annemarie looked after her departing form, turned to van Effen and smiled. 'She can wrap you round her little finger any time, can't she?'

'Any time and any day,' van Effen said cheerfully. 'And, alas, she knows it. "Minx" is the word for her. Something I have to show you, in case you're in the house alone.' He led her to a picture on the wall and pushed it to one side to reveal a red button set flush with the wallpaper. 'What's known to the trade as a personal attack button. If you think you're in danger, suspect it or even sense it, you press this button. A patrol car will be here within five minutes.'

She tried to make light of it. 'Every housewife in Amsterdam should have one of those.'

'As there are a hundred thousand housewives in Amsterdam – maybe two for all I know – it would come a mite expensive.'

'Of course.' She looked at him and didn't or couldn't smile any more. 'I've been with the two of you a few times now and one would have to be blind and deaf not to realize that you're just potty about your kid sister.'

'Tut, tut. I can but sigh. Is it so obvious?'

'I hadn't finished. You didn't have that installed just because you love her. She's in danger, isn't she?'

'Danger?' He caught her by the shoulders, so tightly that she winced. 'Sorry.' He eased his grip but left his hands where they were. 'How do you know?'

'Well, she is, isn't she? In danger, I mean.'

'Who told you? Julie?'

'No.'

'The Colonel?'

'Yes. This evening.' She looked at him, her gaze moving from one eye to the other. 'You're not angry, are you?'

'No. No, my dear, I'm not angry. Just worried. I'm not a healthy person to know.'

'Julie knows about the danger?'

'Of course.'

'Does she know about the postcards?' He looked at her thoughtfully and didn't change his expression as she put her hands on his shoulders and made as if to shake him in exasperation; which was a silly thing to do as van Effen was built along very solid lines. 'Well, does she?'

'Yes. It would be difficult for her not to. The postcards come to this address. One of the Annecy brothers' ways of getting to me.'

'Dear God. This – this is dreadful. How – how can she be so – so happy?' She put her head against his shoulder as if she was suddenly tired. 'How can she?'

'The old saying, I suppose. Better to laugh than to cry. You're not about to cry, are you?'

'No.'

'The old saying doesn't quite apply here. She always was a happy child. Only, now she has to work at it.'

Julie came in with coffee, stopped abruptly and cleared her throat. 'Isn't it a little early in the evening –' She laid the tray down. 'I hope the deafness is a temporary affliction. I said –' She stopped again, the expression on her face showing her concern, moved swiftly to where they stood, put an arm round Anne-marie and gently turned her head until she could see her face. 'Tears. Full of tears.' She pulled a lace handkerchief from her sleeve cuff. 'What's this ruffian been up to?'

'This ruffian hasn't been up to anything,' van Effen said mildly. 'Annemarie knows everything, Julie. Marianne, the kids, you, me, the Annecys.'

'The Colonel, I'll be bound.'

'You'll be bound right.'

Julie said: 'I know, Annemarie. It's a shock. To come all at once, it's a shock. At least it came to me bit by bit. Come. I have the sovereign remedy. A double schnapps in your coffee.'

'You're very kind. If I could be excused –' She turned and walked quickly from the room.

'Well.' There was a demanding note in Julie's voice. 'Don't you see what you've done?'

'Me?' Van Effen was genuinely perplexed. 'What am I supposed to have done now? It was the Colonel –'

'It's not what you have done. It's what you haven't done.' She put her hands on his shoulders and her voice went soft. 'It's what you haven't seen.'

'I see. I mean, I don't see.' Van Effen was cautious. 'What haven't I seen?'

'You clown.' Julie shook her head. 'Annemarie. Her heart is in her face, in her eyes. That girl's in love with you.'

'What! You're not well, that's what it is.'

'My beloved, brilliant dolt of a brother. But don't believe me. Ask her to marry you now. A special licence – which you can obtain at the drop of a hat – and you'd be married by midnight.'

Van Effen looked slightly dazed. 'Pretty sure of yourself, aren't you?'

'No, I'm not. I'm absolutely certain.'

'But she hardly knows me.'

'I'm aware of that. After all, you've only met her, what – twenty, thirty, forty times?' She shook her head. 'The feared interrogator, the writer of books on psychology, the man who can lay bare the innermost secrets of any mind with one piercing glance – well, a hundred per cent for theory, zero for practice.'

'You're a fine one to talk. Specialist in marriage counselling – or should I say match-making? Ha! Six marriage proposals for certain – could have been twenty for all I know – and you turned them all down. There indeed speaks the voice of experience.'

'Don't try to change the subject.' She smiled sweetly. 'Yes, indeed, there speaks the voice of experience. I didn't love any of them. *She* is deeply in love with you. I don't quite understand why.'

'I need a schnapps.' Van Effen opened a nearby cupboard.

'I've just brought you a café schnapps.'

'First of all, I need a schnapps. Then I need a café schnapps.'

'Not a psychiatrist? Why do you think she's so upset?'

'She's soft-hearted, that's why.'

'You should make a splendid match. Soft heart. Soft head.' She took his head between her hands and studied his eyes carefully. 'The hawk-eyed detective lieutenant. What you need is a pair of glasses. And you've missed your cue, haven't you? Half a dozen times, at least.'

'What cue?'

'Oh dear. That wary hunted look makes you more criminal than cop. What cue? "I wouldn't marry her if she were the last girl in the world" should have been your answer to the cue. Standard reaction, I believe.' She smiled again. 'But of course, you're not standard.'

'Oh, shut up.'

'A well reasoned answer.' She sat and took up her coffee. 'Mental myopia. I believe it's incurable.'

'Oh, I don't know. I'm sure you'll find the answer.' Van Effen was his old self, calm, assured, relaxed and very much back on balance. 'I don't particularly care for cool, clinical, slightly superior, slightly amused doctors, but I have to admit you've effectively worked a cure in my case. You've cured me of any interest I might ever have had in that young lady. Or maybe that was what you wanted. I don't know.' She was looking at him with parted lips and uncomprehending eyes. 'I don't need – I don't want, I should say – help, advice or sympathy from you, and not just because they're uncalled-for, unhelpful, unwanted or unsolicited but because I'm perfectly capable of managing my own life without the assistance of a meddlesome young sister. I'll go check if the guard is here.'

He went out leaving Julie to stare numbly at the door he'd closed behind him, disconsolate and disbelieving, and she was still in the same position, still gazing sightlessly at the door, the same expression of hurt and bafflement on her face when Annemarie came into the room. Annemarie stopped, looked in puzzlement at the unhappy face, hurried across the room to Julie's chair, dropped to her knees and said: 'What's wrong, Julie? What's wrong?'

Julie looked away from the door and slowly turned her head. 'Nothing. Nothing's wrong.'

'Nothing's wrong? Oh, God! Nothing. First me, then you. Tears. And you look – you look so woebegone.' Annemarie hugged her. 'Nothing wrong! Julie! Don't treat me like an idiot.'

'I'm the idiot. I've just made a mistake.'

'You? I don't believe it. Mistake. What mistake?'

'The mistake of forgetting that Peter is not only my brother, he's a policeman and heir apparent to the Colonel. You didn't know that, did you?' Julie sniffled. 'Common knowledge. De Graaf is due to retire this year but he's in no hurry to retire as long as Peter is already doing most of his job for him.'

'Never mind the Colonel. Where's that ruffian?'

89

Julie tried to smile. 'Second time tonight he's been called a ruffian by two different girls. I'll bet it's never happened before. He's left.'

'Gone? Gone for the night?'

'No. Just to check on the guard.' Julie smiled again, a more successful effort this time. 'He may be gifted at reducing people to tears but I'm sure he cares for us.'

'He's got a funny way of showing it. What did he *do* to you, Julie? What did he say?'

'Do? Nothing, of course. Say? I stepped out of line, I guess, and he brought me back into line. That's all.'

'You expect me to be satisfied with that?'

'No, I don't, my dear. But can we leave it just for the moment? Please?'

They had finished their coffee by the time van Effen had returned. He appeared to find nothing amiss or, if he did, chose not to comment on it.

'Guard's here,' he said. 'Armed to the teeth. And I have to go now.'

'But your coffee –'

'Another time. I am, as they say, summoned forth. Julie, there's something you must do for me. Could you –'

'Must?' She smiled. 'An order or request.'

'What does that matter.' Rarely for him, van Effen was irritated. 'Do what I ask – please, note the please – or I'll take Annemarie away with me.'

'My word! Such threats. And if she chooses to remain here or I ask her to stay?'

'Rotterdam. Tomorrow morning. Ex-policewoman. You don't disobey orders in the police and remain on the force. Sorry, Annemarie, that was not directed at you. Julie's not being very bright tonight. Don't look shocked, little sister, if you can't see I'm serious then you've become uncommonly stupid. Develop diplomatic flu for the next day or two. Annemarie is in as much danger as you are and I want the two of you here together. Annemarie, nine-fifteen.'

He went to the door and opened it, looked at the two solemn faces and shook his head.

'Exit the gallant Lieutenant into the dark and dreadful night.'

He closed the door quietly behind him.

Four

The tall, thin young man in the dark and dripping raincoat would rarely have called for more than a passing glance or a comment on the fact that he did look rather unprepossessing, an impression increased by the black hair plastered to his head by the heavy rain and that he sported an ill-trimmed black moustache. The moustache, in fact, had not been trimmed at all: he had been in an unusual hurry that morning and had pasted it on ever so slightly askew.

He was standing almost in the middle of the square when he saw her, angling across and coming almost directly towards him. Annemarie, her warpaint back in position again, looked as miserable and bedraggled as the young man, who now stepped out into her path.

'Annemarie, is it?'

Her eyes widened and she looked quickly around. Despite the near torrential rain there were a fair number of people around and a flower and vegetable open-air market only metres away. She looked again at the young man, who was smiling, a rather pleasant smile despite his overall appearance.

'Please don't worry, miss. Hardly the place where anyone would think to carry out a kidnapping. You must be Annemarie – there couldn't be two people answering the description I was given. I'm Detective Rudolph Engel.' He brought a badge from his pocket and showed it to her. 'I could, of course, have stolen this. Lieutenant van Effen wants to see you. He's in his car.'

'Why should I believe you? Why did he send you? He knew where I was. He could have come to see me. What car does he have?'

'A black Peugeot.'

'You would know that, wouldn't you?'

'Yes.' The young man was patient. 'When you've worked

under someone for five years you do know something about him. The Lieutenant said to me, "Miss Meijer is very suspicious. Mention the Amazon, her father, the Colonel and someone's 'lack of courage'." I have no idea what he meant.'

'I do.' She took his arm. 'I'm sorry.'

Van Effen, relaxed behind the wheel of his car, was this morning sporting a homburg hat and a big, black, square beard of the type favoured by Sephardic jews. He looked round as Annemarie opened the passenger door and looked in.

'Good morning, my dear.'

'Good morning, he says. What are you doing here?'

'Sheltering from the rain. It's coming down in buckets. You must have noticed. Come in, come in.'

She sat down and looked at him accusingly. 'Five metres, you said. Never more than five metres away. Sixty seconds in every minute. That's what you said. Where were you? Your promise to look after me! Fine promise.'

'Man proposes, God disposes.' If van Effen was remorse stricken, he concealed it well. 'Besides, you were being looked after. By proxy. Don't tell me you didn't see a rather elderly gentleman hanging around, slightly stooped, grey beard, grey coat and a white stick. He was looking after you.'

'I saw him. That creature! He couldn't have looked after a kitten.'

'Whatever that means. That creature is young, fit, a judo expert and a very accurate shot.'

'Beards,' she almost muttered. 'Beards, moustaches, that's all they can think of. Disguises! Well, thank you, someone was there, but you broke your promise.'

'It was politic to do so. I was close behind and you were less than a hundred metres from your rendezvous when I caught sight of no other than Mr Paderiwski following you even more closely than I was. Mr Paderiwski is shrewd, observant and doesn't like me, which is a nasty combination. He might just have recognized me, especially when I was in close attendance on you. I had taken the precaution of taking two of my detectives with me – think nothing of the fact that we obviously

93

care so much about you – and I decided discretion was the better part of foolhardiness. Hence the switch.'

Engel said through van Effen's open window: 'Anything further, sir?'

'No. Not here. Don't lose sight of our friend.'

'Well, I've already seen him, sir. There can't be another bald, pepper and salt beard with a squint around.'

'Julius Caesar?' Annemarie said.

'None other. I didn't tell Rudolph here what his name was. He wouldn't have believed me. A close but not too close eye on our Julius. And make sure there are always a few people around. I'd rather lose him than lose you. Don't forget what happened to your two colleagues yesterday.'

'I won't forget, sir.' The expression on his face was testimony enough to that. He turned and walked away into the rain.

'Mollified?' Van Effen started the engine and drove off.

'A bit.' She smiled a little. 'Did you have to tell him I was a coward?'

'I did not. Someone was, I said.'

'It doesn't matter, because I am. I don't like riding around in this car, for instance.'

'It takes time to get seats fixed. And what's that got to do –'

'Please. I mean that this car is known. To criminals, I mean.'

'Pfui. There's a couple of hundred like this in the city.'

She said sweetly: 'There's a couple of hundred with the same licence plates?'

'What's that got to do with anything? *You* know the licence number of this car?'

'More or less. Rotterdam. Three nines. We are trained to be observant, remember?'

'But not observant enough to notice that these were clip-on plates, not screwed. Today, this car is registered in Paris with a big 'F' at the side to prove it. I have access to an unlimited number of plates.' She made a face but said nothing. 'You should be interested in more important things. Such as the latest antics of the FFF.'

'Yes?'

'There were no antics. They didn't blow the dyke of the

94

North Holland canal. They called in to both the papers and the police less than ten minutes ago. Positively hugging themselves, they are. Said they never promised they would blow the canal – which is quite true – only that there would be considerable activity in that area at nine o'clock this morning. There were, they reported, scenes of very considerable activity which is again quite true. All rescue and repair teams were there, waiting, as were considerable numbers of police and army, not to mention air force helicopters. They claimed to have taken a good number of aerial photographs of the scenes, just for keepsakes.'

'You believe that, too?'

'Certainly. I have no reason to disbelieve it.'

'But aerial photographs? How could that be possible?'

'It would be all too simple, I'm afraid. There would be any amount of helicopters buzzing about there this morning. An extra one wouldn't be noticed especially if, as is highly likely, it was carrying some official markings.'

'What was the reason behind this pointless and idiotic exercise?'

'It was far from being idiotic and very much to the point. Just in case we missed the point they spelt it out very clearly. They said that in the space of twenty-four hours they had reduced the country, most especially the authorities, to a state of frustrated helplessness. The so-called authorities – they had a number of cynical and very unpleasant remarks to make about the government, the police, the army and those whose duty it was to look after the safety and welfare of dykes, locks, weirs, sluices, dams and I forget what else – were totally powerless to do anything to stop them. All they had to do, they said, was to stop at home, stick a pin into a map, phone the papers, sit back and never go within a hundred kilometres but still guarantee that the law, the army, the repair and rescue teams would be out in full force. It was, they said, both an entertaining and gratifying situation. One can readily understand why they feel that way.'

'And not a word about their purposes, no hint as to what lies behind it all?'

'No hint, but a suggestion that we might soon know what

95

their demands are going to be. They didn't use the word "demands" but they can have meant nothing else. Tomorrow, they said, they were going to flood a really large area of the country and after that they would probably have talks with the government. Can you imagine? The sheer cold arrogance of it all. They speak as if they are an independent sovereign state. Next, one supposes, they'll be calling for an open debate in the UNO.' He glanced at his watch. 'Plenty of time. Two minutes to remove this outfit – no washing or soaking required – and five minutes to put on my Hunter's Horn uniform. I suggest coffee.'

She put a hand on his arm. 'You really are going there, aren't you, Peter.'

'Of course. I've said so. Somebody has to and as I am the only person who's been in contact with them, it has to be me. How else do you think the law would ever get anywhere unless it's prepared, just once in a while, to take the initiative?'

'I wish you weren't going. I feel certain something is going to happen. Something awful. You could be hurt, even killed, or, maybe even worse, crippled for life. You know what they did to those two men. Oh Peter!' She was silent for a moment, then said: 'If I were your wife, I'd stop you.'

'How?'

'I don't know,' she said miserably. 'Appeal to your better nature, love for me, something like, "For my sake, if you care about me, please don't go." Something clever like that,' she said bitterly.

'Well, you're not my wife, and, even if you were, I'd still go. I'm sorry that sounds hard and selfish and cruel, but it's my job and I have to go.' He put his hand on her arm. 'You're a very kind girl and I do appreciate your concern.'

'Kind? Concern?' She caught his wrist and gently removed his hand from her arm. 'Concern!'

'Annemarie!' Van Effen's surprise was genuine. 'What on earth's wrong.'

'Nothing. Just nothing.'

Van Effen gazed ahead for some moments, sighed and said: 'I don't think I'll ever understand women.'

'I don't think so either.' She seemed to hesitate, then said: 'I don't much fancy going to a coffee-shop.'

'If you wish we won't. But why not?'

'I don't much care for wearing this face in public. Where there are decent people around. It doesn't matter back there. And I don't think you are particularly keen on being seen among the same public with a freak like me.'

'I know what lies behind the warpaint so it doesn't matter to me.' He paused. 'Maybe I don't know anything about women but I always know when they're telling fibs.'

'I'm telling fibs?'

'Of course you are.'

'Well, yes, I am. Can't we have coffee at Julie's place. It's only another five minutes.'

'Sure. Time I have. I know you're very fond of Julie. But are you also worried about her?'

'I think she's worried about me. Even though she knew you would be there she didn't like the idea of my going back to that place.'

'You didn't answer my question. You're not, perhaps – well, just a little bit worried about her?' She remained silent.

'The Annecy brothers. Would you believe, I've never even seen either of them? I regard them as a fairly distant menace.'

'The menace I'm thinking of is a great deal nearer to home. Well, not menace. Problem, rather.'

'This is something new on me. A bagatelle, whatever it is. Give me the name of this person or problem and I'll attend to it.'

'Indeed, Lieutenant.' Something in the tone of her voice caught van Effen's attention and he gave her a long speculative look. 'And how do you attend to this bagatelle, when the bagatelle in question is yourself?'

'Ah. Me again. I don't suppose there's any point in repeating the old complaining question?'

'Which is what?'

'What the hell am I supposed to have done this time?'

'By your standards, I suppose, absolutely nothing.'

'I detect a certain sarcasm? Or is it irony? I've noticed an increasing use of it. Not becoming, Annemarie. You should do something about it. Well, what *have* I done?'

'Reduced a lovely girl to tears. Not once, but three times. And when I say lovely, I don't just mean beautiful. I mean the nicest, kindest, warmest person I've ever met. Three times. But it's as I said. By your standards, a bagatelle.'

'Julie?'

'Julie! Who else would I mean? Or do you have a whole collection of ladies that you go around reducing to tears?'

'What's she crying about?'

'What's she – I don't know what to say. I can't believe you're cruel, indifferent. But don't you care that she's upset?'

'Of course I care. I'd care more if I knew why she was upset.'

'I wonder. You'll think it funny. For one thing, you left last night without a good-night hug and kiss. You've never done that before, she says.'

'Funny? It's ludicrous. My men getting hospitalized, a gang of lunatics threatening to inundate our country, another gang of lunatics wanting to hire me to blow up the palace or whatever, nations toppling and I'm supposed to be worried about smooches? A bagatelle? Soon fix that.'

'Of course you will. A double ration of affectionate farewells. Georgie, Porgy, pudding and pie, kissed the girls and made them cry.'

'Shakespeare?'

'English nursery rhyme.' Her voice was very curt indeed. 'Perhaps a bagatelle. What does matter is that she says she hurt two people she loves because she was meddlesome. I suppose she means you and me. Said she thought she was helping but that she was too clever or too stupid for her own good.'

'That's her problem. A little bit of self-analysis never did anyone any harm.'

'Self-analysis! *You* told her she was interfering and too smart for her own good. Anybody's good.'

'Julie told you that?'

'Of course she didn't. She's too loyal – misplaced loyalty, perhaps. Julie would never have said that – she's too unselfish to think about herself. But it sounds exactly like you.'

'I'll say I'm sorry. Very, very sorry.'

'And, of course, you'll tell her that I told you to.'

'No. I must say it's a sad thing to be held in such low esteem by two ladies you love.'

'The Lieutenant is pleased to be flippant,' she said coldly.

'Flippancy? Never. You don't believe me?'

'No, I don't believe you.'

'I care very much about you. But as a matter of principle and in the interests of discipline, a barrier must remain between the officer class and rankers.'

'Oh, shut up!' The tone was one of pure exasperation.

'The principle doesn't seem to be standing up very well,' van Effen said gloomily. 'And the barrier's flat. So much for discipline.'

Annemarie gave no indication that she had heard a word he'd said.

Julie, polite but reserved, had gone to make coffee, Annemarie had headed for the bath and van Effen spoke to the guard, a man called Thyssen, who assured him that all was quiet and that the man he had relieved had had a similarly uneventful night. Julie entered the living-room just as he did: she was still quiet and unsmiling.

'Julie?'

'Yes?'

'I'm sorry.'

'For what?'

'I've hurt my Julie.'

'You? Hurt? How?'

'That's right. Make it easy for me. I know you've been upset, most likely still are. Annemarie told me.'

'Did she tell you why?'

'No. But it didn't take my analytical mind, the one you're always denigrating, very long to figure it out. In retrospect, I could have been more tactful. But things on my mind, lots of things. Apart from those things, you're upset, Annemarie is upset because you're upset, and I'm upset because the two of you are upset. I've got to go out and see some desperate

99

criminals and I can't afford to be upset. I have to be careful, crafty, cunning, calculating, watchful and ruthless and I can't be any of those things if I'm upset, and I'll only be upset if you insist on remaining upset. So you'll have me on your conscience for the rest of your life if something happens to me, such as being shot in the head, thrown off a high building or drowned in a canal. Are you still upset?'

She came close to him; linked her hands behind his neck and put her head on his shoulder. 'Of course I am. Not because of last night, but because of what you've just said. You're the only brother I have and I suppose I have to love someone.' She tightened her grip. 'One of those days the gallant Lieutenant is going to go out into what the gallant Lieutenant calls the dreadful night and the gallant Lieutenant is not going to come back.'

'This is the morning, Julie.'

'Please. You know what I mean. I feel fey, Peter. I feel something dreadful is going to happen today.' She tightened her grip even more. 'I do so wish you weren't going out. I'd do anything in the world to stop you. You know that this is not the first time – that I've felt this way, I mean – it's been three or four times, and I've been right every time. Change your appointment, Peter, please, darling. I know, I just know how I won't feel this way tomorrow.'

'I'll come back, Julie. I love you, you love me, I know you'd be terribly sad if I didn't come back, so I'll have to come back, won't I?'

'Please, Peter. Please!'

'Julie, Julie.' He smoothed her hair. 'You lot certainly do wonders for my morale.'

'What do you mean "you lot"?'

'Annemarie's been at it too. Feeling fey, I mean. Prophesying death, doom and disaster. You can imagine how this cheers me up no end. Tell you what. A compromise. I promise you I won't be lured astray by any bad men or go anywhere with them from the Hunter's Horn. I'll listen to what they say then make my plans accordingly. Basically, I think that I'll arrange to meet them again at a time and place of my own choosing, this being after I've learnt what their plans are for me – or their evil intentions. So, a deal. If you promise me one of your cordon bleu lunches – finest French wines, of course – for one o'clock, I'll promise I'll be here at one.'

Still with her hands linked behind his neck she leaned back and looked at him. 'You will?'

'Just said so. Your eyes are funny. About to weep salt tears for the gallant Lieutenant?'

'I was thinking about it.' She smiled. 'I've changed my mind. I'll think about the lunch menu instead.'

Annemarie came in. She was wearing a bathrobe that was much too large for her and a towel wound around her presumably still very wet hair. She smiled and said: 'It's difficult to move around this house without interrupting private conversations. Sorry I look such a fright.'

'You can frighten me at any time,' van Effen said cheerfully. 'She really isn't too bad looking, is she, Julie?'

'She's the most beautiful girl *you've* ever seen.'

'In my profession you don't get to see many girls, beautiful or otherwise.' He looked at Julie consideringly. 'You're not too bad yourself. But, then, I'm used to your face. It's a toss-up. And who am I to quibble in – or at – such company?'

'It pleases the Lieutenant to be carefree and light-hearted, Julie,' Annemarie said acidly. 'He was anything but this morning. What have you done to him?'

'We've been conducting a mutual admiration party,' van Effen said.

'No, we haven't. And I haven't been appealing to his better nature either – I wouldn't know where to look for that. I think maybe we're slightly unfair to the poor man. Both you and I, it seems, have been full of bad omens and predicting all sorts of awful things that are going to happen to him. He was just suffering from some gloom and despondency, that's all.'

'He wasn't the only one,' Annemarie said. 'Your cloud seems to have lifted a bit, too.'

'You're choking me,' van Effen said.

'Ah!' She unclasped her hands. 'Peter says he isn't going to do anything brave today. Just going to the Hunter's Horn, meeting whoever is there, make arrangements for another meeting and then leave. Going to find out what their plans for him are. Thing is, he's going directly there – where he'll be guarded by heaven knows how many armed detectives – and coming directly back again.'

Annemarie smiled, her relief as obvious as Julie's. 'That *is* good.' The smile slowly vanished. 'How do you know he'll keep his word?'

'A police officer's word –' van Effen began.

'Because he's coming back at one o'clock. For lunch. Extra special. French wines. He knows what I'm like if anyone is late for my meals, far less misses them. Besides, I'd never cook for him again.'

'Banned for life? No, not that. I'll be back. Guaranteed.'

Annemarie said: 'Is he coming for us or for the lunch?'

'The lunch, of course. Us he can see any time.'

'Not or – and,' van Effen said. 'A peaceful hour. I may well be called upon to attend to something about two o'clock. The FFF, I mean.'

'I thought,' Annemarie said, 'that they weren't going to do anything until some undisclosed time tomorrow.'

'I was about to tell you. I was interrupted.'

Julie said: 'Somebody interrupted *you?*'

'She did. She was either being fey, like you, or getting on to me about something or other.'

'What?' Annemarie said.

'How can one remember one instance out of so many? However. The FFF promise to entertain us at two o'clock this afternoon. Same place on the North Holland canal north of Alkmaar as promised this morning – they say the mines have been planted since yesterday, that they elected not to fire them and defy us to find them – and also the Hagestein sluice.'

'The what?' Julie said.

'A sluice. Technically, I believe, a regulable weir. Concrete structure to control the flow of water. South of Utrecht, on the lower Rhine. They may attack one or the other, they say, or both, or neither. The old uncertainty principle. Well, time to dress for my appointment.'

He squeezed his sister's shoulders, kissed her, did the same to an astonished Annemarie, said: 'Someone has to uphold the law,' and left.

Julie looked at the closed door and shook her head. 'There are times, I feel, when someone should pass a law against him.'

Van Effen, attired as he had been for his visit the previous afternoon, parked his car – not the Peugeot – in a side street three blocks away from the Hunter's Horn and made his way to the back entrance of the restaurant. As the Hunter's Horn was situated in a far from salubrious area this door was kept permanently locked. Van Effen had the key. He entered, passed into the semi-darkness of the passageway beyond and had just relocked the door when something hard jabbed with painful force into the small of his back.

'Don't move.'

Van Effen didn't move. He said: 'Who is it?'

'Police.'

'You have a name?'

'Raise your hands.' A torch flicked on behind him. 'Jan, see if he has a gun.'

Hands fumbled at his jacket and he felt his shoulder-holstered gun being removed. Van Effen said: 'So. My hands are up. My gun is gone. May I turn round?'

'Very well.' Van Effen turned. 'Is that the way, Sergeant Koenis, to teach your men to search for weapons?' He lowered his hands and hitched up his trousers. There was an ankle holster, each with its Lilliput, attached to each leg. 'Put on the overhead light.'

The light came on. The man with the gun said: 'Good God. Lieutenant van Effen. Sorry about that, sir.'

'Just as long as you didn't shoot me full of holes, Sergeant. Nothing to be sorry for. Semi-dark, and, with my back to you, my trademarks, scar and black glove, weren't visible. And, of course, you weren't expecting me to enter this way. I'm just glad to see that you and your men are so on the alert.'

'I didn't even recognize your voice.'

'Cheek padding. I must admit it does alter the voice some-what. How many men do you have here, Sergeant?'

'Five, sir. Two with machine pistols.'

'And in the street outside?'

'Another five. Behind first-floor windows. Another two machine pistols.'

'Very gratifying. To see that the Colonel places so high a value on his Lieutenant.' He turned to the young policeman who held the gun in his hand. 'Do you think I could have my property back?'

'Yes, sir. Sorry, sir. Of course.' The policeman was highly embarrassed. 'I won't make *that* mistake again.'

'I know you won't. Go and ask Henri if he'll come here – Henri's the sad-looking man behind the bar.'

When Henri appeared, lugubrious as ever, he said: 'I hear you've been held at gunpoint, Peter. Must have been a rather unusual experience for you. My fault. I forgot to tell the Sergeant that you had your own key. Never expected you to come that way.'

'No harm. Customers. How many?'

'Three only. And, yes, they're regulars. Any more come in when you and your visitors are talking and I'll keep them well away. No one will be able to hear a word you say.'

'Except you, of course.'

Henri almost smiled. 'Except me. The gentleman who was here said they wouldn't find the microphone even if they looked for it. He asked me if I could find it and I couldn't. Not in my own bar. He said he thought it was highly unlikely that they would look anyway.'

'I think so too. Switch on the recorder in the office as soon as they come through the door. I shall be off now and make a respectable entrance through the front door. They've probably got someone watching.'

Van Effen was sitting in the booth nearest the door when the three men entered, Agnelli in the lead. Van Effen stood and shook hands with Agnelli, who seemed no less genial and friendly than he had on the previous occasion.

'Very pleased to meet you again, Mr Danilov,' Agnelli said. 'Helmut, of course, you know.' Paderiwski didn't offer to shake hands. 'And this is my brother, Leonardo.'

Leonardo Agnelli did offer to shake hands. He bore no resemblance to his brother. He was short, squat and had black beetling brows. The brows in themselves meant nothing, he'd just been born that way: in his own ugly way he seemed just as harmless as his brother, which again, of course, meant nothing. Introductions over, van Effen sat down. Agnelli and the other two men remained standing.

Agnelli said: 'This is your favourite booth, Mr Danilov?'

Van Effen looked slightly puzzled. 'I don't have a favourite booth. This is – well, it's just the one furthest away from the rest of the customers. I thought you might appreciate the privacy.'

'We do, we do. But would you mind if we went to another?'

Van Effen gave them some more of the same puzzled frown. 'Not at all. But I think I'm entitled to know why. Stop! I have it. The concealed microphone. A splendid basis for mutual trust.' He appeared to think briefly. 'Might have done the same myself.'

'You're an explosives expert.' Agnelli sounded apologetic. 'Such people usually – always, I believe – have a considerable knowledge of electronics.'

Van Effen smiled, stood, moved out into the aisle and waved a hand toward the empty booth. 'A thousand guilders to the first man to find the concealed microphone which I've just spent hours installing under the fascinated gaze of the proprietor and his customers. A thousand guilders for a few seconds' work. I have a generous nature.'

Agnelli laughed. 'In that case, I don't think we need bother to move.' He sat and gestured that the other two should do the same. 'Not joining us, Mr Danilov?'

'When I'm talking I –'

'Of course. I think we'll all have beer.'

Van Effen ordered, sat and said: 'Well, gentlemen, to the point.'

'Certainly.' Agnelli smiled. 'That's the way I prefer it. We have reported to our leader and he seems to approve our choice.'

'I had hoped to see him here this morning.'

'You'll see him tonight. At the Dam Square. The royal palace, to be precise, part of which, with your expert assistance, we intend to blow up tonight.'

'What!' Van Effen spilled some of the beer which he had just picked up. 'The royal palace! You did say the royal palace?'

'I did.'

'You're mad. You're quite mad.' Van Effen spoke with simple conviction.

'We don't think so. Nor are we joking. Will you do it?'

'I'll be damned if I will.'

Agnelli smiled his easy smile. 'You have been overcome by a bout of righteousness? A law-abiding upholder of justice and the straight and narrow path?'

'None of those things, I must admit. But you must understand that although I operate mainly outside the law and have a past that wouldn't bear rigorous examination, in fact, any kind of examination, I'm a pretty normal citizen in most ways. I've come to like the Dutch, and, although I don't know them from Adam, I've come to respect, even admire, their royal family.'

'Your sentiments do you credit, Mr Danilov. Believe me, I share them. But I hardly think those are your real reasons for refusing. You said yesterday afternoon that you would not become involved in any operation where there might arise even the danger of risk to limb, far less to life. Is that not so?' Van Effen nodded. 'I assure you no such risk will arise tonight.'

'Then you just want to cause a harmless explosion inside the palace—'

'Precisely.'

'And why in heaven's name should you want to cause a harmless explosion inside the palace?'

'You are not to concern yourself with that. It is, as you may well guess, a purely psychological gesture.'

'How am I to know it will be harmless?'

'You'll be able to satisfy yourself on this score when you get there. The explosion will take place inside an empty cellar. There are empty cellars on either side of it. All four doors are lockable and we will remove the keys after they have been locked. There are also empty cellars above. There is absolutely no danger to anyone involved.'

'There's danger to us. The palace is heavily guarded. Word has it that the guards are likely to ask questions of an intruder after they've shot him dead. My aversion to people getting killed includes myself.'

'Please, Mr Danilov. We are not simple-minded. Do I look like a person who would embark upon an operation like this without every detail being meticulously planned in detail beforehand?'

'I'll grant that. You don't.'

'Then you may rest assured that we will encounter no trouble. As an additional assurance, both our leader and I will be there with you. We have no more ambition to end up in durance vile than you have.'

'Maybe your records are not so unblemished either.'

'Unblemished or not, it would go hard with anyone caught with explosives within the precincts of the palace.'

'Very neat.' Van Effen sounded sour. 'So now you know I have a record whereas I don't know whether you have or not.'

'It hardly matters, does it?'

'If it does, it escapes me at the moment. It'll probably come to me when it's too late. What's this bomb like?'

'I'm not sure.' Agnelli smiled. Van Effen had practically committed himself. 'I'm not an explosives expert. Such talents as I have lie elsewhere, more in the organizing field, shall we say. I understand that it weighs three or four kilos and is made of some material called amatol.'

'What are the cellars made of?'

'Made of? You mean the walls?'

'What else could I mean?'

'I really couldn't tell you.'

'I don't suppose it matters. I was just trying to figure the blast effect. If the cellars are deep and have –'

'Those cellars are very deep.'

'So. And with the palace on top they'll have to support a very considerable weight. I don't know how old this particular part of the palace may be, I know nothing about the palace, but the walls would have to be pretty stoutly built. Reinforced concrete is unlikely. Dressed stone, I should guess, and of a considerable thickness. Your little firework is hardly likely to dent them. All the people in the palace will be aware of is a slight shake, if that, a tremor that wouldn't raise any eyebrows at the nearest seismographic station, wherever that may be. As for the sound factor, it would be negligible.'

'Are you sure?' Agnelli's tone was unaccustomedly sharp.

'If my assumptions are correct, and I see no reason why they shouldn't be, then I'm sure.'

'No loud bang?'

'They wouldn't hear it in the palace drawing-rooms, far less out in the Dam Square.'

'How could one ensure that it is heard?'

'Bring along enough spare amatol, let me have a look at the walls and I'll tell you. Tell me, is it your intention just to leave the explosive there, lock the doors, throw away the keys – it will have occurred to you, of course, that there will be duplicates?'

'These we have.'

'And arrange for the bang after you're clear of the palace?' Agnelli nodded. 'Then why on earth do you want me for a simple job like this? I've little enough in the way of conscience but I'd feel downright guilty taking money for a job like this. A young teenager in his first year in a physics or chemistry lab could do this. All you require is a battery, any old alarm clock, some household flex, a fulminate of mercury detonator, a primer and you're off. Even simpler, all you require is a length of slow-burning RDX fuse. What you don't want is an explosives expert – me. It's a matter, Mr Agnelli, of professional pride.'

'This *is* a job for a professional. It's to be set off by remote radio control.'

'A teenager in his second year in a physics or chemistry lab. Can't you do it yourselves?'

'For good reasons we want an expert. The reasons are not for you.'

'You have the technical data for this radio-controlled device.'

'A professional needs an instruction book?'

'Only an amateur would ask a professional such a stupid question. Of course I need an instruction book, as you call it, but it's not instructions I require. These systems are not difficult if you know how they work. Problem is, there are quite a number of different systems: it's not instructions I require but data. As far as the device and the control are concerned, I need to know such things as voltage, wattage, wave-length, radio range, type of detonator, the nature of the triggering mechanism, the type of shielding and a few other odds and ends. You have this? The data, I mean?'

'We have. I shall bring it along tonight.'

'You will not. I have no wish to give offence, Mr Agnelli, but only a rank amateur would suggest that I start to learn about this device on the spot. I want to be so thoroughly familiarized with the data that I can leave them all behind before I go near the place. I shall want those data at least an hour in advance.'

'Or no deal?'

'I wouldn't insult you by threats or blackmail. I assume that a reasonable man recognizes a reasonable request?'

'He does. We'll send it around at, say, six-thirty this evening?'

'Fine.' Van Effen paused briefly. 'Well, well. We have been making diligent enquiries, haven't we?'

'It really wasn't very difficult. We come now to the delicate question of remuneration – although I did promise it would be on a generous scale.'

'You did mention the possibility of permanent employment?'

'I did.'

'Then let's regard this as a test demonstration. You know, efficiency, reliability, professionalism. If I measure up, let's then discuss payment for future jobs.'

'Fair and generous. So fair, in fact, that I feel almost diffident about raising the next delicate point.'

'I would hate for you to embarrass yourself. Let me raise it for you.'

'This is more than generous.'

'My nature. You have given me highly secret and very valuable information for which the police would doubtless reward me handsomely.' Van Effen knew from Agnelli's brief frown then renewed smile that he had indeed guessed correctly. 'I shall not be giving this information to the police. Reasons? One, I am not a double-crosser. Two, I don't like the police and they don't like me – I don't want to be within a long distance of any policemen. Three. Purely selfish and financial – I am certain I can make a great deal more money from working for you on several occasions than I can from betraying you once. Four, I do not wish to spend the rest of my life with a hit man or hit men only one step behind.' Agnelli was smiling very broadly now. 'The fifth is the most compelling reason. From what you have just told me you obviously have informers, contacts inside the palace who would immediately alert you to the presence of the police. As there could and would be only one person who could have betrayed you I could, possibly, be summarily disposed of, although I think you would find it much more elegant to turn me over to the police and suggest that they have a look at extradition requests from Poland and the United States. I think I would prefer the States – I might at least get a semblance of a fair trial there. I am not wanted, of course, under the name of Danilov: but the description of villains is usually pretty thorough and there can't be many wanted men going round with a facial scar and a ruined left hand like mine. You can understand, Mr Agnelli, why I shall be giving the police a very wide berth indeed.'

'I must say that you and the law don't appear to have a great deal in common. Thank you, Mr Danilov, for having done my delicate task for me. That was exactly what I did have in mind. I am quite sure that you are going to be a very valuable member of our team.'

'I can be trusted, you think?'

'Unquestionably.'

'Then I am doubly honoured.' Agnelli raised a questioning

eyebrow. 'I didn't have to remove the magazines from my guns today.'

Agnelli smiled, stood, shook hands and left with his two companions. Van Effen went to the office, listened to the playback of the recording, expressed his satisfaction and thanks to Henri, pocketed the tape and left.

As had now become his custom, van Effen parked his car at the rear of the Trianon but entered by the front door. A nondescript little man, seemingly engrossed in a newspaper, was seated close by the desk. Van Effen spoke to the man behind it.

'I'd like a menu, please.' He paid no attention to the seated man. 'Thank you.' He ticked off some items on the menu. 'I'll have that, that and that. And a bottle of burgundy. In my room at twelve-thirty please. After that I don't want to be disturbed – so no phone calls, please. I'd be glad if you would give me a wake-up call at four o'clock.'

Van Effen took the lift to the first floor, walked down the stairs and peered cautiously round the corner. The little man had gone. He went across to the desk.

'I see you've lost a valued customer, Charles.'

'Hardly valued, Lieutenant. He drinks one tiny jonge jenever once every hour or so. That's his third time here since last night. He is rather obvious, isn't he?'

'He doesn't seem to think so. Will you cancel my lunch, Charles?'

Charles smiled. 'Already cancelled.'

Van Effen left the Trianon a few minutes later, his appearance returned to normal.

'Well,' van Effen said, 'were you worried stiff about me?'

'Of course not,' Julie said. 'You told us there was nothing to worry about.'

'Liar. You, too.'

'Me?' Annemarie said. 'I haven't said a word yet.'

'You were about to. Your concern is perfectly understandable. A jonge jenever, large. The very jaws of death, I tell you.'

'Tell us about brave Daniel,' Julie said.

'In a moment. First of all, I must phone the Colonel. He will be consumed with anxiety about his trusty lieutenant.'

'It's twelve-thirty,' Julie said. 'If I know the Colonel his only concern now is what aperitif he's going to have before lunch.'

'You do him an injustice. And, incidentally, me.' He took the drink from his sister. 'May I use your bedroom?'

'Of course.'

Annemarie said: 'I thought –'

'There's a phone there.'

'Ah. State secrets.'

'Not at all. Come along. Both of you. It'll save me from having to repeat myself.'

He sat down on Julie's bed, opened a bedside cupboard and extracted a phone. Annemarie said: 'That's a curious-looking instrument.'

'Scrambler phone. Any eavesdropper who is locked into your telephone hears only garbled nonsense. A device at the recipient's end works in reverse and makes the jumble intelligible again. Much used by secret services and the better class of spy. Very popular with criminals, too. The original connection was to my apartment but I can also call de Graaf on it.'

He got through immediately. 'Good morning, Colonel . . . No, I have not been attacked, kidnapped, tortured, assassinated or otherwise set upon . . . Quite the contrary. Positively cordial . . . No, there was a newcomer. Romero Agnelli's brother. Genial mafia-type, quite friendly, really, rejoicing in the name of Leonardo Agnelli . . . Yes, it is rather splendid, isn't it, and yes, we've made some arrangements. I am engaged to blow up the royal palace at eight p.m. . . . No, sir, I do not jest.' He covered the mouthpiece and looked at the two startled, wide-eyed girls. 'I think the Colonel's drink has gone down the wrong way. Yes, sir, amatol. Triggered by a remote-controlled radio device, details of which I shall be receiving this evening . . . Certainly I intend to do it. They're depending on me . . . No, it's deep in the cellars. There will be no loss of life . . . Very well.'

He covered the mouthpiece with one hand and gave his

empty glass to Julie with the other. 'I'm to keep a respectful silence while he communes with himself before telling me what to do. I don't need telling and I almost certainly won't agree with what he suggests.'

'Blowing up the royal palace.' She looked at Julie who had just brought in the jenever bottle. 'The palace. Blowing it up. He's mad. You – you're a policeman!'

'A policeman's lot is a hard one. All things to all men. Yes, I'm listening!' There was a long pause. Julie and Annemarie studied his face covertly but closely, but he gave no indication as to what he was thinking although he did permit himself the occasional thoughtful expression as he sipped some more jenever.

'Yes, I understand. Alternatives. First, you can pull me off altogether and you have the means to ensure that I do this, so, of course, I would have to accept that decision. But there's a difference between pulling me off a job and putting me back on to it again. Should this prove to be the first in a series of bomb outrages – and you know better than anyone that those things almost invariably happen in cycles – then I should have to refuse to be assigned to the investigation on the grounds that I was fortunate enough to be given the opportunity to investigate this group's activities and you denied me the opportunity . . . Certainly, sir, you could ask for my resignation on the grounds of refusing to obey orders. I would refuse to resign. You'd have to fire me. And then, of course, you would have to explain to your minister that you fired me because you had made a mistake, because you had refused to listen to me, because you wouldn't give me the chance to stop what may be a new crime wave before it started, because you had backed your own judgment against mine and you had been wrong. Throw as many chestnuts as you like into the fire, Colonel. I refuse to pull them out. And I refuse to resign. Excuse me, sir.'

Julie had sat beside him on the bedside and had put both hands on his telephone arm as if trying to pull it away.

'Stop it, Peter, stop it.' Despite the fact that van Effen had prudently covered the mouthpiece, her voice was low, tense, urgent. 'You can't talk to the Colonel like that. Can't you see

113

that you're putting the poor man in an impossible situation?'

Van Effen looked at Annemarie. From her compressed lips and slowly shaking head it was evident that she was of the same opinion as Julie. Van Effen looked back at his sister and she visibly recoiled from the expression on his face.

'Why don't you hear me out instead of indulging in a repetition of last night's unwarranted interference and blundering into things you know nothing about? You think he's in an impossible situation? Listen to what I say and judge what kind of position I'm in.' She slowly removed her hands and just looked at him, her expression uncomprehending. Van Effen raised the phone again.

'Forgive the interruption, Colonel. Julie says that I have no right to talk to you in this fashion and that I'm putting you in an impossible situation. Julie, alas, doesn't know what she's talking about. Annemarie, who is also here, agrees with her but she wouldn't know what she's talking about either. In fairness to them I must say that, judging by the way they are looking at each other, they don't think I know what I'm talking about either. You people are only on the periphery: I'm the man in the middle. An impossible situation, she says. Consider your alternative.

'I go ahead as planned with Agnelli and company. You, you say, will ensure my safety. In the first place you are duty-bound – you claim – to notify the royal household using as justification the many threats that have been made against the royal family in recent months. You will have the Dam square invisibly cordoned off by snipers. You will have anti-terrorist police squads inside the palace itself. It has apparently never occurred to you that those criminals have their moles and informants pretty thick on the ground and that the presence of even one extra policeman will be immediately reported. I have been warned that if any such thing happened they would know that there could have been only once source, one person, through whom this information reached the police. And I don't think – I *know* – that the palace security is pitiful and that those spies move freely within the gates. Lift that telephone to the palace, to

114

your anti-terrorist squads, to any other policeman, and you might as well reach out for pen and paper and write down and sign my death warrant.' That was, van Effen was aware, pitching it rather strongly, extradition was the worst he had to face, even assuming they had penetrated his disguise, which was uncertain. But now wasn't the moment for such niceties.

'Ensure my safety? You'll ensure my death, van Effen in a better world by midnight. What's one detective-lieutenant less just so long as your pettifogging rules and hidebound regulations are concerned? Maybe – no, I'm sure – that Julie and Annemarie don't like me very much at the moment but I think they'll have the grace to testify at the inquest that I did do my best to save my own miserable skin.

'That, of course, is the absolute worst scenario and I've no intention of being part of it. I've been thinking during our conversation and I've changed my mind about one thing. You've offered me two alternatives. One leads to being fired, the other to the old pine box. I'm not quite in my dotage yet and I think it would behove me to find some form of work where I'll be faced with threats of neither dismissal nor extinction. If you send one of your boys round to Julie's place I'll let him have my written resignation. At the same time I'll give him the tape-recording I had made in the Hunter's Horn this morning. I hope that you and your University friends will be able to make something of it and of the other tape-recorded telephone messages. Sorry about this, Colonel, but you leave me with no option: I seem to have run out of alternatives.' He replaced the telephone in the bedside cupboard and left the room.

When Julie and Annemarie rejoined him he was sitting relaxed in an armchair, legs crossed and jenever in hand. For a man who had just made such a momentous decision he seemed singularly unconcerned.

Julie said: 'May I say something?'

'Certainly. Compared to what the Colonel said and what he is no doubt thinking at this moment your slings and arrows are as nothing.'

She smiled faintly. 'I haven't lost my senses or memory. I have no intention of being – how did you put it so charmingly last night – cool, clinical, superior and handing out unwanted and unsolicited advice. I am sorry for what I said in the bedroom. I didn't know you were in so impossible a situation. But if I go on to say that I also think you've put the Colonel in a fearful fix, you'll probably say that you appreciate that a lieutenant's life is as nothing compared to the Colonel's finer feelings. Well, I still say I'm sorry, but –'

Annemarie interrupted. 'Julie?'

'Yes?'

'I wouldn't bother saying sorry to him again. I don't for a moment believe he's in an impossible situation. Look at him. He's getting high blood pressure through trying not to laugh out loud.' She gave him a considering glance. 'You're not very active. I thought you came through here to write out your resignation.'

He frowned, looked off into the middle distance, then said: 'I've no recollection of saying that.'

'That's because you never had any intention of writing out your resignation.'

'Well, well. We'll make a lady detective of you yet. You're quite right, my dear, I did not. How could I? How could I leave Uncle Arthur alone to cope with the rising wave of crime in Amsterdam? He needs me.'

Annemarie said to Julie: 'If I were to say to him that he is as Machiavellian as he is big-headed, do you think he would fire me? Or just try to reduce me to tears?'

Van Effen sipped his jenever. 'Fortunately, I am above such things. And you must never confuse Machiavellianism with diplomacy, big-headedness with intelligence.'

'You're right, Annemarie. I'm sorry I said "sorry".' Julie looked at van Effen with something less than affection. 'And what are you going to do now?'

'Just sit. Waiting.'

'Waiting for what?'

'The phone. The Colonel.'

'The Colonel!' Julie said. 'After what you said to him?'

116

'After what he said to me, you mean.'

'You're going to have a very long wait.' Annemarie spoke with conviction.

'My dear children – or should I say babes in the wood – you sadly underestimate the Colonel. He is infinitely shrewder than either of you. He knows very well indeed what the score is. He's taking some time to make this call because he's figuring out a way to beat a strategic retreat without loss of dignity, peace with honour, if you will. Now there, if you like, does go a man with a Machiavellian cast of mind – after forty years battling with the underworld one does develop a certain cast of mind. I told the Colonel that he had left me with no place to go. De Graaf, being de Graaf, realized at once what I meant – that *he* had no place to go.'

Julie said: 'Seeing you're so clever, would you mind –'

'There's no need to be unpleasant. Look at me. I am treating you with unfailing courtesy – or should I say chivalry –'

'I suppose. What's the Colonel going to say?'

'That's on consideration – or on re-consideration – well, he's going to give me carte blanche. The 8 p.m. assignation is on.'

'It would be nice to see you wrong for once,' Julie said. 'No, I didn't really mean that. I only hope you are wrong.'

For a time no one spoke. The girls kept looking at the telephone on the coffee table by van Effen's side. Van Effen wasn't looking at anything in particular. The phone rang.

Van Effen picked it up. 'Ah! Yes . . . I accept that. Maybe I did step out of line. But I was provoked.' He winced and held the telephone some distance away from his ear. 'Yes, sir, you were provoked too . . . Yes, I thoroughly agree. A very wise decision, if I may say so . . . Of course, you will be kept in the picture, sir . . . No, they don't trust me . . . Yes, sir, here. Goodbye.'

He hung up and looked at Julie. 'Why aren't you in the kitchen, my girl? Distinctly smell burning. I was asked for lunch –'

'Oh, do be quiet. What did he say?'

'Carte blanche. 8 p.m.'

Julie looked at him, her face still, for what seemed a long time but could only have been a few seconds, then turned and went to the kitchen. Annemarie made a couple of steps towards him, stopped and said: 'Peter.'

'Don't say it. I've already got out of one difficult situation. Don't you and Julie put me in an impossible one.'

'We won't. I promise. You know that we can't help what we feel and you can't blame us for that. But you could blame us if we did start talking about it, so we won't. That's sure.' She smiled. 'Now, isn't that considerate.'

'Very. Do you know, Annemarie, I do believe I'm beginning to like you.'

'Like me?' She gave him a quizzical look. 'So you didn't even like me when you kissed me this morning? Absentmindedness, I suppose. Or do you just go around kissing policewomen as a matter of routine? Something to do with their morale, no doubt.'

'You're the first.'

'And, no doubt, the last. We all make mistakes, whatever I mean by that cryptic remark. Who doesn't trust you?'

'Who doesn't – what?'

'Something you said to the Colonel.'

'Ah. My criminal associates. We parted at the Hunter's Horn professing mutual trust and faith. Didn't stop them from staking a man out at the Trianon. An irritation. No problem.'

'And after lunch?'

'Stay here a bit. The Colonel is going to call me. That will be after we hear what, if anything, the FFF have been up to at two o'clock. The Colonel is convinced that they will not blow up the Hagestein. Frogmen have found no traces of any underwater charges in position.'

Van Effen called his office and asked for the desk sergeant. 'The men on Fred Klassen and Alfred van Rees. They called in at noon?' He listened briefly. 'So van Rees has lost our man. Chance or on purpose, it doesn't matter. I assume you have the licence number. All officers on patrol. Not to approach. Just locate. Note this number and call me here.'

Lunch was an excellent but hardly festive meal. Julie and Annemarie were determinedly over-bright and over-cheerful and the harsh edges of strain occasionally showed through: if van Effen noticed anything amiss he made no comment: her brother, Julie knew, rarely missed anything.

They had coffee in the living-room. Shortly after two o'clock a young motor-cycle policeman came to collect the Hunter's Horn tape.

Julie said: 'I hear that you are awaiting a call from the Colonel. After that?'

'Your bed, my dear, if I may. I don't know when I can expect to sleep tonight or even if I will sleep so I think an hour or two might be of some value. That hour or two, of course, would be helped along by the brandy you have – unaccountably – so far failed to offer me.'

The Colonel's call came when van Effen was halfway through his brandy. It was a brief call and one-sided. Van Effen said 'yes' several times, 'I see' a couple of times, then told the Colonel goodbye and hung up.

'The FFF blew up the North Holland dyke at exactly 2 p.m. Extensive flooding, but shallow and no lives lost. Not according to first reports. The Hagestein weir was not touched. As the Colonel says, he expected this. The frogmen had located no charges and he is convinced that the FFF were unable either to approach the weir or conceal charges. He's further convinced that their blasting techniques are primitive and limited only to simple operations like blowing up dykes and canal banks.'

'But you're not convinced of this, are you?' Julie said.

'I'm neither convinced nor unconvinced. I know no more about it than you do. Maybe the Colonel finds it preferable, more comforting to think along those lines: maybe the FFF want the Colonel – us, the country – to think along those lines. They have all the hallmarks of being a devious and highly organized bunch. That impression, too, may be deceptive. Are they a simple-minded group trying to make us think they are devious or a devious-minded group trying to make us think they are simple? Figure it out for yourselves. I can't. I'm going to rest lightly. Turn on the radio, would you? The FFF have, it seems, got into the habit of making a public announcement after what they no doubt regard as being one of their master strokes. Don't bother to wake me to convey their next dire threat. In fact, don't bother me for anything.'

He had barely dropped off when Julie came in and shook him awake. He opened his eyes and, as was his custom, was almost instantly awake. He said: 'This is the way you don't disturb me? The heavens have fallen in?'

'I'm sorry. A letter came for you.'

'A letter? An exhausted man is torn from his slumbers –'

'It came by special delivery,' she said patiently. 'It has *Urgent* stamped all over it.'

'Let me see.' He took the envelope from her, glanced briefly at the address and postmark, opened the envelope, half extracted the contents, pushed it back inside again and slid the envelope under the pillow. 'And I'm disturbed by this. One of my fellow officers trying to be witty. Next time, be sure the heavens have fallen in.'

'Let me see what was inside that letter,' Julie said sharply. She sat on the bed, laid her hand on his arm and said in a gentle voice: 'Please, Peter?'

Van Effen made to speak, said nothing, reached under his pillow, retrieved the envelope and gave the contents to Julie. It was not a letter, just a plain postcard, blank on one side. On the other side was a crude drawing of a coffin and a hangman's noose.

Julie tried to smile. 'Well, it has been three months since the last one, hasn't it?'

'So?' Van Effen sounded indifferent. 'It's been, as you say, three months. And what's happened in that three months? Nothing. And no reason on earth why anything should happen in the next three months.'

'If it's so unimportant, why did you hide it?'

'I didn't hide it. I put it away in the full view of my little sister whom I didn't want to upset.'

'May I see that envelope, please?' She took it, looked at it and handed it back. 'All the others had come from other countries.

This one is post-marked Amsterdam. That was the first thing you saw and that's why you put it away. The Annecy brothers are in Amsterdam.'

'Maybe. Maybe not. This postcard could have come from any country to a friend or accomplice in Amsterdam who sent it on to this address.'

'I don't believe that. Kid sister or not, I'm all grown up and a big girl now. I can think for myself, I can feel for myself. I *know* they're in Amsterdam. And so, I'm sure, do you. Oh, Peter. It's all too much. One set of madmen threatening to flood our country, another set going to blow up the palace and now this.' She shook her head. 'Everything at once. Why?'

'It is an unusual set of circumstances.'

'It is a – oh, do be quiet. Do you have *no* idea what is going on?'

'I've no more idea than you have.'

'Maybe. Maybe not. I'm not sure I believe you. What are we going to do? What are *you* going to do?'

'What do you expect me to do? Patrol the streets of Amsterdam until I find some character carrying a coffin over his shoulder and a noose in his hand.' He put his hand on her arm. 'Please excuse momentary irritation. There's nothing I can do. Second thoughts, yes. I can go back to sleep, Next time, make sure the heavens *have* fallen.'

'You're hopeless.' She half-smiled, rose, shook her head again when she saw that his eyes were already closed and left the room.

He had barely dropped off for the second time when Julie returned. 'Sorry again, Peter. The Colonel. I told him you were asleep but he said it didn't matter if you were dead, I was to bring you back to life again and get you to the phone. He left me in no doubt that it was very urgent indeed.'

Van Effen touched the bedside cupboard. 'He could have used the scrambler.'

'Probably using a public phone.'

Van Effen went through to the living-room, took the call, listened briefly, said: 'I'm leaving now,' and hung up.

Julie said: 'Where?'

'To meet a person the Colonel says may be a friend. I don't know his name.' Van Effen put on shoulder holster, tie and jacket. 'Things, as you said, Julie, tend not to occur singly. First, the dyke nut-cases. Then the palace nut-cases. Then the Annecy nut-cases. Now this.'

'Whatever "this" may be. Where's your friend?'

'Wouldn't you know. He's in the mortuary.'

Five

The old town of Amsterdam may well be unique in the attraction of its tree-lined winding canals, its medieval charm, its romance, its almost palpable sense of history, its nostalgic beauty. The city mortuary wasn't like that at all. It didn't possess a single attractive feature, it had no charm, medieval or modern, was totally and irredeemably ugly. It was clinical, functional, inhuman and wholly repellent. Only the dead, one would have thought, could have tolerated such a place: but the white-coated attendants, while not much given to whistling at their work, seemed no different from your average office worker, factory mechanic or farm labourer: this was their job and they did it in the best way they could.

Van Effen arrived to find de Graaf and a serious young man, who was introduced as Dr Prins, waiting for him. Dr Prins was attired in the regulation uniform of white coat and stethoscope. It was difficult to imagine what function a stethoscope played in a mortuary: possibly to check that incoming admissions were, in fact, dead on arrival: more probably, it was just part of the uniform. De Graaf was in a dark and sombre mood but this was not due to his surroundings for, over the long years, de Graaf had become more than accustomed to mortuaries: what he was not accustomed to was having to leave his fish course and a bottle of Chablis almost untouched on a restaurant table.

Dr Prins led them to a long, cavernous, tomb-like chamber, the furnishings of which – exclusively in concrete, white tiles, marble and metal – accorded well with the chilled atmosphere. An attendant, seeing Prins approach, opened a metal door and pulled out a wheeled rack that ran smoothly on steel runners. A shrouded form lay on this. Dr Prins took the top corner of the sheet.

'I have to warn you, gentlemen, that this is not a sight for weak stomachs.'

'My stomach couldn't possibly be in worse condition than it is,' de Graaf said. Prins looked at him curiously – de Graaf hadn't seen fit to make mention of the abandoned fish and wine – and pulled back the sheet. What lay revealed was indeed, as the doctor had said, not a sight for queasy stomachs. Dr Prins looked at the faces of the two policemen and felt vaguely disappointed: not by a flicker of expression did they display whatever emotions they might have felt.

'Cause of death, doctor?' de Graaf said.

'Multiple, massive injuries, of course. Cause? An autopsy will reveal –'

'Autopsy!' Van Effen's voice was as cold as the mortuary itself. 'I do not wish to be personal, doctor, but how long have you held this post?'

'My first week.' The slight pallor in his face suggested that Dr Prins was, himself, having some problems with his internal economy.

'So you won't have seen many cases like this. If any. This man has been murdered. He hasn't fallen off the top of a high building or been run over by a heavy truck. In that case the skull or chest wall or pelvis or the femoral bones or tibia would have been crushed or broken. They haven't. He's been battered to death by iron bars. His face is unrecognizable, knee-caps smashed and forearms broken – no doubt when he was trying to defend himself against the iron bars.'

De Graaf said to the doctor: 'He was, of course, wearing clothes when he was brought in. Anyone been through them?'

'Identification, you mean, Colonel?'

'Of course.'

'Nothing that I know of.'

'It doesn't matter,' van Effen said. 'I know who it is. I recognize that scar on the shoulder. Detective Rudolph Engel. He was shadowing a man known as Julius Caesar – you may remember Annemarie mentioning this character in La Caracha.'

'How do you know this?'

124

'Because I was the person who told Engel to do the shadowing. I also warned him that there was more than a degree of danger attached and that he was on no account to be in a position where he would find himself without people around. I reminded him what had happened to the two detectives who had trailed Agnelli. He forgot or disobeyed or was carried away by curiosity or enthusiasm. Whatever it is, it cost him his life.'

'But to murder him in this savage fashion?' De Graaf shook his head. 'Even to kill him at all. Well, it does seem an unbelievable instance of over-reacting.'

'We'll probably never know the truth, sir. But if we do we'll probably find out that he wasn't disposed of just for shadowing but because he'd found out something they couldn't let him live to report. High stakes, Colonel.'

'High indeed. It might help to have a word with this – ah – Julius Caesar.'

'Probably couldn't find him in the first place. He'll have gone to ground, left Amsterdam for healthier climes or, most likely, shaved off his pepper-and-salt beard and got himself a wig for his bald pate and a pair of dark glasses to conceal his squint. Besides, even if we did pull him in, what have we got to charge him with?'

They thanked Dr Prins and left. As they were passing through the entrance hall a man at the desk called the Colonel and handed him a phone. The Colonel spoke briefly, handed back the phone and rejoined van Effen.

'Not destined to be our afternoon, I'm afraid. Office. Just heard from the hospital. One of our men there. Just been fished out of a canal, it seems.'

'What's he doing in hospital? You mean he's not drowned?'

'No. Touch and go, it seems. We'd better have a look.'

'Identity?'

'Not established. Still unconscious. No papers, no badge. But carrying a gun and a pair of handcuffs. So they guessed it was a cop.'

In the hospital they were led to a private room on the first floor, from which a grey-haired doctor was just emerging. He saw de Graaf and smiled.

'My old friend! You don't waste time, I must say. One of your men has just had a rather unpleasant experience. A very close thing, very close, but he'll be all right. In fact, he can leave in an hour or two.'

'So he's conscious?'

'Conscious and in a very bad temper. Name of Voight.'

'Mas Voight?' van Effen said.

'That's him. Little boy saw him floating face down in the water. Luckily there were a couple of dock-workers close by. They fished him out and brought him here. Couldn't have been in the water more than a minute or so.'

Voight was sitting up in bed and looking very disgruntled. After the briefest of courteous enquiries as to his health de Graaf said: 'How on earth did you come to fall into that canal?'

'*Fall* into the canal!' Voight was outraged. 'Fall into –'

'Shh!' said the doctor. 'You'll just do yourself an injury.' He gently turned Voight's head: the blue and purple bruise behind the right ear promised to develop into something quite spectacular.

'Must have run out of crowbars,' van Effen said.

De Graaf frowned. 'And what is that meant to mean?'

'Our friends are being active again. Detective Voight was keeping an eye on Alfred van Rees and –'

'Alfred van Rees!'

'You know. The Rijkswaterstaat man. Locks, weirs, sluices and what have you. Unfortunately it would seem that Detective Voight couldn't watch van Rees and his own back at the same time. Last report, Voight, was that you had lost van Rees.'

'A patrolman found him again. Gave me the address. I drove down and parked by the canal, got out –'

'What canal?' van Effen said.

'The Croquiskade.'

'The Croquiskade! And van Rees. You astonish me. Hardly the most salubrious part of our fair city.'

Voight rubbed his neck. 'I didn't find it very salubrious either. I saw van Rees and another man coming out of this doorway and then they went back in again. Why, I don't know. I wasn't in a police car and as far as I know they've never seen

126

me, never suspected I was following them. And then – well, the next thing I knew I was in this bed. Never even heard a footstep behind me.'

'Did you get the house number?'

'Yes. Thirty-eight.'

Van Effen picked up a bedside phone, told the switchboard it was police and urgent, gave them his office number and said to de Graaf: 'I don't suppose that anyone will still be at number thirty-eight. But we may find something there – if, that is, they didn't see Detective Voight being fished out of the canal. If they did, it'll be as clean as a whistle. Question of search warrant, sir?'

'Damn the search warrant.' De Graaf was obviously rather shaken that his old friend van Rees could be involved in illegal activities. 'Effect an entry by any means.'

Van Effen was through to his office almost immediately, asked for a certain Sergeant Oudshoorn, got him in turn just as quickly, gave him the address and instructions and listened for a brief period.

'No, Sergeant. Take four men. One at the front door, one at the back . . . No warrant. The Colonel says so. Yes. Take the damned door off its hinges if you have to. Or shoot the lock away. Detain anyone you find inside. Don't leave there. Radio report to station and await instructions.' He hung up. 'Sergeant Oudshoorn seems to relish the prospect.'

They told Voight to call home, have dry clothes brought, go home and rest and said goodbye. In the passage-way de Graaf said: 'It can't be. Impossible. Man's a pillar of society. Good heavens, I even put him up for my club.'

'Could be a perfectly innocent explanation, sir. The state of Voight's neck and his immersion in the canal seems to suggest otherwise. Remember, I suggested in Schiphol that perhaps he was a Jekyll by day and a Hyde by night. Maybe I got it wrong. Maybe he's a daylight Hyde.' As they approached the hospital entrance van Effen stopped abruptly. De Graaf stopped also and looked at him curiously.

'One rarely sees an expression of concern on your face, Peter. Something amiss?'

127

'I hope not, sir. Something's been nagging away at the back of my mind but I haven't had time to think about it. Not until now. This call you got while you were lunching – at least, when you were about to have lunch – did it come from the station?'

'Of course. Sergeant Bresser.'

'Where did he get his information from?'

'The hospital I presume. Bresser said he'd tried to find first you, then Lieutenant Valken and failing to find either he'd contacted me. Does it matter?'

'This matters. Young Dr Prins at the mortuary is neither experienced nor very bright. For all he knew or suspected to the contrary, Engel might have fallen off the top of the Haven-gebouw, or been the victim of a street or industrial accident. The mortuary does *not* call in senior police officers unless they know or suspect that the victim did not meet a natural end. So the chances are that the call did not come from the hospital. Bresser's a stolid unimaginative man. Thinking is not his forte. Was it your idea to call me up at Julie's and ask me to come along?'

'You're beginning to get me worried now, too, Peter, although I don't know why. Your name had been mentioned in the call but whether it was Bresser's suggestion you come along or mine I'm not clear. Damn these lunches.'

'Moment, sir.' Van Effen went to the nearest telephone and dialled a number. He let it ring for perhaps fifteen seconds then dialled again while de Graaf watched him at first in perplexity, then in apprehension then with the sick dawning of understanding. He was at the front door and holding it open when van Effen replaced the phone and came running towards him.

Van Effen didn't even bother to knock on Julie's door, which he unlocked with the key he'd fished out coming up in the lift. The living-room appeared to be in perfectly normal condition, which meant nothing. Julie's bedroom was also as it should have been but her bathroom told a different story. Thyssen, the guard, was lying on the floor, perfectly conscious and in apparent danger of suffering an apoplectic stroke, whether from rage or an effort to free himself from the ropes that bound wrists and ankles it was difficult to say. Perhaps he had been having difficulty in breathing through his gag. They freed him and helped him to his feet for he was unable to stand: if the blued hands were anything to go by the circulation of his feet must have been almost completely blocked off too. Whoever had tied him had worked with a will.

They helped him through to the living-room and into an armchair. Van Effen massaged circulation back into hand and feet – not a pleasant process if one were to judge by Thyssen's repeated winces and screwing-shut of the eyes – while de Graaf brought him a glass of brandy. He had to hold it to the man's lips as Thyssen had yet to recover the use of his hands.

'Van der Hum,' de Graaf said referring to the brandy. 'A universal specific and, in the circumstances, despite regulations –'

Van Effen smiled. It wasn't the strained smile of a man deliberately repressing emotion: he seemed quite remarkably unaffected by the turn of events. 'The man who makes the regulations can break the regulations. It wouldn't come amiss, sir.'

They had barely sipped from their glasses when Thyssen recovered enough strength to seize his, lift his trembling hand to his mouth, and drink half the contents in one gulp: he coughed, spluttered, then spoke for the first time.

'God, I'm sorry, Lieutenant! Most damnably sorry! Your sister – and that other nice lady.' He drained his glass. 'I should be taken out and shot.'

'I don't think it will come to that, Jan,' van Effen said mildly. 'Whatever happened is no fault of yours. What did happen?'

Thyssen was so overcome with anger, bitterness and self-reproach that his account was so disjointed and repetitive as to be at times incoherent. It appeared that he had been approached by a Dutch army major – who would ever have harboured suspicions about an Army major? – who had produced a pistol fitted with a most un-Army silencer, forced Thyssen to produce his key and open the door, pushed him inside, followed and advised the girls not to move. He had been followed into the room almost immediately by three furniture-removal men: at least, they were dressed in heavy leather aprons of the type much favoured by their profession: what was atypical about them was that they wore hoods and gloves. Beyond that Thyssen could tell them nothing: he had been taken into the bathroom and tied, gagged and left lying on the floor.

Van Effen went into Annemarie's bedroom – the one that had formerly been his – took one quick look around and returned.

'There's a pile of Annemarie's clothes lying on the bed and a wardrobe missing. They were tied, gagged and carried out in it – to anyone watching an obvious case of legitimate furniture-removing. They must have been keeping tabs on me, sir, about the time you made the call to me from the restaurant. They would have had a furniture van parked nearby and would have moved in as soon as they saw me departing. Very neat indeed. A most uncomfortable trip for the young ladies – but I suppose they must have been too terrified out of their wits to worry about discomfort. Ironic, isn't it, sir, that both of them this morning were full of gloom and woe and foreboding – and prophecies of disaster. Feeling fey was what they called it. They were both convinced that the something terrible was going to happen to me: unfortunately for them they picked the wrong subject for concern.'

De Graaf, a second glass of Van der Hum in his hands, paced up and down. Even forty years in the police had left him without van Effen's ability to mask his emotions: anger and worry fought for dominance in his face.

'What are those devils up to? What did they want – and *who* did they want? Annemarie? Julie? Or both?'

'Julie.' Van Effen handed him the postcard he and Julie had looked at earlier in the afternoon. De Graaf took it, examined both card and envelope and said: 'When did this arrive?'

'Just after lunch. Julie was very upset but I just pooh-poohed it, laughed the matter off. Clever van Effen. Brilliant van Effen.'

'So your friends have returned, the Annecys back in Amsterdam. Lost no time in making their presence known and got at you in the very best way possible. God, I'm sorry, Peter.'

'Feel sorry for the girls. Especially for Annemarie. It was just her fiendishly bad luck to be here when they came for Julie. It was that towering genius, van Effen, of course, who had insisted that she remain here for her own safety. The demands should be arriving quite soon. You will not have forgotten, sir, that the Annecys were – and doubtless still are – specialists in blackmail.' De Graaf shook his head and remained silent. 'It's kind of you not to say so, sir, but you will also not have forgotten that they are specialists in torture, which was the real reason I hunted them down.'

'We haven't been very clever so far,' de Graaf said. 'Things are uncommonly confusing.'

'Kind of you to say "we" sir. You mean me.' Van Effen refilled Thyssen's glass, did the same for his own and sank into an armchair.

After perhaps two minutes, de Graaf looked at him and said: 'Well, surely there's something we should be doing? Shall we start by making enquiries among the flat neighbours, the people living opposite?'

'To check on the *modus operandi* of the kidnappers? A waste of time, Colonel. We wouldn't find out any more than we already know. We're dealing with professionals. But even professionals can make mistakes.'

'I haven't seen any so far.' The Colonel was gloomy.

'Nor have I. I'm assuming that Julie was the target.' Van Effen reached for the telephone. 'With your permission, sir, I'll find out. Vasco. Sergeant Westenbrink. He was the only one who knew where Annemarie lived. They – whoever "they" are – may have put a tail on him and found out by methods I don't care to think about.'

'You think it likely? Or possible?'

Van Effen dialled a number. 'Possible, yes. Likely, no. I don't think there's anyone in Amsterdam who could follow Vasco without his being aware of it: by the same token I don't think that there is anyone in the City who could be followed by Vasco and be aware of it. Vasco? Peter here. Anyone been taking an interest in you since you left this morning? . . . Talked to nobody? Annemarie and my sister Julie have been taken away . . . Within the past hour and, no, we have no idea.

131

Put on your best civilian suit and come round, will you?' Van Effen hung up and said to de Graaf: 'Julie it was. Nobody's been banging Vasco with crowbars.'

'And you've asked him to join you?'

'Us, sir. He's far too valuable a man to be lying low and doing nothing. And, with your permission, sir, I'd like to try to recruit George.'

'Your La Caracha friend? You said yourself he wasn't very good at merging into backgrounds.'

'That's for Vasco. George, on the mental side as you saw for yourself, is very acute and knows the criminal mind probably better than anyone I know: on the physical side he's a splendid insurance policy. So, progress. A very little, but progress nonetheless. I think it's now fairly safe to say that the Annecy brothers and the would-be blowers-up of the royal palace are working in cahoots, or how else would the Annecys know that Rudolph Engel, who had been following one of the palace gang's intermediaries, had been done in and delivered to the morgue?'

'The palace gang, as you call them, could have done the kidnapping. The Annecys could have told them.'

'Two things, sir. What possible motive could Agnelli and his friends have in abducting Lieutenant van Effen's sister? None. The Annecys have a very powerful motive. The second thing is that it doesn't matter a damn whether the Annecys gave Agnelli this address or not: the point is that they sure as hell know each other.'

'And how does this knowledge help us, Peter?'

'At the moment, it doesn't. And it may even actually put us at a disadvantage. They're not clowns and may well have figured out that we have figured out and exercise extra precautions because of that. Precautions against what, I can't imagine.'

'Neither can I. We're doing nothing. There's nothing, as far as I can see, that we can do.'

'One or two small things, perhaps. Alfred van Rees, to start with.'

'What's van Rees got to do with Agnelli and the Annecys?'

'Nothing. As far as we know. But we would at least be doing

something about something. I suggest two tails on van Rees. One to keep an eye on van Rees, the other to keep an eye on the first tail. Just consider how lucky Mas Voight is to be still alive. Then I suggest we investigate van Rees's bank statements.'

'Whatever for?'

'This pillar of the Rijkswaterstaat may be giving the dyke-blowers information that they couldn't get elsewhere. Selling, not giving. Could be, of course, that *if* he's picking up some money that he shouldn't, he might have it stashed away in another account under another name. But criminals – especially people who are not habitual criminals, and I assume van Rees is not – often overlook the obvious.'

'Can't be done. Illegal. Man hasn't even been charged, far less convicted of anything.'

'They've got Julie and Annemarie.'

'So. What connection do they have with van Rees?'

'None. Again, as far as we know. Although I was just thinking of one of the last things Julie said to me, that how extraordinarily odd it was that the dyke-breakers, the palace bombers and the Annecy brothers should all happen along at the same time. Could be a coincidence. Could be too much of a coincidence. Or nothing. Maybe I just hate the whole wide criminal world. Forget it, sir. Just a suggestion.'

The phone rang. Van Effen picked it up, listened, said thank you and hung up. 'This should cheer us all up. There's going to be a radio broadcast of the FFF's latest communiqué in about ten minutes.'

'Inevitable, I suppose. Your suggestion, Peter. Normally, I should dismiss it out of hand. But your suggestions have an extraordinary habit of turning up something.' He smiled without any humour. 'Maybe you share – what's the word? – this precognition with your sister. We'll put those two tails on van Rees – my God, the very idea of putting tails on van Rees – *and* have his liquid assets discreetly investigated. I shall probably be arraigned before Parliament for this. Drag you down with me, of course.' He reached for the phone. 'Let me handle this.'

After he had arranged matters in his customary imperious fashion and put the phone down, van Effen said: 'Thank you.

133

Tell me, sir, do your linguistic friends at the University have all the tapes? Including the one I brought from the Hunter's Horn?' De Graaf nodded. 'When do you expect them to be ready?'

'When they're ready, one supposes. Things move leisurely in the groves of Academe.'

'Think you could hurry them up, sir? National emergency, something like that.'

'I can but try.' De Graaf called a number, spoke to someone he called Hector then, still holding the phone, turned to van Effen. 'Six o'clock?'

'Five forty-five, if possible.'

De Graaf spoke briefly, hung up and said: 'Very precise about our timing, aren't we?'

'Person coming round at six-thirty to the Trianon to give me the radio data for detonating this bomb in the palace cellars.'

'First I heard of it. One finds it uncommonly difficult to keep up with your activities. One finds it rather droll, if I may say so, to find a police officer paying the courtesy of punctuality to a criminal.'

'Yes, sir. Do you know – personally, I mean – any plastic surgeons?'

'Plastic surgeons! What on earth do you want with – well, I should know better, you'll have your reasons. But plastic surgeons? Do you think I know *everyone* in this city?'

'To my knowledge, sir, yes. Or nearly everyone.'

'I could talk to the police surgeon.'

'De Wit is *not* a plastic surgeon, sir.'

'Ah! I have it. My old friend Hugh. Outstanding. Professor Hugh Johnson.'

'Doesn't sound like a Dutch surgeon to me. I mean, he's not Dutch, is he?'

'English. Trained at East Grinstead. I'm told that's the best plastic surgery unit in Europe, if not the world. Man's a genius.' De Graaf smiled. 'Not as smart as the Dutch, though. Not, specifically, as clever as one Dutch lady, a native of Amsterdam, whom he met here on an exchange visit. Six months after they got married he found himself domiciled in this country. Still doesn't know how it happened to him. The very man.' De Graaf cleared his throat in a delicate fashion. 'If you could give me some slight indication as to what you want –'

'Certainly. In the guise in which I meet Agnelli I have scars on my face and hands – remind me to tell you what I'll look like tonight when we meet at the University otherwise you won't recognize me. I want those scars to look even more realistic and, more important to be of such a nature that they can't easily be pulled off, washed off or scrubbed off.'

'Ah. I see. I mean, I don't see.' De Graaf pondered briefly. 'Don't like this at all. You are referring, of course, to Agnelli and his friends and any suspicions they may harbour. I thought you were of the opinion that your *bona fide* status as an internationally wanted criminal was fairly secure.'

'I increasingly believe so, sir. But they don't sound like a lot with whom one can safely take any chances. Might even find a reason tonight to prove – without seeming to, of course – the genuineness and permanence of those scars.'

De Graaf sighed. 'We live in a devious world, a very devious world. Without wishing to give offence, Peter, I must say you seem perfectly at home in it. See what I can do. Damned phone again.'

Van Effen picked it up, listened and said: 'Send a man around with them, will you? Wait a minute.' He turned to de Graaf. 'Sergeant Oudshoorn. Says number thirty-eight is deserted. Neighbours say nobody has lived there for years. Most of the furniture is gone, too. Sergeant Oudshoorn – he's young, enthusiastic, I told you he'd relish this assignment and we did give him a sort of carte blanche – has been investigating some locked cupboards and desk drawers.'

'With the aid of crowbars and chisels, I suppose.'

'I imagine so. I also imagine that it's extremely doubtful that we'll ever have any complaints on that score. Thing is, he says he's come across some odd-looking maps, charts and plans that he can't make head or tail of. Probably of no importance whatsoever. But we're in no position to overlook one chance in a thousand. I've asked Oudshoorn to have them sent round. Do you think that, en route, this messenger might pick up some

135

knowledgeable lad from the City Surveyor's office who might just be able to enlighten us about those maps?'

'Chance in a thousand, as you say. Suppose you want me to do the dirty work?'

'Yes, sir.' He spoke into the phone. 'Tell whoever it is that's bringing the papers round to stop by the City Surveyor's office and pick up someone who will accompany him here. The Colonel is arranging it.'

While de Graaf was issuing his instructions over the phone – he never made requests – van Effen turned on the radio and kept the volume low. When the Colonel hung up the phone he still kept the volume low – the cacophonous racket of the latest number one on the hit parade was not to van Effen's taste – but turned it up when the noise stopped. The modulated voice of an announcer took over.

'We interrupt this programme with a special news bulletin. The FFF, about whose activities you must have all heard or read in the past forty-eight hours, have issued another statement. It reads as follows:

' "We promised to breach the North Holland Canal or the Hagestein weir. Or both. In the event, we chose to breach the canal. The reason we did not damage the Hagestein weir is that we have never been within fifty kilometres of it. In spite of this we have to admit that the turn-out of army, police, air-force helicopters and the experts from the Rijkswaterstaat was most impressive.

' "It should now not be in doubt that we can cause flooding, of a degree according to our choosing, wherever and whenever we wish and that we can do this with impunity: the possibility of detection does not exist. The country's authorities, as we have pointed out before and have demonstrated again, are quite powerless.

' "We are sure that the people of the Netherlands do not wish this state of affairs to continue. Neither, quite frankly, do we. We have certain terms that we wish to be met and would like to discuss those with a responsible member of the government. We suggest that an arrangement for such a meeting, time this evening, location immaterial, be broadcast over TV and radio at

136

6 p.m. this evening. No negotiator below the level of cabinet minister will be considered.

' "We suggest that our negotiator should not be apprehended, held as hostage or subjected to any degree of restraint. Should any of the authorities be so misguided as to do this we would warn them that mines are already in position to the north and south of Lelystad. Precisely how far north and south we choose, in this instance, not to say. The mines, in this instance, are very much larger than on previous occasions and the repair of the breaches will be a matter of days if not weeks. If our negotiator does not return to us by a certain hour to be agreed, then large portions of Oostlijk–Flevoland will be inundated. No warning will be given as to the time of those breaches: they will be some time during the night.

' "We think it almost superfluous to point out that the responsibility for the safety of the Oostlijk–Flevoland and its inhabitants lies exclusively with the government. We do not ask for a great deal – just to speak with a government representative.

' "Should the government ignore our small request and refuse to appoint a negotiator, we shall go ahead and flood the polder. After that, when next we make a similar request accompanied by a similar promise, we think the government may deem it more prudent to be a degree rather more cooperative. We are sure that the citizens of the Netherlands would agree that for the government, motivated solely by affronted pride and stiffnecked outrage, to put this large area and those who live there at such risk, would be intolerable and unforgiveable.

' "The time to cooperate is now, not when incalculable and avoidable damage has been done.

' "The mines are in position."

'That is the message in its entirety. The government has requested us – not ordered, requested – not to pass comment on or discuss this outrageous demand until they have decided what course of action to adopt. It wishes to reassure the people of this country that the government is confident that it has the resources at its command to meet this or any other threat.'

Van Effen switched off the set. 'God save us from politicians. The government, as is its wont, is talking through a hole in its collective hat. It's been caught off-balance, hasn't had time to think – one charitably assumes it can think – and can do no better than trot out old boring, meaningless platitudes. Confident, they say. Confident of what? God's sake, they can't possibly be confident of anything, far less of themselves. Trust us, they say. I'd sooner trust the inmates of a lunatic asylum.'

'Treasonable talk, Lieutenant van Effen, treasonable talk. I could have you incarcerated for this.' De Graaf sighed. 'Trouble is, I'd have to incarcerate myself along with you, as I agree with every word you say. If the government honestly believes that the people will take their meaningless assertions at face value, then they're in an even worse case than I thought. Which, I may add, I didn't think was possible. They are in an impossible situation: do you think it even remotely possible that they don't recognize this?'

'They'll recognize it all right. Just as soon as they begin to think in terms of political survival. If they bury their heads in the sand they'll be turfed out of power within a week. An acute concern about preserving the status quo – their status quo – can work wonders. They have already blundered by having the commentator say that they have been requested – not ordered – to discuss the affair. They have been ordered, not requested, otherwise the commentator, the news-reader, would not have used the term "outrageous demand". There's nothing outrageous in their demand. It's the demands that will be made when the meeting takes place – as, of course, it will do – that will almost certainly be outrageous.'

'Any discussion about this matter can only be speculative,' the Colonel said heavily. 'So it's not worth the speculation. We have other and more urgent matters to attend to.'

'There's a matter I should be attending to at this moment,' van Effen said. 'I have an appointment at the Trianon. Well, a kind of appointment. There's a fellow there who will be expecting me but doesn't know that I'm expecting him. One of Agnelli's stake-outs. He's expecting to see me in my full criminal regalia – he's under the impression that I've been asleep all afternoon, which might have been no bad thing – and I mustn't disappoint him.'

The phone rang. De Graaf answered it and handed it to van Effen.

'Yes. Yes, Lieutenant van Effen . . . I'll wait . . . Why should I?' He held the phone some inches from his ear. 'Some clown advising me to avoid damage to my ear-drums and to –' He broke off as a high-pitched scream, a feminine scream, not of fear but of agony, came from the earpiece. Van Effen jammed the phone against his ear, listened for a few seconds then hung up.

De Graaf said: 'What in God's name was that?'

'Julie. At least that's what the man said. Well, his words were: "Your sister is a bit slow in cooperating. We'll call again when she does."'

'Torture,' the Colonel said. His voice was steady but his eyes were mad. 'Torturing my Julie.'

Van Effen smiled faintly. 'Mine, too, remember? Possibly. The Annecy brothers' speciality. But it was just a shade too crude, too pat, too theatrical.'

'God, Peter, she's your sister!'

'Yes, sir. I'll remind the brothers of that when I meet them.'

'Trace the call, man! Trace the call!'

'No point, sir. I have good ears. I could just detect the faint overlay hiss of a recorder. That could have come from anywhere. And it's what makes me think it's a phoney put-together job.'

'Then why the devil was the call made?'

'Two reasons, perhaps, although I can only guess at the first. I don't think they thought that I would even suspect that the call was not what it purported to be, that I would be so upset over my sister's kidnapping that I would take anything in its connection at face value. Second thing, of course, is that they're not after Julie, they're after me. This – at least to their highly suspect way of psychological reasoning – is part of the softening-up process.'

De Graaf sat in silence, rose, poured himself another Van der Hum, returned to his seat, thought some more then said: 'I

139

hardly like to bring up this point, Lieutenant, but has it occurred to you that next time, or maybe the time after next, the Annecys may decide to abandon the psychological approach and say: "Surrender to us, Lieutenant van Effen, or your sister will die and we'll see to it that she dies very very slowly." Would you do it?'

'Do what?'

'Give yourself up to them?'

'Of course. My appointment at the Trianon is overdue, sir. If there is any message for me, would you call me there. Stephan Danilov, if you remember. How long do you intend to remain here, sir?'

'Until I see those maps or charts or whatever that Sergeant Oudshoorn found, and until I can get Lieutenant Valken here to take over. I'll put him in the picture as far as I can.'

'You have all the facts, sir.'

'One would hope so,' de Graaf said rather enigmatically.

When van Effen had gone, Thyssen said curiously: 'I know it's not my place to speak, sir, but would the Lieutenant really do that?'

'Do what?'

'Give himself up.'

'You heard the Lieutenant.'

'But – but that would be suicide, sir.' Thyssen seemed almost agitated. 'That would be the end of him.'

'It would be the end of someone, and that's a fact.' De Graaf didn't seem overly concerned.

Van Effen returned, via the rear entrance, to his room in the Trianon, called the desk and asked for Charles.

'Charles? Van Effen. Has our friend returned? . . . Good. He will, I know, be in a position to hear every word you say. Kindly say the following into the phone. "Certainly, Mr Danilov. Coffee immediately and not to be disturbed afterwards. Expecting a visitor at six-thirty." Let me know when he's gone.'

Some thirty seconds later Charles called to inform him that the lobby was now empty.

Van Effen had just completed his metamorphosis into

Stephan Danilov when the phone rang. It was de Graaf, who was still at Julie's flat. He said he had something of interest to show van Effen and could he, van Effen, step round. Ten minutes, van Effen said.

When van Effen returned to the flat he found Thyssen gone and his place taken by Lieutenant Valken. Valken was a short, stout, rubicund character, easy-going and a trencherman of some note, which may have accounted for the fact that although he was several years older than van Effen he was his junior in the service, a fact that worried Valken not at all. They were good friends. Valken was, at that moment, surveying van Effen and speaking to the Colonel.

'A reversal to type, wouldn't you say, sir? Cross between a con man and a white slaver, with just a soupçon of a Mississippi river-boat gambler thrown in. Definitely criminal, anyway.'

De Graaf looked at van Effen and winced. 'Wouldn't trust him within a kilometre of either of my daughters. I don't even trust the sound of his voice.' He indicated the pile of papers on the table before him. 'Like to sift through all of those, Peter. Or shall I just call attention to the ones that interest me?'

'Just the ones that interest you, sir.'

'God, that voice. Fine. Top five.'

Van Effen examined each in turn. They showed plans of what were clearly different levels of the same building: the number of compartments in each plan left no doubt that it was a very large building indeed. Van Effen looked up and said: 'And where's van Rees?'

'Well, damn your eyes!' de Graaf was aggrieved. 'How the hell did you know those were the plans of the royal palace?'

'Didn't you?'

'No I didn't.' De Graaf scowled, which he did very rarely and with difficulty. 'Not until that young architect or whatever from the City Surveyor's office told me. You do rob an old man of his pleasures, Peter.' De Graaf regarded himself as merely approaching the prime of his life.

'I didn't know. Just guessed. As I shall be inside that building within three hours you can understand that my thoughts turn to it from time to time. Van Rees?'

'My old and trusted friend.' De Graaf, understandably, sounded very bitter indeed. 'Put him up for my club, by God! Should have listened to you earlier, my boy, much earlier. And we should have expedited the examination of his bank account.'

'No bank account?'

'Gone. Gone.'

'And so, one supposes, has van Rees.'

'Four million guilders,' de Graaf said. 'Four million. Bank manager thought it a highly unusual step to take but – well –'

'One does not question the motives and the integrity of a pillar of the community?'

'Blackballed,' de Graaf said gloomily. 'Inevitable.'

'There are other clubs, sir. Schiphol, I assume, is still not open for operations?'

'You assume wrongly.' The gloom remained in de Graaf's face. 'Heard ten–fifteen minutes ago. First plane out, a KLM for Paris, took off about twenty minutes ago.'

'Van Rees, clutching his millions, relaxing in the first class?'

'Yes.'

'And no grounds for extradition. No charges against him. In fact, no hard evidence against him. That we'll get the evidence, I don't doubt. Then I'll go and get him. When all this is over, I mean.'

'Your illegal penchants are well known, Lieutenant.'

'Yes, sir. Meantime, I suggest that my penchants, your blackballing and the fact that van Rees is at the present moment probably entering French air space are not quite of primary importance. What does matter is that van Rees – who has by this time passed over to the dyke-breakers all they'll ever want to know about sluices, weirs and locks so that they won't even miss him now – was also tied in with the would-be palace bombers. And we are as convinced as can be that the Annecy brothers are in league with the bombers. It was Julie who first expressed the possibility of this idea, how too much of a coincidence can be too much of a coincidence, although I must say – with all due

142

modesty and not with hindsight – that this possibility had occurred to me before.'

'Your modesty does you credit, Lieutenant.'

'Thank you, sir. Well, what we're faced with now is the probability – I would put it as high as certainty – that we are faced not with three different organizations but only with one. That should make things much simpler for us and easier to cope with.'

'O. Of course, of course.' De Graaf gave van Effen the kind of look that stops a long way short of being admiring. 'How?'

'How?' Van Effen pondered. 'I don't know.'

'Heaven help Amsterdam,' de Graaf muttered.

'Sir?'

De Graaf was saved from enlarging on his brief statement by a knock on the door. Valken opened it to admit a tall, lean gentleman with greying hair, rimless glasses and a faintly aristocratic air. De Graaf rose to his feet and greeted him warmly.

'Hugh, my good friend. So kind of you to come and to come so quickly. At great inconvenience to yourself, I have no doubt.'

'Not at all, my dear chief, not at all. The patients of a plastic surgeon do not expire upon the spot if not attended to immediately. With a six-month waiting list one can squeeze in the odd patient here and there.'

De Graaf made the introductions. 'Professor Johnson. Lieutenant van Effen. Lieutenant Valken.'

'Ah. Lieutenant van Effen. The Colonel has explained your requirements to me. Rather unusual requirements, I may say, even in our at-times somewhat bizarre profession – we tend to be called upon to remove scars, not inflict them. However.'

He looked at the scar on van Effen's face, produced a magnifying glass and peered more closely. 'Not bad, not bad at all. You have quite an artistic bent, my dear fellow. Wouldn't deceive me – not when you've spent all your life studying thousands of different scars of every conceivable variety. But a layman is not a plastic surgeon and I doubt very much whether any layman would question the authenticity of that scar. Let me see the dreadful wound concealed by that glove on your left hand.' He did some peering. 'By Jove, even better. You are to be congratulated. Very convenient to have it on your left hand, isn't it? But a trifle suspicious to the nasty criminal mind, perhaps? You are, of course, right-handed.'

Van Effen smiled. 'You can tell just by looking at me?'

'I can tell that left-handed persons don't carry barely concealed pistols under their left armpit.'

'Too late for a transfer now, sir. I'm already identified as being a left-hand-glove wearer.'

'Yes. Well. I see. Your scars more than pass muster. The trouble, I suppose, is that you suspect that those scars might be subjected to some kind of test, such as with a scrubbing brush or even a hot soapy sponge?'

'A hot soapy sponge is all that is needed.'

'Normally, you understand, the perfect non-removable scar would take some weeks to achieve. I gather, however, that time is not on your side. Ah, Colonel. Is that Van der Hum I see?'

'It is indeed.' The Colonel poured a glass.

'Thank you. We don't generally advertise the fact, but members of our profession – well, before an operation, you understand?'

'Operation?' said van Effen.

'A trifle,' Johnson said soothingly. He took some brandy, then opened a small metal case to reveal a gleaming array of surgical instruments, most of them of a very delicate nature. 'A series of subcutaneous injections with a variety of inert dyes. There will be no weals, no puffiness, I promise you. There will also be no local anaesthetic. Takes better that way.' He looked very closely at the facial scar. 'Must have the position, size and colour as before, you understand. Your left hand is unimportant. Nobody, I assume, has seen that scar. I can give you a much more satisfyingly horrific scar than you have now. Now, if I could have some hot water, sponge, soap.'

Twenty-five minutes later and Johnson was through. 'Not my proudest achievement, but it will serve. At least, no one can pull or scrub those scars off. Have a look, Lieutenant.'

Van Effen went to a mirror, looked, nodded and came back.

'First class, sir. A dead ringer for the one I had painted on.'

He surveyed his apparently horribly mangled left hand with melancholy admiration. 'I've really been through it. After such a marvellous job, sir, it seems ungrateful to ask – but how permanent are those scars likely to be?'

'Not permanent at all. Those dyes are of a completely different chemical composition from tattoo pigments. Absorption time varies – two to three weeks. I shouldn't worry, Lieutenant – they're really quite becoming.'

De Graaf and van Effen met Professor Hector van Dam, Professor Bernard Span and Professor Thomas Spanraft in the living-room of van Dam's house. They didn't look at all like professors or, more accurately, what professors are supposed to look like. They looked more like a combination of prosperous businessmen and solid Dutch burghers, all curiously alike, all overweight, all cheerful and all with slightly flushed cheeks which might have come from the over-heated room or the large bottle of wine which circulated freely among them.

Van Dam spoke. 'Well, gentlemen, we think we have the answers you seek. Not too difficult, really. We have in this country linguistic specialists, both occidental and oriental – especially oriental, we have had vast experience of dealing with Asiatic languages over the centuries – as you will find anywhere in Europe. Professor Spanraft has come up specially from Rotterdam. No oriental knowledge in this case. I may start, perhaps, with my own small contribution.'

He looked at van Effen. 'This gentleman you met in some café with the unusual name of Helmut Paderiwski. He is not Dutch and he is most certainly not Polish. He is, specifically and unquestionably, southern Irish. Even more specifically, he is a Dubliner. My qualifications for making so confident an assertion? A year as visiting scholar and lecturer at Trinity, Dublin. Bernard?'

Professor Span made an apologetic gesture with his hands. 'My contribution, even smaller than Hector's, was pathetically easy. I am told that the other two gentlemen the Lieutenant met in the same café with the splendid, if slightly unlikely, names of Romero and Leonardo Agnelli are dark-haired, dark-eyed and of a rather Mediterranean cast of countenance. Gentlemen of such appearance are not exclusively confined to an area south of the Alps. They are even to be found, as you must know, in our own predominantly fair-haired and fair-complexioned society. The Agnellis are two such.'

'You are quite certain of that, sir?' van Effen said. 'I know Italy well and –'

'Lieutenant van Effen!' Professor van Dam was shocked. 'If my colleague –'

Professor Span held up a placatory hand. 'No, no, Hector, the Lieutenant's query was a legitimate one. I gather that the enquiries in which he and the Colonel are engaged are of a most serious nature.' He smiled a deprecatory smile. 'As a mere academic, of course – anyway, Lieutenant, rest assured that those gentlemen are as Dutch as you or I. My life on it. And at a guess – an educated guess, mark you – from Utrecht. You are amazed, perhaps, by my perspicacity? Please do not be. My qualifications? Impeccable. I'm a Dutchman. From Utrecht. Your turn, Thomas.'

Spanraft smiled. '*My* qualifications are strikingly similar to Hector's. This lady who makes all those mysterious phone calls. Young, beyond a doubt. Educated. Perhaps even highly so. Northern Ireland, specifically Belfast. My qualifications? I, too, have been a visiting scholar and lecturer. Queen's, Belfast.' He smiled. 'Good heavens, I may even have taught the young lady.'

'If you did,' de Graaf said heavily, 'you didn't teach her the right things.'

De Graaf turned to van Effen, who was driving a Volkswagen that evening. As it was not impossible that he might be called upon to drive one or more of Agnelli's group that evening it had been deemed more prudent not to use the Peugeot, where the presence of a police radio might have been inadvertently discovered. Car papers and insurance were, of course, made out in the name of Stephan Danilov.

'What do you make of this Irish connection, Peter?'

'I have no idea, sir. We know, of course, that petty criminals have in the past sold Russian and other eastern bloc weapons to the Irish Republican Army; but these, as I say, were petty criminals operating on a relatively petty scale. This, I feel, is something much bigger. The IRA never had any organization worth speaking of in this country. The FFF definitely have. Where can I contact you later on this evening, sir?'

'I wish you hadn't mentioned that,' de Graaf said gloomily. 'Earlier, I had hoped to spend it in the bosom of my family. But now? If the government does decide to send an emissary to parley with the FFF – good heavens, Peter, we completely forgot to listen in to the six o'clock news – the broadcast, rather, that was to state when and where the government would hold this parley.'

'We've only to lift a phone. It's of no significance.'

'True. This emissary I mentioned. Who, do you think, is the logical choice?'

'The Minister of Justice?'

'No other. My lord and master whom you have frequently, actionably and accurately described as an old woman. Old women like to have their hands held. Who do you think would best play the part of nursemaid?'

'You'd make an admirable choice. In fact, I'm happy to say that you would be the inevitable choice. Don't forget to take an umbrella big enough for both of you.' Rain had begun to fall and fall so heavily that the Volkswagen's wipers failed adequately to cope with it. 'You should consider yourself privileged, sir, to have a ringside seat at what may be, at least, a minor turning point in history.'

'I'd rather have my own armchair by my own fireside.' De Graaf reduced visibility even more by drawing heavily on his cheroot. 'But whatever seat I'm in tonight it'll be a damned sight safer and more comfortable than the one you'll be in. Not that I would suppose for a moment that they have armchairs in the palace cellars.' De Graaf, apparently concentrating on increasing the blue fug inside the car, lapsed briefly into silence then said: 'I don't like it, Peter. I don't like it at all. Too many ifs, buts and question marks.'

'I have to admit that I'm not all that madly keen on it myself.

But we've agreed – it's our only way in. And there's another thing I don't like too much and makes me more than glad that your friend gave those scars a degree of permanence. I mean, they may have reservations about me that I didn't suspect before.'

'What makes you suspect now?'

'A rather disquieting remark that one of those gentlemen let drop a few minutes ago – Professor Span, it was. He said he came from Utrecht. He is firmly of the opinion that the Agnelli brothers come from the same place.'

'So?'

'It may have escaped your memory, sir, but Vasco – Sergeant Westenbrink – also comes from Utrecht.'

'Damn it!' De Graaf said softly. The implications had struck him immediately. 'Oh, damn it all!'

'Indeed. Cops and criminals generally have a working knowledge of each other. Two things may help, though. Vasco spent much of his time in Utrecht working under cover and he's been in disguise – sort of – since he took up residence in Krakerdom. Imponderables, sir, imponderables.'

'Your continued existence would seem to me to be another imponderable,' de Graaf said heavily. 'There is no call –'

'Yes, sir, I know, over and above the call of duty. Let's just say in for a penny in for a pound, or, if you like, a calculated risk. By my calculations, the odds are on me.' He pulled up outside de Graaf's house.

'I am glad that I'm not a betting man.' He peered at his watch. 'Six-seventeen. If I want to reach you in the next hour or so you will, of course, be in your room in the Trianon.'

'Briefly only, sir. For about forty minutes, from, say, six forty-five onwards, I'll be in La Caracha.'

'The devil you will! La Caracha. I thought someone was delivering some data or whatever it is in the Trianon at six-thirty and that you were going to study that?'

'I don't have to look at it. I know how to operate radio-controlled detonations. When I explained to them at length the difficulties involved in radio detonation, that was for their benefit and my benefit. Their benefit, to convince them that I really was what I purported to be, a whizz-kid in explosives: my benefit, to find out how much they really knew about the subject, which appears to be singularly little. Work that one out, sir – why so highly organised a group is anything but organized in what would appear to be a very – if not the most – vital department. That's one of the reasons why I said that by my calculations the odds are on me – I think they may really need me and be prepared to lean over just so slightly backwards to give me the benefit of the doubt.

'But the real reason for whatever optimism I have lies in La Caracha. You may remember I asked Vasco to meet me in Julie's flat. I changed my mind about that: I think that the further he and I – in my capacity of Danilov – keep away from the flat the better. So I've arranged to meet him in La Caracha. I also took the liberty of phoning George and asking him if he would be interested in giving me a little assistance. He said he would be more than pleased. I did not – I repeat *not*, sir – co-opt him in your name. I thought there were some things you'd rather not know about – officially, that is.'

'I see. You have a point. I sometimes wonder, Peter, how many things I don't know about, officially *and* unofficially, but now is not the time for brooding. I mean, you haven't the time. And how do you propose to have those two help guarantee your continued existence?'

'They will, I hope, be keeping an eye on me. A close eye. Vasco, as I think I've mentioned, has no equal as a shadower. And George – well, he has other virtues.'

'So I've noticed. May heaven help us all.'

Agnelli's messenger arrived punctually at six-thirty, less than two minutes after van Effen had arrived back in his room at the Trianon. A man, van Effen reflected, ideally suited for his task – a small, drab, unremarkable nonentity of a man who could have been first cousin of the other nonentity who consumed so remarkably few jonge jenevers in the close vicinity of the reception desk in the lobby. He handed over a yellow envelope, said that someone would be around to pick him up at seven forty-five and left, less than twenty seconds after his arrival.

'No,' Sergeant Westenbrink said. He was seated with van Effen and George in a small private room in La Caracha. 'I don't know the Annecys – the two that you didn't put in prison, that is.'

'Do they know you?'

'I'm sure they don't. I never came into contact with them. They left for Amsterdam about three years ago.'

'Ah, I'd forgotten. Either of you hear this broadcast that was supposed to be made to the FFF?'

'It was made,' George said. 'Minister of Justice's house. 8 p.m. Guarantees of immunity – I assume the government believed in the threat to turn the Oostlijk-Flevoland into a new sea.'

'Well, doesn't concern us at the moment. You are sure you want to come in on this, George?'

George seemed to reflect. 'Could be difficult, even dangerous. There might even be violence.' He frowned, then brightened. 'But one does get so tired of serving Rodekool met Rolpens.'

'So. If you'll be kind enough to have your car outside the Trianon – or, shall I say, in the discreet vicinity – by seven-forty. Might leave in my Volkswagen, might be in the car of whoever comes to pick me up. I don't for a moment think you'll lose us but, in any case, you know we'll be heading in the general direction of the royal palace.'

George said: 'Does our Chief of Police know about us – our plans?'

'He knows about you two and that you'll be keeping a very careful watch – I hope – over me. The rest, no. It would never do for us to go around breaking the law.'

'Of course not,' George said.

At precisely seven forty-five, no other than Romero Agnelli himself came to collect van Effen from the Trianon.

Six

As far as one could tell, Romero Agnelli was in high good humour: but, then, as far as one could tell, Romero Agnelli was always in high good humour. Even the torrential rainfall drumming on the roof of the car had no effect on his spirits. The car was Agnelli's, a large and, van Effen had been glad to note, fairly conspicuous green Volvo.

'Dreadful night,' Agnelli said. 'Quite dreadful. And worse still to come, I'm sure. Bad time of the year, this. Always a bad time. Gales, spring tides, north wind – must listen in to the eight o'clock forecast.' Agnelli, van Effen thought, was uncommonly interested in the weather conditions. 'Busy day, Mr Danilov?'

'If you call sleeping being busy, yes, then I've had a busy day. Late in bed last night – late this morning, actually – and I didn't know what hour you'd keep me up to tonight. You have not, Mr Agnelli, been too free with information about your plans.'

'Would you have been in my situation? Don't worry, we won't keep you late. That data I sent round – it proved useful?'

'Everything I required.' Van Effen pulled out the yellow envelope from under his coat. 'Returned with thanks. I don't want to be found with that in my possession. Where's the radio?'

'In the boot. In perfect condition, I assure you.'

'I don't doubt it. Nevertheless, I shall want to see it. I trust the amatol, primers and the rest are *not* in the boot?'

Agnelli looked at him in amusement. 'They're not. Why?'

'I'm thinking of the detonator. Usually made of some fulminating powder, commonly a mercury derivative. Delicate. Doesn't like being jounced around. And I don't like being around when it's jounced around.'

'They're in a room we've hired off the Kalvetstraat.'

'Would it be presumptuous of me to ask why the radio isn't with the explosives?

'Not at all. I want to trigger off the device in the palace from the Dam Square itself. Perhaps you wonder why?'

'Wonder or not, I'm not going to ask. The less I know the better all round. I'm a great believer in the need-to-know principle.'

'So, normally, am I.' He switched on the car radio. 'Eight o'clock. Forecast.' The forecast, which came through almost immediately, was not encouraging. Wind, force seven, north, veering north-north-east, increasing, heavy rains, temperature dropping. Then followed some technical jargon about stationary depressions and a confident, if gloomy, assertion that the weather would continue to deteriorate for the next forty-eight hours.

'Sounds bad,' Agnelli said. His expression did not appear to reflect inner concern. 'Lots of people, especially the middle-aged and older with longer memories, won't be feeling any too happy – especially with the recent comments about the decayed state of the dykes. Same conditions as caused those dreadful floods back in the fifties – and the dykes are in no better condition now than they were then.'

'Putting it a bit strongly, isn't it, Mr Agnelli? Think of the huge storm-surge barriers they've built in the delta area in the south-west.'

'And what guarantee have we that the North Sea is going to be considerate enough to launch its attack against the delta area? Little point in locking your front door if the back door is falling off its hinges.'

Agnelli parked his car in the Voorburgwal, reached into the back seat and produced two large umbrellas.

'Not that these are going to be much help in this downpour. Just wait a few seconds until I get the radio out of the boot.'

Just over a minute later they were standing outside a door to which Agnelli had his own key. Beyond lay an ill-lit and dingy passageway, its floor covered with cracked linoleum. Agnelli furled his umbrella and gave a coded knock on the first door to the right – three taps, then one, then three. The door was opened by the man calling himself Helmut Paderiwski who made an unsuccessful effort to restrain a scowl when he recognized the person accompanying Agnelli, who appeared not to notice it.

'Helmut you have met,' Agnelli said, and led the way into the room. Unlike the corridor, it was brightly lit and was large and furnished in surprising comfort. Leonardo Agnelli gave van Effen a nod and a smile.

Leonardo apart, there were four other people in the room, all young, all pleasant looking and very respectable: two men and two girls, all looking like refugees from some university honours graduate course, the type that would have more than passed muster in any Parisian grand salon: they were also of the type that, in the past decade, had not only been members of, but had organized and controlled so many politically motivated criminal groups in Germany and Italy. They were considerably more formidable than your common-or-garden criminal who was concerned primarily with the accumulation of as much wealth as possible in the shortest time possible but who would rapidly abandon all thought of ill-gotten gains if personal danger threatened, fanatically dedicated people who would stop at nothing to achieve their own cherished Utopias, no matter how bizarre, sick and undesirable those Utopias might appear to the vast majority of their fellow men and women. They could, of course, have been genuine salon intellectuals who sought no more of life than the opportunity to discuss Proust and Stendhal, Hegelian and Kantian philosophies. But seekers after the higher truths did not commonly assemble in such clandestine fashion, especially not in the close vicinity of sixteen-kilo blocks of amatol explosive which van Effen had at once observed neatly stacked in a corner.

Agnelli indicated the two young men. 'Joop and Joachim. They have other names, of course, but are not using them at the moment.' Joop and Joachim, oddly alike in that both were tall, slightly stooped and wore horn-rimmed glasses, bowed slightly, smiled but refrained from reciprocal comment when van Effen said he was delighted to meet them. Agnelli turned to a sweet-smiling dark-haired girl. 'And this is Maria, who has also for the moment forgotten her surname.'

'My, my,' van Effen said. 'Imagine forgetting a name like Agnelli.'

Agnelli smiled. 'I didn't think you would be the man to miss much, Mr Danilov. Yes, my sister. And this is Kathleen.' Kathleen, petite and slender, had blue eyes, dark hair and a slightly humorous, slightly wry expression which in no way detracted from the fact that she was very pretty indeed.

'Kathleen?' van Effen said. 'But that's an Irish name. And, if I don't give offence, you're every man's concept of what an Irish colleen should look like. You know, the one in the song "I'll take you home again, Kathleen"?'

She made a mock curtsy. 'You choose to flatter me, kind sir. No offence. My mother is Irish. I'm quite proud of it, in my own Celtic way.'

Professor Spanraft's putative ex-student, van Effen knew. And, beyond doubt, the girl who had spoken over the telephone to the sub-editor Morelis and others.

'It was promised that I would meet your leader tonight,' van Effen said. 'He is not here.'

'He asked me to convey his apologies,' Agnelli said. 'An urgent appointment that he couldn't break.' If one were in any way courteous, van Effen reflected, one did not break appointments with Ministers of Justice.

'Those are all your group?'

'No.' Agnelli waved a hand. 'Those are all that are with us tonight.'

'Pity I won't be able to further my acquaintance with them,' van Effen said. 'They may be with us but I won't be with them.' He turned towards the door. 'I trust they enjoy their trip to the cellars. I'm sorry, Mr Agnelli. Good-night.'

'Wait a minute, wait a minute!' Agnelli, no longer smiling, was totally taken aback, his face registering his lack of comprehension.

'A minute? Not a second. Not in this company.' Van Effen looked around the other equally startled and puzzled occupants of the room, his eyes and mouth dismissive and more than slightly contemptuous. 'If you imagined that I was going to move into hostile territory – and no matter how good your inside information may be, the possibility of danger is always there – carrying explosives and with this bunch of amateur rubber-neckers traipsing at my heels, you have to be out of your mind.' He reached for the door-handle. 'Get yourself another demolition expert. Preferably from a lunatic asylum.'

'Is that what it is?' Agnelli smiled in relief. 'My dear fellow, those people are not coming with us. Do you think *I* am from a lunatic asylum? Only you, Leonardo and myself.'

'Then what are all those people doing here? And don't tell me it's none of my business. It is. I value my freedom above all things and my freedom is endangered when unnecessary risks are taken. Don't you know that danger lies in numbers? Don't you think it's stupid to have your people holed up so near a place where you intend to carry out an illegal act? Don't you ever operate on the need-to-know principle?'

'This is not our base, Mr Danilov. One night only.' Agnelli was slightly on the defensive, slightly uncomfortable. 'Those people are here simply as observers.'

'Observing what?'

'The effects of the explosion.'

'Effects? The walls of Jericho come tumbling down? There'll be nothing to observe.'

'Psychological effects. Reactions. Guide to our future plans.'

'Effects on whom? The crowds thronging the Dam Square?' Van Effen looked at him incredulously. 'That rain's torrential. There won't be a single living soul in the square tonight.' He looked slowly round the unsmiling faces. 'Sunday-school kids on a Sunday-school picnic. Cheap thrills? Or the feeling that they're not making a contribution, not really participating unless they're on the spot? God help us. Let me see all the gear you have.' Enough moral ascendancy, van Effen thought, was enough.

'Certainly.' Agnelli tried, not too successfully, to hide the relief in his face. 'Joop?'

'Yes, Mr Agnelli.' Joop opened a cupboard and brought out some boxes which he set on the carpet and proceeded to open.

'Primer. Detonators. Battery. The trigger mechanism. The setting on this – here – is activated by –'

'Joop.'

'Yes?'

'Are you detonating this device?'

'No. Of course not.'

'Why not?'

'Because I'm not an expert. Oh, I see. Sorry.' Discomfited, Joop withdrew. Van Effen looked at Agnelli.

'You have the key for the radio box?'

'Yes, of course.' He handed it over. 'Please excuse Leonardo and myself for a moment.' Both men left by a side door. Van Effen unlocked the metal lid of the radio container and studied the controls on top of the radio. He turned the power on, touched a knob here, pulled a switch there, calibrated the gauges on a couple of dials and adjusted two wave-length bands. No one watching – and everyone was watching – could doubt he or she was in the presence of an expert. He then studied the timing dial on the triggering mechanism, produced pad and pencil, made a few rapid calculations then straightened, obviously satisfied.

'Nothing to it, really, is there?' Kathleen was smiling.

'Agreed. Can't imagine why I'm here.' He stooped, locked the lid of the radio container and thrust the key into an inside pocket.

'You do trust people, don't you?' Kathleen said.

'No. Especially kids. But if you remove temptation from the reach of kids then they can't possibly fall into it, can they? I have no wish to be blown up in the cellars of the palace.'

He turned as Agnelli and his brother re-entered the room. Both were dressed as policemen, Romero Agnelli as an inspector, his brother as a sergeant. Van Effen surveyed them.

'You make an excellent inspector, Mr Agnelli. Really most becoming. Your brother looks the part, too, except for one thing: he's really at least five inches too short for the police force.'

'Short legs only,' Agnelli said comfortably. 'He's as tall as anyone when he's seated behind the wheel of a police car.'

'You surprise me. About the police car I mean. You have – ah – come into possession of one?'

'Not exactly. We have, shall we say, a car that looks exactly like a police car. Not too difficult.' He looked at his watch. 'A police car is expected at the palace in about twenty minutes.'

'Expected?'

'But of course. We have friends and we have made arrangements. Joop, be so kind as to pack the equipment, will you?' He indicated two grey metallic cases that stood nearby.

'So you just drive up and walk inside?' van Effen said.

'We believe in keeping things simple. Of course.'

'Of course. No reason required, naturally. You just walk in.'

'Yes.' He indicated the two metal cases Joop was loading with equipment. 'With those.'

'Again, of course. You declare the contents?'

'Electronic detecting equipment. For locating hidden explosives.'

'I didn't know there was any such thing.'

'I don't believe there is. However, in this silicon chip, computerized and electro-magnetic age, people believe anything. The explosives we're looking for have – we believe – been secreted in the basements, somewhere. Underworld tip. So we go to the basements to look.'

'You have your nerve,' van Effen said.

'Not really. Calculated risk and we calculate that the risk is not very high. People don't normally publicize in advance the fact that they intend to do something which is the precise opposite of what they intend to do. And with those uniforms, the police car and the impressive set of credentials we have we don't expect to experience too much trouble. We've even got a set of papers for you.'

'That's fine. Papers. Papers don't matter a damn to me. Nor does the fact that you haven't gone to the trouble to find me a uniform. What –'

'No uniform. You're a civilian expert. The papers say so.'

'Let me finish. You two may – and very probably will – get off with your minimal disguises. But how am I going to disguise my scarred face and the fact that I have a crippled hand? My

157

description will probably be in every paper in the country tomorrow.'

Agnelli looked closely at the scar on van Effen's face. 'If you'll pardon the cruel remark, that really is a beauty. Joachim?' This to one of the two young men. 'What do you think? Joachim, Mr Danilov, is an art school student and also a make-up designer for theatrical groups. He requires quite a large case to carry all his stock in trade. As you can imagine, in an organization such as ours, we find our friend's specialized gifts invaluable.'

'Do you have anything against beards, Mr Danilov?' Joachim said.

'Not as long as they don't make me look worse than I already am.'

'I have several in a suitably auburn shade. In your case, I'm afraid, it would have to be a beard of rather a luxuriant style. I know the one. I'll apply some paste.'

'Just so long as I can get it off again.'

'Forty-eight hours and it will fall off.' Joachim left the room.

'About that black glove, Mr Danilov,' Agnelli said.

'I'm afraid there is nothing they can do with that.'

'How can you be sure?'

'How can I be sure? If you'd a hand like mine don't you think I'd have tried anything – everything – to camouflage it?' Van Effen let just the right note of bitterness creep into his voice.

'Nevertheless, perhaps I might see it?' Agnelli's voice was gently insistent. 'I promise you I won't say "Good God above" or swoon or anything of the kind.'

Van Effen, being ostentatious without appearing to be, turned his back on the rest of the company and peeled off the black glove. He held his hand up to within a foot of Agnelli's face.

Agnelli's normally mobile face became still. He said: 'I promised you I wouldn't say "Good God" or anything of the kind – but, well, I've never seen anything like it before. How in heaven's name did this happen?'

Van Effen smiled. 'Legitimately, believe it or not. Someone

made a mistake when we were trying to cap an oil fire in Saudi Arabia.'

'One trusts he paid for the mistake?'

'There and then. He was incinerated.'

'I see. In which case one might almost imagine you've been lucky.' Agnelli took van Effen's wrist and touched the scars with his finger-nails. 'That must hurt.'

'Not the slightest. Skin's paralysed. Stick a row of needles into it or slice it with a scalpel. Wouldn't feel a thing.' It would be unfortunate, van Effen thought, if Agnelli took him at his word. 'It's unimportant. All that matters is that I can still oppose finger and thumb.'

Joachim came back and Agnelli said: 'Do you mind if Joachim looks at this?'

'If he's the sensitive artistic type I should imagine he'd be better off looking elsewhere.'

Joachim looked and failed to hide the revulsion in his face. 'That's – that's *awful*! I couldn't – I mean – how can you bear to go about like that.'

'I don't have much option. It's the only left hand I've got.'

Joachim said: 'You'd better put your glove back on. There's nothing I – nothing anyone can do about that.'

'Time to go,' Agnelli said. 'Helmut, we'll meet you and the others down in the Dam in about half an hour, perhaps forty minutes. Don't forget the radio.'

'The radio?' van Effen said. 'You're going to operate the radio in this monsoon?'

'We have a mini-bus. Where's the key to the radio?'

'In my pocket,' van Effen said. 'I thought it might be safer there.'

'I'm sure you're right.'

They left, taking the metal cases with them. Agnelli stopped at a door close to the entrance, opened it, went inside. He reappeared, leading a Dobermann pinscher which had about it the homicidal appearance shared by many members of its breed: it was, reassuringly, muzzled.

'Is that animal as fierce as it looks?' van Effen asked.

'I've had the good fortune never to find out. However, he's

not here for the purposes of either defence or attack. Dobermann pinschers can be trained to smell out explosives. Use them at airports. Fact.'

'I know it's a fact. Has this dog been so trained?'

'Quite frankly, I have no idea. For all I know, his olfactory nerves may be completely paralysed.'

'I'm beginning to believe that you might even get off with this,' van Effen said.

They made the best time they could through the drenching rain and were back at the spot where they had parked the Volvo in the Voorburgwal. Van Effen had his hand on the door when he realized that it was not, in fact, the car in which they had arrived: it was, unmistakably, a police car. Van Effen got into the back seat beside Agnelli and said: 'You leave your own car here and come back and find a police car in its place. You know, I now do believe that you are going to get off with it after all. You do have your organization.'

'Organization is all,' said Agnelli.

Everything went off as Agnelli had confidently expected. They were expected at the palace and their credentials received only the most cursory inspection: they and the car were so obviously official that a more detailed examination could only have seemed superfluous: besides, it was raining very heavily indeed and the guards were very anxious indeed to get back to the shelter just as soon as they could.

Agnelli led them to a doorway which was so completely shrouded in darkness that he had to use a pencil torch to locate the keyhole of a door, a keyhole for which, as he had promised, he had the key. He also had a succession of keys which he used two flights of stairs down to open a succession of cellars. He knew the location of every door, every light switch.

'You lived here?' van Effen asked.

'I've been here a couple of times. One has to be fairly meticulous about these things.' He led the way through a completely empty cellar into another equally bare cellar and said: 'This is the place. Not too difficult, was it?'

'I find it hard to believe,' van Effen said. 'They do have security systems here?'

'Excellent ones, I'm told. But security is a relative term. There is no security net that can't be breached. Look at Buckingham Palace for instance. One of the tightest security shields in the world but as has been proved several times in the past year or so any semi-intelligent person – and, indeed, as has also been proved, those of a considerably lower IQ – can go in and out whenever they feel so inclined. Well, Mr Danilov, it's yours.'

'Minutes, only. Open this far door for me – if you have the key.'

Agnelli had the key. Van Effen produced a tape and proceeded to measure the thickness of the walls. He said: 'How come all those cellars are so empty?'

'They weren't a few days ago. They were pretty well filled with old furniture, archives, things that you expect to collect in a royal palace over the years. Not that we were concerned with the well-being of those antiquities, most of which were just ancient rubbish anyway. It was no part of our plan to burn the palace down.'

Van Effen nodded, said nothing, went out – accompanied by Agnelli – and climbed a flight of steps to work out the thickness of the ceiling. He returned to the cellar, made a few calculations on a piece of paper then said: 'We'll use the lot. Those walls are stouter than I would have expected. But the resulting bang should still be quite satisfactory.'

'Always a pleasure to watch an expert at work,' Agnelli said.

'No more than it is to watch a journeyman brick-layer at work. He does his five years' apprenticeship. I've done mine.'

'There's a difference, I suggest, between dropping a brick and dropping a detonator.'

'A skilled tradesman never drops anything.' Van Effen busied himself for not more than two minutes, then said: 'I think I recall you saying that you did have the duplicate keys for the cellars we've just passed through?'

'I did and I have.'

'So no one else can get near this place?' Agnelli shook his head. 'So. Finished.'

Their departure was no more eventful than their arrival had been. Less than ten minutes after van Effen had inserted the detonator into the primer they parked their car just behind a dimly lit mini-bus.

As they stepped out a figure emerged from the shadows. He came up to Agnelli. 'All well, sir?'

'No problem, John.'

'Goodnight, sir.' The man got into the police car and drove off.

'More organization,' van Effen said. 'Formidable.'

The five people they had left in the room close by the Voorburg-wal were all seated in the mini-bus which, being a fourteen-seater, was considerably larger than its name suggested. Van Effen and Agnelli sat in the wide seat in the back.

Van Effen said: 'May one ask how long you expect to wait here?'

'Of course.' Agnelli had become more than his usual smiling self in the past few minutes: He was now positively jovial. He had shown no signs of strain inside the palace but strain there must inevitably have been. 'Not quite sure myself, to be honest. A few minutes, perhaps. Certainly no more than twenty. But first, one must beware lurking and suspicious policemen. Leonardo? Catch.'

He threw something to his brother then stood up himself and shrugged his way into a long grey raincoat. Then he sat, reached below the seat, pulled out a machine which looked like and was a radio transceiver, flicked a switch which made a red light glow, then brought up a headband with one earphone, which he draped over his knee: he reached down again and brought up a microphone the lead of which was, presumably, attached to the transceiver.

'Sorry I have to keep you waiting,' he said, almost apologetically. 'But I, in turn, have to wait a call.'

'More organization,' van Effen said. 'Quite admirable. But there is one area in which your organization falls down.'

'Inevitably.' Agnelli smiled. 'In what respect?'

'No heating in this vehicle.'

'An oversight. Maria?'

'It's by the radio.'

Agnelli reached under the seat and, not without some effort, brought up a large wicker basket which he placed on the seat between van Effen and himself. He opened the lid to reveal a rather splendidly appointed picnic basket.

'What you would have expected, Mr Danilov. A picnic basket for the Sunday-school picnickers. If we cannot have external warmth at least we can provide some of the internal variety.' The contents of the basket tended to bear out his claim. Apart from two rows of gleaming glasses and packets of sandwiches neatly wrapped in cellophane, it held a very promising variety of bottles. 'We thought we might have something to celebrate this evening,' he said, again almost apologetically, 'and I do think we have. A schnapps, perhaps, Mr Danilov?'

Van Effen said: 'I unreservedly withdraw my remarks about your organization.'

Agnelli hadn't even had time to begin to pour the schnapps when the transceiver buzzer rang. He clamped on the headpiece and acknowledged the call then listened in silence for almost a minute. Then he said: 'Yes, they are foolish. They have no place to go. So a little persuasion to tip the balance? Call me back in one minute.' He took off the headpiece. 'Well, who's the volunteer to press the button?' There were no volunteers. 'Well, then, I suggest you, Mr Danilov. You're the man who prepared the charges so, of course, we'll all blame you if the explosion turns out to be a damp squib or, alternatively, the palace falls down, so perhaps it's only fitting that you press the button also. That way the rest of us will all feel blameless while you –'

He wasn't given time to complete his sentence. Van Effen stabbed the button and less than two seconds later, deep and muffled like a distant underwater explosion but very unmistakable for all that – to anyone with normal hearing, the sound must have been audible up to a kilometre away – the reverberation from the detonating amatol rolled across the square. Van

Effen took the bottle from Agnelli's unresisting hand – Agnelli, not smiling and with lips parted, seemed to be seeing something very far away – and poured himself a schnapps.

'Seems I'll just have to congratulate myself. A nice loud bang but the royal walls still stand. As guaranteed. My health.'

'That was splendid,' Agnelli said warmly. He was back on his own usual smiling balance again. 'Perfectly splendid, Mr Danilov. And no damage after all that noise. Unbelievable.'

'Perhaps a little royal wine spilt on the royal table-cloth.' Van Effen made a dismissive gesture. 'I don't want to seem unduly modest – not in my nature, really – but that was next to nothing. Next time – if there is a next time – something a little more demanding perhaps.'

'There'll be a next time. That I promise. *And* a little more exacting. That I also promise.' He paused to sip some schnapps as the others, obviously excited and elated, turned to congratulate van Effen, then held up a hand for silence as the buzzer rang again.

'Ah! You heard it also, did you? Very, very satisfactory. Mr Danilov is a man of his word.' He was silent for almost a minute then said: 'Yes, I agree. I'd been thinking along those lines myself. Most fortuitous, most . . . Thank you. Ten o'clock then.'

He replaced headpiece and microphone, then leaned back in his seat. 'Well, now, time to relax.'

'You relax,' van Effen said. 'Not me. If you're not moving on, I am.' He made to get up and a puzzled Agnelli caught his arm.

'What is wrong?'

'There's nothing wrong with me. It's just, as I've told you, that I've got a very acute sense of self-preservation. As soon as the police come to their senses – if they ever lost them, they're a pretty efficient bunch hereabouts – they're going to start questioning everyone within eyesight of the palace. I should imagine – no, I'm certain – that a minibus with eight odd characters such as us parked in a rainstorm in the Dam would be a prime target for questioning.' He shrugged off Agnelli's hand and rose. 'I've an acute aversion to being questioned by the police. A criminal

– and we are criminals – has to be some kind of retarded lunatic to remain in the vicinity of his crime.'

'Sit down. You're right, of course. Foolish of me – one should never let one's guard down. Helmut?'

Paderiwski, who was obviously in full agreement with van Effen, drove off at once.

Back in the room they had so recently vacated, Agnelli sank into an armchair. 'Thank you, ladies, thank you. Schnapps would be fine. Now, perhaps, Mr Danilov, we can relax.'

'Safer than where we were. But relax? For me, no. Still too close. Instinct? Plain cowardice? I just don't know. Anyway, I have an appointment tonight. Nine-thirty.'

Agnelli smiled. 'You were pretty sure that you were going to keep that appointment?'

'I never had any reason to doubt it. No, that's not quite accurate. I never had reason to doubt that the arranging of the explosion was a simple matter. I had ample reason to question your ability to get us in and out undetected. But, then, I had no reason beforehand to be aware of your rather remarkable organizational ability. I'll have no doubts about you again.'

'Nor we of you – not after tonight's performance. I had mentioned the possibility of finding a permanent niche with us. That's no longer a possibility, it's a guarantee if you're still of the same mind.'

'Of course I'm of the same mind. Tonight, you had a free demonstration. Now, I would appreciate some steady employment.'

'The point I was about to raise. I think you are now entitled to be taken into our confidence.'

Van Effen looked at him in silence, took a thoughtful sip of his schnapps and smiled. 'Not, I feel certain, your full confidence. You are not about to tell me your ultimate aims. You are not going to tell me how you came together. You're not going to tell me how you are financed or by whom. You are not going to tell me where you stay– although, if we're to work together in however limited a capacity, you'll have to give me some intermediate contact phone number. You're not even going to tell me why, in what would appear to be an otherwise highly organized set-up, you require my services at such a late date.'

Agnelli was thoughtful. 'That's a lot of things you seem to be certain that we're not going to tell you. How come?'

Van Effen let a little impatience show. 'Because that is precisely the way I would behave myself. The need-to-know principle. I'm sure I don't have to remind you of that again. What I do believe is that you are about to let me into your very limited confidence about your immediate operational plans. No abnormal prescience on my part. You have to. If, that is to say, I'm to be of any use to you.'

'Correct on all counts. Tell me, Mr Danilov, are you in a position to acquire explosives?'

'Good God!'

'Is that so extraordinary a question to ask of an explosives expert?'

'My astonishment was not at the fact that you ask me. I'm surprised that – well, that such an organized group should embark upon what I take to be an ambitious project without the essentials to hand.'

'We have some of what you call the essentials. We may not have enough. Are you in a position to help?'

'Directly, no.'

'Indirectly?'

'Perhaps. I would have to make enquiries.'

'Discreet, of course.'

Van Effen sighed. 'Please don't be so naive. If it were possible to obtain explosives without official permission in the Netherlands you would already have done so.'

'Sorry. Silly remark. But we have to protect ourselves. Your contact would not, of course, obtain supplies – if he could – in a legitimate fashion?'

'I'm not being indiscreet in saying that, to the best of my knowledge, my contact has never been involved in any legitimate dealings in his life. He would regard it as an affront to his professional code. He is also, incidentally, the only man in the country who knows more than I do about explosives.'

'Sounds like a person whose acquaintance it might be useful to make.' Agnelli studied his glass then looked at van Effen.

'Not by any chance your friend Vasco? The person who introduced us at the Hunter's Horn?'

'Good lord, no.' Van Effen creased his brow and compressed his lips. 'Vasco is hardly what you might call my friend, Mr Agnelli. I got him out of bad trouble, once, and have employed him occasionally on some none-too-demanding errands. But we are not soulmates. I'm quite certain that Vasco knows nothing about explosives, has no access to them and would find it difficult to obtain a child's cap pistol in a toy shop.'

Agnelli turned to his brother and shrugged. 'Had we known that, Leonardo, you wouldn't have spent so much time looking for him this afternoon.'

'Vasco frequently disappears,' van Effen said. 'Has a girl-friend in Utrecht, I believe. You are seriously trying to tell me that you were, also seriously, thinking of engaging Vasco's services?'

'Not exactly, but –'

'He comes in the front door and I go out the back and that's that,' van Effen said. 'He's unstable, unpredictable and highly dangerous, whether he means to be or not.'

'I don't quite understand what you mean by that.'

'And I don't quite understand you. You mean you've never even bothered to check on him, his background?'

'We didn't check yours.'

'You didn't have to,' van Effen said bleakly. 'Not with all those extradition warrants hanging around.'

Agnelli smiled. 'That was this morning and this morning has been forgotten. You obviously know something about Vasco that we don't.'

'Obviously. He's bad. Poison. He's the classic example of game-keeper turned poacher. He's treacherous and a man full of hate. He hates the law and the society that law protects – or is supposed to protect. He's that most dangerous of criminals, an ex-cop gone wrong.'

'A policeman?' Agnelli's surprise, van Effen thought, was splendidly done. 'Police!'

'Ex. No public accusation of wrong-doing, far less a trial. Dismissed without explanation – although doubtless there would have been an explanation made to Vasco. Just try making some discreet enquiries at the Utrecht police station about a certain ex-Sergeant Westenbrink and see what kind of dusty answers you get. My friend George is a different kettle of fish entirely. A firm believer in honour among thieves. An honest criminal, if such a contradiction in terms exists.'

'This George is your explosives friend?' Van Effen nodded. 'He has a second name?'

'No.'

'Do you think he'd work for me?'

'George never works for anyone. He might be prepared to work *with* someone. Another thing. George never works *through* anyone. Not even through me. He's a very careful man. His police record is clean and he wants to keep it that way. He talks to principals only and then it must be face to face.'

'That's the way I like it. Do you think you could get him to talk to me?'

'Who knows? I could ask him. Not here though.'

'Why not?'

'Because I'd advise him against it. He knows I wouldn't do that without reason. Where can I contact you?'

'I'll contact you. At the Trianon.'

'I won't make any comments about how touching your trust in me is. Tomorrow morning.'

'Tonight. Ten o'clock.'

'You *are* in a hurry. No point, I suppose, in asking you the compelling nature of this deadline you so obviously have to meet. Besides, I told you, I have a nine-thirty appointment.'

'Ten o'clock.' Agnelli rose. 'You will of course try to see your friend immediately. I'll put a car at your disposal.'

'Please, Mr Agnelli. Don't be so naive.'

Seven

'That's an Esfahan rug you're standing on,' Colonel de Graaf said. 'Very rare, very expensive.'

'I've got to drip on to something,' van Effen said reasonably. He was standing before the fire in the Colonel's luxuriously furnished library, steam gently rising from his saturated clothing. 'Not for me a door-to-door chauffeur-driven limousine. *I* have to cope with taxis that go home to roost when the first drop of rain falls and with people who seemed anxious to know where I was going. It didn't seem clever to let them know that I was going to the house of the Chief of Police.'

'Your friend Agnelli doesn't trust you?'

'Difficult to say. Oh, sure, it was Agnelli who had me followed – couldn't have been anyone else. But I'm not sure that he's suspicious of me – I think that, on principle, he just doesn't trust anyone. Difficult character to read. You'd probably like him. Seems friendly and likeable enough – you really have to make an effort to associate him with anything like blackmail and torture – and even then you find it difficult to convince yourself. Which means nothing. I assume you had a comfortable evening, sir – that you didn't have to cope with the elements or the thought that you might be shot in the back at any moment.'

De Graaf made a dismissive gesture which could have meant either that such considerations were irrelevant trifles or that they could not possibly apply to him in the first place. 'An interesting meeting, but only to a limited extent. I'm afraid Bernhard wasn't in a particularly receptive or cooperative frame of mind.' Bernhard was Bernhard Dessens, the Minister of Justice.

'A dithering old woman, scared to accept responsibility,

unwilling to commit himself and looking to pass the buck elsewhere?'

'Exactly. I couldn't have put – I've told you before, Peter, that's no way to talk about cabinet ministers. There were two of them. Names Riordan and Samuelson. One – person calling himself Riordan – could have been in disguise. The other had made no attempt at any such thing which can only mean that he's pretty confident about something or other. Riordan had long black hair – shoulder-length, in fact, I thought that ludicrous style had gone out of fashion ten years ago – was deeply tanned, wore a Dutch bargee cap and sun-glasses.'

'Anything so obvious has to be a disguise.' Van Effen thought for a moment. 'He wasn't by any chance very tall and preternaturally thin?'

De Graaf nodded. 'I thought that would occur to you at once. The fellow who commandeered that canal boat from – who was it?'

'At Schiphol? Dekker.'

'Dekker. This must be the man Dekker described. And damned if I don't agree with your bizarre suggestion that this fellow – Riordan or whatever – is an albino. Dark glasses. Heavy tan to hide an alabaster complexion. Black hair to hide white. Other fellow – Samuelson – had white hair, thick and very wavy, white moustache and white goatee beard. No albino, though – blue eyes. All that white hair would normally bespeak advanced years but his face was almost completely unlined. But, then, he was very plump, which may account for the youthful skin. Looked like a cross between an idealized concept of a US Senator and some bloated plutocrat, oil billionaire or something like that.'

'Maybe he's got a better make-up man than Riordan.'

'It's possible. Both men spoke in English, from which I assumed that Samuelson couldn't speak Dutch. Both made a point of stating that they were Irish-Americans and I have no doubt they were. I don't have to be Hector or one of his professorial friends to know that – the north-east or New York accent was very strong. Riordan did nearly all the talking.

170

'He asked – no, he demanded – that we contact the British government. More exactly, he demanded we act as intermediaries between the FFF and Whitehall on the basis that Whitehall would be much more likely to negotiate with another government than with an unknown group such as they were. When Bernhard asked what on earth they could possibly want to discuss with Whitehall they said they wanted to have a dialogue about Northern Ireland, but refused to elaborate further until the Dutch Government agreed to cooperate.' De Graaf sighed. 'Whereupon, alas, our Minister of Justice, seething and fulminating, while at the same time knowing damn well that they had him over a barrel, climbed on to his high horse and said it was inconceivable, unthinkable, that a sovereign nation should negotiate on behalf of a band of terrorists. He carried on for about five minutes in this vein, but I'll spare you all the parliamentary rhetoric. He ended up by saying that he, personally, would die first.

'Riordan said that he very much doubted that Dessens would go to such extraordinary lengths and further said that he was convinced that fourteen million Dutchmen would take a diametrically opposite point of view. Then he became rather unpleasantly personal and threatening. He said it didn't make the slightest damn difference to anything if he, Dessens, committed suicide on the spot, for the Oostlijk–Flevoland dyke in the vicinity of Lelystad would go at midnight if the government didn't agree to talk terms by ten o'clock tonight. He then produced a paper with a list of places which, he said, were in immediate danger of going at any moment. He didn't say whether or not mines had already been placed in those areas – the usual uncertainty technique.

'Among the places he listed – there were so many that I forget half of them – were Leeuwarden, the Noordoost polder in the vicinity of Urk, the Amstelmeer, the Wieringermeer, Putten, the polder south of Petten, Schouwen, Duiveland and Walcheren – did we remember what happened to Walcheren during the war? Both the Eastern and Western Scheldt estuaries were on their list, he said – did we remember what happened there in February 1953 – while Noord and Sud Holland offered a positive embarrassment of riches. That's only a representative sample. Riordan then started to make very sinister remarks about the weather, had we noticed how high the level of the North Sea had risen, how the strengthening wind had gone to the north and that the spring tides were at hand – while the levels of the Rhine, Waal, Maas and Scheldt were near an all-time low – so reminiscent of February 1953, didn't Dessens think?

'He then demanded that they talked to a minister or ministers with the power and courage to make decisions and not a snivelling time-server bent only on preserving his own miserable political career, which was, I thought, a bit hard on Bernhard.

'Riordan then said that, to display their displeasure at this wholly unnecessary hiatus in negotiations, they would detonate one of several devices they had placed in public buildings in the capital. Here the two of them had a whispered conference and then Riordan announced that they had chosen the royal palace and defied anyone to find the explosives before they went off. No lives, he said, were at risk in this explosion, which would occur within five minutes of their departure. He added, almost as an afterthought, that any attempt to restrain them, hinder their departure or have them followed would inevitably mean that the Oostlijk–Flevoland dyke would go not at midnight but at nine o'clock this evening. On this happy note, they left. The palace explosion, as you may know, duly occurred.'

'So I believe.' It seemed the wrong moment to tell de Graaf that it was he, van Effen, who had pressed the button. He shivered and moved to a less damp patch on the Esfahan. 'I think I'm getting pneumonia.'

'There's brandy.' De Graaf waved a hand at once indicative of preoccupation and irritation that one should be unaware of the universal specifics against pneumococci. 'Schnapps, scotch –' He broke off as a knock came on the library door and a uniformed policeman admitted George and Vasco who were, if anything, even more saturated than van Effen had been. 'Two more advanced cases, I suppose.'

George said: 'I beg your pardon, Colonel?'

'Pneumonia. Help yourselves. I must say I wasn't expecting you gentlemen.'

'The Lieutenant said –'

'I know. It just slipped his memory.'

'I have a lot on my mind,' van Effen said. 'Well?'

'We had a good look at them when they left the house to go to that small bus. Also had a good look at them in the Dam Square. Recognize them anywhere.' George paused reflectively. 'Seemed a very harmless bunch to me.'

'Ever seen – or seen pictures of – the youthful assassins that made up the Baader-Meinhof gang? All they lacked were harps and haloes. When I said "Well", that wasn't what I meant.'

'Ah! That. Yes. Well.' George seemed slightly embarrassed. 'When you left the house – we saw you go but didn't approach you as you'd asked us not to in case you were being followed – you know you *were* followed?'

'Yes.'

'We waited across the street for ten minutes then crossed to the lighted window. The rain! Talk about standing under Niagara Falls.' He waited for sympathetic comment and when none came went on: 'Waited another ten minutes. We could hear music and conversation.'

'I'll bet you could. So then, overcome by the rain, impatience or suspicion, you moved in. Light still on. Long-playing cassette on a recorder. Birds flown by the back door. Hardly original. So we still don't know where they're holed up. Not your fault – Agnelli's obsessed by security.'

'Still could have done better,' Vasco said. 'Next time –'

The phone bell shrilled and de Graaf picked it up, listened for some time, said 'Wait a minute, sir' and cupped the mouthpiece. 'Predictable, I suppose. Dessens. Seems the cabinet is a bit shaken about the palace explosion and are convinced that the Oostlijk–Flevoland dyke will go up at midnight. So they're going to parley. They want me along and suggested 11 p.m. I'd like you to be there. 11 p.m.?'

'Eleven-thirty possible sir? I have a couple of appointments.'

De Graaf talked some more then hung up. 'You do seem to

173

have a very crowded appointment book, Lieutenant. I can't
recall your mentioning any of this to me.'

'I haven't had a chance to. I have to be at the Trianon at ten
o'clock to take a call from Agnelli. He's a bit short of explosives
and I've promised to supply him with some.'

'Explosives. Of course. Naturally.' De Graaf hardly spilled a
drop as he poured himself a brandy. 'Having already blown up
the palace' – it was an exaggeration but a pardonable one in the
circumstances – 'one could not expect you to rest on such
trifling laurels. And where do you intend to find this explosive?
I'm sure you won't be wanting more than a few hundred kilos of
TNT or whatever it is.'

'Me? Haven't the time. Haven't the authority, either. But I
thought, perhaps, sir, if you would care to use your influence –'

'Me! The chief of police? To supply illegally-come-by explosives to a group of terrorists?' De Graaf considered. 'I suppose
you would expect me to deliver it personally?'

'Good heavens, no. That's where George comes in. Sorry,
George, haven't had the chance to explain this or anything. Had
a long talk this evening with Agnelli about you and Vasco. I'm
afraid, Vasco, that I've blackened your character beyond all
hopes of redemption. You're a crooked cop, bent as a horse-
shoe, untrustworthy, unpredictable and only a couple of steps
removed from a psychiatric ward. Agnelli was just that little bit
too casual when asking questions about you. I'm certain he
knows you are or were a cop. He comes from Utrecht too. Not
that that should be any bar to his employing you – after we've
made certain delicate alterations to your appearance and history
– in the not-too-distant future.

'George, you're an arms dealer. Heaven knows there are
enough of those around, but you're something special. The
king-pin. Mr Big. A Leopard tank? A SAM missile? Even a
motor torpedo boat? George is your man. And being Mr Big
means you're important. You talk only to principals. No
intermediaries, not even me. Face to face or no deal.'

'I talk to this Agnelli?' George smiled widely. 'You want me
on the inside?'

'I have a feeling that I could do with a little help, sooner

174

rather than later. I've no right to ask you, of course. There's Annelise and your kids. Things might get a little difficult –'

'A little difficult!' De Graaf could put a nicely sarcastic edge to his voice when he had a mind to. 'Difficult. I don't say it's crazy because nothing's crazy if there's a chance, but I don't like it at all. It's based on the assumption that they're not on to you and that's an unjustifiable assumption. Sure, they've gone along with you so far and you with them, but that's only because, so far, it's suited you both. But if they are on to you and they decide a time has come when you're of no further use to them, then when the time comes to discard you it may be in a pretty permanent fashion. Have you the right to ask that of George?'

'I've just done that.'

The phone rang again and de Graaf picked it up. 'Ah. Lieutenant Valken . . . Yes, yes.' De Graaf's face became very still as he listened. 'Never mind if you've never heard it before. Wait till I get a piece of paper and pen.' De Graaf wrote down a few words, told Valken goodbye and hung up. He reached for his glass.

Van Effen said: 'Julie, Annemarie?'

'Yes. How do you know?'

'Valken, your face, brandy. Bad?'

'Bad enough. Phone call from the brothers. They say the girls are as well as can be expected which can mean anything or nothing. They also say they've sent a telegram of condolences to Rotterdam.' He'd picked up the piece of paper he'd scribbled on. 'To David Joseph Karlmann Meijer.'

Van Effen sipped his brandy and said nothing. George and Vasco exchanged glances of incomprehension. At length George said: 'And who might he be?'

'I forgot,' de Graaf said. 'You don't know, of course. Anne's – Annemarie's – father.'

'Yes,' George said. 'I mean no. I don't understand, Colonel. What about Annemarie?'

De Graaf stared incredulously at van Effen. 'You mean, you haven't told them?'

'I don't believe I have.'

'Good God!' De Graaf shook his head. 'The need-to-know

principle, I suppose. One of those days, Peter, you're going to forget to remind yourself of something and that will be the end of you.' De Graaf looked from George to Vasco. 'Annemarie and Julie – Lieutenant van Effen's sister – have been kidnapped. The Annecy brothers.'

'The Annecy brothers.' George was silent for a moment. 'Those murderous fiends. You put two of them away for fifteen years.'

'Correction. Lieutenant van Effen put them away and the two that escaped have been threatening to get him ever since. They've gone one better. They've got Julie.'

'I know Julie well. And what's the significance of this message to Annemarie's father?'

'The significance lies in her father. You will find it hard to believe, George, but the father of that fearful frump who used to frequent La Caracha is one of the wealthiest men in the Netherlands. Maybe the wealthiest. And a very powerful man. He has the ear of the government. He's in a position rather similar to Dassault, the plane maker, in France. There are some areas in which they don't move without consulting him at first or, at least, listening to what he says. He has power and wealth and a daughter and now they have the daughter and may well turn his power and wealth to their own advantage. Anne Meijer is any criminal's dream hostage come true.'

Van Effen put down his glass and looked at his watch. 'It's time, George.'

'God in heaven! I don't believe it. You look at your damned watch and say it's time to go. Doesn't it occur to you to wonder how in the hell they got that information about David Meijer.'

'Some sort of persuasion, I suppose.'

'Persuasion! Torture. They tortured the poor girl!'

'What poor girl?'

'Are you all right, Lieutenant? Annemarie, of course.'

The shake of van Effen's head was very positive. 'No. Not Annemarie. The Annecy brothers – or at least the two we put away – never tortured without a reason, however twisted that reason might be. The reason was either revenge or to get information. Why should they revenge themselves on Annemarie – what has she ever done to anyone? And information – what information could they possibly get from her. They don't know who she is, who her father is. Didn't, rather. As far as they are concerned she's only a friend of Julie's and they took her along for no reason other than the fact that she happened to be there. If they tortured anybody – and I suspect it was only a threat of torture, to get information about me – it would have been Julie. My guess is that Annemarie volunteered that information about herself as a sop to the Annecys, to turn their minds to the thought of unlimited ransom money – maybe she even mentioned her father's influence with the government although people like the Annecys would almost certainly have been aware of that anyway – anything to distract attention from Julie. Annemarie's no fool – if she were, I wouldn't have brought her up from Rotterdam. She knows that the Annecys of this world are above all pragmatists and that anything that would further their plans would be of a great deal more interest to them than hurting me by proxy.'

'Cold-blooded fish,' de Graaf muttered.

'Pardon, sir?'

'You could be right or you could be wrong. Damage both ways. If you're right the Annecys' hands have been greatly strengthened and David Meijer's pocket almost certainly lightened, or will be in the very near future. If you're wrong, you're putting your head in that charming hangman's noose that the Annecy brothers put on their postcards. If you're wrong she'd have talked of many things, principally that Stephan Danilov is Peter van Effen. I can't take the chance that you're not wrong. My orders are that you are not to go through with this.'

George said: 'Normally, Colonel, I wouldn't dream of not complying with your wishes. But these aren't normal circumstances. By refusing your request, I'm not stepping outside the law nor am I making the point that I'm no longer a policeman. I'm just going my own way.'

De Graaf nodded. 'I can't stop *you*. But I can –'

'You can force him to go his own way, too,' George said. 'By resigning. You'd never forgive yourself, Colonel.'

177

De Graaf scowled, refilled his glass, sank into an armchair and gazed into the fire. Van Effen nodded to Vasco and the three men left the room.

Van Effen and George returned to the Trianon to find that the usual watch-dog was not in his usual place. But there was another and, if possible, even more insignificant character seated some distance from the desk and sipping beer instead of jonge jenever. Van Effen had no doubt that this was a replacement from the same stable. The manager called to them as they passed the desk.

'This message has just come for you, Mr Danilov.' He handed van Effen a slip of paper which read: 'May I see you in your room? Two minutes.'

'Yes, of course. Thank you.' Van Effen folded the paper into his pocket and led George to the lift. The promised two minutes later the manager arrived in van Effen's room. He closed the door behind him, looked doubtfully at George and seemed to hesitate.

'No problem,' van Effen said. 'My friend here is on the side of the angels. George, Charles. The manager. Charles, George. George is police.'

'Ah. A word of warning, Lieutenant. I wouldn't use the back entrance tonight – somebody, a stranger to anyone round here – has taken up more or less permanent residence by the back door. He's in an old DAF. And you will have noticed that your old looker-after in the lobby has been replaced by an even more obvious one. There's another man who has just started a meal in the dining-room. He's seated conveniently by the door so that he can see anyone who crosses the lobby. He knows the new shadow. No words exchanged, just a brief look and an even briefer nod. No risk in that, they must have thought – they have no reason to suspect my interest in them. That's why I waited two minutes, to see if either of them made a move. No disappointment – our dining-room friend was at the public phone almost before the lift doors closed behind you. I waited until he finished his call to whatever person he was reporting your arrival. I was watching them from the mirror as the diner left the booth. Brief nod again, no words.'

'When you go bankrupt, Charles, apply to me any time. I'll watch the bogeymen.' The manager left.

'So,' George said. 'We can expect that phone call any minute now. The man in the restaurant has tipped off Agnelli that Stephan Danilov has returned accompanied by George, the explosives expert and illegal arms supplier. One wonders what lions' den or nest of cobras they've chosen for the rendezvous.'

'I don't wonder. There are no lions or cobras in Room 203, which is where we are. Charles tells us that Agnelli – it can only be Agnelli – has two other faithful but not very bright henchmen lurking around the place. Why? Surely it only required one stake-out, the one in the lobby, to advise him of our arrival. The other two are guards, parts of his insurance policy – don't forget Agnelli has no reason to think that we know of their presence. There may even be others that Charles knows nothing about. This is the last place that we would think would be chosen as a meeting point – or so Agnelli must imagine – and so we wouldn't think of arranging a reception committee here. And when he does call, you can be sure that he will announce that he will be here in a matter of minutes so that we can't have the time to arrange one.'

Van Effen was right on both points. Agnelli called in person to say that they would meet at the Trianon and that he and his friends would be there in under five minutes.

'He's bringing friends, plural,' van Effen said after he had hung up. 'I don't think Romero Agnelli trusts anyone.'

From the cordial, guileless expression Agnelli wore on his arrival, one could see that van Effen was wrong; here, patently, was a man one could trust anywhere. Agnelli had brought three men along with him. His brother Leonardo, looking, if that were possible, an even more genial member of the Mafioso than he had done the last time, and two others whom van Effen had never seen before. One of them, a burly, slightly florid, pleasant-featured character of indeterminate age – somewhere between forty and fifty, van Effen would have guessed, but it was difficult to be sure – was introduced as Liam O'Brien: from his accent, no less than from his name, he had to be Irish. The other, a handsome young man, dark and slightly swarthy, was introduced as Heinrich Daniken: he could have been of any nationality. Agnelli did not see fit to disclose what the function of either man was.

Introductions over, refreshments proffered and accepted, Agnelli said to George: 'Do I call you George or do you have another name?'

'Just George.' He smiled. 'I'm an anonymous person.'

Agnelli surveyed the vast bulk before him. 'You, George, are the least anonymous-looking person I've ever seen. Don't you find it rather a drawback in your profession? Whatever that may be, of course.'

'Drawback? It's a positive advantage. I'm a peace-loving man who abhors violence but when you're as big as I am no one ever offers it to you.' George, van Effen thought admiringly, was as consummate and convincing a liar as he'd ever known. 'And, of course, everybody, or nearly everybody – I think particularly of those who are sworn to uphold the law – think that everyone who is as big, fat, cheerful and harmless as I am, must be able to get by very well without being able to think. It's a kind of law of nature. Well, I'm no Einstein, but I'm not yet ready to be locked away in an institution for the retarded. But we haven't met here to discuss personalities, Mr Agnelli, have we? Five questions. What do you want? How much or how many? When? Where? Price?'

The slipping of Agnelli's good-humoured smile was so momentary that only the most alert or observant would have noticed it and even then it could have been as much imagined as seen. 'You do get to the point rather quickly, don't you, George? No time for the little business niceties, I see. Well, that's the way I prefer it myself. Like you, I have no time for beating about the bush: like you, I regard myself as a business man.' He produced a paper from an inside pocket. 'Here's my shopping list. Fairly comprehensive, is it not?'

George studied it briefly. 'Fairly. Well within my limited capacities, I should think. Most of the items are straightforward, especially the explosives. The ground-to-ground wire-guided missiles – these will be anti-tank missiles, although you don't say so – and the SAM ground-to-air missiles are also easily come by, as are the plastic mines, grenades and smoke-bombs.' He paused, sipped some brandy and frowned. 'Something here I don't quite understand, don't even like. I'm not talking about the fact that you seem to be preparing to wage a limited war, even although only a defensive one: that's none of my business.' He handed the list over to van Effen. 'Comment?'

Van Effen studied it for no longer a time than it had taken George then returned the list. 'Specifications.'

'Exactly.' George, not smiling, looked at the four men in turn then concentrated his gaze on Agnelli. 'This is a lethal enough list as it is. But it could be dangerous in other ways, even suicidal, if it got into the hands of whoever prepared this list.'

Agnelli wasn't smiling either. He looked more than slightly uncomfortable. 'I'm afraid I don't understand.'

'Then I'd better enlighten you. Specifications, as my friend Stephan has said. Explosives – no specifications. Missiles, ditto – and that applies to both types. What kind of primers? What kind of detonators? Fuses – you don't even say whether wire or chemical, how slow-burning or fast-acting. No explosives expert ever composed this list. Some amateur did, some bungling incompetent. Who?'

Agnelli studied his glass for some time then said: 'I'm the incompetent. But I did get some bungling help from my three associates here.'

'God help us all,' van Effen said. 'You're not fit to be let loose with a box of kiddies' fireworks. I have to ask you, not for the first time, where the hell are your experts?'

Agnelli smiled ruefully and spread out his hands. 'I'll be perfectly frank with you.' Romero Agnelli, van Effen realized, was about to lie in his teeth. 'We are temporarily embarrassed. The two men on whom we rely have been called away for other duties and won't be back for a couple of days. But we thought – well, you gentlemen are both explosives experts and –'

'That's no problem,' George said. 'We know what to get and

181

can give you simple instructions on how to use them without blowing your silly heads off. The missiles are a different matter. Only a trained man can fire one of those.'

'How long does that take?'

'A week. Ten days.' George was vastly exaggerating, van Effen knew, but the four men's patent ignorance of all things military was so extensive that it was very likely a safe exaggeration. 'And don't ask us, we're no military men, we're no more skilled in those matters than you are.'

Agnelli was silent for some time then said abruptly: 'Do you know of anyone who is. Skilled in such matters, I mean?'

'Do you mean what I think you mean?'

'Yes.'

'I do.' The way George said 'I do', in a tone just one degree short of impatience, made it clear that it was quite inevitable that he should know.

'Who?'

George gave him a look of pity. 'He hasn't got a name.'

'You must call him something.'

'The Lieutenant.'

'Why?'

'Because he is a lieutenant.'

'Cashiered, of course.'

'Certainly not. A cashiered lieutenant is no good to me. I thought you would appreciate that a person like myself can only operate at second or third hand. A middleman, if you like. Or two.'

'Ah! I see. Your supplier?'

'Mr Agnelli. You can't possibly be so naive as to expect me to answer so naive a question. I'll see what can be done. Where do you want this stuff delivered?'

'That depends on how soon you can deliver it.'

'By noon tomorrow.'

'Good heavens!' Agnelli looked incredulous then smiled. 'It looks as if I've come to the right shop. How will it be delivered?'

'By Army truck, of course.'

'Of course.' Agnelli looked slightly dazed. 'This makes things a bit difficult. I thought it would be at least the day after tomorrow. Could I call up tomorrow to finalize time and place? And could you hold up delivery for at least a few hours?'

'That can be arranged.' George looked at van Effen. 'Mr Agnelli can call here? 10 a.m., say?' Van Effen nodded and George smiled at Agnelli. 'Can't say yet, but somewhere between ten and twelve thousand dollars. We offer the best discount rates in Europe. Dollars, guilders or deutschmarks. More, of course, if our – ah – services are required.'

Agnelli stood up and smiled, his old relaxed and genial self again. 'Of course. The price, I must say, doesn't seem too exorbitant.'

'One thing,' van Effen said pleasantly. 'You are aware, aren't you, Mr Agnelli, that if I moved to another hotel and registered there under another name, that the chances of your ever finding either of us again would be remote?'

'Remote? They wouldn't exist.' Agnelli was frowning. 'Why ever should you mention such a thing?'

'Well, a state of mutual trust does exist between us, doesn't it?'

'Naturally.' The puzzlement still there.

'Well, if it does, call off the watchdogs in the lobby, in the dining-room and outside.'

'My watchdogs?' From the expression on Agnelli's face one could see that, far from being baffled, he was stalling for time.

'If you don't, we'll throw them into the canal – suitably trussed of course – and then move on.'

Agnelli looked at him, his face for once expressionless. 'You do play for keeps, don't you? I really believe you would.' He smiled and put out his hand. 'Shame. Very well, watchdogs retired. Shame. But they really weren't up to it.'

When they had gone, van Effen said to George: 'You really should have taken up a life of crime. Too late now. Anyway, you'd have given Colonel de Graaf apoplexy years ago. I'll bet Annelise has no idea quite how splendid a liar you are. You have Agnelli hooked, outfoxed, outgunned and demoralized, not to say dependent: at least, let's hope so. Will you talk to Vasco later this evening and tell him that you've got an offer of employment for him in the capacity of an army lieutenant – after, of course, he's made suitable alterations to his appearance? We mustn't forget that Agnelli has had the opportunity of studying Vasco at close range.'

'There'll be no problem.' George handed over Agnelli's shopping list. 'I'd give a great deal to see the Colonel's face when he sees what he's got to go shopping for in the morning. You'll be seeing him, I take it, in an hour or so. Has it occurred to you that Agnelli might very well be there along with Riordan and this fellow Samuelson?'

'It's an intriguing thought and, yes, it has occurred.'

'Well?'

'Well, what?'

'Well, what, he asks. We *know* that Agnelli is Annecy.'

'We're ninety-nine per cent certain. Don't forget that I never saw either of the two Annecy brothers that we didn't manage to catch and put away.'

'The fact that you don't know him doesn't mean he doesn't know you, of course he does – he must have seen your picture in the papers many times during the period of the arrest and trial. How do you think he's going to react when he sees before him not only the dreaded Lieutenant van Effen but the dreaded lieutenant whose sister he's got tucked away in some dungeon, the sister who, for all you know, he spends his leisure time with, testing out the latest model in thumb-screws?'

'Should be interesting.'

'Colonel de Graaf was right,' George muttered. 'You belong a hundred fathoms down. Just a cold-blooded fish.'

' "Your ten cents will help to kill a British soldier. It's a bargain at the price – the best bargain you'll ever get." That's what the collectors say when they go around rattling their damn tin cans in the Irish bars in the United States. Especially in the Irish bars in the north-east states. Especially in New York. Most especially of all in the borough of Queens where the Irish are thickest on the ground. Ten cents. That's all they ask, just ten cents. And, of course, they rattle their cans whenever they hold Irish nights, Irish dances, Irish raffles, Irish whatever you like.

184

'If you've never heard that there are charitable organizations – charitable they call themselves – which collect for arms, then you live in another century or with your head in the sands. They claim that the millions of dollars that they've collected over the years have gone to support the widows and orphans of the IRA members foully slain by the murderous British. Support widows and orphans! The founder of one such evil organization once made the mistake of telling the truth when he said: "The more British soldiers that are sent back from Ulster in their coffins, the better." Jack Lynch, a former Irish premier, has gone on record as saying that the money is intended for one purpose only – to *make* widows and orphans. British widows and orphans.'

Riordan, an abnormally tall, abnormally thin man, black-haired, deeply tanned and dressed in a near-ankle-length black raincoat which served only to heighten the looming angularity of the man, was literally shaking with rage as he stood facing his audience, his fists ivory-knuckled on the table before him. His sincerity and outrage were unquestionable, his intensity almost terrifying.

'God knows it's bad enough that the contributions to these infamous organizations should come from honest, God-fearing, intensely religious Catholics who are duped into thinking they are contributing to a worthy cause instead of some damnable crew who make Murder Incorporated look like innocent children playing in a kindergarden. The money goes directly to dedicated IRA operatives. Some of it is used to buy guns at black-market sales in New York itself, auctions usually held in razed areas or empty car parks, always by night, nearly always in the Bronx, Queens or Brooklyn. Guns, gentlemen, are rather easily come by in the fair city of New York.' In the depth of his bitterness, Riordan almost spat the words out. 'The rest of the money is used by other operatives who openly travel to the southern and mid-western states where gun permits do not exist. Wherever the guns come from, they all end up in the New York area from where they are shipped out, almost always from New Jersey or Brooklyn, with the warm encouragement and complicity of the stevedore unions and the upright US customs, many of whom are first or second generation Irish and feel blood-brothers to the murderous IRA. As the Customs Service is controlled by the US Treasury Department, it is logical to suppose that those dealers in death operate with the cognisance if not the connivance of the US Government. The Irish influence in Congress is as well known as it is remarkably powerful.'

'A moment, Mr Riordan, if you would.' The interruption came from Aaron Wieringa, the Minister of Defence, a big, florid, blue-eyed and very calm man, a man immensely respected throughout the country and one who would very likely have become premier quite some years ago if he had not been cursed with the unfortunate and crippling handicap, for a politician, of total incorruptibility. 'One appreciates – one can hardly fail to appreciate – that you are a very angry man. We are not, I assure you, nineteenth-century ostriches and I think it would be true to say that there is not a man in this room who does not understand that your fury is totally justifiable. I would not go so far as to concur in your condemnation of Washington and Congress, but that, in the current and particular circumstances, is by the by. Your opinion, as distinct from your recital of verifiable facts, is not of immediate concern.

'What is of immediate concern is why your wrath has seen fit to focus itself on our unfortunate country in general and the city of Amsterdam in particular. I cannot, at the moment, even begin to fathom the reason for it, although I am certain we will not be left in ignorance for long. But nothing you have said so far begins to justify your attempt to blackmail us into acting as intermediary between you and the British Government. I appreciate that you may have, and very probably do have, very powerful reasons for wanting all British troops to withdraw from Northern Ireland, but how you can possibly imagine that we have the ability to persuade Britain to accede to your preposterous demands quite passes my understanding. No conceivable reason exists why they should so accede.'

'A totally conceivable reason exists. Humanitarian motives. Humanitarian motives on your part and on theirs.'

'Our respective governments would be reluctant to see the

Netherlands flooded and countless thousands – maybe hundreds of thousands – drowned in those floods? Before even considering such matters, an answer to my question, please. Why us? Is it that, because of our particular geographical situation, we are peculiarly susceptible to threats of genocide?'

'You have been chosen because Amsterdam is the linchpin in the whole lethal gun-running operation. It is the gun-running centre of Northern Europe and has been for years, just as it has been the heroin centre of Northern Europe. This knowledge is in the public domain, and the continued existence of those two evil practices can only bespeak a deep level of corruption in both government and law-enforcement levels.' An indignant-looking Mr Wieringa made to interrupt but Riordan imperiously gestured him to silence. 'There are, it is true, other towns engaged in gun-running, notably Antwerp, but, compared to Amsterdam, Antwerp operates in a minor league.'

This time Mr Wieringa, speaking in almost a shout which was unknown for him, would not be gainsaid. 'You mean you would find it impossible to flood Belgium.'

Riordan carried on as if he had heard nothing. 'Not all the guns passing through Amsterdam go to Eire, of course. Some go to the RAF. Others go to –'

'The RAF!' It was, almost inevitably, Bernhard Dessens, the Jusice Minister, who rarely if ever contributed anything of significance to any discussion. 'You suggest that the British Air Force is supplied –'

'Be quiet, you idiot.' Riordan, it seemed, could descend below the rhetorical level he usually set for himself. 'I refer to the Red Army Faction, the inheritors of the bloody mantle of the Baader-Meinhof gangsters of the early seventies. Some go to the Sicilian-controlled Mafia-type criminal organizations that are springing up all over Western Germany. But the bulk goes to Eire.

'Do you know what it's like in Northern Ireland, Mr Minister?' Nobody bothered to follow his line of vision to know that he was addressing the Minister of Defence and not the Minister of Justice. 'Can you imagine the hellish conditions that exist there, the hideous tortures practised by both the IRA and UVF, the homicidal insanity that has ruled there for fourteen years? A country ruled by fear that is tearing it to pieces. Northern Ireland will never be governed by representatives of the two communities, Protestant and Catholic working together, because they are far too bitterly divided by religion and, to a lesser extent, race. There are one and a half million people living together in a small area, but in spite of their divisions ninety-nine point nine per cent on either side have never harmed anyone or ever wished to. That ninety-nine point nine per cent on either side are united in only one thing – in abhorring terrorism and in their desire to live only in peace. It is a desire that, as matters stand, can never be realized. Conventional politicians, with all the faults and frailties of their kind, are still those who observe the conventions. In Ulster, conventional politicians are an extinct breed. Moderation has ceased to exist. Demagogues and gunmen rule. The country is ruled by a handful of crazed murderers.'

Riordan paused for the first time, probably as much for breath as anything else, but no one seemed inclined to take advantage of the hiatus.

'But murderers, even crazed murderers, must have their murder weapons, must they not?' Riordan said. 'And so the murder weapons are shipped from Amsterdam, usually, but not always, inside furniture. The weapons are sealed in containers, of course, and if the Amsterdam customs are unaware of this they must be the worst, the blindest, or the most corrupt and avaricious in Europe. Nine times out of ten, the ships unload in Dublin. How they – the containers, I mean – get past the Dublin customs I don't profess to know but I don't think there's any question of collusion – if there were the customs wouldn't have turned up a million dollars' worth of illegally imported arms destined for the IRA four years ago. But most of the guns do get through. From Dublin the arms containers variously labelled, but popularly as household goods, are trucked to a warehouse in County Monaghan and from there to a horticultural nursery in County Louth. Don't ask me how I know but it would be rather difficult not to know: the people thereabouts know but don't talk. From there the weapons are taken to Northern Ireland, not smuggled over the border in the middle of the night by daredevil IRA members, but brought in during daylight hours in cars driven by women, mostly young, surrounded by laughing kids. All very innocuous.

'It's a long, long way from where a machine-pistol is purchased in a mid-Western state until it's in the hands of some maniacal killer crouched in the shadows of some back street in Belfast or Londonderry. A long way. But in all that long way the vital stage, the focal point, the nodal point, the venturi in the funnel, is Amsterdam. And so we have come to Amsterdam.' Riordan sat down.

The breaking of the ensuing silence was far from immediate. There were, altogether, eight men in Dessen's luxurious lounge. Three men had accompanied Riordan to the Minister of Justice's house – Samuelson, whom de Graaf had described to van Effen, O'Brien, who had come to the Trianon, and Agnelli, the man who George had forecast would be there. Samuelson and O'Brien probably thought there was nothing they could profitably add to what Riordan had said and Agnelli had probably yet to recover his full powers of speech. When he had entered the room and seen van Effen, appearance returned to normal, sitting there, his eyes had momentarily widened, his lips momentarily parted and a slight but noticeable amount of colour had left his cheeks, and not momentarily either. Almost certainly van Effen was the only person who had noticed the fleeting sea-change that had overcome Agnelli, but, then, probably, van Effen had been the only person who had been looking for it.

There were also four men on the other side of the negotiating table; the two ministers, de Graaf and van Effen, and they had nothing immediately to say either, and this for two excellent reasons: there was nothing they could immediately say that would be in any way helpful and all had to admit to themselves that Riordan had expressed his viewpoint with a certain degree of logical persuasion, however unreasonable, threatening and preposterous his accompanying demands might have been. It was Aaron Wieringa, glancing in turn at each of his three companions, who broke the silence.

'Before I speak, gentlemen, have any of you any comment to make?'

Van Effen said: 'I have.'

'Lieutenant?'

'Mr Riordan has been surprisingly reticent about one thing. He hasn't said *why* he wants all British influence removed from Northern Ireland. If we are to negotiate on his behalf I think we should have the right to know something of his motivation, his intentions. It may be that his intentions are so awful, so appalling, that we would risk any disaster to our country sooner than comply with his wishes. We have, of course, no reason to believe that Mr Riordan will tell us the truth.'

'The point is well taken,' Wieringa said. 'Well, Mr Riordan?'

'There's no point in swearing that I'll tell the truth, because any liar would say the same.' Riordan had again risen to his menacing height, he seemed to find talking easier that way. 'I have talked about the ninety-nine point nine per cent of good and decent people in that war-torn country who are utterly dominated by the point one per cent of those maniacal killers. Our sole objective is to eliminate this point one per cent and enable the people of Ulster to resolve their own future in an atmosphere of calm and peace and quiet and hope.'

'Elimination?' Wieringa said cautiously. 'What precisely do you mean by that?'

'We will exterminate the evil bastards on both sides. We will excise the cancer. Is that blunt enough for you?' Riordan sat down.

'It sounds like a high purpose,' van Effen said. He made no attempt to disguise the contemptuous disbelief in his voice. 'Noble and humane. Let them resolve their own future. Hardly ties in, does it, with your earlier statement that Northern Ireland will never be governed by representatives of the two communities? Has it not occurred to you that if the most conceivably rabid IRA leader were sitting in that chair he would talk exactly as you are talking now, in order to achieve the same end as you are seeking – to get the British out of Northern Ireland at all costs. What assurance do we have that you are not, in fact, that rabid IRA leader?'

'You have none.' This time Riordan had not risen from his chair and his voice was remarkably calm. 'I can do no more. If you cannot see that I detest the IRA and all its manifestations, you must be blind. I am so appalled at the suggestion that I cannot easily find words to counter it.'

There was another and even longer silence, then Wieringa said: 'I believe one calls this an impasse.'

'Impasse, as you say,' Riordan said. He was still seated, the time for rhetoric had apparently passed. 'But surely there are certain salient factors that should resolve the impasse. Oostlijk –Flevoland, for instance. Leeuwarden. The Noordoost polder. Wieringermeer, Putten, Petten, Schouwen, Walcheren and others. And I did mention that we have the Royal Palace mined?'

'The Palace?' Wieringa said. He didn't seem particularly overcome.

'Tonight's little demonstration was just that. A little demonstration. Just to prove how pathetically easy it is to circumvent your alleged security precautions.'

'Save your breath, Riordan.' Wieringa's voice was curt. No 'Mr' this time. 'The time for threats is past. Only moral considerations remain.'

'Fifty-fifty,' van Effen said.

Wieringa looked at him for some moments, then nodded.

'My way of thinking, too. Thank you, Lieutenant. It is difficult to decide to drown one's country on the basis of a gamble.' He looked at Riordan. 'I am empowered to make decisions. I will call the British ambassador. He will call the Foreign Office in London. We shall make a radio announcement – worded in a suitably cautious fashion, you understand. Those three things I can promise. The outcome of the negotiations, of course, are not for me to predict or influence. That is understood?'

'That is understood. Thank you, Minister.' There was no hint of triumph, not even satisfaction, in Riordan's voice. He stood. 'Your integrity is a byeword throughout Europe. I am content. Goodnight, gentlemen.'

No one wished him goodnight in return.

After the departure of Riordan and his associates there was silence in the room until Wieringa had put through his telephone call. When he had replaced the receiver, he sipped delicately from his brandy glass, smiled and said: 'Comments, gentlemen?' He was a remarkably calm man.

'It's outrageous, disgraceful and dastardly,' Dessens said, loudly and predictably. Now that the need for action and decision-making was over, he was all fire and fury. 'The good name, the honour of the Netherlands lies in the dust.'

'Better, perhaps, than that its citizens should lie under the flood-waters,' Wieringa said. 'Colonel?'

'You had to consider the balance of probabilities,' de Graaf said. 'Your decision, sir, was not only the correct one: it was the inevitable one.'

'Thank you, Colonel. Lieutenant?'

'What can I usefully add, sir?'

'Quite frankly, I don't know. But, according to the Colonel – and it is, I must say, a most handsome admission on his part – you are closer to those villains than anyone else in Amsterdam.' He smiled. 'I do not, of course, use the word "closer" in a pejorative sense.'

'Thank you, sir. I'd hoped not.'

'You're not really very forthcoming, are you, Lieutenant?'

'A certain uncharacteristic diffidence, sir. I may be the senior detective-lieutenant in the city, but I'm pretty junior in this exalted company. What do you want me to be forthcoming about, sir?'

Wieringa regarded the roof and said, almost inconsequentially: 'I had to make a pretty important decision there.' He dropped his gaze and looked at van Effen. 'Did you believe Riordan?'

Van Effen picked up his glass and considered it without drinking from it. He was obviously marshalling his thoughts. Then he said: 'Four points, Minister. There are two things I believe about Riordan, one point I'm not sure whether to believe or disbelieve and a fourth where I definitely disbelieve.'

'Ah! Hence your cryptic remark "fifty-fifty"?'

'I suppose. First, I believe he is definitely not IRA.'

'You do, Lieutenant? In that case, am I not entitled to ask why you pushed him?'

'Confirmation. But I was sure before. That speech of his – that impassioned and violent denunciation of the IRA and all its methods. You'd have to be an exceptional actor to get that amount of hatred into your voice: but you'd have to be an impossibly good one to have a pulse beat like a trip-hammer in your throat.'

'I missed that,' Wieringa said. He looked at de Graaf and Dessens. 'Either of you gentlemen –' He broke off at their mute headshakes.

'Secondly,' continued van Effen, 'I believe that Riordan is not the leader, the driving force, the man in charge. Why do I believe that? I can't give a shred of evidence, of proof. But he's too fiery, too unbalanced, too unpredictable to be a general.'

'You wouldn't fight under him, van Effen?' Wieringa was half-smiling, half curious.

'No, sir. There's someone else. I'm certain it's not Agnelli. I would take long odds it's not O'Brien – he's got sergeant-major written all over him. I'm not saying it's Samuelson. He's an enigma, a mystery. But his presence is totally unexplained and when any presence is as inexplicable as that then a very big explanation would seem to be called for.

'Where I'm uncertain whether to believe his story or not, is about Northern Ireland. Riordan said his only aim was to eliminate the monsters. His voice did carry what might have been regarded as the authentic ring of sincerity and, as I've said, I don't believe he's all that good an actor.' Van Effen sighed briefly, shook his head and sipped his brandy. 'I know this is all rather confusing, gentlemen. Let me put it this way. I believe that he believes what he says, but I don't believe that what he believes is necessarily true. It's one of the reasons why I'm convinced he's not the king-pin. Two things. He was caught outright in a flat contradiction yet appeared to be unaware that any such contradiction existed. Then he seems to be unaware that there could be three sets of fanatics around – the extremist Protestants, the extremist Catholics and the Mediators. That's them. The Mediators could be the most irresponsibly dangerous of all. To achieve the final solution, the Mediators are prepared to drown a million. One could imagine what the final solution would be like in Ulster. No. Let me rephrase that. I can't imagine that.'

'The same thought was in *my* mind.' Wieringa spoke very slowly. 'The very same. Although not so clearly formulated. In my mind, I mean.' He smiled. 'Well, that should be enough for a day – but you did mention that there was something you didn't believe.'

'Yes, sir. I don't believe his threats. His immediate threats, that is. His long-range threats are a different matter. But the ones he mentioned here tonight – and the ones outlined to Colonel de Graaf earlier this evening – I do not believe, with the exception of the threat to Helystad in Oostlijk–Flevoland. The rest I believe to be bluff. Especially the threat to destroy the Palace.'

'If you say that, Lieutenant,' Wieringa said, 'I'm damned if I don't believe you. Why do you say that?'

'Because I don't believe they have any mines laid inside the Palace. They were concerned that the explosion inside the Palace tonight would be heard over a considerable area to convince you that they had, indeed, the ability to carry out their promise.'

Wieringa regarded him with a puzzled expression. 'You sound fairly sure about this, Lieutenant.'

'No, sir. I'm certain.'

'How can you be so sure?'

'I have inside information.'

Wieringa looked at him in a speculative fashion but said nothing. Not so Dessens. He had been totally out of his depth all evening but now he thought he was on secure and known footing and that it was time to assert himself.

"What were the sources of your information, Lieutenant?'

'That's confidential.'

'Confidential!' Whether the source of Dessens' immediate anger was due to the reply or the fact that van Effen had omitted the mandatory 'minister' or 'sir' was difficult to say: he probably didn't know himself. 'Confidential!'

194

'I'm trying to be discreet, sir, that's all. I don't want to divulge my sources because it may cause acute and unnecessary embarrassment. Surely you can understand that – it's so commonplace in the police world that it's hardly worth the mentioning. Why don't you just take my word for it?'

'Understand it! Commonplace! Take your word!' Dessens' mottling complexion was rapidly assuming the hue of a turkey wattle. 'You arrogant – you arrogant – you –' He made a visible effort to ward off the onset of apoplexy. 'I would remind you, Lieutenant' – he put a heavy accent on the word 'Lieutenant' – 'that I am the Minister of Justice' – he put a very heavy accent on that, too – 'whereas you are only a junior officer in the force which I personally –'

'That's unfair, sir.' De Graaf's voice was impersonal. 'Next to me, van Effen is the senior police officer in the city of –'

'Keep out of this, de Graaf.' Dessens tried to let ice creep into his voice but his temperature control had slipped. 'Van Effen! You heard me.'

'I heard you,' van Effen said, then added 'sir' almost as an afterthought. 'I know what I'm talking about because I'm the person who placed that charge in the cellars of the Royal Palace.'

'What! What!' Dessens' complexion would now have made any turkey-cock look to his laurels. 'Good God! I can't believe it.' He was halfway out of his chair. 'My ears deceive me!'

'They don't. Sir. I was also the person who pressed the button that detonated the explosives.'

Dessens said nothing, not immediately. The shocked horror of this threat to the safety of the royal family, this dreadful *lèse-majesté*, held him in thrall. Van Effen returned to his brandy and made no attempt to keep his opinion of the Minister of Justice out of his face.

'Arrest this man, de Graaf,' Dessens shouted. 'This moment!'

'On what charges, sir?'

'On what charges! Have you gone mad as well as – as well as – Treason, man, treason!'

'Yes, sir. This raises problems.'

195

'Problems? Your duty, man, your duty!'

'Problems, sir. I'm the city's Chief of Police. All other policemen in Amsterdam are junior to me.' Every century of de Graaf's aristocratic lineage was showing. 'Nobody in Amsterdam has the authority to arrest me.'

Dessens stared at him, his anger gradually changing to bewilderment. He shook his head and said nothing.

'What I mean is, sir, that if Lieutenant van Effen is to be locked up on a treason charge, then you'd have to lock me up, too, because I'm as much a traitor as he is.' De Graaf considered. 'More, I would say. I am, after all, his superior; moreover, I personally authorized and approved every action the Lieutenant has undertaken.' Inconsequentially, it seemed, but probably to give Dessens time to readjust, de Graaf turned to van Effen and said: 'You forgot to tell me that you personally had detonated those explosives.'

Van Effen shrugged apologetic shoulders. 'You know how it is, sir.'

'I know,' de Graaf said heavily. 'You have so much on your mind. You seem to have told me that before.'

'Why have you stepped outside the law, Colonel?' There was no reproof in Wieringa's voice, only a question. Wieringa had remained remarkably unperturbed.

'We did not step outside the law, sir. We are doing and have done everything in our power to uphold the law. We – Lieutenant van Effen – have gained the entrée – and a highly dangerous entrée it is – into the ranks of the FFF. I think it is more than dangerous, it's close to suicidal. But Lieutenant van Effen has persuaded me – and I most reluctantly agree with him – that it's our last best hope. Our only hope.'

Dessens looked at the two policemen dazedly but his mind was beginning to function again, at least after a fashion. 'How is this possible? Van Effen's face must be known to every criminal in Amsterdam.' He had forgotten how junior van Effen had been only moments ago.

'It is. But not the van Effen you see before you. His appearance, voice and personality have changed to such a remarkable extent that I'd wager my pension that neither of you would recognize Stephan Danilov, which is the pseudonym he has temporarily and conveniently adopted.' He might have wagered something else, van Effen reflected; de Graaf was so wealthy that his pension was a matter of total indifference to him. 'Whether the FFF have uncritically accepted Stephan Danilov at his face value, we have no means of knowing. It seems incredible to me that, so far, they appear to have done. If they have not done or will not do so the city of Amsterdam will be requiring a new senior detective-lieutenant. They will also be requiring a new police chief, which the Lieutenant will probably regard as a trifling matter, because I shall have to resign. The Netherlands, of course, will be looking for a new Minister of Justice, because you, Mr Dessens, are also a party to this. Only Mr Wieringa can look forward to a safe tenure.'

Dessens looked stricken. 'I haven't said that I'm a party to anything.'

Wieringa took him gently by the arm. 'Bernhard, if you would, a word in your ear.' They walked away to a distant corner of the lounge, which was fortunately as large as it was luxurious, and began to converse in low terms. Wieringa appeared to be doing most of the conversing.

Van Effen said: 'What weighty matters do you think our revered cabinet ministers are discussing?'

De Graaf forgot to reproach van Effen for his unseemly and unconstitutional levity. 'No prizes for guessing that. Mr Wieringa is explaining to Mr Dessens the principle of Hobson's choice. If Dessens doesn't go along, the Netherlands is still going to be looking for a new Minister of Justice. If Dessens hadn't forced you to divulge your confidential information he wouldn't have found himself in the impossible situation he does now. Hoisted, to coin a phrase, on his own petard.' De Graaf seemed to find it a moderately entertaining thought. He settled himself comfortably in his chair, sighed and reached out for the brandy bottle. 'Well, thank heaven everything's over for the day.'

Van Effen considerately let de Graaf pour himself some brandy and sip it before producing Agnelli's shopping list. 'Not quite complete, I'm afraid, sir. There's this little item.'

De Graaf read through the list, his face stunned, then read through it again. His lips were moving, but at first no sound came. He had just got around to muttering: 'This little item, this little item,' when Wieringa and Dessens returned. Wieringa looked his normal imperturbable self, Dessens like a Christian who had just been given his first preview of the lions in the Roman arena.

Wieringa said: 'What little item, Colonel?'

'This.' De Graaf handed him the paper, put his elbow on the arm of his chair and his hand to his forehead as if to hide his eyes from some unspeakable sight.

'High explosives,' Wieringa read out. 'Primers. Detonators. Grenades. Ground-to-ground missiles. Ground-to-air missiles.' He looked at van Effen consideringly but with no signs of consternation on his face. 'What is this?'

'A shopping list. I was going to ask the Colonel to get it for me.' Dessens, who had adopted precisely the same attitude as de Graaf, made a slight moaning sound. 'As you are the Minister of Defence, the Colonel would have had to approach you anyway. I'd also like to borrow an Army truck, if I may. With a little luck I may even be able to return it.'

Wieringa looked at him, looked at the paper in his hand, then back at van Effen again. 'Balanced against this shopping list, as you call it, the loan of the odd army vehicle seems an eminently reasonable request. All this I can obtain without any great difficulty. I have heard a considerable amount about you, van Effen, and I have learnt a great deal more tonight. I would hesitate to question your judgement.' He thought for a moment. 'I think I would question my own first, so I don't question yours. No doubt it's just idle curiosity on my part, but it would be nice to know *why* you require those items.'

'The FFF seem to be short of explosives and offensive weapons, so I have promised to supply them with some.'

'Of course,' Wieringa said. 'Of course.' The Defence Minister appeared to be virtually unshockable; certainly, nothing showed in his eyes. Nothing was to be seen in the eyes of de Graaf or Dessens either, but that didn't mean that they were shock-proof: their shading hands still cut their eyes off from the dreadful realities of the harsh world outside.

'They also seem to be short of explosive experts, so I volunteered my services.'

'You know something about explosives?'

De Graaf reluctantly uncovered his eyes. 'He knows a great deal about explosives. He's also a bomb disposal expert. I wish,' he said bitterly, 'that this was something simple, like defusing a ticking 500-kilo bomb.'

'Yes, sir.' Van Effen was addressing de Graaf now. 'I've also recruited George and Vasco, George as another person versed in the way of explosives and Vasco as a trained missile launcher. You will understand that I did not have time to consult you on those matters.'

'You can't think of everything,' de Graaf said dully. He discovered, to his apparent astonishment, that his brandy glass was empty and set about rectifying this.

'Nothing illegal about recruiting those two men, Mr Wieringa. They're police sergeants. And they weren't recruited – they volunteered. They know the dangers. There's nothing to be done about the explosives, sir, but if you could have an armourer deactivate the missiles I'd be very grateful.'

De Graaf lowered his glass. 'So would I. So would I.' Not much in the way of life had come back into his voice.

Wieringa said: 'I suppose I'm just being idly curious again but why are you and your two friends taking these appalling risks?'

'Calculated risks, sir. I hope. The reason is simple. The Colonel has said that we have gained an entrée into the FFF. That's not quite accurate. We have been accepted – or appear to have been accepted – on the fringes. We're just on the outer strand of the spider's web. We don't know where the spider is. But if we deliver the requested items, we'll find out. They're not likely to leave missiles and missile launchers in a safe deposit box in the Central Station.'

'Impeccable logic, van Effen, impeccable logic. Except, of course, for one tiny little flaw.'

'Sir?'

'The spider may gobble you up. The scheme is mad, quite mad – which is the only reason it might just succeed. I'd be intrigued to know where and when you arranged this.'

'About an hour and a half ago. Over a drink with Agnelli.'

For the first time, Wieringa's monolithic calm cracked.

'Over a drink with Agnelli? Agnelli? Agnelli! One of those men who have just left?'

'I was Stephan Danilov then. Well, can't think of anything else so, with your permission, I'll be on my way. The weather forecast should be interesting tonight – latest reports say flood-level danger inside the next forty-eight hours might even exceed that of February 1953. That will be the time for our friends – and it doesn't leave a great deal of time for negotiations with the British Government. You will remember that I said I didn't believe in Riordan's short-range threats: I'm convinced that the long-range threat, the massive flooding of the country, has been arranged and is totally real. One small point, Colonel. Riordan's allegations against the integrity of our customs. They're ludicrous. I know that. You know that. The world doesn't. I'm convinced that the transfers are taking place in the Ijsselmeer, Waddenzee or the open see. It's a Navy job. God knows we've got a bad enough name already as a gun-running entrepot: I wonder what it will be like when all this is over.' Van Effen smiled. 'Still, it's not a job that can be handled by a junior police officer: only the ministries of Defence and Justice can cope. Good-night, gentlemen.'

'Moment, Peter, moment.' It was de Graaf and his distress was apparent. 'Surely there's *something* we can do to help?'

'Yes, sir. There is. Do nothing. Absolutely nothing. *Any* attempt to help us will probably help us into our graves. Those are clever and desperate men so please, please, don't try anything clever and desperate yourselves. Don't have the truck followed, not in any way, no matter how clever you think you are, nothing. No helicopters, no blind barrel-organist, nothing. And nothing so futile and puerile as fitting a concealed location transmitter bug to the truck – unless they're mentally retarded, it's the first thing they'd look for. Nothing. Do *nothing*.'

'We take your point,' Wieringa said drily. 'Nothing.' His

tone changed. 'But from what you've just said, Lloyd's of London wouldn't insure you for a ninety-nine per cent premium. But you go. For the last time – why?'

'You heard what Mr Dessens said – the good name and honour of the Netherlands in the dust, and you with its citizens full fathom five. We can't have that, can we?'

'Your sister?'

'What about my sister?'

'The Colonel told me tonight. God only knows how you carry on as you do. I couldn't. Kidnapped.'

'She's part of it.'

'I would not care to be the unfortunate man who abducted her when you meet up with him.'

'I've already met up with this unfortunate man.'

'What!' For the second time Wieringa's self-control deserted him, but he recovered quickly. 'When?'

'Tonight.'

'Where?'

'Here. Agnelli.'

'Agnelli!'

'I should have shot him full of holes? There's a law against it. I'm a policeman. I'm supposed to uphold the law. Sworn to it, in fact.'

He left. Wieringa said: 'I begin to believe some of the stories about van Effen. The not-so-nice ones. God, Arthur, that's his *sister*. No blood in his veins. None. Ice.'

'Yes, sir. Let's hope Agnelli has not hurt Julie.'

'What do you mean?'

'Then he's a dead man. Sure, sure, van Effen's sworn to uphold the law – but only in front of witnesses.'

Wieringa stared at him, then nodded slowly and reached for his glass.

Eight

At noon on that February day the streets of Amsterdam were dark as dusk. At noon on that same day the streets were as deserted as those of any long-dead city. The cloud cover driven by that icy northern wind must have been black and heavy and thousands of feet in depth but it could not be seen: the torrential slanting rain that bounced knee-high off those same deserted streets limited visibility in any direction, including vertically, to only a few yards. It was not a noontide for the well-advised to venture out of doors.

Van Effen, George and Vasco were among the very few who seemed to be singularly ill-advised. They stood in the porchway of the Trianon hotel, sheltering from the monsoon-like rain behind the side glass panels. Van Effen was subjecting Vasco to a critical examination.

'Not bad, Vasco, not at all bad. Even if I hadn't known it was you, I don't think I would have recognized you. I'm quite certain I would have brushed by you in the street and not given you a second look. But don't forget that Romero Agnelli had the opportunity of studying you very closely over the table at the Hunter's Horn. On the other hand, the clothes you wore on that occasion were so outlandish that he probably didn't spend much time examining your face. It will serve.'

Vasco had indeed undergone a considerable metamorphosis. The long blond locks that had straggled haphazardly over his shoulder had been neatly, even severely, trimmed and parted with millimetric precision just to the centre left. His hair was also black, as were his eyebrows and newly-acquired and immaculately shaped moustache, all of which went very well with his shadowed, thinned-down cheeks and heavy tan. All dyes were guaranteed waterproof. He was the maiden's conceptualized dream of what every young army officer should look like. Shirt, tie, suit and belted trench-coat were correspondingly immaculate.

'They could use him in those army advertisements,' George said. 'You know, your country needs you.' George, himself, was still George. For him, disguise was impossible.

'And the voice,' van Effen said. 'I'm not worried about Agnelli, he's hardly heard you say more than a few words. It's Annemarie. I don't know whether she's a good actress with her emotions under control or not, but I rather suspect not. It would rather spoil things if she flung her arms round your neck and cried "My saviour!"'

'I have a very bad cold,' Vasco said hoarsely. 'My throat is like sandpaper.' His voice reverted to normal and he said morosely: 'Whose throat wouldn't be in this damned weather. Anyway, I'll be the strong, silent type: I shall speak as little as possible.'

'And I,' George said, 'shall lurk discreetly in the background until one of you have advised the ladies – if the ladies are indeed there – of my presence. But make it fast.'

'We'll make it as fast as we can, George,' van Effen said. 'We appreciate it's a bit difficult for you to lurk discreetly anywhere for any length of time. And I have no doubt whatsoever the ladies will be there.' He tapped the newspaper under his arm. 'What's the point in holding a couple of trumps if you don't have them in your hand?'

The FFF's latest announcement had been very simple, direct and to the point. They had now with them, they said – crude words like 'abducted' and 'kidnapped' had been studiously avoided – two young ladies, one of them the daughter of the nation's leading industrialist, the other the sister of a senior police officer in Amsterdam. They had then proceeded to name names. Condolences, the FFF had said, had been sent to both parents and brother, together with assurances that they were being well cared for and expressing the pious hope that they would continue to remain in good health.

'I do look forward to meeting those cardplayers,' George said wistfully. 'Crafty bunch of devils, aren't they? I wonder what

American university – or it could be Irish – offers a combined course in terrorism and psychology?'

'They're not exactly mentally retarded,' van Effen said. 'But, then, we never thought they were. Another push up the back for the arm of the government – and another push into an even more impossible situation. Just ending their message with those prayerful good wishes. No threats, no hints of reprisals or what might happen to the girls, no possibility of torture or even death. Nothing. The old uncertainty principle in full operation again. What, we are left to wonder, do they have in mind. That's left to us – and, of course, it's only human nature to come up with the worst possible scenario. Bad enough to have the country threatened with inundation, but for the tender-hearted and romantic – and even among the so-called stolid Dutch there are an uncommon number of those around – the thought of what dreadful terrors may lie in store for two beautiful and innocent young damsels could be a great deal worse.'

'Well, there's one consolation,' Vasco said. He was practising his *in extremis* voice again. 'I'm sure that's the last threat about your sister's well-being that you'll be getting, Lieutenant.'

'Stephan,' van Effen said.

'Stephan. I know. But I won't apologize this time.' Vasco's voice was back to normal. 'Once I clap eyes on that lot there's not the slightest chance I'll forget.'

'My mistake,' van Effen said. 'I'm the person who's doing the forgetting – about your undercover years. I agree with you – there'll be no more threats to Julie. By the same token, I don't even think they'll bother to try to extract any money from David Meijer. Apart from the fact that they appear to have unlimited funds of their own, David Meijer is much more important to them as David Meijer – the man who, however unofficially, has very much the ear of the government and is in a position to influence them, to swing whatever decision may be under consideration. Not that I think that the government has any decision under consideration. I think that matter has been effectively taken out of their hands now. The ball, in the American phrase, is now very much in the court of the British.'

'I wouldn't very much like to be in the position of the British either.' George said. 'They face a position that, if it's possible, is even worse than the one our government had to face. Are they going to be dictated to, even by proxy, by a bunch of what are essentially no more than terrorists, no matter what lofty motives they may ascribe to themselves? What will happen in Northern Ireland if they did pull out – would there be strife, and murder, even massacre that might cost more than any lives that could or would be lost in the Netherlands – and, of course, we can have no idea of how many lives that might be – hundreds or hundreds of thousands. Or do they just dig in, refuse to move and sit back and let the Hollanders drown and make themselves the lepers of the world, ostracized, perhaps for generations to come, by all nations – and although this is a wicked old world there must be still quite a few left – who still subscribe to some ideals of decency and humanity?'

'I do wish you'd shut up, George.' Rarely for him, van Effen sounded almost irritable. 'You put the damn thing all too clearly. In a nutshell, it's a toss-up between what value is put on the lives of x number of citizens in Ulster against y number of citizens in the Netherlands.' Van Effen smiled without much mirth. 'It's difficult to solve an equation when you don't even have a clue as to what the factors are. Imponderables, imponderables. The physicists who ramble on about the indeterminates and uncertainties in quantum mechanics should have this one dumped on their laps. Me, I'd rather spin a coin.'

'Heads or tails,' George said. 'What way do you think the coin would land?'

'I have absolutely no idea because, of course, no one ever knows which face of the coin is going to show. But there's one factor that is at least faintly determinate, even although that is wildly uncertain, and that is human nature. So at a wild guess, just as wild as guessing at the toss, I would say that the British would give in.'

George was silent for a few moments, one massive hand caressing his chin, then said: 'The British haven't got much of a reputation for giving in. Feed any of them enough beer or scotch or whatever and like as not someone will end up by telling you that no unspeakable foreigner has ever set foot on their sacred soil for a thousand years. Which is true – and it's the only country in the world that can claim that.'

'True, true. But not applicable – or at least of importance – here. This is not a case of Churchill declaiming that we will fight in the streets, hills, beaches or wherever and that we will never surrender. That's for martial warfare and in martial warfare the parameters and issues are clearcut. This is psychological warfare where the distinctions are blurred out of sight. Are the British any good at psychological warfare? I'm not sure they are. Come to that, I'm not sure that any country is – too many indefinables.'

'I don't think, anyway, that it's a factor of either martial or psychological warfare. If there's any factor that's going to count, it's the factor of human nature. This is how it might just possibly happen. The British will bluff and bluster, rant and rave – you have to admit that they yield first place to none when it comes to that – throw their arms in the general direction of a mindless heaven, appeal for common justice and claim they're as pure and white and innocent as the driven snow, which, at this moment of time and conveniently forgetting their not-so-distant bloody history, they have some justification in claiming to be. What, they will ask, have we done to precipitate this intolerable situation and why should they, luckless lambs being led to the slaughter etc, be forced to find an impossible solution to an impossible problem which is none of their making? All quite true, of course. Why, they will cry, is no one in the world lifting a finger to help us, specifically those idle, spineless, cowardly, incompetent etc, Dutch who can't bear to separate themselves from their cheese and tulips and gin even for the few moments it would take to eradicate this monster in their midst.

'Nobody, of course, is going to pay a blind bit of attention to what they are saying. And when I say "they" I don't mean the British people as a whole, I mean Whitehall, their government. And here's where the first real bit of human nature comes in. The British have always prided themselves on their compassion, fair-mindedness, tolerance and undying sympathy for the under-dog – never mind what a few hundred million ex-subjects of the British Empire would have to say on that subject – and their kindness to dogs, cats and whatever else takes their passing fancy. That they may be happily existing in a world of sheer illusion is irrelevant: what is relevant for them is that what other people may regard as sheer hypocrisy is, for them, received truth. It is an immutable fact of life – British life, that is – so that if we poor Dutch even as much as got our feet wet, their moral outrage would be fearful to behold. Their indignation would be unbounded, ditto their consternation, the principles of all they think they hold dear destroyed, their finer sensibilities trampled in the mud. *The Times* letter department would be swamped in an unprecedented deluge of mail, all of it demanding that the criminals responsible for this atrocity should be held to account. X number of heads on x number of chargers. John the Baptist raised to the nth.

'And now the second real bit of human nature. Whitehall is acutely aware who the John the Baptists would be. The government – any government, come to that – may regard themselves as statesmen or cabinet ministers but deep down in their cowering hearts they know full well that they are only jumped-up politicians strutting their brief hour upon the stage. Politicians they are and politicians in those fearful hearts they will always remain. And in their little egoistic political minds they are concerned, with rare exceptions – our Minister of Defence is one – only with security of tenure, the trappings of office and the exercise of power. Their egos are their existence and if you destroy their egos you destroy their existence or at least consign them to the political wilderness for many years to come.

'There would be a landslide defeat for them at the next election or, much more likely, they would be turfed out of office very promptly. For your average cabinet minister, such a possibility is too appalling for contemplation. So we won't get our feet wet. Motivated not by their own miserable fear, cowardice, greed and love of power but by the overriding dictates of common humanity, Whitehall will gallantly bow its head to the terrorists.'

There was a considerable silence, interrupted only by the hissing and drumming of rain on the window panes and streets and the constant rumbling of distant thunder. Then George said: 'You never did have a very high opinion of politicians, did you, Peter?'

'I'm in the sort of job where I have the unfortunate privilege of coming into contact with far too many of them.'

George shook his head. 'That's as may be. But that's a very, very cynical outlook to adopt, Peter.'

'We live in a very, very cynical world, George.'

'Indeed, indeed.' There was a pause and this time George nodded his head. 'But sadly I have to agree with you. On both counts. About the world. And about the politicians.'

Nobody had anything more to say until a van drew up before the hotel entrance – it was, in fact, the mini-bus that had been used in the Dam Square the previous evening. Romero Agnelli, who was driving, wound down the window and slid back the door behind him.

'Jump in. You can tell me where to go.'

'Jump out,' van Effen said. 'We want to talk to you.'

'You want to – what's wrong, for God's sake?'

'We just want to talk.'

'You can talk inside the bus.'

'We may not be going anywhere in that bus.'

'You haven't got the –'

'We've got everything. Are we going to stand here all day shouting at each other through the rain?'

Agnelli slid the door forward, opened his own and got out, followed by Leonardo, Daniken and O'Brien. They hastily mounted the steps into the shelter of the porch.

'What the hell do you think you're doing?' Agnelli said. The suave veneer had cracked a little. 'And what the hell –'

'And who the hell do you think you're talking to?' van Effen said. 'We're not your employees. We're your partners – or we thought we were.'

'You think you –' Agnelli cut himself off, frowned, smiled and hauled his urbanity back into place. 'If we must talk – and it seems we must – wouldn't it be a little more pleasant inside?'

'Certainly. This, by the way, is the Lieutenant.' Van Effen made the introductions which Vasco hoarsely acknowledged, apologizing profusely for the state of his throat. Agnelli, it was clear, had no idea who he was, even going as far as to say that Vasco couldn't possibly be anything else than an army officer.

Inside, seated in a remote corner of the lounge, van Effen unfolded his newspaper and laid it on the table before Agnelli. 'I suppose you can see those headlines?'

'Um, well, yes, as a matter of fact, I can.' He could hardly have failed to for the banner headline was the biggest the newspaper could produce. It read, quite simply, 'FFF BLACKMAILS TWO NATIONS' which was followed by a number of only slightly smaller headlines which were concerned primarily with the perfidy of the FFF, the heroic resolution of the Dutch government, the dauntless defiance of the British government and one or two other lies.

'Yes, well, we rather thought you might have read something like this,' Agnelli said. 'And we did think you might have been a little troubled. But only a little. I mean, I personally can see no reason for concern, or that anything has radically altered. You knew what the reasons for your employment – sorry, engagement – were and you knew what we were doing. So what has changed so much overnight?'

'This much has changed,' George said. 'The scope of the thing. The escalation of the plan. The sheer enormity of the matter. I'm a Dutchman, Mr Agnelli. The Lieutenant is a Dutchman. Stephan Danilov may not be Dutch born, but he's a damn sight more Dutch than he is anything else and we're not going to stand by and see our country drowned. And country, Mr Agnelli, means people. It is certain that none of us three operates inside the law: it is equally certain that none of us would ever again operate outside the law if we thought that our actions would bring harm to any person alive. Quite apart from that, we're out of our depth. We are not small-time criminals but we do not act at an international level. What do you people want with Northern Ireland? Why do you want the British out? Why do you blackmail our government – or the British? Why do you threaten to drown thousands of us? Why threaten to blow up the Royal Palace? Or haven't you read the papers? Are you all mad?'

'We are not mad.' Agnelli sounded almost weary. 'It's you

209

who are mad – if you believe all that you read in the papers. The papers have just printed – in this instance, what your government has told them to say – in a state of national emergency, and the government do regard this as such, they have the power to do so. And the government have told them what *we* told them to say. They have followed our instructions precisely. We have no intention of hurting a single living soul.'

'Northern Ireland is still a far cry from blackmailing the Dutch government for a little ready cash,' van Effen said. 'This, we thought, had been your original intention and one with which we'd have gone along. Quite willingly. We have no reason to love the government.' He stared off into the far distance. 'I have no reason to like quite a number of governments.'

'On the basis of what you have told me,' Agnelli said, 'I can quite understand that.' He smiled, produced his ebony cigarette-holder, fitted a Turkish cigarette and lit it with his gold-inlaid onyx lighter, all of which demonstrated that he was at ease, in charge and back on balance again – assuming, that is, that he had ever been off it in the first place. 'Cash is the basis, gentlemen, and only cash. Precisely how it is the basis I am not yet permitted to divulge but you have my assurance that it is the sole and only motivation. And you also have my assurance – which you can take or leave as you choose – that we have no intention of bringing harm to anyone. And, quite honestly, in saying so we are not so moved, perhaps, by humanitarian considerations as you are. Organized crime on a large scale is big business and we run our affairs on a business-like basis. Emotion is nothing, calculation all. Killing not only pays no dividends, it is counter-productive. A robber is pursued by the law, but only within reasonable limits: but he who kills in the process of robbery is relentlessly pursued. No, no, gentlemen, we are in the business of conducting a purely psychological warfare.'

George reached across the table and touched another headline. 'Kidnapping young ladies is another form of psychological warfare?'

'But of course. One of the most effective of all psychological forms of blackmail. It touches the strings of one's heart, you understand.'

'You are a cold-blooded bastard,' George said genially. When George was at his most genial he was at his most menacing and the slight compression of Agnelli's lips showed that he realized that he was in the presence of menace. 'I wonder how you would like it if your wife, sister or daughter were held with a gun at their heads or a knife at their throats? And don't throw up your hands in horror. Blackmailers never hold hostages without accompanying threats of what will happen if their blackmailing ends are not achieved. As often as not such threats are carried out. What would it be in this case? Turning them over to some of the less uninhibited among your employees for a few hours' innocent pleasure? Torture? Or the ultimate? We are, as we have repeatedly told you, not men of violence. But if any harm were to come in any way to those young ladies, totally harmless and innocent as we believe them to be, we would be capable of actions that you would regard as being acts of unimaginable violence. I do wish you would believe me, Mr Agnelli.'

Agnelli believed him all right. The atmosphere in the Trianon's lounge was acceptably cool but a sheen of sweat had suddenly appeared on Agnelli's forehead.

George said: 'Why, for instance, did you kidnap this Anne Meijer? Is it because her father runs a minor kingdom of his own and may be presumed to have a powerful voice in government?' Agnelli nodded silently. 'And this' – he twisted the paper to have a glance at it – 'this Julie van Effen. She's only a policeman's sister. There are thousands of policemen in the Netherlands.'

'There's only one van Effen.' Agnelli spoke with a considerable depth of feeling. 'We know there's a nationwide hunt up for us but we also know who's leading it. Van Effen. If we have his sister, and we do, we may clip his wings a bit.'

'You don't sound as if you care for this man very much?' Agnelli said nothing, the look in his eyes said it for him. 'And you still ask me to believe that you wouldn't subject those girls to some subtle or not so subtle forms of persuasion to achieve your ends?'

'I don't really care whether you believe me or not.' Once again Agnelli was beginning to sound more than a little tired. 'I believe you are quite capable of doing what you say you would do if you found out we are deceiving you. I have no doubt that you are heavily armed. I suggest you come along and see and believe for yourselves. That includes seeing our hostages this afternoon. If you don't like what you see you can leave or take any other measures you think appropriate. There's nothing else I can say and I can't speak fairer than that.'

George said: 'Stephan?'

'We'll go along. Mr Agnelli's explanations may be a bit thin, but if we are to believe in the essence of what he says – and I have no reason to think that we shouldn't – then I think we all may have a great deal to lose if we are raising objections to a state of affairs that do not exist. It wouldn't be very bright of us to cut off our own noses. As Mr Agnelli says, let's go and see for ourselves.'

'Thank you, gentlemen,' Agnelli didn't mop his brow, perhaps because he wasn't the brow-mopping kind, but almost certainly because he would not have regarded it as a very politic thing to do. 'I was by no means convinced that you would come to see it my way – you are exceptionally difficult negotiators, if I may say so – but I am glad you have done.' Moderation, reasonableness, courtesy – Agnelli could generously afford all of those now that he had had, as he thought, his own way. 'Now, where's the truck?'

'Nearby garage.'

'Garage? Is it safe –'

'I own it,' George said. 'Goodness sake, do you think this is the first time?'

'Of course. Silly question.'

'We have one or two questions,' van Effen said. 'We're committed now and we've no more wish to take chances than you have. I don't for a moment suppose we'll know where this place is until we get there. Have you a place of concealment for this truck?'

'Yes.'

'How many people are going out there?'

'Apart from yourselves? The three of us, Mr Riordan whom you haven't met but have read about, Joop and Joachim. Why?'

'Please. My turn for questions. You travel in the mini-bus?'

'Well, no. We'd hoped there would be plenty of room in the truck.'

No, indeed, van Effen thought. They wanted to keep the closest possible eye on the three of them and the precious contents of the truck. 'How many cars?'

'Cars?' Agnelli looked faintly surprised. 'No cars. Why?'

'Why?' Van Effen looked at the ceiling, then at George, then back at Agnelli. 'Why? Tell me, Mr Agnelli, have you ever transported stolen Government property before?'

'This will be a new experience for me.'

'I want two cars. One to follow the truck at two or three hundred metres, the other to follow the first car at a similar distance.'

'Ah! Well, now, I appreciate this. You do not wish to be followed.'

'I have a rooted objection to being followed. One chance in a million. We do not take that chance.'

'Good, good. Joop and Joachim. I'll phone now.'

'Last question. We forgot to discuss this. Do we return to the city tonight?'

'No.'

'You should have told us. We do require a tooth-brush or two. However, we guessed right and packed some gear. Three minutes in the lobby.'

Back in his room van Effen said: 'George, I've said it before and say it again. Your career has been a wasted one, ruined and misplaced. That was splendid, quite splendid.'

George made a mock-modest gesture of depreciation. 'It was nothing.'

'How to establish a moral ascendancy in one easy lesson. They're going to go out of their way not to step on our toes. And did you gather the impression, George, that they need us more than we need them. Or, at least, that *they* think so?'

'Yes. Intriguing.'

'Very. Second, they know that they're not going to be followed. It was our suggestion, so that makes us trustworthy?'

'Anyone can see that. It will also, we trust, make them relax their vigilance.'

'We trust. Third, again thanks to you, it is certain that Agnelli has no idea whatsoever who I am. Agnelli is sadly in need of a course of instruction from you. He's a poor dissembler and over-reacts too easily. It is not possible, that, knowing who I was, he could have sat at the same table without giving himself away. Lastly, it seems fairly certain that we'll be safe until or unless they find out who we are or until we are no longer of any use to them – when they have achieved whatever it is they want to achieve, that is. But I think the latter unlikely. I could understand them wanting to dispose of us if we were to betray their identity but their identity is already well known – the names of those in Dessens' house last night will probably be in every major newspaper in Europe this morning. Or by night-fall. And the TV and radio. I asked Mr Wieringa to make specially sure about that. And didn't you love all this talk about limiting themselves solely to pure psychology and being interested only in cash returns? You believed him, of course?'

'You can always trust a man like Mr Agnelli.'

Agnelli, O'Brien and Daniken were waiting in the lounge when the two men descended. Van Effen said: 'Fixed?'

'Yes. But one thing we overlooked – or I overlooked. I said I'd call them back. I didn't know whether to ask them to come here or not.'

'We'll let them know when we move out in the truck.'

'Why not call them from here?'

Van Effen looked at him as if in faint surprise. 'Do *you* ever make two consecutive calls from the same phone?'

'Do I –' Agnelli shook his head. 'And to think that I thought *I* was the most suspicious, most security-conscious person around. Do we move now?'

'The heating in Dutch army trucks is rather sub-standard. I suggest a schnapps. We have time?'

'We have. Very well. Until the Lieutenant comes, I assume.'

'He doesn't join us. We join him. That's why I suggested a schnapps. Takes him a little time.'

'I see. Rather, I don't. He's not going to join –'

'He's leaving by the fire escape. The Lieutenant has a penchant for unorthodox exits. Also, he's bashful about calling attention to himself.'

'Unorthodox. Bashful. I understand now.' Standing by what appeared to be a freshly painted army truck in an otherwise empty, brightly lit small garage, Agnelli surveyed the rather impressive figure of Vasco who was now attired in what was obviously a brand new Dutch army captain's uniform. 'Yes, I understand. The desk staff in the Trianon would have found the change rather intriguing. But I thought – um – the lieutenant was a lieutenant?'

'Old habits die hard. You don't change a man's name just because he changes his suit. Promoted last month. Services to Queen and country.'

'Services to – ah, I see.' Agnelli, it was clear, didn't see at all. 'And what's this bright orange dagger flash on the radiator?'

' "Manoeuvres. Do not approach." '

'You don't miss much and that's a fact,' Agnelli said. 'May I look inside?'

'Naturally. I wouldn't like you to think that you'd bought a pig in a poke.'

'This, Mr Danilov, is the most unlikely looking pig in a poke that I've ever seen.' Agnelli had inspected the neatly stacked and, in the case of the missiles and launchers, highly gleaming contents of the truck and was now actually rubbing his hands together. 'Magnificent, quite magnificent. By heavens, Mr Danilov, when George here is given a shopping list I must say that he delivers. I wouldn't have believed it.'

George made a dismissive gesture. 'A little assistance from the Lieutenant here. Next time, something a little more difficult.'

'Splendid, splendid.' Agnelli looked towards the front of the truck and at the heavily side-curtained bench seat behind the front seats. 'That, too? I see, Mr Danilov, that you share my passion for privacy.'

'Not I. Senior Dutch army officers on manoeuvres.'

'No matter. Mr Riordan, I am sure, will be delighted. When you meet him you will understand why. He is a man of a rather striking appearance and rather difficult to conceal, which is a pity, as he does like his privacy.' Agnelli was silent for a moment, then cleared his throat and said: 'In view of all this and the very, very stringent security precautions you have taken, Mr Danilov, I do feel a bit – in fact, very – diffident about asking – but, well, do you mind if Mr O'Brien here carried out a closer inspection?'

Van Effen smiled. 'I've often wondered what Mr O'Brien's function might be. But this? Well, I'm slightly puzzled. If Mr O'Brien knows more about explosives and arms than we three do, then he must be Europe's leading expert and our services would seem to be superfluous.'

'Explosives, Mr Danilov?' O'Brien was an easy smiler and had a pleasant light baritone voice, a natural for the rendering of 'When Irish eyes'. 'Explosives terrify me. I'm an electronics man.'

'Mr O'Brien is being modest,' Agnelli said. 'He's an electronics expert and one of the very best in the business. Security. Alarms. Installation – or deactivating.'

'Ah. Burglar alarms. Photo-electric rays, pressure pads, things like that. Always wanted to meet one of those. It'll be a pleasure to watch one at work. Little enough scope, I would have thought, for an electronics man around an army truck. Wait a minute.' Van Effen paused briefly then smiled. 'By all means go ahead, Mr O'Brien. I'll take long odds against you finding one, though.'

'Finding what, Mr Danilov?'

'One of those dinky little location transmitters.'

Agnelli and O'Brien exchanged glances. Agnelli said: 'Dinky little – I mean, how on earth –'

'Because I removed one this morning. Rather, the Lieutenant did it for me.'

Agnelli, as van Effen had said, would never stand in line for

216

an Oscar. He was perplexed, apprehensive and suspicious, all at the same time. 'But why should one – I mean, how did you suspect –'

'Don't distress yourself.' Van Effen smiled. 'Perfectly simple explanation. You see –'

'But this is an army truck!'

'Precisely. Far from uncommon on Army trucks. Use them on their silly war games, especially at night, when there's no lights permitted and strict radio silence. Only way they can locate each other. The Lieutenant knew where they were usually concealed and found and detached this one.'

Vasco opened a map compartment by the driver's seat, removed a tiny metallic object, and handed it to van Effen, who passed it over to O'Brien.

'That's it, all right,' O'Brien said. He looked doubtfully at Agnelli. 'In that case, Romero –'

'No, no,' van Effen said. 'Go ahead and search. Be happier if you do. Damn truck could be littered with them, for all I know. Speaking personally, I wouldn't know where to start looking.'

Agnelli, trying with his usual lack of success to conceal his relief, nodded to O'Brien. Van Effen and George left the truck and wandered idly around, talking in a desultory fashion. Agnelli, they could see, was displaying a keen interest in O'Brien at work, but none in them. In a far corner van Effen said: 'Must be an interesting profession being a professional dismantler of alarm systems.'

'Very. Useful, too. If you want to get at the private art collection of some billionaire or other. Or into a secret army base. Or bank vaults.'

'It's also useful if you want to blow up a dyke or a canal bank?'

'No.'

'I didn't think so either.'

Although it was only just after 1 p.m. when they left the garage it could well have been night-time for the amount of light left in the sky. And although it seemed impossible that the amount of rain could have increased, it undoubtedly had: the truck was equipped with two-speed wipers but might almost as

217

well have been equipped with none at all. And the wind blew even more strongly from the north. Apart from the occasional triple tram the streets were deserted. One might almost have thought that the efforts and intention of the FFF were wasted: Holland, it appeared, was about to drown under the weight of its own rainfall.

Agnelli had made his phone call from the garage. Shortly after leaving it, at a word from Agnelli, Vasco, who was driving, pulled up outside an undistinguished café off the Utrechtsestraat. Two cars were parked there, both small, both Renaults. Agnelli got out and spoke hurriedly to the invisible drivers of the cars: he had need to hurry, he had no umbrella and his gaberdine raincoat offered no protection at all to the pitiless rain.

'Joachim and Joop,' he said on his return. 'They are following us to a restaurant just this side of Amstelveen. Even the FFF must eat.' Agnelli was probably back to his smiling again but it was impossible to say. The inside of the truck was almost totally dark.

'If they can follow us,' van Effen said. 'In this weather, I can see that my precautions were superfluous. I thought we were to meet your brother and Mr Riordan. I must say I shall be most interested to meet your Mr Riordan. If the newspaper accounts are anything to go by, he must be a most extraordinary character.' He ignored George's heavy nudge in the ribs.

'He's all that. They've elected to remain in the cars – I don't suppose they fancied getting wet. We'll meet up in De Groene Lanteerne.'

Riordan was indeed an extraordinary character. For some extraordinary reason – known only to himself – he had elected to dress himself in a sweeping, neck-buttoned, black-and-white shepherd's tartan cloak with matching deerstalker, of the type much favoured by Highland lairds and Sherlock Holmes. As the cloak ended six inches above his knees and hence made him look even more incongruously tall and skeletal than ever, he couldn't possibly have been trying to make himself as inconspicuous as possible. He had greeted everyone civilly enough –

when he wasn't declaiming against the IRA he was, it seemed, a normally grave and courteous man – raised his eyes at the sight of Vasco's uniform, readily accepted its explanation and thereafter remained silent, not from any wish to disassociate himself from those at the table but because he was carrying a large, very intricate and expensive-looking radio and had a pair of earphones clamped to his head. He was listening, Agnelli explained, to weather forecasts and Dutch and international news broadcasts. Agnelli didn't have to explain why.

Lunch over, Riordan elected to continue the journey in the truck, earphones still in place. He ensconced himself in the right-hand corner of the rear bench seat and seemed to approve of the heavy side curtain which he pushed as far forward as possible. Vasco drove south during the dark afternoon making the best speed possible which, because of the near zero visibility, was no speed at all. Van Effen was particularly impressed by the carefully polite attention Vasco paid to Agnelli's would-be meticulous instruction as how to drive through Utrecht. As Vasco had been born, bred, lived all his life and been a police driver in Utrecht, it said much for Vasco's heroic patience that he three times followed directions that he must have known to be wrong.

About mid-afternoon, Riordan unhooked his earphones. 'Progress, gentlemen, progress. The Dutch Foreign Minister and Defence Minister – that's that excellent Mr Wieringa of theirs – arrived in London this afternoon and are meeting with their counterparts. A communiqué is expected. It shows that we are being taken seriously.'

Van Effen said: 'After those scare headlines, those banner headlines in the papers today, and all the emergency news flashes on TV and radio, did you seriously expect *not* to be taken seriously?'

'No. But gratifying, none the less, gratifying.' Riordan re-affixed his earphones and leaned back into his corner. The expression on his face was an odd mixture of the expectant and the beatific. A man with a mission, Riordan wasn't going to miss out on anything.

Some twenty minutes later the truck pulled off to the right on to a B-road and, a couple of kilometres further on, left on to a still more minor road. It stopped at a building which appeared to be fronted by a brightly-lit porch.

'Journey's end,' Agnelli said. 'Our headquarters – well, one of them – and our overnight stop. I think you'll be quite comfortable here.'

'A windmill,' van Effen said.

'You seem surprised,' Agnelli said. 'Hardly uncommon in these parts. Disused but still functional, which is also not unusual. Large extensions and quite modernized. It has the additional attraction of being a long way from anywhere. If you look to this side you'll see the place of concealment I promised for the truck. Disused barn.'

'And that other barn-like structure beside it?'

'State secret.'

'Helicopter.'

Agnelli laughed in the darkness. 'End of state secret. Obvious, I suppose, since we told people that we had taken aerial photographs of those rather stirring scenes north of Alkmaar on the Noord Holland canal.'

'So you're now the happy owner of both army and air-force property?'

'No. Not air force. Indistinguishable, though. A lick of paint here, a lick of paint there, some carefully selected registration numbers – but it's unimportant. Let's go inside and see what we can find in the way of old Dutch cheer and hospitality.' Now that he had, as he thought, completed his mission with a hundred per cent degree of success he was positively radiating a genial cordiality. It could well, van Effen thought, represent his true nature: nature had not designed him for the cut and thrust, riposte and parry that he had been through that afternoon.

'Not for me,' George said. 'I'm a businessman and a businessman always likes to –'

'If you're referring to payment, George, I can assure you –'

'Payment? I'm not referring to payment.' George sounded pained. 'I'm referring to standard business practices. Lieutenant, is there an overhead light? Thank you.' George produced a sheaf of papers from an inside pocket and handed them to Agnelli. 'Inventory of goods. You have to sign the receipt but not until I have checked the conditions of all the items – you will understand that I had no time to do so this morning – and see how they survived the transport. Standard business ethics.' No one seemed to find it peculiar that George should use the word 'ethics' in connection with stolen goods. 'But some of that hospitality wouldn't come amiss. Beer for me?'

'Of course,' Agnelli said, then added delicately: 'Would you be requiring any help?'

'Not really. But it is customary for a purchaser or purchaser's agent to be present. I would suggest Mr O'Brien. Electronics experts are accustomed to small fiddly things and detonators are small fiddly things. A carelessly dropped detonator, Mr Agnelli, and there wouldn't be a great deal left of your windmill. There wouldn't be a great deal left of the people inside it, either.'

Agnelli nodded his satisfaction and led the way to the porch that had been added to the windmill. A tall, shock-haired and unshaven youth whose most notable facial characteristic was the negligible clearance between eyebrows and hairline, moved to bar their entrance. A machine-pistol was held loosely in his right hand.

'One side, Willi.' Agnelli's voice was sharp. 'It's me.'

'I can see that,' Willi scowled – it was the kind of face that wasn't built for much else – and stared truculently at van Effen. 'Who's he?'

'Hospitality,' van Effen said. 'Our genial host, no doubt. God help us. Is this the kind of hired help you have around here?'

Willi took a threatening step forward, lifting his gun as he did so, then subsided gently to the ground, clutching his midriff as he did so: the blow he had received there had been no friendly tap. Van Effen took his gun, removed the magazine and dropped the gun on top of the wheezing Willi. Van Effen stared at Agnelli, his expression a nice mix of consternation and disbelief.

'Frankly, I'm appalled. I don't like this one little bit. Is this – I mean, is he typical – you have retarded morons like this on your team? People who are going to hold – no, people who are holding nations to ransom having – having – words fail me. Have you never heard of the weakest link in the chain?'

'My own sentiments exactly,' Riordan said gravely. 'You will remember, Romero, that I expressed my reservations about this fellow. Even as a guard, the only possible function he could serve, his limitations have been cruelly exposed.'

'I agree, Mr Riordan, I agree.' It would have been untrue to say that Agnelli was discomfited, but his ebullience was in temporary abeyance. 'Willi is a disappointment. He shall have to go.'

Willi had now slipped over on to his side. He was conscious enough, propped on one shaky elbow and grimacing with pain. Van Effen looked over his all but prone form to the opened doorway beyond. His sister was there, Annemarie by her side, Samuelson just behind them. The expression on both girls' faces were markedly similar – slightly wide-eyed, slightly shocked, totally uncomprehending. Van Effen let his eyes rest on them for a brief moment then looked indifferently away.

'Have to go, Mr Agnelli? Have to go? If he goes, I go. Can't you see that you're stuck with him, want it or not. Stuck with him either above ground or below. Let him go and the first thing he'll do is talk his head off to the first policeman he meets. No drastic methods, preferably, but his silence must be assured. I hope the rest of your Praetorian guard is a cut above this character.'

'The rest of the Praetorian guard, as you call them, are more than a cut above this unfortunate.' Samuelson, rubicund, smiling and looking even more prosperous than the previous evening, had gently pushed the girls apart and stepped out on to the stoop. He smelt of some very expensive after-shave lotion. Rubbing his chin with an immaculately manicured hand, he peered down at Willi then looked up at van Effen. 'You do have a direct way with you, my friend. At the same time one must admit that you come to some remarkably quick conclusions in a commendably short time. I must confess that I have occasionally felt tempted to do just what you have done, but, well, explosive violence of that kind is not my forte. Ah, yes, I saw it all. Very economical, very.' He extended a hand. 'Samuelson.'

'Danilov.' Judging from both his bearing and his speech, van Effen was in no doubt that he was in the presence of the man who mattered. His speech. Samuelson had said so few words the previous evening that his country of origin had remained uncertain. De Graaf had thought him Irish-American. De Graaf, van Effen thought, had been wrong. This man was English-American. Perhaps even an Englishman who had spent just long enough in the United States to pick up a slight American over-tone. Van Effen gestured to the fallen man. 'Sorry about this, Mr Samuelson. One does not usually treat a host's staff in so summary a fashion. On the other hand you must admit that it's not the average guest who finds himself confronted with a sub-machine gun.'

'A well-taken point, Mr Danilov.' Like Agnelli, Samuelson seemed much given to warm and friendly smiles. 'A breach of hospitality. It will be the last – as you yourself have personally assured. All is well, Romero?'

'Perfect, Mr Samuelson. Everything there, everything in order. Exactly as Mr Danilov guaranteed.'

'Splendid. Mr Danilov does have a certain aura of competence about him. Come in, come in. Wretched evening. Absolutely wretched.' That, thought van Effen, made him English for sure. 'And good evening to you, Captain. I understood you were a lieutenant.'

'A very very recent captain,' Vasco said hoarsely. 'Sorry about this throat.'

'Dear me, dear me.' Samuelson sounded genuinely concerned. 'A hot toddy, and at once.' Samuelson did not seem to find it at all amiss that a regular army captain should be in their company: but a man with so smoothly unlined a face could take many things in his stride without registering reactions of any kind. 'Let me introduce our two charming guests. Miss Meijer, Miss van Effen.'

Van Effen bowed briefly. 'Those are the two who figured so prominently in the headlines this morning? Their photographs didn't do them justice.'

Agnelli said: 'Mr Danilov and his friends were rather concerned about their well-being, Mr Samuelson.'

'Ah, yes. Compatriots, of course. No need, no need. As you can see, both in excellent health.'

There were five other people in the room, all men. Two were earnest looking, intellectual looking youths cast in the mould of Joachim and Joop. The other three were older, bigger and a great deal tougher looking, although that didn't mean that they were in any way more dangerous: apart from the fact that they lacked sunglasses they looked uncommonly like the Secret Service men who guard an American president. There was nothing criminal in their appearances. Samuelson didn't see fit to introduce them: as a result, indeed, of some signal that van Effen had not seen they all quietly left the room.

'Well, now.' Van Effen looked at Samuelson, Agnelli and Riordan in turn. 'I don't know which of you I should address. It doesn't matter. We have delivered the material – one of our number is at present checking the explosives and armaments to see that they are in the best possible working order. We understood that some call might be made on our services – our expertise, if one might put it that way. If you don't require us, there's no point in our remaining. We have no wish to impose ourselves on anybody.'

Samuelson smiled. 'You would rather go?'

Van Effen smiled in turn. 'I think you are perfectly well aware that we would rather stay. I'm as curious as the next man. Besides, it would be most interesting to know what is going to happen without having to wait to read about it in the newspapers.'

'Stay you shall,' Samuelson said. 'We will probably have need of your expertise. We do, in fact, have plans for you. But first, perhaps, a soupçon of borreltje. 5 p.m., and 5 p.m., I understand, is the prescribed hour. Leonardo' – this to Agnelli's brother who had just entered with Daniken – 'be so kind as to have some hot water brought from the kitchen.' This, van Effen felt certain, made Samuelson the man who called the tune. 'And some honey. We must do something about this fearful cold the Captain has. Come. Join me.'

A log fire burnt in an open hearth built into the windowless back wall. Adjoining this was a circular oaken bar, small but quite splendidly stocked. Samuelson moved behind this as Riordan said: 'You will, of course, excuse me.'

'Of course, James, of course,' Samuelson said. Van Effen felt faintly surprised. Riordan didn't look like a man who had a first name. Riordan nodded to the company and mounted a circular stairway.

Van Effen said: 'Mr Riordan doesn't approve of our heathenish practice of having a borreltje at this hour?'

'Mr Riordan doesn't disapprove. He doesn't drink himself, nor does he smoke, but he doesn't disapprove. I may as well tell you – for you will find out anyway and I don't wish to cause anybody any embarrassment – that Mr Riordan regularly goes upstairs at this hour for prayer and meditation. He does this several times a day and one cannot but respect a man with such deeply-held beliefs. He is very devout – and is, in fact, an ordained minister of the church.'

'You surprise me,' van Effen said. He thought briefly. 'No, on second thoughts you don't surprise me. It seems very much in character. For such a devout character, I must say, the Reverend has certainly let loose a storm of cats in the dovecotes of Europe today.'

'You must not think ill of Riordan, nor underestimate him.' Samuelson spoke very seriously. 'He is an evangelist, a missionary fired by a burning zeal. He is genuinely appalled by what is happening in Northern Ireland and believes that if blood must be spilled to bring peace to that troubled land then that's how it will be. In his own words, he's prepared to use the devil's tools to fight the devil.'

'And you support him in all of this?'

'Naturally. Why else should I be here?'

It would have been interesting, van Effen thought, to know just why else he should be there but it seemed hardly the time and place to raise the question. He hoisted himself on a bar stool and looked around.

The two girls were in whispered consultation. Agnelli and Daniken had already occupied the two stools at the further end of the bar. Vasco, who had been wandering round looking at the paintings and brass and copper work on the walls, made his unconcerned way over to the bar and sat down beside Daniken whom he began to engage in hoarse conversation.

'Mr Samuelson.' It was Julie. 'I think I'll go to my room. I have a bit of a headache.'

Van Effen remained casually still, drumming his fingers idly on the bar-top, a man perfectly at ease with himself. He was, in fact, very far indeed from being at ease with himself, the last thing that he wanted was that either of the girls should go to their rooms. Samuelson, who had been stooping down behind the bar, came to his unwitting rescue.

'My dear Julie!' If he weren't so certain that he knew what Samuelson would say next, van Effen could have hit him. 'Not to be thought of. Here we have a fine Tio Pepe. Guaranteed cure for any headache. Would you deprive me of your company?'

They would obviously have cheerfully done just that but just as obviously deemed it prudent to do as he told – prisoners tend to do what their gaolers tell them – and came and perched reluctantly by the bar, Julie close to her brother. She glanced at him briefly, a glance which told him quite clearly what she thought of violent characters who spoke off-handedly about sticking undesirable characters under the ground, then looked away. Almost at once she looked back again, fortunately not too quickly: something had just touched her right thigh. She looked at him, frowning slightly, then glanced downwards. Almost at once she turned away and made some confidential remark to Annemarie, just as Samuelson's head cleared the bar again. Magnificent, van Effen thought, she was magnificent, the best in Amsterdam wouldn't be good enough for his sister after this.

She accepted her sherry from Samuelson with a correctly pleasant if somewhat forced smile, delicately sipped her drink, placed it on the bar-top, opened her handbag on her lap and brought out cigarettes and lighter. She *was* magnificent, van Effen thought. She lit the cigarette, returned the cigarette case but not the lighter to her bag and, while still talking quietly to Annemarie while watching, without seeming to, the men at the bar, dropped her hand till it touched van Effen's. A moment later, the lighter and the folded note, the top of which had been protruding between the fore and middle fingers of van Effen's was safely inside her closed bag. He could have hugged and kissed her and made a mental note to do so at the first available opportunity. In the meantime, he did the next best thing, he downed his borreltje in one gulp. He had never much cared for it but this one tasted as nectar must have done to the gods. Samuelson, ever the attentive host, hurried across to replenish his glass and van Effen thanked him courteously. The second borreltje went the same way as the first.

Julie locked the bedroom door behind her, opened her bag and brought out the note which she began to unfold. Annemarie looked at her curiously.

'What have you got there? And why are your hands shaking, Julie?'

'A billet-doux that I have just got from a love-lorn suitor in the bar. Wouldn't your hands shake if you'd just got a billet-doux from a love-lorn suitor in the bar?' She smoothed out the note so that they could both read it together. It had been meticulously typed so obviously it was not a scribbled note put together at the last moment.

'*Sorry about the appearance and the thick accent,*' it said, '*but you will understand that I can't very well go around in my ordinary clothes and using my ordinary voice.*

'*The dashing young army captain is Vasco. You will understand why he has developed this sore throat. Annemarie might just have been a little startled to hear his normal voice. Agnelli would have been very startled.*

'*George is with us. Couldn't bring him in at first because George can't be disguised. Couldn't have you hugging him with feminine shrieks of delight.*

'*You don't know us and you don't want to know us. Stay away from us but don't make it too obvious. Distant, remote and extending to us as much courtesy as you would to any other common criminals.*

'*Don't try to do anything clever. Don't try to do anything. The men, probably, are not dangerous but watch the girls. They're shrewd and have nasty devious feminine minds.*

'*Destroy this note immediately. I love you both.*'

'And signed,' Julie said, 'with his own unmistakable signature.' Her hands still weren't too steady.

'You said he would come,' Annemarie said. Her voice was like Julie's hands.

'Yes, I did, didn't I? Didn't expect him quite so soon, though. What are we going to do – cry with relief?'

'Certainly not.' Annemarie sniffed. 'He might have spared us the bits about feminine shrieks of delight and shrewd and nasty devious feminine minds.' She watched as Julie ignited the note over a wash-basin and flushed the ashes away. 'So what do we do now?'

'Celebrate.'

'In the bar?'

'Where else?'

'And ignore them totally.'

'Totally.'

Nine

The barn that served as a garage was cold and draughty and leaking and couldn't have served as a barn for many years: the air was heavy with the unsavoury smell of musty hay although there was no trace of hay to be seen. But it was clean and well lit, enough to show that the army truck's freshly painted bodywork had vanished under a thick encrustation of mud.

George and O'Brien were bent over what appeared to be some kind of check-list when van Effen entered. George looked over O'Brien's shoulder and lifted an interrogative eyebrow. Van Effen gave a brief nod in return, then said: 'About through?'

'Finished,' George said. 'All present and correct, I think.'

'Think,' O'Brien said. 'Check, re-check and cross-check. Never saw a man so meticulous about anything.' Julie and Annemarie had taken what seemed like an unconscionably long time before making their departure. 'But I did learn a little about explosives. And a lot about drinking beer.'

They switched off the lights, padlocked the doors – George pointedly pocketing the key while making some remark to the effect that signed receipts came first – and entered the mill. Julie and Annemarie were seated at a table by the fire, each with a small glass before her, a sure indication, van Effen knew, that they had read the note he had left with them. He noted, approvingly, that both girls regarded their entry with an open curiosity: it would have been an odd person indeed who would have registered indifference when encountering George's vast bulk for the first time. Across the fire-place, and seated at another table, Samuelson was just replacing the hand-set of a rather splendid-looking radio transceiver: when obtaining new equipment the FFF obviously didn't patronise second-hand markets.

'All well?' Samuelson said.

'All well,' O'Brien said. 'Just about managed to stop George testing the detonators with his teeth. That's quite an arsenal you have there, Mr Samuelson.'

'Sign here, please.' George laid three copies of the inventory on the table before Samuelson who signed them, thus confirming that he was, indeed, the man in charge, smiled and handed them back to George who solemnly handed over the garage padlock key.

'A pleasure to do business with you, George. How would you like the fee to be paid?'

'Not time for the fee yet,' George said. 'The inventory is only a promise. Wait for the guarantee – let's see if the damn things work.'

Samuelson smiled again. 'I thought businessmen always demanded cash on delivery.'

'Not this businessman. If, of course, you decide not to use them, then I'll present the bill – you understand that I can't very well return them to the ordnance store. Or if you decide to dispense with our services.'

'Still a pleasure, George. I'm quite certain we'll be requiring both your goods *and* your services. Well, gentlemen, we'll be hearing a rather –' He broke off, looked at van Effen, patted the radio and said: 'You know what this is, don't you?'

'A transceiver. RCA. The best, I believe. If you'd a mind to, you could reach the moon with that.'

'It can reach Amsterdam, which is all I want. Helmut. Helmut Paderiwski, whom you have met, I believe.'

'Yes. I rather wondered where Helmut was.'

'Our voice in the capital. He has just arranged for our latest message to be made known.' He glanced at the wall clock. 'Exactly eight minutes. TV and radio. We've decided not to bother about newspapers any more. I am not being smug when I say that we can now get instant coverage whenever we wish it. I think you'll all find it a rather interesting message – messages rather. Don't you think we should give them – ah – advance notice, Romero? Mr Danilov here has said that he likes to know what's going on before he reads or hears about it.'

'If it is your wish, of course.' Agnelli was his usual smiling self. 'But I would rather they saw it on TV. I think it would be interesting to see what the reaction of the average Dutch citizen would be.'

'We'll wait. It's unimportant. Although I'd hardly call those three average Dutch citizens. Ah! Our provision party has returned.'

The two girls van Effen had met the previous evening in the room off the Voorburgwal entered, each carrying a shopping basket. They were followed by a young man who was having some difficulty in coping with a huge hamper he was carrying.

'Welcome back,' Samuelson said benignly. 'A successful expedition, I see. Ah! Introductions. Mr Danilov, of course, you've met. This is George, this is the Captain who for some obscure reason is called the Lieutenant. Maria. Kathleen. You look puzzled, Mr Danilov.'

'That's a lot of food.'

'True, true. But a lot of mouths to feed.'

'It's a fair way to Utrecht.'

'Utrecht? My dear fellow, we shop at the local village store. Delighted to have our trade. Ah, the factor of anonymity.' He laughed. 'Romero. If you would be so kind.'

Romero led van Effen to the front door, opened it and gestured. At the foot of the steps stood a dark blue van. Emblazoned on its side, in golden lettering, was the legend *Golden Gate Film Productions*.

'Ingenious,' van Effen said.

'It is, rather. Not a famous enough name to attract national attention but we're certainly well enough known locally. Been here for almost a month now. We have a camera crew almost continuously on the move around the area. An isolated spot, this, and it brings a touch of colour into their otherwise drab lives. No trouble at all in recruiting house and kitchen staff: we are generous employers and very well thought of locally.'

'You'd be even better thought of if they knew that this is probably the only area in the Netherlands that's immune from flooding.'

'There's that, there's that.' Agnelli seemed quite pleased with the idea. 'War film, I need hardly say. Hence the helicopter. Had to get official permission, of course, but that was a mere formality.'

'I'd wondered how you'd managed that. You do have your nerve, that I must say.'

'Just had a thought. This newly acquired truck. Change of paint and it can move around in complete freedom. War film – army truck. Follows, no?'

'Yes. This is your brain-child, of course?'

'Yes. But why "of course"?'

'You do have a certain talent for devious organization.'

The TV announcer, soberly suited and tied and ominously grave in expression, looked as if he were about to pronounce a funeral oration.

'We have just received what is called an interim communiqué from London. It says that the talks about the Dutch crisis are continuing and that a further communiqué can be expected within the hour.

'It was expected that some further statements would be received from this terrorist organization calling itself the FFF. Those have arrived some fifteen minutes ago. They are not so much statements as threats of the very gravest nature.

'The first of those states that they, the FFF, expect to hear by midnight that a definite and affirmative answer – that is an answer agreeing to the FFF's demands – will be announced before 8 a.m. tomorrow. If they do not hear such confirmation by midnight, the Oostlijk–Flevoland dyke will be blown at five minutes past midnight. The citizens of Lelystad are advised to begin to take precautionary measures now. If they fail to do this, the FFF now disclaim all responsibility for their fate.

'The second statement makes the announcement that the FFF have in their possession a number of nuclear explosive devices which they will not hesitate to use, if the need arises, to achieve their ends. The FFF hastens to assure the people of the Netherlands that those nuclear devices are not of the calibre of hydrogen or atomic weapons. They are tactical battlefield devices intended for delivery by plane, rocket or shell-fire. All are of American manufacture, some still on the secret list. All have been obtained from NATO bases in Germany. They have the serial numbers of those devices – they are clearly stamped on each one – and the US forces in Germany can confirm that those devices are, in fact, missing. If, that is, they are prepared to give this confirmation.'

There was a pause while the newscaster broke off to accept and glance at a sheet of paper that had just been handed him by a studio colleague: judging from the stricken expression on the colleague's face, he had already read the message.

Van Effen looked around the room. No newscaster, he felt certain, had ever had so rapt an audience. The faces of George and the Lieutenant were expressionless, but that was only because, in certain circumstances such as those, they hadn't much use for expressions: but their eyes were very still. Julie and Annemarie looked shocked. Kathleen and Maria were smiling, but their smiles were half-hearted and more than tinged by apprehension: no question, they had known what was coming but they still didn't like hearing it. Agnelli, O'Brien and Daniken looked thoughtful but not particularly gratified. But the normally genial Samuelson was revelling in every moment of it. True, he was still smiling, but there was no warmth in his smile: there never can be in the smile of a hungry crocodile that has just spotted his unwary lunch.

'We have here,' the announcer said, 'a further message from the FFF. They say they are prepared to release those numbers at any time, but they feel a practical demonstration to prove their possession of those nuclear devices would be much more convincing. Accordingly, they intend to explode one of those devices in the Ijsselmeer in the early afternoon of tomorrow. The power of the charge will be in the range of one kiloton – that is to say, the equivalent of one thousand tons of TNT. This is expected to cause a certain disturbance of the water but the probable height of the accompanying tidal wave – tsunami is the term for it – is not precisely known. It is hoped that the inhabitants of the coastal settlements of the Ijsselmeer will not be too inconvenienced. Inconvenienced!' The newscaster almost spluttered the word which was obviously not in the script – or the repetition of it. He recovered himself. 'The demonstration has been delayed until the afternoon in order to allow British cabinet ministers plenty of time to fly across and join their Dutch colleagues in watching this demonstration. The precise time and place will be announced later. The device, they add, is already in position.

'Finally, they demand some money. This money, they say, will be returned. It is not blackmail money, or ransom money, merely a temporary loan to cover operating expenses. Details of the methods of payment will be announced later this evening – this is to give the parties concerned time to arrange for the transfer. The demand is for one hundred million guilders from the government, twenty million from Mr David Joseph Karlmann Meijer, the Rotterdam industrialist.' The newscaster laid down his paper. 'Viewers will not need reminding that Mr Meijer's daughter, Anne, is being held hostage by the terrorists.' Samuelson touched a switch before him and the screen went blank.

'I wish,' Samuelson said in a complaining voice, 'that he wouldn't call us "terrorists". "Philanthropists" is the word. I rather liked that touch about operating expenses. Anne, my dear, do sit down. You're over-excited.'

Annemarie, who was clearly and very understandably over-excited was on her feet, face pale, lips compressed, her hands unclenching and clenching into ivory-knuckled fists.

'You monster,' she whispered. 'You utterly evil monster.'

'You think so, my dear?' He looked round the room, smiling. Van Effen was one of those who smiled back at him: there were witnesses. 'Not at all. Philanthropist. Equitable redistribution of excess wealth. Besides, it's not even that. As you heard, merely a temporary loan. Don't tell me that the wealthiest man in the Netherlands can't afford that money. I know all about your father.'

'You murderer,' she said softly. Her hands were hanging straight by her sides now, and they were still. 'You murderer.' The tears were rolling down her cheeks and now Julie was on her feet, her arm around the girl's shoulders. 'You know all about my father. You know then that he has had two major heart attacks this year. You know that he came out of hospital

234

only four days ago after his last heart attack. You've killed him.' Her voice, like her shoulders, was shaking. 'You've killed him.'

Samuelson had stopped smiling. He frowned and said: 'I did not know this. Before God, I didn't.' Without apparently even pausing to think he reached out for the handset of his RCA and pressed a button. He must have received an acknowledgment almost immediately for he started talking into the mouthpiece rapidly and urgently, clearly issuing instructions in a language that no one there knew but which George, from a few odd words, recognized as being Yiddish. He replaced the handset, rose, walked around behind the bar, poured himself a brandy, not a small one, and drank the contents in two or three gulps. This performance was watched with some astonishment but no comment was made.

Van Effen rose in turn, walked round to the bar in turn and poured brandy in turn – two brandies. He carried these round to Anne and Julie, waited until they had both sipped from them and resumed his seat.

'Fine lot you are when it comes to ladies in distress.' He looked at Agnelli. 'That was a nice line in threats.'

'You think they were meaningless threats, Mr Danilov?' Agnelli didn't seem at all reluctant to speak, like others in the room he probably found it embarrassing not to look at Samuelson who was on his second brandy and paying attention to nobody. 'I assure you they were all genuinely intended. And will be carried out.'

'So much for your word, Agnelli.'

'I don't understand.'

'You'd have to have a damned short memory not to. Only a few hours ago you promised us that no harm would come to any Dutch people. You warn all the Lelystad people to take the necessary precautions against the breaching of the dykes. Good God, man, it's pitch black outside and coming down in torrents. They won't be able to *see* to take precautions.'

'They don't have to see. Flood level won't be more than half a metre. We've checked and checked the area. Plenty of second-floor rooms and attics – although they could remain on the ground floor if they didn't mind getting their feet wet. And plenty of boats. We've checked that also. The message was primarily for intimidation. Surely you can see that?'

'That's as maybe. Where's old Elastic Conscience?'

'Elastic what?'

'Elastic who. Riordan. The praying priest. The god-fearing Reverend. Why wasn't he here watching?'

Agnelli smiled faintly. 'He regards TV as the work of Satan. Could be right, for all I know. As you saw, he's practically married to his earphones. There was a simultaneous radio broadcast.'

'You *do* really have those nuclear devices? I find it frankly incredible.'

'I can show them to you.'

'Well, that answers that. So this man of peace and goodwill is prepared to play around with lethal explosives.'

'You heard what Mr Samuelson said to you a short time ago.' Agnelli looked quickly at the bar. Samuelson, still looking at nothing and nobody but with something peculiarly tense in his stance, appeared to be on yet another brandy. 'Mr Riordan's prepared to use the devil's tools to fight the devil.'

'Too late in the day to talk about pious, hypocritical platitudes, I suppose. How did you get them – those nuclear devices?'

'You heard. NATO. West Germany. Specifically, US bases.'

'I heard that. I didn't ask where. I asked *how*.' Van Effen looked away for a moment, then back at Agnelli. 'I know. The RAF. The Red Army Faction.'

'Yes. I would have told you but since you've guessed it or know – yes.'

'Jesus! The holy father upstairs must really have the original, twisted, double-dyed, infinite-stretch elastic conscience. The RAF! And only last night, according to the papers – correct me if I'm wrong – he was telling Wieringa, the Defence Minister, that the RAF were the inheritors of the bloody mantle of the Baader-Meinhof gangsters of the early seventies. The fact that his own hands are stained a bright red doesn't appear to worry the Reverend at all. God, I should have thought of this right away. It's only a couple of weeks since there was this successful break-in at a US army ammunition depot outside Hanover. The RAF claimed responsibility and their claim was generally accepted: the RAF is rather good at this and the Americans rather poor at guarding their installations. No mention of nuclear devices. It would have been in character for the RAF to have made specific mention of this: one supposes that they did but that the US Army, or the army through the government, put a stop order on this. Anti-nuclear sentiment is high enough already in Germany without the added knowledge that there's a bunch of woolly-headed hare-brained young terrorists on the loose with nuclear weapons in their suitcases.'

'No prizes for your guesses, Mr Danilov. Had to be that way. And it was.'

'Your information, of course, comes from the same source as the nuclear devices.'

'Where else?'

'Joachim and Joop. And the two other baby-faced choirboys who were here when we arrived this afternoon.'

'Who else?'

'The leisure-time terrorists, as the West Germans call them – nights and weekends only. Since the egregious Christian Klar was captured – along with two lady friends, Mohnhaupt and Schultz I think they were called – and charged with the murders of diverse politicians, prosecutors, bankers and industrialists, the RAF have pulled in their horns and are reported to have moved into neighbouring countries. I suppose Holland was the natural, the inevitable first choice. Should be like a second home to them.' Van Effen thought briefly then smiled. 'On the one hand the RAF, on the other your blackmailing demands on the Dutch Government. Don't you find it rather a splendid thought, Mr Agnelli, that the Dutch Government are going to pay the RAF for nuclear devices to be used against the Dutch people?'

Agnelli didn't have the opportunity to say whether he did or not for the call-up buzzer on the RCA rang at that moment. He lifted the handset, spoke an acknowledgement, then said: 'Mr Samuelson, for you.'

Samuelson came and took the handset, listened, said: 'Thank

you, Helmut, thank you very much,' hung up and looked at his watch. 'Four minutes. I'm going to my room, Romero, but will be down for dinner. So will Mr Riordan. There'll be a news flash on TV in four minutes. Please don't miss it.' On his way to the stairs, he stopped by Annemarie's table. 'I am sorry, Miss Meijer.' No 'my dear', no 'Anne'. 'I did not know.'

When the news flash came, interrupting some appropriately lugubrious offering from Handel by the Concertgebouw, it was very much what van Effen expected. 'The now notorious terrorist group, the FFF,' the newscaster read, 'have announced that, for reasons they do not wish to discuss, the demand for twenty million guilders from Mr David Meijer has been withdrawn, effective as from now. Miss Anne Meijer will be released and returned to her father as soon as is conveniently possible. The sum now asked from the Government has been correspondingly increased to a hundred and twenty million guilders.'

Apart from a slow shake of the head, which could have meant anything but probably indicated a total lack of understanding, Annemarie did not react at all. Julie smiled in delight and hugged her. George clapped a hand on van Effen's knee and said: 'Well, now, my friend, what do you think of that?'

'Splendid,' van Effen said. 'Quite splendid. Bit unfair on policemen's sisters, though. They should have let her go as well.'

'I must admit,' van Effen said, 'that it does make it a bit more difficult to kill him, should that unfortunate need arise. If, of course, our friend Samuelson was moved solely by humanitarian principles. One must not misjudge the man. Perhaps he recalled the days when he used to say his prayers at his mother's knees and his heart was touched. Equally well, he may be an even more calculating villain than we've given him credit for.'

'I can't see how you can possibly say that,' Vasco said. They were pacing to and fro on the front porch. It was bitterly cold, now, and the wind of gale force dimensions. They had a certain degree of privacy out there – it had been impossible to conduct a private conversation inside – but only a certain degree. There was a loft over the garage, approached, as was the custom in that area, by an external stairway. Earlier on they had seen one man go up those stairs and another come down: almost certainly a change of watchman who would have taken position behind the loft window. There were probably others similarly stationed in the other barn and in the windmill itself. Whether the purpose was to keep insiders from going out or outsiders from coming in, it was impossible to say. All that could be said was that it was done with great discretion. Civilian staff were employed in the windmill and even the hint of the maintenance of a guard – almost certainly an armed guard – would have done much to destroy the credibility of the *Golden Gate Film Productions*.

'I not only say that he may be an exceedingly cunning villain,' van Effen said. 'I believe it. Sure it was moving, touching, heartrending even, a fundamentally decent man overwhelmed by his own decency. You noticed the terms of the communiqué. Miss Anne Meijer will be released as soon as conveniently possible. For conveniently possible read inconveniently impossible. People will know that the poor man is trying desperately to return Annemarie to the bosom of her family but finds it impossible to do without jeopardizing his own plans and safety. But he has made the offer. Mr David Meijer, who has not, I assume, accumulated his millions or billions or whatever without having some faint glimmer of intelligence somewhere, will know exactly what the score is and that his daughter is as much a pawn as ever and that he can still be counted on to do the right thing – as far as Samuelson is concerned – about bringing his influence to bear on whatever the government's decision may be. The government whose decision matters, of course, is the British one. He can't influence that. But he can influence the Dutch Government to influence the British one, which is just about as useful from Samuelson's viewpoint.

'And think what would have happened *had* David Meijer died while his daughter was still in the FFF's custody. Unlikely, but that's not the point. People range from the soft-headed to the incurably romantic. The "died-of-a-broken-heart" syndrome has always had a powerful following. Sure, people do die of a broken heart but it's over the months and the years and not overnight. No matter. If he had died the public reaction to Samuelson and the FFF would have been one of total revulsion and rejection. Attitudes would harden, resistance stiffen, and the average man in the street would say: "The hell with this cold, ruthless, murderous monster. Never give in to him, never. Let him do his worst and see if we care." That, I should imagine, is the last thing that Samuelson and company want.

'Going back to that communiqué. Notice the noble, dignified and selfless fashion in which he refused to give the reasons for his decisions. I didn't know that David Meijer had a heart condition but for all I know it may be common knowledge. If it's not, I'll take long odds that it soon will be. Helmut Paderiwski, whom Samuelson calls our voice in Amsterdam, will make good and sure of that and that *his* voice will be heard. Radio and newspapers will be anonymously and discreetly told that David Meijer has a severe heart condition – the truth of that can soon be established – and hints dropped that his gallant hostage daughter had been pleading for his life. For the newspapers, it's a natural, a human-angle story to tug at the very heart strings. Suitably dressed up in the usual sickening journalese, this will be manna to Samuelson, a big plus, an image that puts him in line for tabloid canonization. No matter what he's done or is threatening to do, popular sympathy is going to swing behind him and make it all the easier for his demands to be granted. The whole world loves a reformed rogue, a bandit with a heart of gold. A toast to the Robin Hood of Amsterdam.'

'This I do believe,' George said. 'Among the other accomplishments that you don't know I have, is a smattering of Yiddish. Not much, not even a working knowledge, but a smattering. I wondered what senseless instructions he was trying to give in Yiddish to this fellow Paderiwski in Amsterdam. I don't wonder any more. It makes sense.'

'Lastly, of course, there's the Dutch reverence for the guilder. What praise, people will say, can be too high for a man who spurns twenty million guilders – the fact that he doesn't have it and probably wouldn't have got it anyway is quite irrelevant – at the sight of a tear-drop in the corner of the eye of a lovely maiden. The twenty million, admittedly, is added to the government's bill, but who ever cared about robbing a government. You still think, Vasco, that Samuelson was motivated only by humanitarian considerations?'

'When you put it that way, I have to admit that I don't. He has to be what you say – a crafty conniving villain. Well, it's all very well you having convinced me. It's an unfortunate fact that fourteen million other Dutchmen didn't hear you. I'm convinced that they're going to stay convinced to the contrary.'

'Not all of them. Give some of them time and they'll work it out. The great majority won't. And that's what the frightening thing is about Samuelson. It took me quite a time to figure out the angles here and I'm in the heart of this whole messy business. Samuelson's got a computer mind. He did it all on his feet, within seconds and it would seem automatically, although of course it wasn't automatic at all. Man's brilliant. And he's highly dangerous. It would behove us to have a very long spoon when we're supping with Samuelson.'

'Back to the devil again, is that it?' George said. 'He's the key. Nothing else fits the lock. He's the one who says that Riordan is prepared to use the devil's tools to fight the devil. I wonder if Riordan uses a long spoon to sup with Samuelson. It must cost thousands of dollars a day to run this operation. Maybe tens of thousands. Agnelli hasn't got that kind of money and I doubt whether Riordan ever earned a penny in his life.'

'Samuelson beyond doubt. The paymaster.'

'Pity we're in no position to check with Interpol.'

'Wouldn't do us any good even if we were. If he's as clever as I think he is. Interpol will never have heard of him. Interpol simply has no idea as to who the world's outstanding criminals are. That's why they're outstanding. May not even have a criminal past at all – I say criminal past as distinct from criminal record. He'll have no record. And perhaps, as I say, no past. He may even be what Uncle Arthur suggested he was – a bloated plutocrat, a man who has made his immense fortune in oil or shipping or something of the kind.'

'Then we would have heard of him.'

'We may or may not have heard of him – under another name,

of course. May not even be a photograph of him in existence. Some of the world's wealthiest men are never photo-
graphed.'

George said: 'If he's as wealthy as we think he may be, why is
he trying to extract more from other sources?'

'Show. I'm convinced that Samuelson neither wants nor
needs money. But for all I know he may have persuaded his
partners that his funds are drying up and he's now making a
show about money to divert attention from the fact that money
is of no value to him and that his interests lie elsewhere. Agnelli
makes no secret of the fact that he's very interested in money
and this may be Samuelson's way of keeping him happy. He has
a large staff to keep happy and they'll be keenly interested in
seeing Samuelson displaying a keen interest in money. He
seems to need us – for what precise purpose we don't yet know,
we may well be here on only a contingency basis – but we need
money too. And Riordan, above all, has to be kept happy, for
Riordan above all needs unholy money to achieve his holy
purposes.'

'Unholy money for unholy purposes,' George said. 'Split
mind. Dichotomy. There must be something in this Irish-
American connection. We know there are men who are willing
to trade heroin for bags of gold to help a so-called worthy cause.
Purblindness. That the word?'

'Something like that. In medical terms, tunnel as opposed to
peripheral vision. We have to accept that it's an illness and try to
treat it as best we can.'

'How do we go about treating this ailment? The good doctor
has something on his mind?' Despite his vast bulk George
shivered in the bitter wind. 'A prescription? A nostrum?'

'Too late for medicine.'

'Surgery? I wouldn't even know which end of a scalpel to
hold.'

'You don't have to. In the best medical parlance, surgery, at
this moment, is contra-indicated.'

George cleared his throat delicately, which is no easy thing to
do in a gale-force wind. 'You have suddenly developed a
new-found regard for the well-being of murderous villains?

242

Criminals who are prepared to drown God knows how many thousands of our fellow countrymen?'

'No such sea-change, George. I know they have their quota of hard men and psychopathic nut-cases around here but do you seriously doubt for a moment that we could kill Riordan, Samuelson and Agnelli and get the girls away unharmed?'

'*I* know we could – I take back my ludicrous suggestion about your tender heart. Tungsten steel, more like.'

Vasco's expression didn't exactly register shock but it did hold a certain amount of apprehension and disbelief.

'You're a policeman. Sir. Sworn to uphold the law. I mean, give them a fair trial and hang them in the morning.'

'I'm my own court of law and I'd shoot them down like wild dogs if I thought it would solve anything but it wouldn't. Two reasons – one psychological, one practical.

'The psychological – curiosity, nosiness if you like. I am not convinced that those three are ordinary criminals. I am not convinced that Romero Agnelli is the murderous, ruthless killer we think he is. He bears no resemblance to his two brothers I put behind bars, who were Grade A vicious sadists. The fact that he hasn't laid a finger on either Julie or Annemarie helps bear that out. Or Riordan. He's no psychopath. Loony as a nut or nutty as a loon and a demagogue of some note – but only an occasional demagogue. But being loony doesn't necessarily mean that you're certifiable: there are quite a number of people tidied up – institutionalized, as they say – in lunatic asylums who are convinced that they are the only sane people around and that there exist great numbers of people, those responsible for wars, hunger, diseases, genocide, heroin pushers and those who talk glibly of nuclear annihilation, not to mention a few other trivial matters, who should be where they are, and who's to say they're not right?'

'And then there's the factor of demagoguery.'

'Dema what?' Vasco said.

'People who are supposed to go in for ranting and raving. A word that has fallen into disuse. A word associated with the likes of Hitler, Mussolini and a few dozen nationalistic leaders in the world today. There are good demagogues and bad ones.

243

Originally it meant people who were opposed to established rules of law, usually bad rules. Christ, if you like, could have been called a demagogue. Riordan, I admit, is no member of the Holy Trinity, but I believe him to be a sincere and honest demagogue, however misguided. I do not believe him to be evil.

'Samuelson is the nigger in the woodpile – if one can use such racist language in these days. He's the real enigma. You know that he's English?'

Both men shook their heads.

'He is. A wealthy man. Obviously, a very wealthy man. Sure, rich men are normally under a compulsion to become even richer, but there's a limit even to that and I believe Samuelson has reached that limit. As sane and stable a man as you could ever hope to meet. Beneath that bonhomie and geniality I think he's an obsessed man. A driven man. I would like to know what drives him. What do you think of Kathleen?'

Both men stared at him, then George said: 'Wait a minute.' He disappeared inside the mill and reappeared shortly afterwards with three very large glasses of brandy in his hands. 'If we are to continue this discussion in Verkhoyansk temperatures – what do you mean "Kathleen"?'

'What I said. How does she strike you?'

'We hardly know her,' George said. 'A lovely child, of course.'

'There you go again. You and your middle-aged propensities. Vasco?'

'I agree with George. I've never seen –' he broke off. 'She seems kind and gentle and –'

'An accomplished actress? A case-hardened spy?' Vasco said nothing. 'The feminine equivalent of the smiler with the knife under the cloak?'

'No!' Vasco was vehement.

'No, indeed. When she was watching that TV announcement tonight, you weren't. You were watching her. Not that I blame you, she's as watchable as anyone in the Netherlands. But that's not why you were watching her. Apropos of nothing, Vasco, I think you'd make an excellent Inspector. Under, of course, the watchful eye of George, whom I hope to persuade to leave his ill-chosen role of restaurateur.'

'Me?' George stared at him as if either or both of them had taken leave of their senses.

'You. You're wasted. Keep La Caracha, of course. Annelise is the best cook in Amsterdam and you could always hire a couple of thugs, preferably ex-convicts, to take over your distasteful duties as bouncer. But that's by the by. What did her eyes tell you, Vasco?'

'Her eyes?' Vasco was momentarily confused.

'Kathleen's. You were watching her eyes, not her face.'

'How did you know —'

'A combination of craftiness, cunning, deviousness and experience. Practice is all. Fear, distress?'

'Something like that. Distinctly unhappy. Edgy. Odd thing was, she was looking like that *before* the announcement was made. She knew what was coming or thought or was convinced she knew what was coming and didn't like it one little bit.'

'Another driven person,' van Effen said.

'If we're talking about drivers and driven people,' George said, 'you could also include Maria Agnelli. A great lip-licker is our Maria. We've all met people who lick their lips when they're in a state of sadistic anticipation but when you're in a state your lips don't tremble. Hers did. Nervous apprehension. Revulsion, if you like.'

'I missed that,' van Effen said.

'Well, we've each of us got only one pair of eyes,' George said reasonably. 'But you only had to have half an eye to see that Samuelson enjoyed every moment of the broadcast. So what do we have? Three driven people. One of those driven people, Samuelson, is also the driver, going hell-bent, one might say, round a series of hairpin bends down a pretty precipitous. mountain slope. The other two are driven, terrified of going over a precipice at the next hairpin.'

Vasco said in a complaining voice: 'You're going too fast for me. You make those two girls sound relatively harmless, maybe even nice. Joachim, Joop and those two other baby-faces in the mill here – Baader-Meinhof, RAF or whatever you call them – they are not nice.'

'They wouldn't agree,' van Effen said. 'They are the new Messiahs, dedicated to the creation of a nobler and better world. It's merely because of the blind folly of this misguided world that assassination and the deployment of tactical nuclear weapons have become their stock-in-trade.'

'And those two girls are their associates and allies,' Vasco said. He sounded very bitter indeed. 'Or do you dip your hand into this witches' brew of murder, mayhem, blackmail, terrorism and theft and bring them out pure as the driven snow?'

'A little dusting of soot, perhaps. Camouflage. A little coercion here, a little blackmail there, misguided love, misguided loyalty, a warped code of honour, a false sentimentality, a judicious mixture of truth and lies.'

' "Conned", I believe is the word you're after,' George said. 'But they weren't conning anyone when they kidnapped Julie.'

'Of course they were. Sure, they hoped to discourage me, but that was only the ostensible reason. Romero Agnelli would never have thought that up on his own and as for hurting my sister I've already given it as my opinion that he would be reluctant to tread on a beetle. The orders came from his brothers Giuseppe and Orlando, that delightful duo I put away all those years ago.'

'But they're in prison.'

Van Effen sighed. 'Vasco, Vasco. Some of the most powerful and vicious gangs in the world are controlled by bosses temporarily confined to maximum-security blocks in prisons. Palermo, Cagliari, Ajaccio, Marseilles, half a dozen cities in the United States, even London and Amsterdam and Naples – there's where the criminal overlords – overlords still with powers of life or death – hang out in their prison cells. It's Romero's brothers who have the orders for the sending of those menacing postcards to me, who ordered Julie's kidnapping. But they're not after Julie. I don't believe they're even after me. Convicted criminals, oddly enough, don't usually harbour grudges against the cops who caught them: their resentment is reserved for the judges who sentenced them. Italy is a classic example of this.'

'If they're not after you or Julie,' George said slowly, 'then my towering intellect tells me they're after something else. And to think that Samuelson had the staggering effrontery to say that Riordan was prepared to use the devil's tools to fight the devil.'

'And I said that one would require a very long spoon to sup with the devil.'

'Speaking about the devil,' Vasco said, 'and with all due respect, of course, what the devil are you two talking about?'

'The devil,' George said. 'Or devils. Part of the flooding – or non-flooding of the country – and it may even be a pre-condition – will be that Romero's murderous brothers be released from prison or, heaven help us, be given a free pardon.'

There was a brief hiatus while George returned inside the mill to get some more anti-pneumonia specific. When he returned van Effen said: 'Well, so much for theory. I think we've got everything right except Samuelson's ultimate motivation. We're not even wrong about that – we just don't know. Now, practicalities: that shouldn't take too long. Our options are limited and, besides, it's too damned cold.

'We have agreed that now is not the time to dispose of the three boss villains here. There are other and non-theoretical reasons. Samuelson may *not* be the C-in-C, although I'm convinced he is. There may be others. He has to have someone in the vicinity of the Ijsselmeer to trigger off that damned nuclear device of theirs. They also told us, unwisely, that this is only a stop-over HQ. The other will be their main one and, almost certainly, the one from which they intend to make their final strike. We have to find it so, for the moment, we have to go along with them.

'I'm more than prepared for the fact that they'll breach the dykes north and south of Lelystad and flood the east and south Flevoland areas shortly after midnight because I'm equally certain that the British are going to temporize and not throw in the towel before the first bell rings. With any luck there should be no loss of life – human life, that is: I wouldn't care to guess what is going to happen to the livestock. This nuclear device to be detonated in the Ijsselmeer tomorrow afternoon presents a more serious threat – my guess is that it would be in the Markerwaard – and I wouldn't much care to be in the vicinity of Marken or Volendam when it went off. Nasty things, tidal waves, especially when the height is unpredictable. Things might even be unpleasant in Hoorn or Amsterdam itself, although I doubt it. After all, this is meant primarily as a demonstration for the British cabinet or whatever. The big bang will come later – considering the steadily worsening conditions that should be at the next high tide afterwards. Or the one after that. In daylight, anyway.'

Vasco said: 'Why daylight?'

'You think they have this helicopter just to make a non-existent film? They want it to take them some place a land-based vehicle can't reach. An island, perhaps, though that seems unlikely. The point is that it's very difficult to land a helicopter in gale force winds although highly-trained air-sea rescue pilots do it regularly. But to try it in a gale in total darkness and driving rain – in zero visibility, that is – is foolhardy to the point of suicide – especially if you happen to have as part of your cargo some potentially unstable nuclear devices. So, daylight.'

'We might be here for a couple of days yet?' George said.

'My guess is that we'll be off first light in the morning. They'll want to establish themselves in their HQ, near the scene of action. Those ground-to-ground and ground-to-air missiles – they have been deactivated?' George nodded. 'How are you when it comes to deactivating tactical nuclear devices?'

'I've never even *seen* a tactical nuclear device. If I could examine one or see a blue-print, well, yes, perhaps. Otherwise, no. I know I wouldn't feel a thing but I still don't much fancy being vaporized.'

'Well, we'll have a look at them later on tonight. They're somewhere on the premises. We don't even have to look. You heard what Agnelli said – "I can show them to you now." '

'Won't that make them suspicious?' George said. 'That we didn't ask to see them right away? They'll be thinking we have been having a conference and have dreamed up some devilish scheme.'

'Let them think what they like and be as suspicious as they like. We're as safe as men in a church. We, my friends, are indispensable.' George and Vasco looked at each other, then at van Effen, but said nothing. 'We're also not very bright. Joop, Joachim or some of their psychopathic Red Army Faction pals stole those nuclear devices from the US NATO arms dump near Metnitz on the night of February 3rd. Something else happened on that same night.'

'February 3rd,' George said. 'Of course. We really are not very bright. That was the night the De Doorns ammunition dump was blown out of existence. Samuelson's explosive experts trying to replenish their supplies. An enormous crater. No replenishments and, of course, no experts. No wonder the FFF were so desperate for our supplies and services. We're probably the only people around who could set off a squib. Lloyd's of London would approve of this.'

Vasco said: A marvellous insurance policy, to be sure. But has the thought occurred to you that Joop or one of his lunatic associates may know how to trigger those nuclear devices?'

'The thought has occurred,' van Effen said. 'So we'll just have to attend to the lunatics or the devices, won't we? Or both. But before we start attending to anything I suggest we go inside, have a wash and brush up, find out how thoroughly they have examined our luggage, listen to the next riveting communication from the Dutch or British governments or the FFF, then join our genial hosts for dinner. One would imagine that a man of Samuelson's resources could run to a cordon bleu chef.'

Romero Agnelli greeted them genially on their entrance and at once pressed jonge jenevers on them. 'You must be needing this after your long stay outside. I mean, it's pretty cold tonight.'

'Not for us,' van Effen said. 'We're fresh-air fanatics.'

'I thought that applied only to the English. Anyway, I trust you enjoyed your stroll.'

'If you call pacing up and down your verandah a stroll, then, yes, we did.' Van Effen knew that Agnelli was perfectly well aware that they had not once left the verandah.

'And, of course, the opportunity for a private conversation.'
Agnelli was still smiling.

'Well, yes. Pondering our probable future, about which we know precious little. After all, you and your friends are hardly very communicative. We don't know what we're here for, what services we are expected to perform, where we're going, even when we're going.'

'That last I can tell you – eight o'clock tomorrow morning. As for the rest, well, you and I are great believers in the need-to-know principle.'

'True, true. But there's one thing that we do need to know – where do we sleep tonight? On the floor?'

'Dear me, no. Mind you, this is no Amstel but we do have accommodation of sorts. Come, I'll show you. I've already had your baggage brought up.'

He led the way up the curving staircase and along to a door at the end of a passageway. The room beyond was of moderate size with three single beds. Agnelli indicated a door at the far end of the room.

'Bathroom. No marble bath, no gold taps, but serviceable enough.' He looked at his watch. 'Dinner in twenty minutes.' He left, still smiling.

Van Effen and George sat on their beds, engaged in desultory conversation, while Vasco looked around. In this particular kind of looking-around Vasco was a specialist, very meticulous, very thorough. After a few minutes he said: 'Clear. No bugs.'

George hoisted his medium-sized suitcase on to his knees. It was one of those fancy cases with combination locks, four figures by each of the two keyholes, eight in all. George peered at it closely.

'Combinations as set?' van Effen said.

'As set. But not untouched. Very tiny scratches. This case is brand new, never been used before. Normally, I wouldn't be seen dead with this junior-executive status symbol but Annelise gave it to me for my birthday and it would have been more than my life's worth to have left home without it. It's been opened and closed and in very short order, too. I don't know of a safe-breaker in the Netherlands who could have done this.

Anyone who knows his job can open a conventional safe – a pair of good ears or a doctor's stethoscope can hear the tumblers click. No tumblers in this type of lock.'

Van Effen said: 'I'll bet O'Brien could open the vaults of the Amsterdam-Rotterdam bank with a bent hairpin.'

'I wouldn't doubt it.' George adjusted the combination figures and opened the case. 'A very neat character. Everything exactly where it was except of course where it's naturally settled in the process of being carried.'

'Yours, Vasco?'

Vasco unlocked his case. 'Untouched. Spare Smith & Wesson magazines still there.'

'Naturally.' Van Effen opened his own case – it hadn't even been locked – lifted out a rather battered toilet bag and took from it a burgundy-coloured aerosol can with a chrome top. The side of the can bore the legend: Yves Saint Laurent – Pour Homme – Mousse à Raser. The aerosol, in fact, contained no shaving foam.

'Well,' George said, 'nobody's been touching or sniffing the contents of that lot.'

'Obviously.' Van Effen replaced the aerosol. 'If they had they'd still be here. Horizontal on the carpet. I doubt if they even opened my toilet bag. If there was anything worth finding, they must have reckoned, it would have been in George's thief-proof case.' He took a small tablet of soap from his toilet bag and handed it to Vasco. 'You know what to do with this.'

'Hygiene is all.' Vasco went into the bathroom while van Effen and George crossed to the window opposite the beds and opened it. As far as they could judge in the darkness they were about fifteen feet above the cobbled courtyard below, a courtyard shrouded in almost total darkness.

'Very satisfactory, George, don't you think?'

'Very. Only snag is that you'll have to make a pretty long detour to keep in the darkness in order to reach the back of the barn. And have you thought of anti-personnel land-mines – you know, the nasty kind that jump three feet in the air before exploding?'

'George, this place is run and staffed entirely by local villagers. If, say, a laundry-maid was just kind of accidentally blown in half –'

'True. Point taken. But if you were to run into a patrolling member of the FFF –'

'Anybody out on patrol on a night like this has to be a head case. Gale, driving rain, bitter cold, thunder and lightning due any time –'

'But –'

'I'm not going to run into anyone. Someone might run into me. Velvet gloves. Vasco's taking his time, isn't he?' They moved to the bathroom door, tried to open it and found it locked. Van Effen rattled the door handle.

'Put out your light,' Vasco said. They did as he asked. Vasco opened the door of the bathroom which was in total darkness. 'Sorry about that, gentlemen, but I didn't want the watcher in the shadows to know that he was being watched by another watcher in the shadows. Not, mind you, that our fellow-watcher is very much in the shadows.'

The bathroom window was, in fact, directly opposite the door in the loft of the barn that held the army truck on the ground floor. The man standing in the doorway was making no great effort to conceal his presence and the courtyard light projecting from the mill verandah was quite strong.

'Doesn't seem to me to be guarding against anything very much,' van Effen said. 'Unenthusiastic. Don't blame him. Must seem like a pretty useless exercise on a night like this.'

'And a pretty freezing exercise, too,' George said.

'He generates his own heat,' Vasco said. 'Wait.'

They didn't have to wait long. After less than two minutes the guard reached behind him, lifted a bottle to his lips and took what appeared to be a very considerable swig from it.

'No mineral water, that's for sure,' van Effen said. 'Let's get inside.'

They closed the bathroom door behind them and switched on the bedroom light. Vasco handed van Effen a small metallic object sheathed in polythene. Van Effen dropped it in his pocket.

'I've stuck the two pieces of soap together and left them in hot watcr,' Vasco said. 'Should be mushed together again pretty soon. I have an idea. Just after I got into the bathroom I saw a man crossing the courtyard towards the barn. That's when I switched off the light. He disappeared round the back of the barn, you know, where the outside stairs are, and then joined the man who was then standing at the loft door. Changing of the guard, so to speak. That was exactly at seven o'clock. It occurred to me that it might be very convenient if the condition of my throat has deteriorated so badly that I will be unable to join you for dinner. It might be very convenient if we found out how regularly they changed guards.'

'It would indeed,' van Effen said. 'An excellent suggestion, Vasco. Should have thought of it myself. Promotion guaranteed – if, that is, we survive this lot. I'm sure Samuelson will be most distressed. Probably insist on sending you another toddy.'

'Make sure it's a large one, if you please. I'm feeling very weak.'

'Mr Danilov. George.' As van Effen and George descended the stairs into the living-room, Samuelson advanced to greet them, beaming as if they were long-lost friends. 'Just in time for the next TV broadcast. Then dinner. But where's our dashing young Lieutenant?'

'Our young Lieutenant isn't feeling at all dashing. Throat's worse. Flu, I think.'

Samuelson clucked his tongue and shook his head. 'Damn flu's everywhere these days. This awful weather. Most important that he's reasonably fit tomorrow. Herta!' This to a flaxen-haired young girl who was setting the table for the evening meal. 'A toddy. A strong one. Take it up to the Lieutenant's room. Dear me, dear me. Ah!'

Agnelli had just turned up the volume of the TV set and a rock band, which had been playing, mercifully, in apparent mime, faded from the screen to be replaced by the accustomed announcer looking, if possible, even more lugubrious and funereal than he had on the previous occasion.

'With reference to the threats being made against our country by the unidentified group calling themselves the FFF, the

Ministry of Defence has just issued a statement. The British Government and ours are in constant contact but no announcement as to the results of those negotiations can yet be made pending the outcome of discussions between Whitehall and Stormont. Stormont is the parliament or governing body of Northern Ireland which is, of course, next to ourselves, the country most closely concerned with the outcome of those negotiations. Whitehall, it must be said, finds itself in a most difficult and peculiar position. Ulster, Northern Ireland, that is, although an integral part of Great Britain, retains a certain degree of autonomy as far as decisions relating to its own future is concerned. When further news comes to hand the country will be immediately informed.

'The FFF have informed us that they will issue a further communiqué after this broadcast. This will be transmitted to you at 8 p.m.

'In the circumstances, the latest report from the meteorological office is relevant. The wind, due north, is Force Nine and strengthening. Torrential rain is sweeping over most of Scandinavia and is heaviest of all over the Netherlands. The North Sea is expected to reach its highest level for at least the past quarter century inside the next forty-eight hours.'

The announcer's image faded and Agnelli switched off the set.

'Dear me, dear me,' Samuelson said. 'Things do look very unpromising. Or very promising. All depends upon one's point of view.' He gestured towards the bar. 'Romero, see to it that our friends are not neglected. Excuse me, ladies and gentlemen. I shall be back shortly.' He disappeared up the stairs.

While the Agnelli brothers busied themselves behind the bar van Effen wandered aimlessly around the room apparently admiring the paintings and the bronze and copper artefacts that decorated the walls. He paid particular but very brief attention to the telephone: the telephone number had been carefully and thoroughly inked out, which neither surprised nor disturbed him. He was reasonably certain that he could, later that night, have given that number to the police HQ in the Marnixstraat in Amsterdam, which would have enabled them to pinpoint the exact whereabouts of the windmill, but that would not have suited his purpose: the answer to the machinations of the FFF lay elsewhere. Samuelson, presumably and for reasons best known to himself, had gone upstairs to use another telephone to deliver the text of the next FFF communiqué.

Dinner that night was a rather odd affair. Not that there was anything odd about the food. Obviously, there wasn't a cordon bleu chef within miles. The Dutch, taken by and large, are not gourmets. Your standard Dutch cook or housewife consider it a matter of personal pride and honour and an insult to their guests if they can see any part of the plate under the mound of food that covers it: the food was palatable enough but Michelin would not have come there a second time.

What was odd was the contrasting behaviour of the diners. Samuelson, Romero Agnelli, van Effen and George were in an expansive, genial and talkative mood. Daniken made an occasional contribution but was clearly no conversationalist. The Rev. Riordan, apart from delivering a lengthy and, in the circumstances, extremely hypocritical blessing before the meal, remained grave and thoughtful and totally silent throughout the meal: Riordan, van Effen reflected, if not quite deranged or demented, was totally detached from reality and possessed of an incredible naiveté. Leonardo was equally silent. He, too, was thinking, but only of his stomach: for a man of his diminutive stature, he was an awesome trencherman. They spoke only when spoken to, smiled but seldom and for the most part were remote and withdrawn to the point of being dispirited.

At one point van Effen said to Romero Agnelli: 'And where's our friend O'Brien tonight? He's not down with the flu, I trust?'

'O'Brien's as fit as a fiddle. He's elsewhere.'

Van Effen said: 'Ah.'

Samuelson smiled. 'You really are a singularly incurious person, Mr Danilov.'

'Would it help any if I knew where he was or what he was doing?'

'No. Romero has spoken to me several times about your need-to-know philosophy. It is one with which I am in entire agreement.' He glanced at his watch. 'Romero, it lacks one minute to eight o'clock.

It was the same newscaster. He looked as if he had just heard that his entire family had been wiped out in an air crash.

'We have here the latest communiqué from the FFF.' He didn't sound at all like a newsreader, he intoned the words like a minister delivering a funeral oration. 'It is very brief and reads as follows: "We place no credence in the Ministry of Defence's statement. We think the Dutch and British governments are either stalling or don't believe in our threats. Or both. We do not intend to stall. We do intend to make them believe our threats. The dykes north and south of Lelystad will be breached a few minutes after midnight. The nuclear device in the Ijsselmeer will be detonated at 2 p.m. tomorrow. We beg you to believe that these two incidents will be regarded as the merest trifles compared to the disaster that will engulf the Netherlands within twenty-four hours of the detonation of the nuclear device." That is the end of their communiqué.

'We have also had a further statement from the Ministry of Defence. They say that they have no comment to make on this latest communiqué on the basis that there is no way that they can predict the irrational workings of the minds of terrorists.' Samuelson clicked his tongue and shook his head sadly. 'They say they are prepared to believe that the terrorists are insane enough to carry out their insane threats' – more cluckings and shakings from Samuelson – 'and can do no more than warn all local authorities to carry out all possible means of protection.

'Netherlands experts and British nuclear scientists have agreed on the probable results of such a nuclear explosion. It is assumed that this will take place in the Markerwaard. If this device is located in or near the centre of the Markerwaard, the tsunami – the tidal wave – reaching the shores should be of minor proportions, averaging between sixty and seventy centimetres. Should it be placed close inshore the wave could be several times as high and the local results could be disastrous.

'The nation will be immediately informed of any further developments.'

Agnelli switched off the set. Samuelson, half-smiling, looked

256

at van Effen and said: 'Do I detect just a trace of a half frown, Mr Danilov?' Van Effen made no reply. 'Romero has told me that you are prepared to react in an extremely violent form to any threat to the lives of your fellow citizens or, rather, to the citizens of your adopted country. Romero is of the opinion that you and your two friends are highly dangerous men. I concur. You are, I believe, heavily armed.'

Van Effen opened his jacket to demonstrate that he wasn't carrying his shoulder-holstered Smith and Wesson, then turned to Agnelli, who was sitting next to him, crossed his knees and pulled up his right trouser leg to show that he wasn't carrying his Lilliput either. 'I do not consider guns as being an essential part of dressing for dinner. Do you think I would be so mad as to start a gun-fight in the company of four beautiful young ladies? Any ladies, come to that?'

'No. My mistake. The nuclear device is in the Markerwaard but is located precisely in its centre. Do you believe me?'

'If I had your unpleasantly suspicious mind I would say that I'd wait until five past two tomorrow afternoon to find out. As it happens, I believe you. Now, Mr Samuelson, you know that I do not normally probe into anyone's affairs but I must confess to being just a little concerned about those nuclear devices. My two friends and I are acknowledged explosives experts but we know nothing about nuclear devices. We wouldn't recognize one if we saw it, far less know how to arm it, activate it or deactivate it. But we do know they are nasty, jiggly and unpredictable things. I do know you have some on the prem- ises, although I don't know how many. What I do know is that I have a healthy regard for my own skin. I assume you're transporting them elsewhere – they can be of no use to you here. I have no wish to be aboard whatever form of transportation is taking those devices from here to wherever elsewhere may be.'

Samuelson smiled. 'Mr Daniken here shares your sentiments exactly.'

'What has Mr Daniken got to do with it?'

'Mr Daniken is our helicopter pilot. He doesn't want to carry those things.'

'I didn't refuse to, Mr Samuelson,' Daniken said. 'I said I was highly reluctant because of the great risk involved. I agree with Mr Danilov. I don't know how unstable or temperamental those damn things are. Flying conditions are atrocious, just on the limit. With an updraught or wind shear we can go up or down a hundred feet in two seconds. We could make a heavy landing, a crash landing or, heaven help us, just crash.'

'You and Mr Danilov can relax. Should have mentioned it before, but we made our minds up just before dinner. No helicopter. We have decided to use the army truck with which Mr Danilov and his friends have so thoughtfully provided us. Those devices are quite small and can easily be concealed in what looks like a couple of extra long-range petrol tanks. We'll have three men dressed in uniforms, Ylvisaker as a full-scale lieutenant-colonel, and the rest –'

'Where did you get the uniforms?' van Effen said.

'I told you,' Samuelson said patiently. 'We're making a war film. The rest of us go by helicopter.'

'Must be some helicopter.'

'A war film, I said. A gunship. The end of the Vietnam war caught the US Air Force on the hop and they had over-produced. Going for a song. Elderly but fully serviceable. Stripped of armament, of course, but we ordered dummies. I suggest we move to more comfortable chairs for our brandies, liqueurs or whatever.'

Van Effen said: 'If I may be excused, I'd like to have a look at the Lieutenant.'

'Give him my sympathies,' Samuelson said. 'I suggest he might appreciate another toddy.'

'Thank you. I'm sure he would. If he's not asleep, that is.'

Vasco was not asleep. He was comfortably seated in a small armchair that he had brought into the bathroom. Using the pencil beam of the variably hooded torch which was an indispensable item of his travelling equipment, van Effen handed Vasco the glass.

'Compliments of Mr Samuelson.'

'Very civil of him. Well, it's eight-twenty now and the same character is still on watch. Judging from his performance with that bottle he must be half sloshed by this time. Like me, as you can see, he's found an armchair. I'm surprised he hasn't dropped off by this time. Anyway, I'll keep watch until they change guard. The toddy will help sustain me through the long watches of the night.'

Van Effen gave him a brief resumé of the Ministry of Defence's statement and the FFF's reply, promised that he and George would be back by nine o'clock and left.

He returned to the living-room to find that the group seated in armchairs had been considerably depleted.

'The Lieutenant seems to have benefited from that first toddy. He doesn't sound quite so hoarse. Very drowsy but not too drowsy to attack the second toddy. His thanks. And dear me, dear me, the lovely young ladies have departed. Shame. But I'm not surprised. They were hardly what you might call gay and vivacious at the table tonight.'

'They said they were tired,' Samuelson said. Julie, van Effen knew, had not been tired. She was a notoriously poor air traveller and the thought of travelling in a helicopter – she'd never been in one in her life – must have been a nightmare. 'Whatever have they done to make them tired?'

'Nothing. They're just nervous and apprehensive.'

'Just like George and myself.'

Samuelson surveyed him dispassionately. 'I doubt whether you and your big friend have ever been nervous and apprehensive in your lives.'

'There's always a first time. And where's the holy father?'

'You know the Reverend doesn't drink. But it's not that. Every night before he goes to sleep he spends an hour in meditation and prayer.'

Van Effen said sombrely: 'Let's hope he includes in his prayers the souls of the victims of his nuclear toys.'

The silence that followed, of which van Effen seemed to be quite unaware, was, to say the least, embarrassing. It was Romero, in a clear attempt to break the silence, who said hastily: 'Speaking of those nuclear toys, as you call them, I told you earlier I could show them to you. As an explosives expert, I thought you might be interested –'

'Not I.' Van Effen waved an indifferent hand. 'Same old principles – need-to-know and would it help any if I saw them?' He was aware of George's momentary slight frown but knew that no one else had seen it. Van Effen paused, as if something had just occurred to him, then said: 'Someone has to be able to trigger off those nuclear devices. Don't tell me it's Joop and his psychopathic pals.'

'It is indeed, as you say in your disparaging fashion, Joop and his psychopathic friends.' The words held a rebuke but the tone didn't: it required no telepathy to realize that Samuelson shared van Effen's opinion of the Red Army Faction. 'When they got hold of those devices in Metnitz, they also obtained copies of the operating instructions. One would have been useless without the other.'

'Remind me not to be within five kilometres of Joop and company when they arm either of those devices. A palm-reader once told me I had a long life-line but she could have been wrong. How is this device in the Markerwaard to be detonated?'

'Pre-set timing device.'

'And the two other devices?'

'By radio control.'

'God help us all. Make that ten kilometres.'

'You don't trust them?'

'I wouldn't trust Joop and his friends with a firework. They are fanatics and fanatics have unstable minds. Unstable hands also, probably. No, I don't trust them. Neither, I suspect, do you.'

'You still wouldn't like to see those devices?'

'I presume you're not lunatic enough to keep those in the mill.'

'They're a kilometre away in a secure underground cellar.'

'I've no intention of going out in that monsoon. And though you might not be lunatic I think you're guilty of a grave error of judgement. To detonate any device by radio doesn't call for the mind of an Einstein but it can be tricky and a job for experts.

Joop and his band of trusty experts have never detonated a charge in their lives.'

'And how would you know that?'

'That's being simple-minded. Why did you have to call me in for the palace job?'

'True, true. Would your scruples, or your objections to monsoons, prevent you from having a look at the operating instructions? We have them in this room.'

Van Effen looked at him then looked away. The TV was on, showing a weirdly dressed quartet who were presumably singing, but, perhaps fortunately, in silence: the volume control had been turned off. Samuelson and his friends were presumably expecting another newscast. Van Effen looked back at Samuelson.

'Scruples? What you have in mind, of course, is that we should do your work – your dirty work – for you instead of those deranged amateurs. Do you know what would happen if those explosions resulted in the deaths of any citizens?'

'Yes. You would ensure that I joined the departed. I wouldn't like that at all.'

'Let's see the plans.'

Romero Agnelli removed a couple of papers and handed one each to van Effen and George. George was the first to speak and that only after a few seconds.

'This isn't a half-kilo device. It's only for the equivalent of fifty tons of TNT.'

Samuelson came very close to smirking. 'The equivalent of ten tons would have suited me equally well. But it's useful to exaggerate the terror potential, don't you think?'

George didn't say what he thought. After less than a minute he looked up and spoke again. 'Only moderately complicated and very precise. Two snags. The first is that Joop speaks fractured English and people who have difficulty in speaking only the simplest form of a language usually are pretty hopeless when it comes to reading or writing it. The second snag is the jargon.'

'Jargon?'

'Technical terms,' van Effen said. 'They might as well be in Sanskrit as far as Joop is concerned.'

'Well?'

Van Effen handed his paper back to Agnelli. 'We'll have to think and talk about it.'

Samuelson tried, not altogether successfully, to smother the smile of a man who knows he has won his point. For the next minute or two they remained, sipping their brandies in comparative and apparently companionable silence, when the singers, if such they were, slowly faded from the screen to be replaced by the now familiar figure of the tragedy-stricken newscaster.

'The government have just announced that they have just received two more demands from the FFF. The first of those concerned the demand for a hundred and twenty million guilders and how it is to be transferred. The government does not say whether it will accede to the request and refuses to discuss the nature of the transfer. The second demand is for the release of two prisoners who were imprisoned several years ago for crimes of extreme violence. The government refuses to disclose the names of the prisoners.

'We would remind viewers that we shall be on the air again at midnight to find out whether the FFF have, in fact, breached the Flevoland dykes.'

Agnelli switched off the set. 'Satisfactory,' Samuelson said. He was actually rubbing his hands together. 'Eminently satisfactory.'

'Seems like a pretty silly and stupid broadcast to me,' van Effen said.

'Not at all.' Samuelson was positively beaming. 'The nation now knows that the government has received details of our demands and, as they have not outright rejected them it probably means that they are going to accede to them. It also shows how weak the government is and in how strong a position we are.'

'That's not what I mean. They've been stupid. They didn't have to make that announcement at all.'

'Oh, yes, they did. They were told that if they didn't we would radio the communiqué to Warsaw who would be just too delighted to re-broadcast it to Western Europe.'

'You have a transmitter that can reach as far as Warsaw?'

'We haven't got a transmitter, period. Nor do we know anyone in Warsaw. The threat was enough. Your government,' Samuelson said with considerable satisfaction, 'is now reduced to such a state of fear and trepidation, that they believe anything we say. Besides, they would look pretty silly, wouldn't they, if the announcement came through Poland?'

Van Effen refused the offer of a second brandy, he had every reason to keep a clear mind for the next hour or two, and said goodnight.

Samuelson looked at him in some surprise. 'But you'll be coming down to see the midnight broadcast?'

'I don't think so. I don't doubt your ability to carry out your threat.'

'I'm going too,' George said, 'but I shall be back down. Just going to see how the Lieutenant is. Incidentally, Mr Samuelson, if I may –'

'Another toddy for the young lieutenant. Certainly, my friend, certainly.'

'He may have a bit of a head in the morning,' George said, 'but he should be halfway towards recovery in the morning.'

Vasco, was in fact, in excellent health and showing no signs of an incipient headache.

'Still the same lad. I should imagine the changeover will be at nine. Some guard. Spends most of the time with his chin on his chest then jerks awake.'

'Let's hope his relief is of the same cast of mind. Me, I'm going to have a snooze. If he's still there at, say, nine-twenty, give me a shake. If he's relieved at nine, shake me at ten. How do you operate the radio on that army truck? And what's its range?'

'Unlimited. Well, a hundred, two hundred kilometres, I'm not sure. Operation is simple. Just lift the receiver and press the red button. The transmitter is pre-set to the nearest army command base which is always manned.'

'I particularly don't want to talk to the army. I want to talk to Marnixstraat.'

'Easy. Standard tuning dial, standard wave-bands and a switch beside the button for illumination that picks out the wave-lengths very easily indeed.'

Van Effen nodded, stretched out on a bed and closed his eyes.

Ten

George woke van Effen at 10 p.m.

'New sentry took over at nine. Hardly seems an improvement on the other one except, that is, from your point of view. He's middle-aged, fat, wears two overcoats, is sitting in the armchair with a rug over his knees and, you'll be pleased to hear, also has a bottle in his hand.'

'Sounds like my kind of man.' Van Effen rose and changed his trousers for a pair of denims.

Vasco said: 'What's that? Your battle uniform?'

'What's Samuelson going to say if he sees me in sodden trousers or even dry trousers that are so wrinkled that it will look as if I'd fallen into a river?'

'Ah. Well, you're going to get wet enough, that's for sure. Rain's heavier than ever. There are times when we can hardly see the lad in the loft doorway.'

'Suits me fine. That barn wasn't built yesterday and old floor-boards in old lofts tend to creak. With rain like this drumming on the roof he won't be able to hear a thing. Besides, judging from George's general description, the sentry is probably half deaf anyway.' He strapped on his Smith and Wesson, shrugged into his jacket and put the aerosol can in one pocket and the hooded torch in the other.

'Velvet gloves,' George said.

Vasco said: 'What's that?'

'Silenced pistol and a knockout gas canister. That's what he calls velvet gloves.'

Van Effen dug into an inside pocket, brought out a small leather wallet, unzipped it, took out the metallic contents, examined them, then returned them to the wallet and pocket.

'Skeleton keys and picklocks,' George said approvingly. 'No self-respecting detective should be without them.'

Vasco said: 'What happens if you don't come back, sir?'

'I shall be back. It's five past ten now. I should be back by ten-thirty. If I'm not back by eleven go downstairs. Say nothing. No doomladen speeches, no warnings that their end is nigh. Kill Samuelson. Cripple the Agnelli brothers and Daniken, and, if Riordan is there, him also. Remove all weapons of course and one of you keep an eye on them and make sure that nobody tries to stagger out of the room and summon help while the other gets the girls. As your guns are silenced, there should be no interruptions. Then get the hell out of it. If anyone gets in your way, you know what to do.'

'I see.' Vasco looked and sounded more than slightly shocked. 'And how do we get the hell out of it?'

Van Effen touched the pocket where he had replaced his wallet of skeleton keys and picklocks. 'What do you think those are for?'

'Ah. The army truck.'

'Indeed. As soon as you get under way, call up the army or the cops. Give them the approximate location of this place – we know it's somewhere between Leerdam and Gorinchen – and leave the rest to them.'

Vasco said: 'They might try to escape by helicopter.'

'You have the alternative of shooting Daniken in both shoulders or taking him with you. I'm virtually certain that none of this will happen. I don't want it to happen and that's not primarily because by the time it happens I'll probably be dead. It would be a confession of failure and I don't like being associated with failure. It would be a most unsatisfactory conclusion: in fact, it would be no conclusion at all. Samuelson has another headquarters and, as we have agreed, other associates: O'Brien has almost certainly departed this evening to associate with those other associates. Even although I doubt it, some of those associates may – I repeat may – be in a position to carry out his plans to a successful conclusion.' He opened the window. 'Back at ten-thirty.'

He slid down the two knotted sheets and vanished into the shadows.

George and Vasco went into the darkened bathroom. Vasco said: 'He *is* a cold-blooded bastard, isn't he?'

George said: 'Um.'

'But he's a killer.'

'I know he has killed and would do so again. But he's very selective, is our Peter. Nobody who has ever departed this world and at his hands has ever been mourned by society.'

Four minutes later Vasco caught George by the arm. 'See?'

They saw. The sentry had just taken a long swig from his bottle, laid it on the floor beside him, clasped his hands over his rug and appeared to relapse into some kind of yoga-like contemplation. The shadow that had loomed behind him resolved itself into the unmistakable form of van Effen, whose right hand curved round and held the aerosol can an inch or two from the sentry's face for a period of not more than two seconds. He then pocketed the aerosol, hooked his hands under the man's knees and eased him forward several inches to ensure that he wouldn't topple sideways from his armchair, picked up a bottle from the floor, poured some of the contents over the sentry's face, emptied the remainder of the contents over the front of his clothes, wrapped the fingers of the unconscious man's right hand round the bottle, thrust hand and bottle partly under the rug, tightened the rug to ensure that hand and bottle would remain where they were then vanished into the gloom.

'Well, now,' Vasco said, 'there's one character who isn't going to report himself for dereliction of duty because of dropping off into a drunken slumber.'

'Our Peter doesn't do things by halves. Let's see now. A two-second burst. He should come to in about half an hour. Peter explained those things to me once.'

'Won't he know he has been drugged?'

'That's the beauty of it! Leaves no trace. That apart, what would you think if you woke up with your clothes reeking of schnapps or whatever and your hand clasped round an empty bottle?'

The stairs, broad and very creaking and just behind where the sentry slept, led directly to the floor of the barn, now converted

267

into a temporary garage. Torch in hand, van Effen descended quickly, loosed the bolts on the retaining half of the entrance door and turned his attention to the army truck. The exterior was as it had been except that the number plates had been changed. He then wriggled under the truck, scraped clear an area on the underside of the chassis just forward of the rear axle and attached to it the magnetic clamp of the metallic device which Vasco had removed from the bar of soap. Thirty seconds later he was in the driver's seat and through to the Marnixstraat.

'Put me through to Colonel de Graaf, please.'

'Who is speaking?'

'Never mind who's speaking. The Colonel.'

'He's at home.'

'He is not. He's there. Ten seconds or you're an ex-policeman tomorrow.'

In just ten seconds the Colonel was on the phone. 'You were a bit harsh on that poor lad.' His voice held a complaining note.

'He's either a fool, an incompetent or was improperly instructed. He was told to keep open an anonymous line.' Van Effen spoke in Polish, which the Colonel understood as well as he did. Dutch police changed their wave-lengths at infrequent intervals and had done so again only that day. As in every major city in the world, villains occasionally picked up police wave-lengths. But the probabilities against a villain who understood Polish picking up a changed wave-length were astronomical. 'Please switch on your recorder. I don't know how much time I have and I don't want to repeat myself.'

'Proceed.'

'I shall spell names backwards. We are south of – this is a name – Utrecht – and between – two other names – Leerdam and Gorinchen. You have that?'

'I have that.'

'Do not attempt to locate and do not attempt to attack. "The Principals are elsewhere"' – it was an outright lie but the Colonel was not to know that – 'and it would achieve only the deaths of five people who don't deserve to die. You know the people I mean?'

'I know.'

'We have here the army truck. You know which one. It has changed the identification plates. I will give you the new numbers. Backwards.' Van Effen did so. 'It will be carrying the nuclear devices you know about.'

'What!'

'I have attached a magnetic transmitter bug to this vehicle. Have an unmarked police car in the vicinity as from, say, 7 a.m. It is to track this truck at a safe distance. This police car will also be in radio contact with two or three Army Commando trucks lying to the west. I am becoming increasingly convinced that this truck will be heading towards the Scheldt area. There will be three people in that truck, all dressed in Dutch army uniforms, including a bogus lieutenant-colonel called Ylvisaker, who may even call himself by that name. I want that truck seized along with its occupants and the seizure to be kept in complete secrecy. If you release that news then the responsibility for the flooding of the country will lie in your hands.'

De Graaf's voice took on an even more complaining note. 'You don't have to threaten me, my boy.'

'I apologize. I am under intense pressure and have to make my points in as impressive a way as I can. One other thing. Have TV and radio announce – or just say, if you like – that they are to be of good heart and that you are closing in on the Rotterdam and Scheldt areas. The reason to be given is that you want every citizen thereabouts to be on continuous alert and report anything abnormal to the police. This is purely psychological and I don't believe our friends are very good at psychology. But please, please, apart from taking this truck in complete secrecy, no other attempts at interference.'

'Understood. I have someone with me who would like a word with you and who speaks Polish even better than you and I do.'

'Spell his name backwards.'

De Graaf did so and Wieringa's voice came on the phone. 'Congratulations, my boy.'

'Those may be a bit premature, Minister. I can't for instance, stop the breaching of the Flevoland dykes or the detonation of the Markewaard device. A further thought has occurred to me. You might have the media include in their broadcasts about the

Rotterdam area that Whitehall and Stormont have arrived at an agreement to begin active and immediate negotiations.'

'The two parliaments might not like it.'

'I'm a Dutchman. Instruct them to like it.'

'Some obscure psychological motive again, I suppose. Very well, I agree. Frankly, my boy, how do you rate our chances?'

'Better than evens, Minister. They trust us. They have to trust us.' He explained briefly about the De Doorns ammunition dump and the RAF's inability to handle radio-controlled devices. 'Apart from that, I'm not only sure but know that they don't distrust or suspect us. They are basically naive, complacent, over confident and sure of themselves. They lack the devious minds of honest detectives. I have to move, sir. I'll call again as soon as whenever possible.'

In the Marnixstraat, the Minister of Defence said: 'You agree with van Effen's assessment, Colonel?'

'If that's what he thinks then that's what I think.'

'Why isn't that young man – well, young compared to us – not Chief of Police somewhere?'

'He'll be the chief here in the not too distant future. In the meantime, I need him.'

'Don't we all,' Wieringa sighed. 'Don't we all.'

Van Effen climbed up to the loft, patted the sentry lightly on the cheek, got no reaction and left. Three minutes later he was inside the bedroom. Vasco looked pointedly at his watch.

'Ten thirty-three,' Vasco said accusingly.

'Sorry. I was detained. Anyway, that's a fine way to welcome back a man who may just have escaped the jaws of death.'

'There was trouble?'

'No. Clockwork.'

'You didn't unpick the garage lock,' George said, also accusingly.

'Another warm welcome. Where are the congratulations for a mission successfully accomplished? Would you have picked that lock if, at the window next to our bathroom, you had seen the Reverend Riordan, who seems to meditate on his feet and pray with his eyes open, gazing out pensively over the court-yard? Instead, I unbolted the garage doors from the inside.'

'I hope you remembered to re-bolt them.'

'George!'

'Sorry. What detained you?'

'Wieringa, the Defence Minister. He was in the Marnixstraat with Colonel de Graaf. If you refrain from asking questions, I'll tell you word for word how our conversations went.'

He did so and at the end George said: 'Satisfactory. You fixed the bug, of course. So why did you go to all this devious trouble of getting hold of the operating instructions for the devices?'

'Have you ever known of a cop – or soldier – for that matter – who never made a mistake?'

George pondered briefly then said: 'Present company ex-cepted, no. True, we may yet need that information – Ylvisaker and his friends might just miss the road-blocks. But you didn't tell them that we were going by helicopter?'

'I did not. For the same reason that I didn't take up Samuel-son's unspoken offer to tell us where we are going. If I had done, his immediate reaction – our Defence Minister's that is – would be to have called his counterpart in Whitehall to send over a Nimrod, the British bomber that is a virtual airborne radar station and which could have tracked us from here to wherever we're going without our knowing a thing about it.' He smiled. 'You wear, what shall we say, George, a rather peculiar expression. The same thought had occurred to yourself?'

'It had.' George looked thoroughly chagrined. 'I thought it rather a good idea, myself.'

'I don't. I have no doubt that the Royal Air Force would have been delighted to comply and I have equally no doubt that within a very short time of our arriving at our destination we would have a visit from our paratroopers and commandos who don't tend to beat about the bush very much. I don't much care for that idea. Three reasons. I don't want a fire-fight, a blood bath. Killing or capturing – killing, more likely – Samuelson and his friends would not be the final solution. There may be – in fact I feel certain there will be, don't ask my why, I don't know – enough of his men left to carry out the ultimate threat.

Thirdly, I don't much care for the idea of the young ladies being hurt or worse. I wouldn't much like to gun down – wound, I mean, not kill – a countryman who was threatening the life of one of the girls.'

Vasco said: 'Julie and Annemarie?'

'All four.'

George said mildly. 'The other two are criminals.'

'They associate with criminals. Different matter entirely. Anyway, if the government were to commit this crass folly, we would be in a position to expose them and dictate our own terms. Wieringa and the Colonel would back us up and they're the only two people who matter. However, this is all academic. It's not going to happen. Moment, gentlemen. These denims are rather damp.'

When he'd changed, he said: 'Our absent friend O'Brien is missing in more than one way – he's also the missing key. I'd give a great deal to know where he is at this moment. He won't have gone to their other hang-out for his expertise in de-bugging and de-fusing alarm systems wouldn't be called for there. One could speculate endlessly as to where he has gone to exercise his skills but that would be a waste of time.'

'I'm neglecting my duties,' Vasco said. 'If I may be excused. George, would you come and switch the light on again?'

He turned off the light, went into the bathroom and closed the door. No sooner had George turned the light on than Vasco tapped on the door. George switched the light off again and the bathroom door opened.

'This may interest you,' Vasco said.

The sentry's head was nodding, intermittently and at irregular intervals. After a few seconds of this he held it in an upright position then shook it from side to side. After a few more seconds of this – it was too dark to see what his expression was registering but it was, very probably, one of confusion and apprehension – brought up his right hand from under his rug, looked at the bottle still clutched in it, upended it and apparently established the fact that it was empty, placed it on the floor and pushed himself back in his seat.

'He's going to drop off again,' Vasco said.

272

'Not him,' van Effen said. 'He's making a major decision.'

The sentry made his major decision. He lifted his rug to one side, pushed himself groggily to his feet and took a few staggering steps that brought him perilously close to the loft doorway.

Vasco said: 'He's drunk.'

'Again, not him. He's seen his bottle is empty and assumes because of that and the fact that he reeks of schnapps that he ought to be drunk and acts accordingly. Auto-suggestion, I believe they call it. It could have been a bit awkward if his relief found that he couldn't wake him. Enough.'

In the bedroom van Effen said: 'I think we should go downstairs in a few moments. Including you, Vasco, if you feel strong enough.'

'I'm a captain in the Dutch army. I'm brave.'

George said: 'You told Samuelson you wouldn't be down.'

'My mind changes along with the circumstances. It was freezingly cold out there. I require brandy. More importantly, I want to see their reaction to the news that the hunt for the FFF is now being concentrated in the Rotterdam-Scheldt area. Even more important is that I want those missiles, explosives and other nasties transferred from the truck to the helicopter.'

'Why?' George said.

'The roads between here and the Rotterdam-Scheldt area will be alive with patrols tomorrow morning, police and army, but mainly, I suspect, army. My personal conviction is that Ylvis-aker will be intercepted. I want those missiles because the FFF want them mounted for some offensive or defensive purposes and that should give them, from our point of view, owing to the fact that the missiles are totally useless, a splendid sense of false security.'

'You should have been a lawyer, a politician, a Wall Street broker or a criminal specializing in fraud,' George said.

'Such devious minds don't belong on the ranks of the police forces.'

'Hark at who's talking. I have also the hunch that the explosives, grenades and other sundries may prove to be more useful to us than to them. Just a hunch. Vasco, what do you know about the regulations concerning the transport of missiles?'

'Absolutely nothing.'

'Then let's invent some.'

'I'll wager, sir, that I can invent better regulations than you can.'

'Gentlemen, gentlemen!' Samuelson's crocodile smile would have shamed an archangel. 'Delighted to see you. I thought you weren't coming down, Mr Danilov.'

'I just couldn't sleep,' van Effen said with a transparent honesty that would have shamed the same archangel. 'As a Dutchman, even an adopted one, I just couldn't – well, you understand – well, you know, Flevoland.'

'Of course, of course. I understand. *And* the Captain – sorry, Lieutenant. Delighted to see you, my boy. I take it you are feeling better?'

'My voice is not but I am,' Vasco said hoarsely. 'Thanks to your kindness, Mr Samuelson.'

'The universal specific. I suggest another.' He looked at van Effen and George. 'Brandies, gentlemen? Large ones?'

'You are very kind,' van Effen said. He waited while Samuelson gave instructions to Leonardo. 'You know that I am a normally incurious person, but two things take my attention. The ladies have returned. I was given to understand that they were still in a state of nervous exhaustion.'

'As far as I can understand, they still are. Your second question?'

Van Effen smiled. 'My second question may give the answer to my first implied question. I see your TV is on again. I have by now come to understand that this means that you are expecting a further communiqué or statement or whatever in the near future.'

'You understand correctly.' It was Samuelson's turn to smile, the usual avuncular one. 'Both questions answered. You will excuse me a moment, gentlemen. I must tell the Reverend that it is earphones time.'

Leonardo brought them their drinks. Van Effen thanked him

and led the other two out on to the terrace. No one raised an eyebrow. Apart from the fact that they had already established reputations as eccentric fresh-air fiends, if they wished to have a private conversation they had already had a long time to have held it upstairs.

Van Effen closed the door and said: 'Well, what do we make of that?'

'The four young ladies who appear to have recovered from their nervous exhaustion? They're talking among each other, not animatedly, not very cordially, but they're talking. And I don't for a moment believe they've come down to watch this next broadcast.' George sipped his brandy thoughtfully. 'Somebody wants to talk to us.'

Van Effen nodded. 'Julie. Could be Annemarie, but my hunch is Julie.' He looked across at the loft door where the sentry was now pacing to and fro, perfectly steady on his feet and looking every inch a man devoted to his job. 'When we get back inside – which will be in a very few seconds, it's like an ice-box out here – I want you to wait a few discreet minutes, then wander aimlessly around, playing the role of a genial, middle-aged Lothario – just act your natural self, that is – and see if you can't have a word with Julie. Just a few words and don't let her talk more than a few words with you. If necessary, just say the word "helicopter". She'll know what I mean, I'll try to get next to her and no one can hear a word on a helicopter. I don't want to go near her myself. If Samuelson has got a leary eye for anyone, it's for me.'

'A bagatelle,' George said.

They re-entered the living-room, both van Effen and Vasco giving exaggerated shudders: George was too big and well-covered for that sort of thing.

Romero Agnelli smiled. 'Back so soon, gentlemen?'

'Fresh air is one thing,' van Effen said. 'The Polar ice-cap another.' He looked up at the flickering but silent TV set. 'Mr Samuelson not down yet?'

'He's hardly had time to get upstairs and back, has he,' Agnelli said reasonably. 'Your glasses, gentlemen.'

At the bar, van Effen said: 'It's a wild night outside and

getting wilder. Do you seriously think it's safe to fly tomorrow?'

'Do you fly?'

'As a passenger, a lot. I have – had – a pilot's licence. Never been in a helicopter in my life.'

'I have a licence for a helicopter. Total solo flying time – about three hours. In weather like this, you wouldn't get me within a hundred miles of the pilot's seat in a helicopter. Daniken's had thousands of hours. Superb pilot.'

'Well, that's a relief.' Van Effen was aware that George and Vasco had drifted away: his eyes made no attempt to follow them. 'Nice to think we might get there – wherever there is.'

'If Daniken wasn't sure he wouldn't take off.'

They continued an amicable discussion along those lines for two or three minutes until Samuelson reappeared, to all appearances his usual urbane and good-humoured self.

'Any moment now, ladies and gentlemen. I think we should take our seats.'

It was the same lugubrious announcer and he seemed to have aged considerably since his last appearance.

'We have two announcements to make, both concerning the FFF. The first is that London and Stormont, the Northern Ireland parliament, have arrived at an agreement to begin active and immediate negotiations with our government. Such negotiations have, in fact, already begun.'

Samuelson beamed.

'The second is that the government advises all citizens of the Netherlands to be of good heart. The Ministry of Defence suspects, although it has no reason to believe, that the FFF will be switching its scene of operations from the Ijsselmeer, where the dyke breaches and the explosion of this nuclear device are promised to take place tomorrow. This is because the FFF have established a practice of not striking twice in the same area. The balance of opinion is that they will concentrate on the south-west, most likely in the Rotterdam-Scheldt. The reason given for this announcement is that the government wants every citizen in that area – repeat *every* – because it affects every citizen, to be on continuous alert and report anything in the slightest way abnormal to the nearest police or army post. It is appreciated that this statement will also be picked up by the FFF, but the government regards this as the lesser of two evils compared to whatever use it may be to the FFF.'

Samuelson was no longer beaming. Van Effen, forehead furrowed and lips pursed, looked at George, then, without altering his expression, at Samuelson and said: 'I don't think I like this very much.'

'I don't like it at all.' His expression was almost a mirror image of van Effen's and the fingers of both hands were drumming on the arms of his chair. After a few seconds he turned to van Effen and said: 'And what do you make of *this* development?' It was significant, van Effen thought, that Samuelson should have asked him first: it didn't speak too highly for his confidence in his associates. Van Effen waited about twenty seconds before he replied: he already had the answers to most possible questions but Samuelson wouldn't have been too impressed by an immediate answer.

'I think they're bluffing. Or, at least, counter or double bluffing. They may believe that you intend to strike next in some other spot entirely and that this is intended to put you off your guard and relax while they close in on where they fondly imagine you are, or they may not be bluffing and this may be intended to restrict your movements. Either way, they're not very bright, but, then, the Minister of Justice, the Minister of Defence and the Chief of Police of Amsterdam are hardly renowned for their outstanding intelligence.' George coughed softly into his hand but retained an impassive expression.

Samuelson looked doubtful. 'Don't forget I've met Wieringa. He didn't strike me as a fool.'

'He's not a fool. He's honest, straightforward and the most popular man in government but lacks the devious intelligence to rise to the very top. Plots and counter-plots are not for him. Another thing, if the authorities knew where we were don't you think we'd have had a visit from a battalion of paratroopers or commandos – or both – quite some time ago?'

'Ah!' The thought seemed to cheer Samuelson up.

'And still another thing. I'm told you have another operations

277

centre somewhere. Why don't you call them and see if they've suffered any harassment?'

'An excellent idea.' Samuelson nodded to Romero Agnelli, who dialled a number, spoke briefly and hung up.

'Nothing,' he said.

'Again excellent,' Samuelson said. 'So we're in the clear.'

'No, we're not.' Van Effen shook his head in a discouragingly definite fashion. 'Lieutenant, is there any chance that it may have been discovered that the truck and weapons are missing from the armoury from which we took them?'

'The truck?' Vasco said hoarsely. 'Possible but unlikely. The weapons, no. The regular inventory isn't due for another two weeks.'

Van Effen said: 'Mr Samuelson, it's not really for me to say, but shouldn't we change the identification numbers on that truck?'

Samuelson also smirked. 'Already done.'

'Well done. But there's more to it than that.' Vasco spoke huskily and unhappily. 'The authorities, as Mr Danilov says, may be operating in this area. Mention was made of both police and army posts. That means there may be police *and* army road blocks. Police road blocks present no danger. Army ones do. They know the missiles in transport – which is in itself an extremely rare occurrence – always travel in convoy. If you want to get them to their destination they'll have to travel by helicopter.'

'Not in *my* helicopter, they won't,' Daniken said firmly.

'Mr Daniken, I believe you to be an expert helicopter pilot.' Vasco's voice being in the assumed condition it was, it was difficult for him to speak coldly, but his eyes were cold enough. 'The cobbler should stick to his last. I'm an expert on missiles. A missile cannot be armed until it's in flight. It's obvious that you've never been in military helicopters. What do you think the Russian gunships use in Afghanistan? Pea-shooters?' Daniken remained silent. 'I also think the other weapons and explosives should be removed otherwise you're more than liable to be asked what armoury you've taken them from and to what armoury or army unit you're taking them. Mobile army con-

trols tend to be very curious, very alert and very persistent –
especially when they know there's a national emergency alert
out.'

Daniken looked unhappy. 'But the detonators –'

'The detonators,' George said comfortably, 'will be in their
velvet sockets, wrapped in cotton wool, in a lead-sheathed steel
box and resting on my lap.' He let a note of irritation creep into
his voice. 'Do you think I want to have myself blown up, far less
your damned helicopter?'

'I shouldn't imagine so.' It was Samuelson who spoke. 'What
do you think, Romero?'

'I don't have to think, Mr Samuelson.'

'Neither do I. Totally agreed, gentlemen. Excellent precautions. We shall drive the truck down to the helicopter tonight
and transfer the missiles and the rest of it after the staff have
retired, which may be rather late especially as they, too, will be
watching their TV sets at midnight. Not that it matters that
much. They are well accustomed to the mysterious goings-on of
film companies.' He paused. 'I wonder if one of you three
gentlemen would care to supervise the transfer of those ma-
terials.'

'I will,' George said immediately. 'No coward like a big
coward.' He looked at Daniken. 'It looks like being a rather
bumpy flight tomorrow. As this is an ex-military helicopter, I
assume you have clamps, lashings and other devices to secure
things that have to be secured?'

'We have,' Daniken said. He still looked distinctly unhappy.

'Seems to be all,' van Effen said. 'Mr Samuelson, I'd like
another snooze before this midnight broadcast. Not that I'm
convinced that we'll see anything. Even if there are ships or
helicopters around with searchlights, visibility in this driving
rain will be zero. George? Lieutenant?'

'Me, too,' George said. 'Any more of this brandy and I'll be
dropping those detonators all over the place.'

Vasco was already on his feet. Without as much as a glance at
the four girls they left and made their way up the stairs. In the
corridor above van Effen said admiringly: 'You really are a
couple of fearful liars. Have a word with Julie, George?'

'Certainly not.' George spoke in a lofty tone. 'We professionals operate on a higher level.' He produced a folded bit of paper from his pocket and replaced it.

'Splendid. Vasco, we approach our bedroom door. Has anything occurred to you?'

'Visitors.'

Once inside, van Effen carried on a brief conversation about the weather, the best way of securing the missiles and other weapons aboard the helicopter and their conviction that the truck should have no trouble in getting through to its destination while Vasco carried out his usual meticulous inspection. After a few minutes he returned from the bathroom and put his fingers to his lips.

'Well, me for bed,' van Effen said. 'Any gallant volunteers to keep the midnight watch?'

'No need for anyone to keep a watch,' Vasco said. 'I have a travelling alarm.'

Seconds later all three were within the bathroom which had both the mirror and overhead lights on. Van Effen and George had gone in first, from darkened bedroom to darkened bathroom followed immediately by Vasco, who left the now lit bedroom door slightly ajar and turned on the light as he entered. He then switched on the overhead shower in the bath.

'One doesn't have to be a genius to know that O'Brien is elsewhere,' Vasco said. 'He could never have been responsible for the crude device that's attached to the underside of my bed. The one device that can't be de-activated without a listener knowing is inside a shower head – the listener can hear it being unscrewed – and even if there were other bugs in here, which there aren't, no one can hear a thing over the sound of a shower. Odd, but a fact.'

'You're just like our big friend here,' van Effen said. 'You should have joined the criminal ranks years ago. You'd have made a fortune. Well, the FFF should now have a tape-recording reassuring them that there's no way they can fail. Let's have a look at that note, George.' George did so and van Effen read it out.

' "Something goes on which neither Annemarie nor I understand but which may be of use to you. We have become quite friendly with our two lady criminal 'kidnappers' and if they are criminals so are Annemarie and I. Hardened criminals don't go around looking as if the day of judgment is at hand and trying all the time not to have tears in their eyes. They do." '

Van Effen broke off and looked thoughtfully at George. 'Anyone see Julie slip this note to you?'

'No.'

Vasco was perturbed. 'What if Julie, I'm sorry, sir, your sister – you must remember I don't know her – has told them about us?'

'Rubbish!' George said. 'As you said, you don't know her. Peter's faith in her intelligence, judgment and intuition is total, as is mine. In fact,' George added confidentially, 'she's a lot cleverer than he is.'

'That was quite uncalled for,' van Effen said coldly. ' "Kathleen is quite definitely the one who is under the most pressure. She is definitely afraid of Samuelson or something that Samuelson might do. Maria is under less pressure but doesn't seem to like what her brother Romero is up to. But she seems to like *him* and I have to admit that he has been very kind and courteous to us since they took us away.

' "I think that, in their own way, they are as much prisoners as we are. I think Kathleen and Maria are here under a form of coercion just as Anne and I are here under coercion, but a different kind of coercion." '

' "Coercion," ' Vasco said. 'That's the word you used. On the verandah, remember?'

'I remember. "We're here – Annemarie and I – simply because we were abducted. They are here, I'm sure, because they have been misled, lied to, because appeals have been made to their love or loyalty or some misguided sense of honour or all three. I think that they, especially Kathleen, have been lured here under totally false misapprehensions".'

'Jesus Christ!' For once George's massive calm had deserted him. 'I've heard of rare cases of telepathy between twins but she's only your young sister. That's what you said, almost word for word.'

'Nothing to do with telepathy. Great minds tend to think alike. Still question her intelligence, judgment and intuition, Vasco?'

Vasco shook his head very slowly, several times, and said nothing.

Van Effen looked at George. 'Hah! And you still think she's cleverer than I am?' George stroked his chin and said nothing. Van Effen read on and his face became very still. 'Maybe you were right at that, George. Listen to this last paragraph.'

' "I know why Maria is here. Despite her disapproval of what Romero is up to, there is a genuine bond of affection between them. As for Kathleen, I have mentioned that she is afraid of Samuelson and whatever he has in mind. I have also mentioned misguided love and loyalty. I am convinced that she is Samuelson's daughter." '

There was a considerable silence then George said: 'I take back what I said about her being smarter than you. She's smarter than the three of us put together. She has to be right. There's no other explanation.'

Van Effen set fire to the note and flushed the ashes away. Then they turned off the shower and left.

Vasco shook van Effen by the shoulder. 'It's time, Mr Danilov.'

Van Effen opened his eyes and, as always, was instantly awake. 'I didn't hear the alarm bell.'

'Turned it off – I've been awake for some time. George!'

Only Samuelson, the Agnelli brothers and Daniken were in the living-room when the three men arrived.

'Just in time, gentlemen, just in time,' Samuelson said. Even though normally cheerful he seemed to be in uncommonly good humour that midnight, a condition that could possibly have been accounted for by the bottle of brandy and glass by his side, but which was almost certainly due to an anticipatory euphoria. 'Ten minutes and we're all back in bed.'

'Not me,' George said. 'I'm staying here. Your loading supervisor, remember. When do we begin the transfer?'

'Of course, of course. Half an hour, say. Leonardo, we are neglecting our guests.'

While Leonardo proceeded to remedy the neglect, van Effen looked at Samuelson. He bore no resemblance to Kathleen but that meant nothing: she probably took after her Irish mother. Van Effen didn't doubt his sister's conviction.

The same announcer, whose depth of depression seemed to be matched only by his remarkable stamina, appeared on screen just after midnight.

'It is with regret that we have to announce that we will be unable to show live the threatened breaches of the Flevoland dykes when and if they occur. It is impossible for our TV cameras to operate in conditions of total darkness and torrential rain. We are, however, in constant radio-telephone touch with a number of observers and will inform you at once as soon as any positive news is at hand.' His image faded from the screen.

'Pity,' Samuelson said. He seemed in no way disappointed. 'It would have been a stirring spectacle. Still, we shouldn't have long to wait.'

They had very little time to wait. Less than a minute elapsed before the announcer re-appeared, replacing a phone on his desk.

'The Oostlijk–Flevoland and Zuidslijk–Flevoland dykes were breached simultaneously some ninety seconds ago. Both breaches appear to be fairly massive but the appalling weather conditions make it impossible to gauge their extent or the severity of the flooding. The authorities say they must wait until the first light of dawn before the scope of the disaster can be accurately assessed. We shall, however, be on the air every hour on the hour to give you what fresh details are available.' He paused to look at a sheet of paper that had just been handed to him.

'A phone call has just been received from the FFF. The message reads: "Markerwaard 2 p.m. today." '

Eleven

Two men were to play particularly important parts in the morning hours of that day.

One of those was Sergeant Druckmann, who was accompanied by two other officers. All three were in plain clothes. Their unmarked police car was mud-covered and slightly battered. It carried an unusual amount of electronic equipment, two separate sets of radio transceivers and a radar tracking device, so much, in fact, that, unusually, it was located on the floor just in front of the right-hand rear seat. The operator sat on the left-hand rear seat with a large-scale road map on his knees. The equipment was, for the moment, covered by a carelessly thrown rug. The car had been in position since six-thirty that morning in a side road just north of Gorinchen.

Two other unmarked police cars, similarly equipped, were within a few miles of them. But it was Druckmann's car that was to matter that morning.

The other man to matter was one Gropious, dressed in the uniform of a corporal in the Dutch army and sitting beside a private at the wheel of a small Dutch army troop carrier. Two other soldiers sat in the rear. Nobody would have used a photograph of Gropious on a recruitment poster for the Dutch army. His uniform was shabby and rather wrinkled and his long blond locks fell every which way under a hat that was more than slightly askew: the Dutch, for some reason best known to themselves, permit their soldiers to grow their hair to a length that would have had any British soldier confined to barracks for a fortnight. But the blond locks were not his own.

The uniform, like the wig, was a fake. Gropious was undeniably a soldier but no corporal: Lieutenant-Colonel Gropious, of the Dutch army commandos, was a particularly tough specimen of a particularly tough and élite corps.

284

The 7 a.m. broadcast that morning – the first breakfast-time broadcast in Dutch TV history – had been at once gloomy and slightly reassuring. Hundreds of square miles of the Flevolands had been inundated but to no great depth. As far as was known, no lives had been lost: the loss in livestock could not be estimated until later in the day. Hundreds of engineers were already pouring even more hundreds of tons of boulders and quick-setting concrete between hastily erected and, it was admitted, inadequately secured vertical steel plates. At best, it was also admitted, this could do no more than slightly reduce the effects of the next high tide and operations would have to cease at least three hours before that.

In the living-room of the windmill, where some dozen people were having breakfast, Samuelson was in high good humour.

'Exactly as predicted, ladies and gentlemen, exactly as predicted.' He looked in turn at van Effen, George and Vasco. 'I keep my word, do I not, gentlemen? Maximum psychological impact, yet not a life lost. Things *are* going our way.' He paused and listened to the thunderous drumming of the rain on the verandah, gradually lost his expression of good humour, drummed his fingers on the table, looked at Daniken and said: 'What do you think?'

'I don't like it much,' Daniken said. He rose and walked out to the verandah, closing the door behind him. He was back inside ten seconds.

'The wind's about the same,' he said. 'That is, gale force. I could fly in that. But the rain is the heaviest I've ever seen, even worse than the onset of the monsoon in India. Visibility is zero. I can't fly in that and keep our flight plan as it is.'

'You mean you won't fly?' Samuelson said. 'You refuse to fly?' Samuelson didn't seem unduly perturbed.

'Not even if you ordered me. I will not be the person who will be responsible for the end of all you wish for. *I* am the pilot and refuse to be responsible for the deaths of twenty-two people. Which I will be if we stick to our flight plans. Mass suicide is not for me.'

Van Effen cleared his throat delicately. 'I am normally, as you know, the most incurious of persons, but I don't like this talk of mass suicide, not least because it involves me. Is the need to leave on time a matter of complete urgency?'

'Not really.' It was Romero Agnelli who answered. 'Mr Samuelson does the honour of leaving all the organization to me.'

'And exceptionally good you are at it, too.'

'Thank you.' Agnelli smiled almost apologetically. 'I'm just a stickler for timetables.'

'I don't think you need to worry too much about timetables,' van Effen said. 'I know this country, you people don't. I'm sure George and the Lieutenant will confirm that downpours of this extraordinary order rarely last more than an hour or so, never as long as two. As I am in this unusually questioning mood, what's all this about flight paths or flight plans or whatever?'

'No reason why you shouldn't know,' Samuelson said. He was obviously relieved by van Effen's statement and was in an expansive mood. 'Daniken has radio-filed a flight plan to Valkenburg, near Maastricht, and this has been accepted. We are, today, filming a scene in hilly countryside and the only hilly countryside in the Netherlands is in the province of Limburg where Valkenburg lies. Romero has even had the foresight to book us hotel accommodation there.'

'Where, of course, you have no intention of going.' Van Effen nodded his head twice. 'Neat, very neat. You take off for Limburg, which lies in a roughly south-south-easterly direction, then Mr Daniken descends and alters course. The Netherlands is a very flat country so one has to fly very low to keep beneath the radar screen. As a pilot myself, I know that altimeters are notoriously inaccurate at very low altitudes. It wouldn't do us a great deal of good if a sudden downdraught were to bring us into contact with a block of high-rise flats or even one of those massive TV antennaes which are such a feature of this country. Mr Daniken has to see where he is going and I have to say that I am in one hundred per cent agreement with Mr Daniken.'

'Mr Danilov has put it even better than I could,' Daniken said. 'I am in one hundred per cent agreement with him.'

'And I agree with you both,' Samuelson said. 'Leonardo, be

so kind as to tell Ylvisaker to delay his departure with the truck until further notice. I do not wish him to arrive at our destination before we do.'

Ylvisaker, resplendent in his lieutenant-colonel's uniform, and his two companions, dressed in the uniforms of a sergeant and private of the Dutch army, departed at 8.45 a.m. The wind had not eased but the rain, as van Effen had predicted, had lessened to no more than a heavy drizzle.

At 8.46 a.m., Cornelius, the policeman in the rear of Sergeant Druckmann's car, said: 'They are moving out, sergeant.' Druckmann picked up his microphone.

'Sergeant Druckmann here. Target Zero has just moved out. Will A, B, C, D, E, please acknowledge.'

The five army patrol vehicles acknowledged in alphabetical order.

Druckmann said: 'Two minutes, three at the most and we should be able to know what route Target Zero is taking. After that, we shall report at minute intervals.'

At 8.47 a.m., twenty-two people filed aboard the giant helicopter. All, except the four girls, van Effen and George, were dressed in Dutch army uniforms. Samuelson said goodbye to four umbrella-carrying staff who had come to see them off, assuring them that they would be back the following evening. All the soldiers, with the one exception, were armed with machine-pistols: the exception, Willi the feckless guard, was burdened only by a pair of handcuffs.

At 8.49 a.m., Daniken lifted off and headed towards the south-south-east.

Also at 8.49 a.m., Sergeant Druckmann reported: 'Tracking Target Zero at two kilometres. Target Zero is now one kilometre north of Gorinchen. From there the three main exit routes are east, south and west. Two minutes and we should be able to let you know which direction he is heading.'

Van Effen turned to Romero Agnelli, who was sitting beside him, cupped his hand to his ear and said: 'Two things intrigue me.'

Agnelli smiled and lifted his eyebrows.

'I was led to believe that the armament on this gunship had been dismantled and replaced by dummies. Those guns are for real.'

'The armament was dismantled and replaced by dummies. Then we replaced the dummies. These things aren't hard to come by if you know where to look. What was the other thing?'

'Why isn't Daniken climbing? We're still under a hundred metres.'

'Look to your left and you'll see why.'

Van Effen looked. Less than fifty metres away another, much smaller helicopter, was flying alongside them. Even as van Effen looked the pilot slid back his window and waved an arm. Van Effen looked forward. Daniken was waving in return. The pilot of the small helicopter closed his window and began to climb. Daniken gently eased the gunship around until it was heading due south.

'Neat,' van Effen said. 'Very, very neat. In weather like this there will be precious little private flying in the country today. The odd bored air controller might just amuse himself by tracking this helicopter to Valkenburg. *That* helicopter, of course, *is* heading for Valkenburg.' Agnelli nodded. 'Your idea, of course.'

Agnelli smiled and made a deprecating motion with his hand.

'Target Zero is heading west on the Sliedrecht road,' Druckmann report. 'Which patrol is in the vicinity?'

'Patrol A.'

'Ah! Colonel Gropious, sir?'

'Yes. I am seeing a road block one kilometre east of Sliedrecht. Close up until you have them visually. But not too close.'

'I understand, sir. Target Zero is travelling at a very leisurely pace – perhaps "circumspect" is the word I'm looking for. Just below fifty kilometres. I estimate they should be with you in just under twenty minutes.'

'Thank you, sergeant.'

Ylvisaker leaned back luxuriously in his seat and lit a cigar. 'This,' he said with a sigh, 'is the life. Thank God we're not aboard that damned helicopter.'

That damned helicopter was bumping and lurching its way in a generally west-by-south direction. 'Generally', because Daniken was at pains to avoid towns, villages or settlements of any size. It was, van Effen thought, a totally superfluous precaution. There was no earthly reason why, say, a lone farmer should report the passage of an unidentified and probably unidentifiable helicopter. Helicopters were ten a penny in the Netherlands.

Van Effen looked around the gunship. Most of the passengers looked distinctly unhappy and their complexions offered an interesting variety of shades of colour. Annemarie and Julie, who were sitting together, had adopted remarkably similar attitudes – clenched fists and eyes screwed tightly shut. Van Effen himself was untroubled: Daniken was a superb pilot.

He cupped his hand to Agnelli's ear. 'How much further?'

'About fifteen minutes.'

'Reasonable accommodation?'

Agnelli smiled. 'It's a nice little place.'

Judging by the standards of Samuelson's taste, the nice little place, van Effen thought, was probably about the size of the royal palace in the Dam Square.

The blue and yellow sign read: 'ROAD CHECK AHEAD. PLEASE STOP AT THE RED LIGHT'.

Ylvisaker's driver slowed and said: 'What do we do now?'

Ylvisaker took a leisurely puff at his cigar. 'Drive on, my man.'

Gropious's driver lowered his binoculars. 'Target Zero for sure, sir.' He raised his binoculars again. 'And the given number.'

Gropious's vehicle was in the left-hand lane, facing oncoming traffic. On the right-hand side, and slightly behind them, was another troop carrier. Two soldiers, both holding umbrellas, were leaning against their vehicle. Both were smoking cigarettes.

'Would you look at that sloppy bunch,' Ylvisaker said. 'Umbrellas! Cigarettes! I'll bet there's not an officer nearer than Rotterdam. And these, mind you, are the gallant troops sworn to defend NATO to the death.'

As they came to a halt at the red light, Gropious and his two men, all three trailing machine-pistols in their left hands, approached the stolen army truck, Gropious going to the front of the truck and his two men to the rear. Ylvisaker opened his door.

'What's all this then, Corporal?'

'Colonel!' An embarrassed Gropious, perceptibly stiffening, executed as military a salute as could be expected from a slovenly corporal. 'Colonel. If I had known –'

Ylvisaker smiled tolerantly. 'What is it, Corporal?'

'Orders, sir. We are under instructions to stop and examine all vehicles, army trucks included, which may be carrying illegally obtained weapons. We were given the registration number of one particular army truck. This is not the one.'

Ylvisaker displayed some mild interest. 'Are you searching for anything in particular?'

'Missiles, sir. Ground-to-ground and ground-to-air missiles. I must admit, sir, that I don't even know what they look like except that they're copper coloured and over two metres long.'

'Duty is duty, Corporal. I see you have two men at the rear. Instruct them to open up and search. Just, you know, for the records.'

Gropious gave the instructions, the rear doors were opened and no missiles were found.

'My apologies, Colonel,' Gropious said. He hesitated, then produced a notebook and pencil. 'My instructions are to make a note of the identification of every person passing through this check-point.'

Ylvisaker reached inside his uniform jacket. Gropious said: 'No, no, sir. In your case, no papers are necessary. Just your name, Colonel.'

'Ylvisaker.'

'Colonel Ylvisaker.' Rather laboriously, Gropious wrote down the name in his notebook. How ironic, he thought, that such a confrontation should occur between a lieutenant-colonel posing as a fake corporal and a civilian – and criminal – posing as a lieutenant-colonel. He put his notebook away and lifted his machine-pistol at the same instant as his two soldiers at the rear of the truck.

'Move,' Gropious said, 'and you're dead.'

No sooner had Gropious and his men brought Ylvisaker and his two men out on to the roadside than Sergeant Druckmann's car drew up behind them. Druckmann and his men got out, Druckmann carrying a considerable number of metal objects in his hand. Druckmann looked at the scruffy corporal with the straggling blond locks and said hesitantly: 'Colonel Gropious?'

'It is indeed.' Gropious removed his hat, took off his wig and threw it beyond the roadside. 'Those damn things itch.'

Druckmann said: 'Congratulations, sir.'

Gropious, who without his wig now looked remarkably like a lieutenant-colonel, shook his hand warmly. 'And the very same to you, Sergeant. Your name, please? All I know is that all the police cars were manned by sergeants.'

'Druckmann, Colonel.'

'An excellent piece of work, Sergeant Druckmann. Most professional. And what, may I enquire, is all that ironmongery you're carrying?'

'Handcuffs and leg irons, sir. I understand that those are not standard army issue.'

'Splendid. Kindly have one of your men attach them at once.' He turned to one of his soldiers. 'Instruct all patrols to return to base. I suggest, Sergeant Druckmann, that you instruct one of your men to do the same for the police cars. Emphasizing, of course, the need for complete secrecy.'

'At once, Colonel. But there is no need to emphasize secrecy. All of us, myself included, have been threatened by Colonel de Graaf with the equivalent of Devil's Island.'

'Ah! Our redoubtable Chief of Police in Amsterdam.'

'Yes, sir. Whose prisoners are those – yours or ours?'

'They are now the property of the nation. We will drive to my base, call up Mr Wieringa, the Defence Minister, and Colonel de Graaf and see what is to be done with them. Meantime, let's have a look at Ylvisaker's truck – well, his stolen truck.'

Inside the truck Druckmann said: 'I really know very little about what's going on. Those three men are FFF?'

'They are indeed and they face three charges. The first is impersonating army officers. The second is being in possession of a stolen army vehicle.' Gropious opened the lids of the two fake long-range petrol tanks to reveal the squat, cylindrical shapes of two bronze-coloured metal objects. 'The third, of course, is to have them explain how come they are transporting a couple of nuclear bombs along the roads of our fair countryside.'

The lids were lowered and they stepped outside. Druckmann said: 'May I smoke in the Colonel's presence?'

'The Colonel is about to do the same.'

After a few moments, Druckmann said: 'Well, all right. I volunteer.'

Gropious smiled. 'To drive this truck to base?'

'I'm a fearful coward, Colonel. I shall take great care.'

'I have a great deal of time for fearful cowards, sergeant. By the time we get there we shall have two US experts from Germany standing by to de-activate those damned things. I shall lead the way, red lights flashing and all that sort of thing, you will follow close behind and your police car will follow close behind you. You have this consolation, Sergeant Druckmann. If you're vaporized, we're all vaporized.'

The time was 9.27 a.m.

At precisely 9.27 a.m. Daniken touched down outside another isolated windmill-cum-farmhouse, considerably larger than the one they had so recently left. Two men and two women, umbrellas in hand, came hurrying out to meet them. It was clear that Samuelson and his friends, judging from the smiles on the faces of the four, were not only known and welcome but also expected.

With the power shut off the interior of the gunship was almost deathly quiet. Van Effen said to Agnelli: 'Well, yes, you do have a certain gift for organization.'

Agnelli smiled and said nothing.

The living-room of the windmill, which had a similar verandah outside, was considerably larger and even more luxurious than the one they had left behind. There were ten people in the room – Samuelson and the Agnelli brothers, van Effen and his friends and the four girls. Daniken, van Effen guessed, was presumably parking – and concealing – his helicopter in a nearby barn. Riordan had gone upstairs, no doubt to indulge in another bout of meditation and prayer.

Samuelson, relaxed in an armchair before a crackling wood fire, sighed like a man well content with himself.

'Clockwork, my friends, just clockwork. The penultimate stage successfully completed. I know it's still relatively early in the morning, but, then, we shall be having an early lunch. Something in the nature of a *soupçon* of jonge jenever, I think.'

'An early lunch?' van Effen said. 'We are moving on?'

'Just after two o'clock.' Samuelson gestured towards a TV set. 'After we've seen what happens in the Markerwaard.'

'I see.' Van Effen made it abundantly clear that he didn't see at all. 'Well, wherever.' He shrugged. 'How many of those establishment do you own in the Netherlands?'

'None. The owners of this house, for instance, are presently basking in the sunshine of the Bahamas. The Golden Gate pays well. This, as you are aware, is the dead season for farming. A local farmer, also well rewarded, looks after the cattle and sheep. There are no problems. Do you know where you are, Mr Danilov?'

'I haven't the faintest idea.' Long experience had taught van Effen to lie with total conviction: he knew exactly where he was.

'After so short a flight, still somewhere in Holland. Does it matter?'

'You are a singularly incurious person. We are in the vicinity of Middelharnis. You know of it?'

'Middelharnis?' Van Effen frowned then said: 'Over Flakkee.'

Samuelson smiled, nodded and said nothing.

Van Effen set down the glass that Leonardo had just given him. His face was stonily bleak and his eyes very cold.

'The Haringvliet,' he whispered. 'You're after the Haringvliet.' He had been well aware of this for some quite considerable time.

The Haringvliet dam was variously referred to as the valve or the sluice gate of Holland. It blocked the entry to the Haringvliet estuary and many waterways beyond. In the late spring and early summer, when the snows in the Alps, Germany and France melted, it diverted the waters from the swollen Rhine, Waal and Maas rivers past Rotterdam and into the New Waterway which joined the North Sea at Europort simply by keeping its massive hydraulically operated, electrically powered gates closed. It could also, when the level of the river water rose too high, and the level of the North Sea was considerably lower, release water directly into the North Sea simply by opening as many of its gates as was deemed necessary. At this time of the year, however, with the river water shrunk to its lowest level, its main task was to keep out the North Sea except at the very latest of neap tides. The flooding, the damage and the deaths that would inevitably result from the destruction of the sluice gate of Holland were incalculable.

'Yes, Mr Danilov.' Samuelson must have been convinced that his life was in danger, but he remained outwardly calm. 'I am, as you say, after the Haringvliet.'

Van Effen nodded just once, briefly. 'Hence the nuclear weapons. I hope to God they detonate en route and blast Ylvisaker and his friends into outer space.'

'A most uncharitable wish, to say the least.' Samuelson sipped his drink: if he was perturbed, he hid the fact uncommonly well. 'I see you are wearing your Smith and Wesson, Mr

Danilov. I have no doubt your friends are similarly armed. Romero, Leonardo and I carry no arms – it's a point of principle with us. If you choose to shoot me, there's nothing I can do about it. But wouldn't you consider it rather unfair to shoot a man merely because you're labouring under a vast mis-apprehension?' Samuelson seemed to be positively enjoying himself.

'Go on.'

'The nuclear devices are most definitely not intended for use on the Haringvliet dam and this for three reasons. Firstly, I don't relish the prospect of vaporizing myself. Secondly I want the sluice gates to remain intact and in perfect working order. Thirdly, I intend to take over the dam.'

Van Effen sipped his drink in silence for a few moments, as if to take time out for thinking. Not only had he known that the Haringvliet was Samuelson's target, he'd been equally con-vinced that Samuelson had had no intention of destroying it.

'How very ambitious. And how do you intend to set about this takeover?'

'It's already half done. About forty hours ago a skilled electrician carried out a very delicate and all but undetectable job of sabotaging three turbo-generators.'

'The devil he did. He was an employee?'

'Naturally.'

'And Dutch?'

'Yes. Twenty thousand dollars, I've always found, has a most profound influence on even the most patriotic of souls. Besides, he had no idea what we had in mind. He, of course, was given the opportunity to trace the source of those faults and when he failed they called in experts from Rotterdam. Those four are currently lodged in a cellar beneath us. They are being well fed and cared for as you can see for yourself any time you wish.'

'That will not be necessary. And then, of course, you sent in your own four experts.'

'Yes. Alas, all four have criminal records and have served prison sentences but they have the saving virtue that they are probably the four best safe-crackers in the country. They also have a considerable knowledge of electrics.'

295

'Such men could not have been easy to come by,' van Effen said. He paused then said: 'Wrong. They could have been easily come by.' He looked at Romero Agnelli. 'Your brothers in prison, of course. They must have the names and track records of every outstanding – by their standards – criminal in the country.'

'They are very able men,' Samuelson said, 'but better at safe-cracking than electrics.'

'Their purpose being, of course,' van Effen said, 'to locate and deactivate all the alarm systems in the dam – pressure pads, rays, panic buttons and whatever. Also to discover the location of both on-duty and off-duty guards.'

'Not to deactivate. Not yet. Might not even be necessary,' Agnelli said. 'The rest, yes. There were one or two points about which they were uncertain so they asked permission to bring in the best turbo-generator experts in the country.'

Van Effen nodded. 'And, of course, they got the best expert in a totally different field. O'Brien. Very clever, I must admit.'

Samuelson waved a hand. 'All Romero's work. He would have made an excellent divisional officer. Has O'Brien returned, by the way?'

Leonardo left the room and returned with an O'Brien who was totally unlike his real self owing to the fact that he had acquired a beard and a moustache.

'Sorry about this,' O'Brien said. Wincing more than slightly he tore off both moustache and beard. 'As I'm going aboard with you, I thought the sudden transformation of a civilian engineer into a Dutch army sergeant-major might have caused some eyebrow raising.'

Samuelson said: 'How is everything?'

'Ready to go,' O'Brien said.

'One point,' George said. 'How are we to recognize those four – ah – colleagues you have on the dam. We don't want to point guns at the wrong people.'

'A good point,' Agnelli said. 'All four are dressed in very light blue overalls.'

'And carrying only tools in their tool-bags?'

'The odd pistol. A few gas grenades. Useful things like that.'

'I'd like some of those,' van Effen said. 'Gas grenades, I mean. In a small satchel or suitcase. Like Mr Samuelson, I'm averse to unnecessary violence and the people on the dam are, after all, my adopted countrymen. If it's necessary to restrain any of them I'd much rather do it with a whiff of gas rather than a bullet.'

'My sentiments exactly,' Samuelson said. 'You shall have them.'

'One further point,' van Effen said. 'How are you going to account for the presence of two civilians in an army group?'

'Aha!' Samuelson smiled broadly. 'Civilians, but not just ordinary civilians. You are two senior members of the Amsterdam police specialist anti-terrorist squad. That should fit the bill rather nicely, don't you think?'

'That's nice,' van Effen said. 'I always wanted to be a policeman. How do you propose to gain entrance to the dam, Mr Samuelson?'

'Nothing simpler. We land on the roadway on the dam. First, of course, we send a radio message to the dam to the effect that there is a suspicion, nothing more, that the FFF may be thinking of making an attack on the dam either from the sea or from the river side and that patrol boats will be approaching from the river side and a destroyer from the sea side. We, of course, shall be there first – it's only a few minutes flying time from here. They will be ordered to maintain complete radio silence – no transmissions, no receptions.'

'The simplicity of true genius,' van Effen said. 'You have your nerve. The young ladies, of course, remain behind?'

'Most certainly not. I wouldn't have Kathleen and Maria miss this splendid dénouement for all the world. The rear of the helicopter will be screened off and the four ladies will remain in hiding until we have taken over.'

'It has occurred to you that the other two girls might scream for help or attempt to overpower Kathleen and Maria?'

'They find it difficult to scream for anything when they're gagged and difficult to attack anyone when their hands are tied behind their backs. As an additional precaution, Joop will be with them. Joop is very useful with a gun.'

'You think of everything,' van Effen said. He hoped Joop wasn't too useful, for then Joop would have to die.

Samuelson rose, went to a desk and brought out two sheets of paper. 'These are the ground and elevation plans of the Haringvliet dam. Leonardo, go and bring the others here. I want every man to know exactly what to do, to know exactly where every guard will be on duty, where the off-duty guards and workers are, and where each man on duty may reasonably be expected to be. There will be no slip-ups.'

Daniken returned just as Leonardo left. In seconds only Leonardo returned, bringing with him Joop, Joachim and the two nameless RAF youths that had been at the other windmill, four older men in their thirties and forties whom van Effen had not seen before and two of the guards he had seen before. The last six looked very tough, very competent. They all crowded round the table, followed by van Effen, Vasco, George, Samuelson, Romero Agnelli, Daniken and O'Brien. Only two men were missing – Willi, who was locked up in a cellar somewhere and Riordan, who was presumably above such mundane and secular matters.

Although it was Samuelson who had called the meeting it was Romero Agnelli who conducted the meeting. His organizational abilities were indeed quite remarkable. He pointed out to each man exactly where he was to go and what was expected of him. He also insisted that they coordinate their watches so that each man should know exactly what time he should be at any given place. This took about five minutes. He then started it all over again. When he started a third time van Effen, accompanied by George and Vasco, headed resolutely towards the bar. Samuelson, smiling, came after them and moved behind the bar.

'You get easily bored, Mr Danilov?'

'I don't have to be told the same thing twice, far less three times.'

'You have a point. Maybe I am overdoing it a bit.' He looked at his watch. 'I find this a bit worrisome. I should have thought the truck would have been here by this time.'

'Ylvisaker struck me as being a pretty competent character,' van Effen said. 'Engine trouble, heavy traffic, burst tyre, anything. Anyway, you can soon find out. You've said you have a radio transmitter here. The Lieutenant is an expert operator – and, of course, he knows the frequency of the truck.'

'Would you, Lieutenant? Thank you.' Samuelson pointed across the room. 'There.'

Vasco seated himself at the transceiver, adjusted his headphones and started transmitting. After two minutes he took off the head-phones and returned to the bar.

'Nothing, Mr Samuelson. Can't raise him.'

Samuelson pursed his lips. 'You're sure?'

'Sure I'm sure.' Vasco spoke with just a faint trace of irritation. 'I know what I'm doing. If you don't believe me, let Daniken try. He knows what he's doing too.'

'No, no. I'm sorry, Lieutenant. Worried, you know.'

'Two things may have happened,' Vasco said. 'He may have had an accident. That's the more serious and less likely happening. What's more probable is that the on-off switch is in the off position.'

Samuelson's brow cleared slightly but only slightly. 'If he's late, why doesn't he call us?'

'Does he know how to operate the radio?'

Samuelson's brow cleared even more. 'Quite honestly, I don't know.' He looked up as an aproned maid approached him.

'Sorry, sir,' she said. 'I thought you might like to know that there is to be a government broadcast in two minutes. Less.'

'Thank you, thank you.' Samuelson hurried round the bar, gestured to Agnelli to end the lecture and switched on the TV set. Within half a minute, the announcer appeared on the screen, a much younger one than previously, but one who had clearly been trained in the same mortician's school.

'The government have three announcements to make. The first is that the British government and Stormont have agreed to withdraw all British troops to barracks. As the troops are scattered all over Northern Ireland this is expected to take several hours but the process is already under way. Although no statement to this effect has been made, this is taken to be indicative of London's intentions.'

Samuelson beamed in satisfaction. At that moment, Ylvisaker was the last thing in his mind.

'The second is that the British Foreign Minister, Defence Minister, the chief of the Imperial General Staff and the First Sea Lord are en route to Amsterdam in a VC10 to witness the detonation of this nuclear device in the Markerwaard at 2 p.m.

'The third is that the government have offered an amnesty to the two as yet unnamed prisoners whose release has been demanded by the FFF.

'We will, of course, be back on screen at 2 p.m.'

'Well,' van Effen said, 'it looks like wholesale surrender.'

'Matters are certainly proceeding quite satisfactorily,' Samuelson said modestly. 'We will each take a minimum of luggage with us. This can be concealed in the rear of the helicopter – soldiers on active duty do not carry suitcases around with them. Lunch will be at twelve-thirty, so we have about two and a half hours to wait till then. I do not think it would be a good idea to indulge in any more jonge jenevers so I suggest we rest. Although we are not returning tonight we have quarters prepared for you, to which you will be shown. Tell me, Lieutenant, do you intend to have a snooze?'

'Not I.'

'Then perhaps you would be kind enough to come down, say, every twenty minutes, and try to contact Ylvisaker?'

'If you think it's worth trying, certainly. I'll go upstairs, have a wash, pack what little equipment I have to pack and be down in twenty minutes. After that, I might as well stay down.' Vasco smiled. 'No furtive trips to the bar, I promise you.'

The room to which van Effen and his companions were shown was almost a duplicate of the one they had left in the other windmill. Vasco carried out his usual meticulous search and pronounced the room clear.

Van Effen said: 'Samuelson is rather concerned about the non-arrival of Ylvisaker and his friends who, I think we may take it, are at present being detained at Her Majesty's pleasure.

More importantly, Samuelson seems to think that it's all over bar the shouting. The possibility of failure doesn't now exist for him. That's a very dangerous state of mind to be in – dangerous for him, I mean.'

George said: 'And what do you think he'll do when he gets to the dam.'

'Take it over. I can't see that giving him any trouble. Then he'll tell the government that he has done just that. Coming so soon after the nuclear explosion in the Markerwaard, it should have a devastating effect on the government who will all too clearly appreciate the implications and realize that the FFF has the nation by the throat.'

'And then,' Vasco said, 'they blow a few bits of concrete off the dam just to show they mean business.'

'Nothing like that,' van Effen said. 'Nothing so crude. The explosives are Agnelli's idea. Apart from being a first-class organizer, Agnelli is a very prudent fellow. I believe that the explosives are for back-up purposes only, just in case something should go wrong.

'What I do believe is that O'Brien knows as much about the controls of the hydraulic gates as the man who designed them. They just open the sluices.'

'And if the authorities cut off the power from the mainland, if you can call it that?' Vasco said. 'Then, perhaps, the explosives?'

'There have to be standby generators. O'Brien will have checked on that. As far as the safety of the country is concerned, the sluice gates of the Haringvliet are the most vital installations in the country. Imagine the sluice gates being open at low tide and a major power failure occurs? They simply cannot afford to rely on a single source of power.

'For the moment, however, and much more importantly, Samuelson and Agnelli have been kind enough to provide us with a detailed outline of their plans.'

George rubbed his hands. 'And now we make our own plans.'

'Now we make our own plans.'

Some forty minutes after Vasco had gone down to the living-room he was joined by Samuelson. Vasco, sitting on the radio chair and idly leafing through a magazine, looked up at his entrance.

'Any luck, Lieutenant?'

'None. I've called four times – every ten minutes, not twenty, as you asked. Nothing.'

'Good God, good God!' Unmindful of his own admonitions, Samuelson went behind the bar and brought back two jonge jenevers. 'Ylvisaker is wildly overdue. What on earth can have happened to him?'

'I've been thinking, Mr Samuelson. He hasn't blown himself to pieces or the news would be all over the country by now. Let's assume he's had an accident or had a breakdown. Let's further assume he doesn't know how to operate the radio. What would you have done, sir?'

'Gone to the nearest phone and informed us. It's difficult to move far in any direction in this country without coming across a house with a phone or a public call box.'

'Exactly. Does Ylvisaker *know* the telephone number of this place?'

Samuelson stared at him then said: 'Ylvisaker has never been here. Wait.'

He hurried from the room and returned within a minute, his face grim. 'The consensus of opinion is that Ylvisaker does *not* know this number.'

'But you know the precise route he was taking?'

'Of course. Two men, a fast car. Bound to intercept. Thank you, Lieutenant. I'm glad to see that there are some minds still working around these parts.'

'Shall I keep on trying, Mr Samuelson?'

'It's a faint chance, isn't it?'

Vasco shrugged. 'Very faint. But nothing else for me to do.'

'Thank you.' Samuelson brought him another jonge jenever. 'Another trifle like this is not going to hurt a mind as clear as yours.'

'That is kind. I think I'll have it on the verandah, if I may. It *is* a bit overheated in here.'

302

'Of course, of course.' Samuelson hurried from the room.

The car was a tan-coloured BMW with Antwerp number plates. Vasco watched the car and its two occupants disappear round a corner, finished his drink in a thoughtful manner, then returned inside. He went to the radio, switched wave-band and wave-length and said softly in Flemish: 'Record.' He spoke for no more than twelve seconds, then switched back to the previous wave-band and length. He tried again for Ylvisaker and was answered by the same silence. He refreshed his drink at the bar, resumed his radio chair, glanced through a magazine and again called the missing truck with the same lack of response. He tried twice more in the next twenty minutes with the same lack of response. He was still trying to make contact when Samuelson returned. He looked at Vasco, went behind the bar and returned with two more drinks.

'Breaking my own rules, I know, but you've earned it and I feel the need for it. Nothing?'

'Dead. I know Mr Danilov makes a point of being incurious about everything but I'm a serving army officer. Just how important are those nuclear devices to you?'

'Almost entirely psychological. If necessary, I would have used them to blow off both the northern and southern approaches to the Haringvliet dam.'

'Whatever for? No senior military commander in the Netherlands would dream of attacking the Haringvliet dam. Bombers? Never. Fighter planes? Never. Not only is your gunship more than a match for any fighter, not only do you have ground-to-air missiles, you will have a large number of hostages whose lives they would never imperil. Destroyer? Torpedo boats? Ground-to-ground missiles are heat-seeking. They're lethal.'

'Not bombers?'

'What would happen if they breached the Haringvliet dam?'

'Of course. Well, no point in trying any longer. Perhaps we should both have a brief rest before lunch.'

Vasco gave van Effen and George a brief resumé of what had happened.

Van Effen said: 'So you've convinced Samuelson of his total invulnerability and ensured that we will have two fewer hard men to cope with abroad the dam. Whom did you notify?'

'Rotterdam police.'

'I think, George, that we may make a policeman of him yet. Well, another hour or so before lunch.'

'Snooze for me,' Vasco said. 'Four jonge jenevers in succession are too much for my delicate constitution.'

'What did you say?'

'Dutch hospitality. You know what it's like.'

Lunch was more than adequate but less than convivial. Samuelson tried to maintain a cheerful façade but he was deeply worried about the fate of his nuclear devices and his worry was almost palpable with the result that the last half hour of the meal was consumed in almost total silence.

Over coffee, Samuelson said to van Effen: 'Do you think it possible that Ylvisaker and his men could have been seized by the authorities, army or police?'

'Highly unlikely. I don't see how they could have been. Your security is total. Even if they had been, the question is, would Ylvisaker or his men have talked?'

'About the Haringvliet dam? No. Until we got here today only Riordan, Agnelli, Daniken and O'Brien were privy to the plans.' Samuelson smiled faintly. 'Your famous need-to-know maxim, Mr Danilov.'

'One does not want to sound cynical or callous, but what the hell are you worrying about, then?'

'As you can see,' the TV announcer said, 'the weather is as atrocious as ever with correspondingly poor visibility, such as one would expect as dusk approaches. The rain is extremely heavy and the wind, between Force eight and nine, has backed to the north-west. We have four cameras in position – one near Hoorn and one near Volendam, on the west side of the Markerwaard and one on the opposite shore near Helystad. This one, I'm afraid, is virtually useless: in spite of its lens hood the rain is

304

driving straight into the lens. We have a fourth camera in a helicopter and we understand they are having a very rough time indeed. The time is 1.58. Our first shots will be taken from the helicopter.'

A white-capped, storm-tossed sea appeared on the screen. Detail was blurred and shifting, because the helicopter was being, it was clear, severely buffeted about, hence making it impossible to maintain a steady camera direction. Another voice took over from the studio announcer.

'Helicopter camera here. I can assure you that my friend in the studio was not exaggerating. The conditions are abominable and I have to confess that the only person who is not sick is, most fortunately, the pilot. We are flying at seven hundred metres, give or take fifty metres every time this damn machine is going up or down, which we hope is a safe height if the nuclear explosion and its accompanying water spout should occur, which God forbid, directly beneath us. It is now precisely 2 p.m. and' – his voice rose almost by an octave – 'there it goes! There it goes! Me and my big mouth. It *is* directly beneath us!'

The camera lens had been extended to maximum zoom. The surface of the Markerwaard boiled whitely and then erupted a great column of water climbing vertically skywards towards the helicopter's camera.

'Would you look at that?' the excited voice went on. 'Would you just look at that?' It seemed rather a superfluous question, as, unquestionably, almost every eye in the Netherlands was looking at nothing else. 'And the air is full of spray. Our pilot is moving as quickly as possible to the north-west – we want to get out of this area as quickly as possible. We are making poor time against this north-west gale, but he is clearly hoping that that same gale will blow the spout and spray away from us. So do I.'

Van Effen looked at Samuelson. He appeared to have gone into some kind of trance. The only sign of movement came from his hands. His fingers were interlocked but his thumbs were revolving slowly around each other.

The studio announcer appeared. 'I am afraid the helicopter's lenses are clouded by that spray. We regret that none of the other three cameras are in visual contact. The detonation appears to have occurred almost exactly in the centre of the Markerwaard.'

The helicopter commentator's voice came again. 'Sorry about that. What with the spray and rain we are at the moment quite blind. We are still moving steadily north-west. Wait a minute, wait a minute. We have eyes again.'

The spout was collapsing on itself. The camera, zoom half retracted, was only momentarily on the spout, then began panning the surrounding area. A circle of water could be seen moving steadily outwards from the centre.

'That,' the commentator said 'must be the expected tidal wave. Doesn't look much like a wave to me, but, then, from this altitude it is impossible to gauge the height of the water.'

The picture faded to be replaced by the studio announcer. 'We are trying to – wait, wait, we have Volkendam.'

A camera, at full zoom, showed a swell of water, little more than a ripple, it seemed, rapidly approaching the shore-line. A commentator said: 'I agree with my colleague in the helicopter. This is hardly my idea of a tidal wave. However, I understand those tsunami tend to increase in height as the water shallows. We shall see.'

There wasn't, in fact, much to see. With the wave less than a hundred metres from land, the commentator estimated its height as just under a metre, which was pretty much in accordance with the scientists' predictions. Samuelson gestured for the set to be switched off.

'A few wet feet, no more,' he said. 'And not a life lost. An impressive performance, wouldn't you say, Mr Danilov?'

'Most impressive.' True, probably not a life had been lost. Not that day. But the years to come might well record a different story: the radio-active fall-out would have fallen or would be falling over the already flood-beleaguered Flevolands. But it hardly seemed an appropriate moment to point this out to Samuelson.

Samuelson said: 'Romero, radio the message to the Haringvliet dam. Emphasize the need for absolute radio silence. Where the devil are those two who went in search of Ylvisaker and his friends?' Nobody knew where the devil they were. 'Five good men lost to me. Five!'

'It's annoying, Mr Samuelson,' Vasco said. 'And worrisome. But it can have no effect on the outcome. We have seventeen men. With the element of total surprise in our favour I could guarantee to take the Haringvliet with only four men.'

Samuelson smiled. 'That's a comfort. We leave in twenty minutes.'

They left in twenty minutes. All the soldiers were armed, all carried either rucksacks or satchels. Neither van Effen nor George were armed, at least not visibly, but they, too, carried satchels, both crammed with gas grenades. In addition, van Effen had taken the precaution of taking his Yves Saint-Laurent aerosol.

As they climbed aboard the gunship, van Effen said to Samuelson: 'Gas, not guns?'

'Gas, not guns.'

Twelve

The gunship touched down on the Haringvliet dam roadway at 2.38 p.m.

Romero Agnelli, dressed as a major and in nominal command of the party, was the first down the steps. A fair-haired, youngish man with horn-rims detached himself from a small group of observers, hurried forward to greet Agnelli and shook him warmly by the hand.

'Damned glad to see you, Major, damned glad. Have you seen what those devils have just done in the Markerwaard?'

'That we have,' Agnelli said sombrely. 'That we have.'

'How seriously do you take this threat to the Haringvliet?'

'Well,' Agnelli said reasonably, 'there's no threat now. Quite frankly, I don't take it seriously at all, but, as soldiers, ours is not to reason why. Quite frankly again, the country is in a state of near panic and ninety-nine per cent of all intelligence reports and agitated phone calls we receive turn out to be groundless. This, I say, may be the hundredth, although, as I say, I don't believe it.' He took the man's arm and led him a few steps from the helicopter as soldiers followed down the steps and others opened the loading doors. 'May I have your name, sir?'

'Borodin. Max Borodin. Manager. What on earth are those things they are unloading?'

'Missiles and their launching platforms. We'll have one facing the North Sea, the other the river. Ground-to-ground missiles and ground-to-air missiles. Heat-seeking. Lethal.' Agnelli did not add that they could be swivelled on their platforms to cover both road approaches to the Haringvliet dam. 'Totally superfluous precaution. The FFF are a mad lot but not mad enough to launch a frontal attack on the Haringvliet dam. We expect a destroyer and patrol boats to be standing by shortly. Again, quite unnecessary.'

'Unnecessary or not, you've taken a great load off my mind. Who are those two rather portly and harmless-looking civilians?'

'Portly they may be. Harmless they are not. Senior police officers from Amsterdam. Very much specialists in a very specialist anti-terrorist squad. They'll be wanting to look for any weak spots in your defences. Pure formality but they insist. We shall leave two soldiers by the missiles to keep watch. Inspector Danilov – that's the less portly one – also insists that my men accompany us. He wants, understandably, that they should familiarize themselves with the general layout of the interior of the dam.'

Twenty minutes it was and a very surprising twenty minutes it turned out to be for Mr Borodin, not least when four blue-overalled mechanics produced Kalashnikov machine guns which had been assembled from their toolbags. It was a completely painless – phsyically, that is, but not mentally for many of those concerned – and bloodless operation. Borodin, his staff and his guards had simply no chance. They all finished up in one of the many giant cellars in which the dam abounded. Agnelli was about to turn the key in the lock when van Effen stopped him.

'No. Rope. Tie them. Come, come, Mr Agnelli, you're the man who never overlooks anything.'

'I've overlooked something?'

'You've overlooked the fact that O'Brien may not be the only man in the world who can pick any lock in the world.'

Agnelli nodded. 'Of course. Rope.' Rope was fetched, enough to secure a hundred men. When Borodin and his men had been bound hand and foot, Samuelson, looking every inch the successful Roman general back from Gaul and making his ritual entry of triumph into the city of Rome, led them all up to the control room. Van Effen and his two friends lingered some way behind while van Effen opened a small tin and brought out six sodden balls of cotton-wool. These they stuffed into their nostrils. Vasco winced.

'What the hell is this? Sulphuric acid?'

'You'll get used to it,' van Effen said.

'And what was this rigmarole about people being able to pick locks? It's a million to one against there being another O'Brien down there.'

'We're going to need rope. Lots of it. There's a couple of hundred yards of it down there.'

Vasco looked at George. 'The man thinks of everything.' He shook his head. 'Agnelli is not the only one who overlooks things.'

They entered the control room. It was wide and very spacious with serried ranks of control panels lining the right-hand wall and paralleling tables. O'Brien was in the vicinity of them but not examining them: van Effen knew he didn't have to.

'Ah!' Samuelson said. 'The very man, Lieutenant. I want to talk to Wieringa, the Minister of Defence.'

Vasco showed no surprise, merely thought for a few seconds. 'The Defence Minister will be out at Volkendam, I imagine. Doesn't matter where he is. No problem. Wherever he is, office, car or plane, he's never more than an arm's length from a telephone. I'll call the War Office and they'll patch him in.'

'How long will it take?'

'A minute. Less.'

'A minute!'

'In the Netherlands,' Vasco said with a trace of loftiness, 'the Army has over-riding priority.' In less than the specified time he handed the phone to Samuelson, who took it, his eyes the eyes of a man whose dreams have come true. Or a madman whose dreams have come true.

'Mr Wieringa? This is the leader of the FFF, the Fighters For Freedom. I trust you appreciated our little demonstration in the Markerwaard this afternoon. I have some more rather unwelcome news for you. We have taken over the Haringvliet dam. I repeat, we are in complete control of the Haringvliet.' There ensued quite a lengthy pause, at least on Samuelson's part before he continued: 'I am glad, Mr Wieringa that you appreciate the significance of this. Any attempt to retake the Haringvliet, by force or by stealth, will have disastrous effects on Holland. I might also add that we have mined the dykes at Hollandsch Diep and the Volkeral. We have observers there.

Any attempts to send divers to investigate will compel us to radio-detonate those mines.

'At 4 p.m. we will be giving a slight demonstration of what awaits your country if our demands are not met immediately by opening a few sluice gates for a few minutes. You might find it instructive to have a helicopter around to take a few pictures so that the people of the Netherlands may understand what lies in store for them.

'I do hope you speed up negotiations with the British government.'

'That was quite a performance, Mr Samuelson,' van Effen said. 'You really do have those two dykes mined?'

Samuelson laughed. 'Of course not. Why should I. That pusillanimous lot now take our every word for gospel.'

Van Effen and his two friends drifted unobtrusively into the space between the table and wall controls and opened their satchels while Samuelson and his men talked excitedly and congratulated themselves. In the space of just over two seconds ten gas grenades, fairly evenly spaced around the room, exploded. The effects were spectacular. Within a few seconds everyone was staggering about and most were unconscious before they crumpled to the floor. Van Effen snatched a key from Agnelli's pocket and the three men hastily left the room, closing the door behind them. Their noses were protected but they could hold their breath for only so long.

'Five minutes and we'll be able to go back in there,' van Effen said. 'They'll be asleep for half an hour at least.' He handed Vasco the key. 'The ropes. Cut Borodin free and tell him to do the same for the others. Explain.'

Vasco entered the cellar and cut an astonished Borodin free, then handed him the knife.

'Cut the others free. We're police officers – genuine ones. The one with the scarred face is Lieutenant van Effen of the Amsterdam police.'

'Van Effen?' Borodin was, understandably, dazed. 'I've seen his picture. That's not him. I know his face.'

'Use your head. So does nearly every criminal in Holland.'

311

'But the FFF –'

'Are having a short nap.' Vasco gathered up the spare ropes and left at a run.

Van Effen approached the man on the seaside missile site. 'Mr Samuelson wants you. Quickly. Control room. I'll keep watch.' The man was just disappearing from sight when van Effen crossed to the other man on the river missile site, his hand round the burgundy Yves Saint-Laurent aerosol with the special fragrance. He lowered the man to the roadway and headed for the helicopter.

The man from the first missile site that van Effen had visited stopped when he saw George, who waved him on encouragingly. As the man passed, George chopped him on the back of the neck. For George, it was just a little chop, but the man, had he retained consciousness would probably have regarded it in a different light. George lowered him gently to the floor.

Van Effen pulled back the curtain and said: 'Ah, there you are, Joop. Keeping a good watch, I see.' Joop's good watch lasted for all of another two seconds before he slumped to the floor. Van Effen produced his Smith and Wesson, waved it in the general direction of Kathleen and Maria and sliced Annemarie's and Julie's bonds free. He raised both girls to their feet, helped them free their gags, and, gun still in hand, put his arms round their shoulders. 'My beloved sister. And my dear dear Annemarie.' The eyes of Kathleen and Maria were as round as the proverbial saucers.

'You took your time about it, didn't you,' Julie said. There were tears in her eyes.

'Gratitude was ever thus,' van Effen sighed. 'There were problems.'

'It's over?' Annemarie whispered. 'It's all over?'

'All over.'

'I love you.'

'I'll have you repeat that when you are in a more normal state of mind.'

The two seated girls were still staring at them. Kathleen said: 'Your brother?' Her voice was husky, her voice disbelieving.

'My brother,' Julie said. 'Peter van Effen. Senior detective-lieutenant of the Amsterdam police force.'

'It's a nasty shock, I will admit,' van Effen said. 'There may be an even nastier one awaiting you. There are those whom you might like to see or who might like to see you. When they wake up, that is.'

All of the FFF were still sound asleep, bound hand and foot, or in the process of being so bound.

'Not bad, not bad,' van Effen said. 'And what else have you been doing with your time?'

'Would you listen to him,' Vasco said. He tightened, with unmistakable enthusiasm, the last knot on the rope binding Samuelson's legs. 'To start with, half the police cars and vans in Rotterdam and Dordrecht should be on the dam inside fifteen minutes. I thought that up all by myself.'

'A promising officer, as I said.' Van Effen turned to Kathleen, who was staring at her father, her face ashen with shock and fear. 'Why, Kathleen?'

Instead of replying, she reached inside her handbag and brought out a small pearl-handed gun. 'You're not going to take Mr Samuelson. You didn't know he was my father.'

'Yes, Kathleen, I did.'

'You did?' Her voice faltered. 'How did you know?'

'Julie told me.'

Julie stepped between the gun and van Effen. 'You'll have to shoot me first, won't you, Kathleen. I'm not being brave because I know you could never do it.'

Vasco moved quietly forward, removed the gun from the suddenly nerveless hand and replaced it in her handbag.

Van Effen said again: 'Why, Kathleen?'

'I suppose it will all come out, won't it?' She was crying openly now. Vasco put an arm around her trembling shoulders and instead of resisting she seemed to lean against him. 'My father is English. He was a Lieutenant-Colonel in the Guards, not under that name. His father was an Earl, who left him a fortune. His sons, my brothers, went to Sandhurst. Both were killed in Northern Ireland, one a lieutenant, the other a second lieutenant. My mother was killed by a renegade off-shoot of the IRA. He's never been the same man since.'

'I guessed as much. He may be tried in this country or be extradited by the British.' Van Effen sounded as tired as he undoubtedly felt. 'In either case, diminished responsibility will apply.'

'You mean he's mad?' she whispered.

'I'm no doctor. Some kind of temporary derangement, I should imagine. Tell me, Maria, had either Romero or Leonardo anything to do with the murder of my wife and children?'

'No, no, no! I swear it. They wouldn't hurt a fly. My two other brothers in prison. I *know* they arranged it. They are hateful, evil men. I will testify to that in court. I promise.'

'That could mean another five or ten years to their sentence.'

'I hope they remain there till they die.'

'No charges will be brought against you and Kathleen. Accessories are one thing, accessories under duress another. Vasco, be so kind as to release that young lady and put a call through to Uncle Arthur. Tell him all. George, take those four ladies out for a restorative. There's bound to be a suitable supply in their mess or canteen or whatever. If not, the helicopter is not exactly bereft. Beware of suicide attempts.'

Julie said: 'I don't think that anyone is going to commit suicide.'

'Your feminine intuition, I suppose. Well, I agree. And, George, you could bring something back here. I feel very weak.'

George smiled and ushered the four girls from the control room.

Vasco was two minutes on the telephone then turned to van Effen, his hand over the mouthpiece. 'I believe Uncle Arthur would like a word with you. May I – ah – join the ladies?'

'By all means.' Van Effen picked up the phone as he heard the first sound of screaming police sirens. Colonel de Graaf's congratulations were fulsome in the extreme. So were those of Wieringa, who eventually handed him back to de Graaf.

Van Effen said: 'I am, Colonel de Graaf, becoming tired of

being the handmaiden who does all the dirty washing for you. I want a new job, increased salary, or both.'

'You shall have both, my boy. An increased salary is inevitably what goes with my job.' He coughed. 'Six months, say? A year?'